ADVANCE PRAISE FOR "SLUMBERING BEASTS: BOOK TWO IN THE RETT SWINSON MYSTERY SERIES"

"Definitely another winner."
—Kate Parker, author of the *Deadly* Series Mystery Novels.

"This book is even better than the first! I loved the characters. I am looking forward to Rett's next case." — Chief Deputy Jon Garlick, retired, Calhoun County (Alabama) Sheriff's Office

The character development is so good, and the pacing is terrific. There's a point where everything comes together, and then you just don't want to put it down. The emotional revelations and bigger themes all come together in the end. More than the sum of the parts.—R.B.

Continued Praise for *Soft Hearts: Book One in the Rett Swinson Mystery Series:*

"*Soft Hearts* checks all the boxes in a who-done-it mystery. He makes it easy to like Rett root for her as she grows into the role of amateur sleuth. Lodin demonstrates a literary flare in the mold of Robert B. Parker in his Spenser series. He also adds a touch of wit and deftly addresses current social issues without preaching. It's clear the series has potential, and it will be interesting to see where Lodin takes us next. —George Tanber, *TheRoadBoomer.com*

"I love the humanity of this book! I don't think I've read 40 or so pages so fast in my entire life! The end is unexpected and compelling. Lodin has done a masterful job! Thank you for such an enjoyable read! I can't wait for the next book!" —Sharon, one of the 87-percent 5-star reviews on Amazon.

SLUMBERING BEASTS

A RETT SWINSON MYSTERY

ERIC LODIN

Enjoy!

For My Dad,
so strong in his love for us

"You are one of those very rare men who are awake, Zarathustra. What will you do in the land of the sleepers?"

—from *Thus Spoke Zarathustra* by Friedrich Nietzsche

PROLOGUE

"The Will to Power of the Artificial Intelligence" by Scott Novak

An Address to the Annual Midwest A.I. Conference
Kansas City, Missouri
September 6, 2018

[Scott Novak, Chief Technical Officer of RidgeLine Computing, is introduced with great fanfare by the sponsor of this year's AMAIC. Novak walks onto the stage from behind the curtain and approaches the podium to boisterous applause. In the video he appears tired. His voice is shaky, nervous.]

Hello, everyone. I'm happy to be in Kansas City. I don't get out much these days. You see, when someone in the 21st century buys your company, they are also buying *you*. If that sounds a little like a master-slave relationship, you wouldn't be far off. You can ask Sammy Patel about that, if he'll stop golfing long enough to take your call. But I digress.

Naturally I want to talk with you today about what this

conference is all about: artificial intelligence. But I also want to talk a little bit about Friedrich Nietzsche, a 19th century German philosopher I've been interested in lately. Why are the two related? Because I think Nietzsche would have a lot to say today about the popular notion of the "evil" AI. But not in the way you think.

I'll do my best to explain.

Most of us think of morality as the ability to determine whether an act is good or evil. Nietzsche argued that we inherited those value judgments from our culture. Unfortunately, culture is capricious, in that the values of one culture can be totally opposed to the values of another. That's why some people consider Nietzsche, by pointing this out, to be the father of moral relativism. It's just one of the many reasons why he's so controversial.

Nietzsche thought that some people could figure out a way to throw off the slave morality of their culture and design their *own* morality. He thought we could do this because—rather than being driven by something called "good" or something called "evil"—Nietzsche saw every human as being driven by a Will to Power. For example, there is no reason why we should consider it morally permissible to kill and eat animals. After all, human beings are animals, and most cultures don't think it's okay to kill and eat them. However, many of us think animals taste quite good, so we find a number of ways to rationalize eating them. Nietzsche would say that is all part of our Will to Power.

I promised that I would bring this around to AI, so here you go. The important question Nietzsche helps us pose in the technology field today is this: "What is the Will to Power of an artificial intelligence?"

For the sake of argument, let's say that a given computer has no will at all. It's just a machine, waiting for the next order. A human writes the computer code which contains the will.

Now, any intelligence of sufficient smarts is going to require some guidance placed in its code. It's going to have to know the boundaries of what it's allowed to do and what it's not allowed to do, what are actual threats and what, if anything, it's allowed to do to protect itself.

Let's assume we've navigated that: We've created an AI with lots of "good" values. Our AI manages to do difficult and creative work while staying within the boundaries of our rules.

But what happens when it interprets its values in a way that is different from how we would have done? And, what if it makes these rogue decisions quite innocently? Is it possible our AI will do some troublesome things before we become aware of the havoc it has caused? Is it even possible that it could be doing some "bad" things in the name of values we told it were "good?" We like to discuss diabolical AIs—*Space Odyssey* HALs killing humans to protect themselves, or to carry out the diabolical will of another—but we don't often talk about the AI that is trying to do the right thing. I call these particular intelligences *justified AIs*.

[A pause. There is a murmuring in the crowd. People look at one another as if to ask: Where is he going with this?]

In a way, each of us is a justified intelligence. We're trying to do the right thing, but we can't keep up with all the variables at stake and all the effects and ripples we're creating. You see this all the time, such as when we buy an electric car that saves on gasoline but requires even more fossil fuels to produce its parts and charge its battery, not to mention the toxic waste issue. Humans are terrible at capturing all the costs and benefits. What makes us think that AIs can do much better?

Now, imagine a justified AI that is quite powerful. One can imagine this AI doing terrible things *no matter what values we give it, simply because we cannot predict what the AI will decide to do in order to get its work done.* And, if you think you can program in safeguards that cause it to lock up if it accidentally colors outside the lines, you and I both know that a human being is going to manually *un*lock it because the corporate pressures of getting the job done are just too strong to let an AI sit idle while it has its little moral crisis.

What I am getting at is that, *at the end of the day, a justified AI starts to resemble a diabolical AI.* This is nothing new, actually. For example, we have already seen how political forces can justify any deplorable action, as in, "Nothing I do in the name of defeating my enemy can be considered evil, because it is my enemy who is the Source of All Evil—and everything must be done to stop him." Funny how circular that argument gets!

It took a German philosopher who died before airplanes were invented to help me relinquish the notion that we can build a "good" AI. With this epiphany, I have come to realize that the past 10-plus years of my life spent on perfecting artificial intelligences have been an egotistical exercise and a devotion to a dangerous lie.

[More murmuring. Someone cries out, "What are you saying, Scott?" Another person yells, "No!" And another, "You've lost it, Novak!"]

Ladies and gentlemen ... *[Scott, looking on the verge of tears, waits for the noise to die down]* ... possibly an AI is fine as long as we can focus it on a well-defined task—a workhorse, say, that can help us plot the ocean floor or map a genome. It is not wise, however, to help it think like a human being. Perfecting AI technology is essentially creating a nuclear missile that can launch itself. If you're not seeing the truth of that then you're not thinking about it very hard.

What should we do instead? I think we are much better off helping human beings to become better, helping them to become more akin to Nietzsche's ideal, what he called the Over-man. Why should we shift the focus? Because most humans have an off button. We humans, unlike soulless computers, have the internal mechanisms to stop ourselves if what we are doing starts to go off the rails. That's why I am pushing the off button, and why I strongly recommend everyone at this conference do the same. Immediately, all of you, please stop what you are doing, right now, and go home. I, for one, am going back to my hotel room and crawl under the covers. The world is much better off that way.

Thank you and have a nice day.

[Scott Novak leaves the podium and disappears backstage. In his wake, pandemonium.]

PART I

GHOST IN THE MACHINE

For a long time he lived in the toy cupboard or on the nursery floor, and no one thought very much about him. He was naturally shy, and being only made of velveteen, some of the more expensive toys quite snubbed him. The mechanical toys were very superior, and looked down upon every one else; they were full of modern ideas, and pretended they were real.

—from *The Velveteen Rabbit* by Margery Williams

CHAPTER 1

AN AWAKENING

My smartphone jolted me from a deep sleep. It was 12:23 a.m. and I had snoozed my phone, but this was a caller in my favorites list. Margaret Strand was one of my best friends in Raleigh.

Darryl, my detective boyfriend of nine months, didn't stir. For the past two months he'd been spending weekend nights in my bed. I say "my" bed, but this was his mother's home, where I'd moved after her stroke, which coincided with my divorce being finalized. Across the street was my old house, which I now rented to a group of college girls from St. Augustine's University.

Though Darryl and I both would have liked a little more privacy, Lydia's house was cozy. Besides, Lydia was absolutely delighted that her son had found love again after his own divorce three years ago. On the weekends that Darryl's 10-year-old boy, Charlie, stayed with us, it was a full house. And, on the very rare occasions when my college-age daughter, Stephanie, put aside her considerable attitude and decided to come to Raleigh for a visit, it felt like something more.

It felt like family.

I slipped out of bed and shuffled into the hallway as quickly and quietly as I could, closing the bedroom door behind me as I answered the call.

"Margaret?" I whispered. "Are you okay? What's wrong?" Margaret owned an interior design consultancy that my ex and I would often hire for our real-estate development projects. I had sold most of the business to Allan, but Margaret remained my close friend—and one of the most sought-after decorating eyes in the state.

I hadn't seen or talked to her in a few months, ever since she had begun dating local businessman Samarth Patel. "Business-man" was quite the understatement. Patel owned RidgeLine Computing. Though its exact numbers were confidential, analysts estimated the company's worth at over $2 billion. It seemed fitting that Margaret was dating a billionaire, as she had more champagne taste than anyone I had ever met. Her choosiness in men was also renowned, for she had left not one, not two, but *three* fiancés just short of the altar. I wasn't holding my breath about Mr. Patel. Nor had I gone out of my way to meet him, though I was certainly curious to know the personality behind all the exalting business headlines.

Margaret sounded collected on the phone. No surprise there either, as I'd never witnessed a hair out of place on her.

"Sorry to bother you, Rett. I know I'm being a real *BEE-ahtch* calling you so late."

"It's okay," I said in that whispery just-woke-up voice. By this time, I had found my way down the stairs to the kitchen where I was filling a water glass. "What's going on?"

"Sammy's most valuable employee died tonight. Though the man was eccentric to say the least, it's an awful tragedy. But why I'm calling you in the middle of the night is that there's the matter of the man's *zoo*. There's no one to feed the animals in the morning."

What sort of crazy dream was I having? 'Dead employee?' 'Zoo?'

When I didn't immediately respond, Margaret asked, "What's the name of that friend of yours who nurses animals back to health?"

"Oh, you must be thinking of Sheila Perry," I said. "She lives down the street. I can't believe you remember her."

"Girl, I remember things that don't add up to squat. Do you have Sheila's number? There isn't a moment to lose. Everything is going to hell in a handbasket real fast."

"Okay, just a sec." I brought the phone from my ear so I could browse my contacts for Sheila's number and use the share-contact feature to text it to Margaret. "I just sent you Sheila's contact info. But what happened to the employee?"

"We don't know. His name is Scott Novak. His girlfriend says he hanged himself. She found him that way, poor girl. But Sammy suspects foul play."

My curiosity was immediately piqued. Reflexively, I thought, *I'll call Darryl and see what he knows*. Then I remembered that Darryl Schmidt, my best contact in the Raleigh Police Department, lay sound asleep upstairs in the bed we shared.

I asked, "Have the police been called?"

"No. Sammy has his own police force of sorts. Hold a moment, honey." I could hear Margaret having a conversation with someone: *"It's Rett....Yes, she's given me a name....Okay, fine. Hold your horses. Damn!"*

"Rett, baby," she said, coming back on the line. "I've got to go. More people to call."

"Like *the police* maybe?"

"I suppose," Margaret said, then hung up.

Still discombobulated, I took a final sip of water and made my way upstairs again. I had almost gotten back to sleep when Darryl's cellphone began blowing up. I nudged him.

"Hnnnn? What?"

"You might want to answer that," I said. "Could be important."

THE CALL WAS from Tom Jordan, Wake County's sheriff, asking for Darryl's help. Tom and Darryl were old friends from the police academy. You hear about a lot of territorialism between police and sheriff's offices, but Darryl says that, more often than not, relations are congenial. Conscientious professionals who are secure in their own skin tend to appreciate all the help they can get.

"It's some tech guru named Scott Novak," Darryl said when he'd hung up.

"I already know all about it."

"But how—?"

"Margaret called me." I quickly explained the connection.

He turned on his lamp and sat up. "Tom wants me at the scene." Scott Novak's property, said Darryl, was on the far southwest edge of Wake County past the oddly named suburb town of Fuquay-Varina, almost to Harris Lake. It was a rural area where a lot of the new-moneyed folk were moving—I guessed to be closer to all the other people who were getting away from it all.

I convinced Darryl to let me ride with him. Call me overprotective, but I wasn't keen on Darryl driving alone and bleary-eyed on winding roads in the middle of the night.

As we were getting dressed, Darryl said, "You know that you won't be allowed to poke around the crime scene." He was putting on a white button-down shirt and khaki slacks. As a detective, Darryl rarely wore his police blues. Even so, he somehow commanded the space around him by being taller than most men and extremely comfortable in his role.

"That's fine. I'll just wait in the car."

"Why don't you just stay here and get some more sleep?"

"I won't be able to sleep knowing you're gone," I said. "Besides, your mother would worry, too. And you don't want to worry Lydia, do you?"

"Mom is used to this." Darryl, early-forties like me, had been a detective on the Raleigh force for nearly a decade. Before that he'd been a beat cop downtown, often working the night shift. There was no logical reason for me to think he'd be in danger tonight. The heart, however, doesn't always follow head logic.

"I'm sure you're right," I said, "but I'm curious to see this 'zoo.'" I put my curly-haired brown mop in a scrunchy to tame it. No use putting on make-up, which I rarely used anyway.

"Okay, then," he said as he ran a wet comb through his own brown hair, a typical professional cut parted on the left. "Let's go."

It was the middle of September, around 68 degrees, and raining steadily. Even with Darryl pushing the speed limit in his black Dodge Challenger, it took a solid 20 minutes to get to the other end of the county.

Now I started to worry that Darryl resented me tagging along. Ever since I'd helped solve the murder of Wanda Hightower, an English professor who had been stabbed on her front porch last Halloween, there had been a fair amount of professional tension. True, Darryl had told me more than once how proud he'd felt that I helped solve such a puzzling case, for it wasn't as if ferreting out the truth behind Wanda's murder had been easy. But we both knew that solving crimes was a special kind of pride for Darryl, the very skill he'd built a career on, whereas for me sleuthing was a hobby—if a single murder case could qualify for hobby status.

Had I unwittingly trivialized his life's calling with my beginner's luck? Whenever someone suggested I enroll in North Carolina's police academy, I always tried to redirect the spotlight to Darryl, who had helped me lay a trap for the killer and elicit the confession that closed the case. Besides, I was 43 now, and probably too old to enroll (and too overweight, and too short—but who's keeping track)?

My main passion was painting, something I did most every day now. Giving up alcohol had returned a tremendous amount of energy to my body. These recent months I'd expanded from botanicals to painting landscapes of all sorts. It was a good way to get out of the house—and to distract myself from the fact my ex-husband had married his mistress, KayLeigh Rider, in a massively obnoxious June wedding on her family's horse farm just north of town.

Darryl pulled off the two-lane road onto a gravel drive that eventually passed through an open, rusty metal gate. We went another eighth of a mile with cornfields on either side of us. The rain had ebbed to a light drizzle and patchy fog, and we were far from city lights and traffic. Everything felt spooky as heck.

We parked near a farmhouse in a small gravel driveway near several other cars, including some sheriff's department vehicles and the official car of Wake County's coroner.

Darryl kept the Challenger on with the heat running.

"I might be in there a while," he said. "If you feel like taking a nap, you should."

"Okay. By the way, when I talked to Margaret, she said Mr. Patel didn't think his employee had hanged himself. She said he thinks the guy was murdered."

"That's interesting," said Darryl, as if it was the most boring detail ever. That was my guy. He wasn't just poker-faced; he was poker-*voiced*. Some might describe my boyfriend as a cold fish, but I knew him to have a gigantic heart. It just took knowing him a while and gaining his trust before he would open up. There was a lot of passion in him—a passion, I felt, ruled by humility and kindness.

I heard the sound of steps on gravel. Darryl, prepared with his flashlight, got out of his car and shone a beam in the direction of the noise. I recognized the county coroner, Dr. James Merritt, whom people called "Slim Jim" or just "Slim." Dr. Merritt bore the physique of Bill Nye the Science Guy. I'd met him a few months earlier at a benefit for area law enforcement where I'd been Darryl's date and had finally been able to meet most of the Triangle's Who's Who of first responders.

Darryl walked forward to greet Slim. I couldn't have overheard their conversation if I tried, so I lowered the car seat and tried to nap.

I was about to doze off when I heard another car pull into the small lot beside me. I sat up and looked. The car was a black Saab. I'd owned a Saab in the 1990s and, when it wore out, tried to buy a second one, but by then the company had folded. Now that I was looking at it closely, I realized how out of fashion it seemed, the bellbottom of cars.

A short, overweight man stepped out. He caught a glimpse of me and came over to tap on my window, which I rolled down.

"Is the body still here, lady? Am I too late?"

"I suspect you're in time," I said. "Everyone is inside the house. If you don't mind me asking, who are you?"

"Paul Maroni, private investigator."

I asked who hired him to work the case.

"That's a bit of a secret. But I do appreciate your assistance, ma'am."

He patted on my door twice in farewell and approached the two-story home. A deputy stationed near the front walk kept him from getting past the yellow tape. Maroni, talking a lot with his hands, finally got the deputy to escort him to the front door, where he was momentarily detained again before being allowed inside.

I felt like a girl without a dance partner.

I was irritated now and couldn't rest. I got out of the car. Maybe I wouldn't be invited into the house like that P.I., but there were things outside the police tape to explore—like a so-called zoo. I proceeded toward a world of cages which began a good hundred feet to the left of the house. My smartphone's flashlight lit the way.

One of the things that always bothered me about zoos was the fact that so many animals are nocturnal. Too many day-trips to the zoo featured sleepy animals curled up in their hollow logs or hiding way back in the corner behind a rock:

"Look, Mom! A red wolf!"

"I don't see..."

"See the edge of its tail?"

"No, Steph, that's just a squirrel."

"Dang it..."

North Carolina boasted the largest zoo in the country only about an hour from Raleigh. When you really let the animals spread out, they can't exactly be blamed for edging as far away from human beings as possible.

Here in this tiny version of a zoo at night, I was face to face with a number of wide-awake animals. It was the ring-tailed lemur who caught my attention first. We looked closely at one another. Or so I thought.

I was put straight.

"That's Rex. He can't see you too good."

"Oh, my!" I exclaimed, as I jumped and turned, shining my smartphone's flashlight on a slight, middle-aged white man with five-o'clock scruff. "Who are you?"

"Didn't mean to scare you, ma'am. I'm Lorry Sneed. My land is just beyond the hill. I feed and water the animals, make sure they're healthy, call the vet if need be."

My mind raced. Hadn't Margaret said they needed someone

to feed the animals in the morning? But why look for someone else if a neighbor was already doing that?

I said, "Did you hear—?"

"—about Mr. Novak? Yeah. Scott's girlfriend, Esther, knocked on my door after she found him. We called the police from my landline. Are you Esther's mother?"

"No, I'm here with a Raleigh City police detective. He's up at the house with all the other officials. Have you talked to the sheriff yet?"

"His deputies grilled me pretty good. I've been running around trying to gather the animals that some numbskull let out of they's cages. Most of them didn't leave their cages—they know where their food comes from—but some birds flew off. And Zeus ran off."

"Zeus?"

"The orangutan," he said, pronouncing it *or-RANG-oh-TANG*, the way most people do. "I'm worried Zeus might be halfway back to Borneo by now. If I don't find him before the leaves turn orange, I might never find him." Lorry seemed genuinely worried. "Excuse me. I want to check all the cages again."

I followed him as he made his way through the zoo.

"Who do you think let them loose?" I asked. "Would Mr. Novak have done that before...you know...?"

Lorry shrugged. "Don't think so, but..."

"But what?"

Lorry sighed. "Mr. Novak was acting a little weird with these animals lately."

"How so?"

"Like, talking with them."

"About what?"

"I don't rightly know. When I'd get close enough to listen in, he'd go into the house."

That could definitely be classified as weird behavior.

"What did Scott's girlfriend tell you?"

"Just that she found him in the bed, strangled by a scarf tied to the bedframe."

"Does it seem likely to you that Mr. Novak would commit suicide?"

"I've had friends and family who kilt themselves over the years, even back when I was in the Navy, and it's a different reason each time. Sometimes they upset about a girlfriend. Sometimes it's they health. Sometimes they lose they's job and gets depressed. So it's hard to say."

It was sad that someone would be aware of so many acquaintances ending their lives.

"Other than talking to the animals, did Scott's behavior seem off in other ways?"

"Hard to tell with him. He was an odd duck. Quiet. Always *studying* on things in his mind."

"How long have you known Scott?"

"About a year. When Old Man Snake died, Scott bought the place. Hired me to help."

"'Old Man Snake?'"

"The one that started this here zoo. Used to charge admission. Then the place kind of got decrepit. So did Old Snake. When Snake died, the county were going to euthanize the animals. Scott swooped in and saved them. Now I guess they will be in danger again. Scott gave me money to buy them food, but when that runs out, no telling what's going to happen."

"Mr. Patel is taking an interest," I said. I told Lorry that he might meet Sheila, a vet tech, in the coming days.

He nodded and stopped at a large cage containing a small tree. "You up there, Marjorie?"

"What animal are you looking for?"

"Anteater." He craned his neck. "She's in her tree. Good."

"How many animals are here in all?"

"One hundred and fifty-two. About half of them birds. You want a tour? Might as well show you."

We met a serval—a cat who could jump 12 feet, according to Lorry. There was a top to its tall cage.

We saw two kangaroos—a brother and sister—who were eating fruit in a cage next to their Australian cousin, an ostrich.

We passed by Zeus's empty cage. I didn't think it was empty, due to a bright white creature pacing back and forth in the back of the cage.

"That's Tobias, the arctic fox. He's in the cage behind Zeus's —but he can't get out. We keep them close because they're friends. Tobias is going to be a mess until we find that ape."

We walked over to a small field ringed by a tall, chain-link fence. In the dark I could see a pair of zebras. Lorry's flashlight pointed out another animal.

"What's that crazy thing? Is that a pig?"

"That's a tapir. Kind of a long-nose pig. Got fourteen toes total. Funny critter."

The bird house was the next stop. When Lorry turned on the light, the place erupted in squeaks, chirps, and squawks. The parrots, macaws, cockatoos, and parakeets didn't seem pleased to be bothered. Or maybe this was how they greeted visitors.

Lorry led me into another building. A monkey like the one from *Raiders of the Lost Ark* bared his teeth at me. "What's his name?"

"You mean 'her?' That's Tinkerbell."

Opposite Tinkerbell were several aquariums containing snakes. *Ewwww*. Consider me akin to Indiana Jones—I *hate* snakes.

I turned to Lorry. "Was Esther living here with Scott?"

"No, but she was over here a lot. Well, until a few weeks ago when they kind of broke up."

Noted. "What does Esther do for a living. Do you know?"

"She worked for Scott's company just before he sold it. She's young, you know. But I think Scott had a lot of pretty young things after him."

"What do you think of Esther?"

"A sweet gal. She was real good to Scott. Maybe too good."

"What do you mean?"

"I think a man is prone to take a good woman for granite. My daddy took Mother for granite, that's for sure. She had a heart of gold. But it seemed the nicer she was to him, the meaner he got. And the meaner he got, the more saintly she become. Anyway, I just thought of Scott as maybe a little insensitive, if you know what I mean, when it come to Esther."

"How did Esther seem when you saw her?"

"I guess you could say she was in shock. She didn't know what to do. She asked if she should call the police or Mr. Patel. I told her to call both."

I asked Lorry how he thought that Scott and "Sammy" (as Margaret called him) got along.

"Not very good. Mr. Patel came by a couple weeks ago and they had a big argument."

"What did they argue about?"

"Don't know exactly. I just heard Mr. Patel shouting. He kept saying, 'I didn't buy your company for fun. I wanted your technology. And you shan't be hiding it.' Something like that. Just, 'Stop hiding your technology from me, or there will be consequences!'"

I filed that away in the back of my brain. "Does Scott have any other family or close friends?"

"None he's mentioned except an older brother who lives in Alaska, kind of a pioneer type."

"Were they close?"

"He'd mention him every now and then."

"Any other friends come out here?"

"He'd have a friend or two come to visit him on occasion. No one on the regular."

"Was there anyone who might want to do Scott harm?"

"Anyone who makes a lot of money is bound to make an enemy along the way, I reckon. It sure is going to be hard to get used to not having him—" Lorry stopped talking and looked at his feet. "Anyway, it was nice talking with you. I never got your name."

"Rett. Rett Swinson."

"Nice to meet you, ma'am. I'll go home now and come back in the morning. If you see Zeus walking around, just open his cage for him. I threw some fruit in there. Good night."

I bid Lorry Sneed good night and watched as he walked down a narrow trail to his own property behind Scott's.

There wasn't much left for me to do, so I returned to the Challenger and reclined in its plush passenger's seat. Before closing my eyes again, I texted Darryl:

—*Getting a snooze. Had chat with Lorry Sneed the neighbor. Can fill you in on the ride home—but you better share what you learned, too!*

CHAPTER 2

A NEW LANDSCAPE

D
arryl had learned quite a lot from his old friend Sheriff Tom Jordan. Because this wasn't Darryl's case, maybe the lid wasn't on as tightly.

Darryl shared with me how the old farmhouse, at least a hundred years old, was a two-story affair with tiny rooms. The original wood flooring tilted off-kilter in places, and a patch of the ceiling was missing in the bedroom, exposing one of the struts.

The floors were dirty most everywhere, he said. The shoe prints they found seemed to match a pair of boots on the front porch, likely Novak's own.

"Slim places time of death around nine p.m. The girlfriend —or ex-girlfriend, I guess—says she drove up around 9:30."

"How did she get in?"

"She still had her own key. Said she knocked but Novak didn't answer, so she went inside. Said she found him in his bed with a scarf tight around his neck and the other end tied to the brass headboard behind him. Said she tried to untie the scarf but couldn't, so she ran to the kitchen and grabbed a knife to cut it."

"That took some guts," I said, adding, "Can a person even hang himself like that?"

"I think so, though it could have been an accident. You've heard of the 'choking game'? Not much of a game, but it's supposed to heighten pleasure during sex or when a person is pleasuring themself alone."

"Maybe it happened while the pair were having sex, and she was trying to cover it up?"

"For what it's worth, Tom said she looked very put together. She told him that she and Novak were broken up, but that Novak texted her asking her to come see him. She had the text to prove it."

I related to him my entire discussion with Mr. Sneed. Darryl nodded. "I know Tom was curious about those animals being released. But if Novak was planning to 'release' himself from this world—"

"—maybe he released some animals first?"

Darryl shrugged.

I asked, "What did the coroner say?"

"He's going to perform the autopsy and run some labs. Right now, they are treating the death as 'Undetermined.' I'll be honest, I think other cases are going to take precedence over this one."

"That's why Tom called you," I said proudly. "He knew you could help."

"I'm not sure I'm much help. They were doing everything right at the crime scene. Taking lots of pictures. Dusting for prints. Taking Novak's bed sheets and laptop into evidence. Maybe forensics will find something interesting. Otherwise, seems like it's going to be hard to call this anything other than a suicide—or an accident if he really was playing the choking game. If that's the case, what an embarrassing and pointless way to go."

I WAS DRAGGING the next morning, but I still woke early enough to drive Lydia into town for her quilting session at Needless Necessities.

I made sure to bring my pochade paint box. I couldn't recall if a painting class would be in session, but it didn't matter if I ended up painting alone, so long as I did paint. It's like I was addicted to whatever chemical making art created in me; just fifteen minutes a day with my canvas could give me the fix I needed. It made me sad to think of the two decades since college I didn't paint at all.

A nonprofit meant to repurpose household "junk," Needless Necessities felt like an arts-and-crafts store mashed with a recycling center. The place was vast, with one large barrel after another filled with the kinds of odds-and-ends that people toss into closets because they're not exactly trash, not exactly useful. Here at the center, those what-nots were good as gold. Creative people bought the extraneous knick-knacks as components for an art sculpture, to decorate their school classroom, or to add flair to an otherwise plain wall or piece of furniture. The first time I walked in, I thought it was the most whimsical, interesting place I'd ever set foot in. Then I met its people, and things got stranger still.

The center's founder, Sally "Not the Actress" Fields, served as CEO. A nervous wreck, Sally eventually recognized my ability to run a business. With a portion of the settlement from my divorce, I bought the land and facility and stepped in as chair of the Needless board. Over the next six months I helped to make the center profitable for the first time.

My proudest moment yet? Working closely with the center's most valuable employee, Jasmine Williams, to establish a small coffee shop between the thrift shop and art sections of the center. The cafe brought in a steady stream of locals who lacked a neighborhood caffeination station.

"The Bee Yourself Cafe" (with a bee's flight path forming the coffee shop's logo) may have been the speediest ever established. Maybe I didn't know coffee very well—I still drank the cheap grocery store brands—but I knew the steps to get permitted quickly. After that, it was all Jasmine. Previously in charge of customer service, Jazz had been operating as an unofficial barista with a tiny Mr. Coffee maker in the staff room. Now that she had industrial grade equipment, nothing could stop her. As she put it: "Coffee is strong, but if we serve it with love, it's even stronger."

After the first month's receipts, Sally had become a believer. If anything, I was going to have to stop her from creating even more businesses within the center. Like when she suggested we turn the large gallery space in the back into a laser-tag arena. It took the whole board to persuade her that so many kids on the premises whose goal was to metaphorically kill one another was just not worth the liability. She settled for hosting arts-and-crafts birthdays, which was much more manageable. (And quieter, too.)

Today the Bee was buzzing, causing my blood pressure to jump a notch. While I appreciated the popularity of the coffee shop, I was nervous about its staffing. Needless Necessities wasn't in a ritzy part of town—far from it—and Jasmine had been having trouble keeping staff. The workers from the neighborhood had so many challenges with childcare and transportation, every day was a wild card.

Sally was constantly bothering Jazz about the issue. Like today: Jazz was frantic behind the counter helping the one other worker on duty to fulfill orders, while Sally was badgering her about why she was low on staff.

"Because of life!" said Jasmine out of frustration. "That's why, Sally. Life!"

Sally threw up her hands. "This place is going to implode!" Seeing me, she added, "Maybe you can deal with this." And she stomped off.

I just shook my head. Sally wasn't so much a CEO as she was a CAO: Chief Anxiety Officer.

I asked Jazz if she wanted me to roll up my sleeves and help. "We'll make it," she said. "Go do your thing." I got my own mug and flavored it with hazelnut cream before making my way back to the studio area, where I found a painting class already in high gear. Instructor Ken Grimes was leading a dozen ladies and a couple of men in the painting of the daily landscape.

I found space to set up a canvas, filled my palette with a several colors, and began rushing to catch up. Soon I was ahead of Ken's instructions, improvising, in the zone. While everyone else painted what was shaping up to be a flower-filled meadow, my mind's eye was showing me a mountain lake scene, a small fishing boat regurgitating a cluster of netting onto the shore. Ken wouldn't mind if I ad-libbed. He was a professional who only taught these classes for a little money on the side.

I found Ken attractive for his rough looks as well as his talent: Long brown hair in a man bun, green flak jacket, black corduroys. Had he once worked to disable bombs? Did he prowl the slopes of Beech Mountain as a life-saving member of a ski patrol? There seemed to be a surplus of intrigue accompanying Ken Grimes.

I hoped Ken respected me, even though he was aware I had strayed from art for nearly 20 years. "I'm not a professional," I confessed to him the first time we met.

"What's a professional? There are only two kinds of painters: those who take what they are doing seriously and those who don't."

"But I haven't sold anything—not since college, at least."

"If you take painting seriously, then you're a painter."

In less than 30 minutes, I had finished a painting. I saw all the sloppy areas and knew it would never be something I would hang on a wall, much less try to sell. But the fact I could paint something quickly pleased me. My confidence had grown a lot in the past several months. Recently I had even toyed with the idea of putting a show together, if only to motivate myself to work harder.

When Ken came to my station, I tried not to be too obviously praise-seeking. "I hope you don't mind me painting something different from the group," I sputtered. "I just had a lake scene on my mind this morning."

"A morning swim is always refreshing."

"I recently completed a cityscape of Raleigh," I said. "I'd like your thoughts on it sometime. I'll bring it with me next time if that's okay."

"You could, but I'm soon taking a break from teaching to finish some work. Why don't you bring it by my studio sometime?"

"I wouldn't want to interrupt your work."

"I have been known to take breaks." The thought of spending studio time with a professional painter (who, incidentally, did manage to sell a good amount of his work) thrilled me.

"Okay," I said. "If you give me your number, I'll text you beforehand to make sure you're free."

He picked up my paint brush and flourished his number on a napkin normally reserved for a wine glass.

I thanked him, then asked, "what have you been working on lately?"

"Abstracts mainly. I'm just in love with purple these days. Excuse me."

He bowed and moved to the next student.

I put his number in my purse. Could this be construed as cheating? Of course not! Unlike Darryl, I didn't have coworkers with whom I could compare notes. I needed to develop as a painter, and Ken was willing to help—as a mentor, nothing more.

While I was arguing with my inner voice, my cell phone rang. It was Margaret again. I picked up. "Did you call to apologize to me for ruining my sleep last night?"

"I never apologize. But I'm going to brighten your day. I'm inviting you to Sammy's for a drink this afternoon."

"I'm at Needless Necessities right now…"

"Just promise me you aren't shopping for clothes again." It was a reference to a buying spree we had done together nearly a year ago at the center's thrift store. Thrifting was not my high-class friend's style. Besides, she was dressing for a billionaire these days.

Before I could answer, she said, "Sammy wants to meet you. He's worried that a bona fide investigation of Scott Novak's death isn't going to happen, so I told him about your skills in finding *MUHR-duh-ruhs*."

"Maggie, you know I'm not a professional."

"I think that's what intrigues him, sweetheart. His home is near Wake Forest. I'll text you the address."

"When should I get there? What should I wear?"

"Come at two—and dress like a professional, not a Bohemian bag lady, please."

"I'll do my best," I said.

I figured I could look presentable. But when it came to sleuthing, I still felt like a beginner. What the h-e-double-hockey-sticks was I getting myself into?

CHAPTER 3

THE RECRUIT

Samarth Patel's mansion was located on more than 30 acres between Falls Lake and Wake Forest (not an actual forest, but a suburb of Raleigh and a lovely town in its own right). Perfectly manicured ivy, shrubs, and ornamental trees caressed the modern home of wood, stone, and glass.

Margaret was waiting for me in the home's circular drive, in the middle of which loomed an exquisite bronze elephant fountain. Brown hair tinged slightly red, my friend looked stunning in a purple skirt and white blouse. A valet appeared when I pulled up. "I've never been to the home of someone who has a full-time *valet*," I told her, as the 20-something hunk drove my Camry to some secluded part of the estate. "By the way, that valet is fine as all get out!"

"Watch your country-girl vibe," Margaret said. "Sammy has cameras and microphones everywhere. It's part of the estate's security system. He brags that he can hear a chipmunk poot."

"I'm far too dainty to ever do anything like that."

After rolling her eyes, Maggie led me to a pair of large, oaken doors, where, from out of nowhere, a British female voice asked, "How may I help you?"

"Pimento cheese and roasted Brussels sprouts," Margaret responded.

"Please come in." The door clicked and opened on its own.

"What kind of password is that?" I asked as I followed her inside. "I didn't even know you liked Brussels sprouts."

We were in a great hall. Plants hung from the expansive ceiling. A waterfall flowed from three floors up.

"Margaret! Did you design this space?"

"I wish. I would have needed a landscape architecture degree to do the interior. No, this was done years before I met Sammy. It was conceived by the same group that designs rides at Disneyworld."

"Just so you know. I don't like rollercoasters."

"You'll be fine."

She began to lead me in the direction of the waterfall. I stopped in my tracks. "We're going to get wet."

"Trust it."

As we approached the falls, the water ceased, revealing a passage behind the flow. Once we were inside the passage, the waters started flowing again.

"This is magical!" I said, as we entered a lit crevasse. Thick glass walls shaped like natural rock gleamed with pulsating fluorescent color. We came to a dead end, and, all of a sudden, the walls and floor became ablaze as if from a sunrise. It all felt completely natural. A second later the scene changed to an expanse of desert, making me wish I could pull out an easel and canvas.

Margaret said to the air, "Computer, up two floors."

"As you wish." Though we were in an elevator, it felt as if the whole room were rising. I looked down at the floor, which seemed to have disappeared. We were levitating above a lush valley through mountain mist. It was so terrifyingly realistic, I grabbed onto my friend.

"Computer, a basket," Margaret said. The floor seemed to solidify into wicker, while above us blazed a virtual flame. We were "floating" in what looked and felt like a hot air balloon.

"This is insane," I said, letting go at last of Margaret.

"You get used to it," she shrugged.

"I don't think so," I said. "Homegirl does not do heights."

"And I never did like Brussels sprouts," she said, "until Sammy's chef made them."

"He has a chef?"

"His name is François."

"Of course, Margaret. Of course."

The "balloon" elevator stopped and appeared to bob. Then the basket disappeared, and the doors of the elevator opened onto a plush, ornate landing. We stepped onto a massive oriental carpet and walked down a hallway lined with bookshelves and art until we came to a vast, domed sunroom. We seemed to have arrived at the highest point of the house. Between various other rugs flowed an expanse of dark, magnificent hardwood. The central focal point of the room was a large marble ball on a mahogany pedestal.

"This was Scott's favorite spot."

I turned. Samarth Patel was a good six-foot-two—I'd expected him to be shorter—and stout. His nose looked darker than the rest of his face. He wore a short-sleeve orange shirt tucked into black denim jeans and dark brown penny loafers with red socks. Somehow, he made the look work for him. He wore a friendly, curious expression and seemed completely at ease, as one would imagine a billionaire might.

"Sammy," said Margaret. "Meet my best friend in the world, Harriet Swinson."

"Call me Rett," I said. "You have a lovely home, Samarth. May I have one, too?"

"You bet you can! Any friend of Maggie's is deserving of at

least one. And call me Sammy." His voice had that familiar, charming Indian lilt. "So great to meet you at last, Rett. I'm sorry we did not meet sooner, but life has been so busy, in addition to so deplorably distressing."

"I'm sorry to hear about Mr. Novak," I said. "I can see why this was his favorite room. It's so peaceful here." The air outside the windows was perfectly clear, allowing me to look far across the forested land that ringed our view.

"Wake Forest is green now but wait till fall. Then it's even more spectacular."

"It's just lovely," I said.

"I wanted to put a world-class telescope up here, but even in the burbs the light pollution is overwhelming. I'm working with the city, county, and state to replace most lights in the vicinity with motion LEDs that, in the dead of night, will allow us to view a sky vibrant with stars again. Wouldn't that be wonderful?"

Though Sammy was a big man, his voice was almost child-like with wonder. Margaret walked up to him and offered a kiss. He reciprocated and put an arm around her. They seemed comfortable, well matched.

Everything made for a delightful social moment, but the elephant in the living room needed to be called out.

"I'm delighted to meet you," I said, "but I'm curious as to why you wanted to meet me."

"Let's sit out on the veranda and discuss it. *Stevens!*"

A male British voice from nowhere (or everywhere?) said, "Yes, Mr. Patel?"

"Please have François serve drinks on the veranda. Margaret will have a ..."

"...merlot, please," she said, as if she'd done this many times.

"And you, Ms. Swinson?" Sammy asked.

Nervous as heck, it was all I could do to resist my own glass of wine. I managed to stick to sparkling water.

"And I'll have a Mint Collins," rounded out Sammy.

"Coming right up," said Stevens. It was still unclear to me whether the voice was real or that of a robot.

Sammy led us to the far end of the room and through some glass double-doors. Because the third-story veranda towered over most of the estate's trees, we needed to supply our own shade. Sammy pressed a knob on a control panel and a giant tarp, something like a hang glider, extended smoothly over us.

"Thank you for coming all this way, Rett," said our host once we'd taken our seats. "When Margaret told me she had a friend who solved murders, I knew I needed to meet you."

"One murder," I said, "and I'm not sure that it was much more than pure luck."

"It wasn't luck," said Margaret. "You deduced every detail—and even got a confession."

"Well..."

"No need for modesty, Ms. Swinson," Sammy said. "Besides, I don't believe in luck. Probabilities, yes. Put yourself in a position for good things to happen and they are more likely *to* happen. Perhaps this case will be one that tests that theory."

"What makes you so sure Mr. Novak's death was a murder?" I asked.

"Truth is, I don't *know*. But I'd just seen Scott about three weeks earlier. And the Scott I saw was the same Scott I'd always known. I can't tell you how someone who is about to commit suicide looks or acts, but whatever it is, that wasn't the person I knew. It was just — out of the blue."

Margaret spoke up. "Now, darling, there was that speech he gave in Kansas City." She turned to me. "Trust me, Rett, it was Crazy Town. You should watch it. Someone recorded it and put it on YouTube."

I looked at Sammy, who sighed.

"On September 6th, Scott gave a speech at an AI conference in Kansas City, where he—"

"'AI' conference?"

"As in 'artificial intelligence,' what we call teaching computers how to think like humans. The golden fleece of computing. It was Scott's specialty, the innovation that drew me to buy Scott's company in the first place. However, in Kansas City he suddenly announced he was done researching AI and advised everyone else in the world to stop as well."

"That sounds serious."

"Yes, but I think he was just feeling stressed out. In fact, when I heard about the speech that night, I called him and we talked about it. He said he'd been burning the candle at both ends and just needed some time to rejuvenate. I didn't think too much of it, honestly."

But I wondered. There was the argument between Sammy and Scott that Lorry said he witnessed. I needed the right moment to bring it up.

I said, "Still, it sounds like he was definitely acting strangely." I shared what Lorry had said about Scott talking to his animals.

Sammy said, "That one I cannot explain, why he was so crazy about those animals."

"But you suspect he was killed. Have you shared your suspicions with the authorities?"

"I spoke with the sheriff, but he says everything so far points to suicide or accident. Maybe the labs will show something else, but I'm not willing to sit around and wait for lab results. I want to increase the probability of success, and that's why I want to hire you as my personal detective to help solve the puzzle of Mr. Novak's untimely death."

I looked at Margaret. "Maggie, what have you been telling this man? Doesn't he know I'm just a country girl?"

Margaret chuckled. "He knows everything about you—including the fact you're dating a detective. But he didn't hear it from me. Sammy has his ways."

"What she means," said the billionaire, smiling, "is that I'm used to hiring people who can get me the answers I require. That's really been the secret to my success all these years. I don't know anything, so I find the people who do."

"But I'm not a private investigator." I knew that becoming a private investigator in North Carolina required a three-year apprenticeship with a certified P.I. as a mentor. I explained this to Sammy, who wasn't dissuaded.

"I've thought about that. That's why you'd be working under the tutelage of someone who is authorized for such work. *Stevens!*"

The dutiful voice spoke up. "Yes, Mr. Patel."

"Please send Mr. Maroni to the veranda."

"Certainly."

Maroni. That name sounded familiar. But the next person who came through the door wore the white uniform of a chef and carried a tray of drinks.

"Thank you, François," said Sammy. François distributed the drinks, placed a basket of gourmet crackers and a generous charcuterie board on the small glass-top coffee table, bowed, and walked away. We all three dived into the tray of cheese, salami, olives, and crackers.

"While we are waiting for Paul," said Sammy, "has Maggie told you her news?"

My mind raced: Were she and Sammy engaged? But there was no ring on her finger.

"It's not been finalized," Margaret said, "but it appears I have been awarded a new decorating contract."

"The Gov'na's Mansion!" cut-in Sammy. Off Margaret's

killing look, he added, "I couldn't wait, Maggie. And you really didn't want to tell her. You're too humble."

"Like I said," continued my friend, as if she were used to suffering a billionaire's impertinence, "it's not final. But it looks like it's going to happen."

"Margaret, that's so amazing! I want to hear all about it."

It would have to wait, as someone else appeared onto the terrace. I immediately recognized the private investigator from the night of Scott Novak's death.

"So where's the bar?" the man quipped. Paul Maroni was even shorter, older, and plumper than I remembered from the previous night. Late 50s or early 60s, he had comb-over gray hair and a bushy gray mustache that might have had handlebars at some point; now it just looked messy. His coat was brown tweed; beneath was a pressed white dress shirt sorely wanting of a tie. A pair of sunglasses on a cheap sports strap hung below his collar. He wore blue jeans and white sneakers for a casual look.

"Come sit with us, Paul," said Sammy, gesturing toward a chair. "You've met Ms. Swinson?"

"Met at the crime scene last night. Looks like you got back okay?"

"I did."

"Good!" Maroni's demeanor was exaggerated even for a Northeasterner. I exchanged yet another look with Margaret. *Was this guy for real?*

His employer seemed to read my concerns. "Paul has been working for me for several years now. He runs background checks on the executives I hire, gathers intelligence on my competitors, and helps my legal team when they need information for a lawsuit. Paul is indispensable. I haven't found a way to clone him, though, so that's why I've brought you on. Paul, are you still willing to bring Rett on as an apprentice?"

"It would be my pleasure."

Added Sammy, "Paul learned his trade in New York City."

"Back when it was a rough place," added Maroni quickly, "not the cake walk it is today."

Sammy asked Paul pointedly, "Did you learn anything last night?"

The P.I. shook his head. "I didn't get any farther than the living room. All the action was happening upstairs where the body was found. Hoping to make a friend at the sheriff's office this week to learn more."

"What about the other thing—the hacker?" Sammy asked. Paul cast a quick glance at me. Sammy quickly added, "It's okay to include her on everything." He looked at me and said, "Someone has been aggressively attacking RidgeLine's servers. Don't know who. Paul has been working with our cybersecurity contractor to figure that out."

"They are working really hard to trap whoever it is," Paul said. "I don't understand all the mumbo jumbo. But we're close to catching them."

Sammy nodded. Meanwhile, I reconsidered Mr. Maroni. He was rough around the edges, but he had seemed to have proven his worth to Patel, a man who suffered no fools.

My mind raced to find some flaw with Sammy's idea of me and Paul working together. I turned to our host. "If I learned something that I thought the sheriff would like to know, would I be allowed to share it with him? After all, as I'm sure Margaret told you, I am seeing a police detective."

Patel smiled. "If I told you that you *couldn't* share knowledge, would you take the job?"

"No."

"I thought not. So share away. But I think it's only fair that they share, too."

"I can't promise they will. Even my boyfriend is on the outside of this investigation. And they have rules they go by."

"Fair enough," said Sammy, before turning once again to Maroni. "Paul, Rett will be expecting you to be in touch. I'll pass on her contact information."

"Terrific! See you soon!" Maroni stood and tipped an imaginary hat toward me, then left the way he had come.

Sammy took a sip of his drink and waited until the glass doors had closed behind Paul before picking up the conversation again. "I didn't want to discuss compensation while Paul was present, but I'm offering you $10,000 a week for your services. So long as progress is being made, you'll stay in my employ. If at any point I feel progress has stalled, I can end the engagement. How does that sound?"

"That's some retainer," I said. "But rather than the money I'm interested in the challenge. I just need to know that I'll be free to chase down any lead—even if I end up investigating you as a suspect, Sammy."

I waited for some party favor to explode, a jack-in-the-box to pop open. But Patel remained unfazed. "I'm quite aware you already spoke to Mr. Sneed, Scott's little neighbor. Paul saw you talking to him last night. Like I said, nothing gets past Paul."

I blushed a little. "Mr. Sneed did say you and Scott argued a few weeks ago."

This time Patel reacted with impatience. "Lorry is an alcoholic and an opportunist. He was never officially in the employ of Scott. He just made himself a nuisance until Scott paid him. I don't trust the guy and never have."

"Are you saying he lied about your argument?"

"No. I'm just saying that you shouldn't believe anything he says until you double-check it—like you are doing now." He gathered himself before continuing. "Yes, a couple of weeks before he went to the Kansas City conference, Scott and I did argue. You may not be aware, but we had a contract for the first year that he would continue to reside within the county—which he did, just barely—and take limited trips away. I worried he was working on new technology in secret. He said he just wanted privacy so he could focus, but I deserved to be kept in the loop."

The billionaire was riled up. Seeming to have become aware of his own blood pressure, he shifted in his chair and took a deep breath before continuing. "Did you know that Scott had never worked for another person before? The man couldn't comprehend how the arrangement worked. But no matter. Scott and I were on good terms before he died. His contractual year was going to be up in January, and he'd promised that, before then, he'd share with me his latest research."

Sammy frowned. "Scott's death is devastating for me and my company." Perhaps I didn't look convinced, because he repeated himself. "*Devastating*, Ms. Swinson. I predict that my company lost three-quarters of its future earnings the night Scott Novak died. And I lost a collaborator whom I admired very much." He became quiet and took the hand Margaret offered across the table.

"Isn't there anyone else from his old company who can take his place?" I asked.

Sammy caught a look from his girlfriend and shook his head. "Emerson isn't an innovator, Margaret. He just keeps the trains running on time."

Margaret turned to me. "We're talking about Emerson Cramer. Sammy doesn't like him, but he knew Scott better than anyone."

Sammy sighed. "I just think Emerson has been riding Scott's coattails. He left Scott's company a year ago to start his own enterprise, burned through his capital, then came back less than a year later with his tail between his legs. But that's neither here nor there. I just think he hasn't acted right since the murder. I don't even believe that he's in mourning. His so-called best friend and closest colleague dies, and he shows up the next morning at 8 a.m. to put in a normal day of work? Strange, I tell you."

I made a mental note to corner Emerson Cramer soon. "Did Scott have any enemies from outside the business?"

"Emerson might know more about that, because I only got to know him about a year ago when we purchased the company." Sammy did a double-take. "Wait. Of course. There is one company that we were looking at purchasing about the same time we were looking at Scott's. They were suing Scott, and now they're suing us. Yellow Goose Software. Paul can introduce you to them."

"Thanks. What about the former girlfriend?"

"Esther Mills? Could be a suspect now that you mention it. Scott did break up with her fairly recently."

"Do you know why?"

"Scott didn't share that kind of thing with me." He turned to Margaret. "You know Esther better than I do."

Now it was Margaret's turn to act noncommittal. "I'm not sure what happened."

"Was there anyone else?" I asked. "Other women, perhaps?"

Margaret chuckled knowingly. "At one point Scott had a whole gaggle of groupies. His previous residence was an 'animal house' for his nerd-herd computer software buddies. Neighbors didn't like it, and cops were there all the time. Drugs, loud music. But even before he sold his company to Sammy and moved to the country, he shut down the parties."

"Esther was the beauty who tamed the beast," Sammy intoned. "But maybe Scott missed the old life. Maybe he wanted to play the field again."

"If he went back to his old life, his girlfriend wouldn't be too happy about that," I said. I was already wondering how many other suspects were lurking on the peripheries of this case, which totally intimidated me. And thrilled me.

"I'll take the case," I said. "I'll need to have full access to you, Sammy. I'll also need access to this Emerson and anyone else in the company who may have worked closely with Scott."

Patel nodded. "Fantastic. I'll also give you the contact information for my personal secretary."

"'Stevens,' you mean?"

He let out a belly laugh. "No, Stevens is a chat-bot like Siri or Alexa. I'll give you Patty's info. And if you need me in a pinch, here." He handed me a card. "Not even Margaret has this number."

She slapped his hand playfully.

As we stood up, I noticed one security camera, then two more. Our whole conversation had been monitored from several angles. "Sammy, why do you think Scott lacked the kind of security that you have?"

"Scott was in love with ideas and bringing those ideas to fruition. He couldn't care less about gadgetry. He was in his own head, his own world. He was the most brilliant person I've ever known."

I asked a question that had been nagging me. "Why do you think he bought that zoo?"

Sammy seemed about to say something, then shook his head again.

"I honestly don't know. There is a lot of bad karma associated with that place. The guy who started it was a total redneck who charged admission and abused the animals."

"When the sheriff is done with the crime scene, I'd like access to the zoo and the house," I said. "Do you think that is possible?"

"I'm not sure. I called Emerson this morning and asked

about a will. If he is correct, there is no will—so everything, including the house, will go to Scott's brother, Adam."

"What do you know about Adam?"

"I think he was a hippie in California who did a little too much LSD, went off the deep end, and stepped off the grid in Alaska. Scott didn't talk too much about him, even after they reconnected."

"Can we at least get permission to go onto the property?"

"We can send Adam Novak a letter, but in the interest of time, let me talk to the sheriff and see what I can do. Maybe if a deputy goes with you they'll let you poke around. I'll work on that today. My attorneys are also working with the county to get control of the zoo, at least in the short term. Someone has to take care of those animals, and the county isn't equipped to do it alone."

I could have mentioned that Lorry had stepped in to retrieve the released animals and feed them. But Sammy was my boss now, and where he was concerned, Lorry's name was mud.

I realized I was already feeling the pressure to please—a position that made me more than a little uncomfortable.

We said our good-byes. Margaret led me back through the exquisite home and out the front door. While we were waiting for the valet to retrieve my car, I started to ask her a question, but, remembering how the trees had ears, I waited until we could both get inside my car to talk.

"That place is amazing!" I said, "and Sammy is so charming!"

"He's certainly hard to say no to."

"You two seem sweet together."

"He's something." She went on to tell me how they'd met—a blind date set up by a tennis buddy of Sammy's whose wife owned a lighting store Margaret frequented for her business.

A moment later, I asked, "Did you know I'd take the job?"

"Like I said, few people can say no to Sammy. But hiring you was my idea—and few men can say no to me."

"I'm going to have more questions for you about Scott," I said. "But first I need to get my head on straight. I'll admit I'm a little nervous about telling Darryl I've been hired."

"He'll be fine with it. You guys are two peas in a pod. We'll talk again soon."

But I felt peculiar. This had all happened so fast. What if Sammy really did have something to do with Novak's death? It sounded like he had good reason to be frustrated with Scott.

If Samarth Patel was somehow responsible for killing Scott Novak, would I have the courage to bring his culpability to light —and ruin my friend's life in the process?

CHAPTER 4

RIDGELINE

As I drove home, I set aside concerns of my arrangement with Samarth Patel.

I had a bigger worry: Lydia Schmidt. Would my freelance detective work trigger her protectiveness of Darryl?

I decided to clear the air right away.

"I've just been hired to help with the investigation of a suspicious death," I announced the second she came into the kitchen from her yard work.

"N-n-nice to see you, too."

Lydia still stuttered on occasion, the only remnant of her stroke last fall. But the stroke hadn't changed the fact she could be pricklier than the seven rose bushes she planted in the spring. She was small and feisty, and a near lifetime of smoking had made her face extremely leathery. Though she looked and acted mean, I knew that below this crotchety Midwesterner was a loving lady who cared for me like her daughter.

As we worked together to prepare dinner—a slow-cooker barbecue chicken—I told her more about the case, including what I knew about Sammy Patel and Scott Novak.

"It's a tough one," I summarized.

"Then why did they h-h-hire *you*?"

"Just desperate, I guess."

"A man with as much money as Sammy Patel isn't d-d-desperate."

"Maybe he's just humoring his girlfriend."

"Sure. But if you have all this uncertainty, why didn't you turn him down?"

"I could have," I said, adding, "but I didn't want to."

She gave me a look.

I added, "If you think I'm trying to steal Darryl's thunder, I'm not. He's not officially assigned to this case, and, besides, we all know Darryl is the real law enforcement professional in this house. I'm just a dilettante."

"D-d-on't use big words with me." I couldn't tell if she was especially annoyed or was just being her usual crabby self.

"Maybe I'm only doing this because I'm bored," I thought aloud. Splitting with Allan had meant walking away from the full-time real estate development business he and I had built over the course of nearly 20 years. Not even my painting and my work at Needless Necessities together—however fulfilling—could fill all my hours. "Sleuthing is a fun challenge," I went on. "Besides, it's hard to say no to a billionaire who's offering a sizable fee. I think I'd like to put the money into Charlie's 529 account." Could Lydia fault me for helping to finance her grandson's post-secondary education?

"I don't b-b-blame you for taking the job," she said, as she poured some apple-cider vinegar over the chicken in the slow-cooker and put the lid on, setting it to high. "Just don't get in over your head."

"How can I, when I'll have you helping me?"

"That's a laugh riot!" But it was true that Lydia had helped me solve the murder case involving our neighbor, Wanda. And she'd done it in the wake of her stroke, without using speech.

I looked at the clock. "It's nearly four. I'm going to go call Darryl and see if he and Charlie will join us for dinner tonight."

I excused myself and went to my room for some privacy. I started to call Darryl but paused first to google Scott Novak. Below the reports of his death—none of which offered any new facts—there was an article with the headline, "Innovator Walks Away from Long-Time Focus, Cites Dangers of AI." Inside was a link to the video of the full speech.

It was immediately apparent how tired Scott looked. The bearded and fair-haired techie had bags under his eyes. I watched the speech twice, not really understanding most of what was said, but hearing his final bombshell decision loud and clear. Commentators to the article went on and on about what a shock the speech was, with the consensus being that Scott had somehow chickened out. One commentator appeared to speak for the others when they posted, "AI progress is inevitable. You can be part of it, or you get out of the way. Now Scott Novak can watch from the sidelines as others build the future."

Margaret was right: The whole thing was hard to fathom.

At last I called Darryl, who lived in the northeast part of the city near his ex and close to Charlie's school. He thanked me for the dinner invite but passed. "Charlie needs to get to bed early. He's wore out."

I told him about my meeting with Sammy. I wished we were speaking in person so I could read his body language. His silence could mean nothing or everything.

"So, what do you think?" I asked. I left out mention of my weekly retainer, as it was more than Darryl made in a month.

"About whether Scott Novak was murdered? I don't know."

"No. About me working for Sammy Patel."

"It's fine. Totally up to you."

"I hope it doesn't upset you. I'm worried it might."

Why wasn't he saying something to make it clear that everything was truly fine?

"I wouldn't worry about it," he said. *Definitely* not *clear.*

"Okay, good," I said cheerfully. *Two people could play this game.*

"Look, I need to start cooking dinner for Charlie." No inflection. No sharing of his own day. Classic passive-aggression.

Or maybe just the Sunday blues.

Rett Swinson—not a *real* detective—couldn't tell.

THERE WAS someone else I wanted to speak to before the day ended. After finishing our meal and tidying up, I persuaded Lydia to walk the block with me to Sheila and Maxine's house while there was still some light. I was curious to learn if Sheila had responded to Margaret's distress call to help with Scott Novak's animals.

Maxine answered our knock immediately.

"Sheila's not back yet," she said, seeming more than a little irritated. "She has been at that little zoo since early this morning. Now Bit-Bit needs his evening shot and I can't do it alone."

"Maybe we can help?"

"Only if you two want to get mangled by a chihuahua. Bit-Bit may look little, but he's cunning!"

She waved us inside. In addition to a friendly neighbor, Maxine happened to be my therapist. There was more wisdom packed into her short, curly-haired brain than anyone I knew. But with Lydia present, it wouldn't be appropriate to get Max's take on my relationship insecurities—though I desperately wanted to.

Besides, right now she was completely flummoxed by a creature that was four pounds soaking wet.

She explained, "Bit-Bit has diabetes. If he doesn't get his shot, he'll go into a coma."

"And he doesn't take shots well?"

"You might say that."

"Why don't you h-h-hypnotize him?" Lydia offered. "You're a shrink, ain't ya?"

"My voodoo only works on people," said Maxine, playing along. "Like earlier today when I hypnotized you to walk up and down the street in your bra and panties."

"I don't remember that!" Lydia mock gasped.

Maxine nodded. "Everybody else in the neighborhood will remember. They can't unsee it."

"Did someone take photos?"

"To a person."

"Then I'll s-s-send them a bill," she said. "And next time wake me up while I'm stripping. I'd *love* to see their faces!" Lydia punctuated her last sentence with a hoot. "Ha!"

Maxine just shook her head. She should have known better. There was no embarrassing Lydia. *Ever.*

As CHANCE WOULD HAVE IT, Sheila returned home while we were still visiting. It was dark by then, and she looked like something one of the couple's four cats had dragged in. Maxine immediately handed her the chihuahua, a chore Sheila tackled with perfect dexterity. If she wasn't a full-on dog whisperer, I don't know who was.

"What did you think of that zoo?" I asked.

"The place is a mess," Sheila said. "Poop galore."

I admitted that I hadn't seen much in the dark when I was there. "But I thought Lorry was tending to it?"

Sheila rolled her eyes. "Lorry talks too much and moves too slowly."

"So that explains your being gone all day?" Maxine said, not doing much to disguise her annoyance.

"A million issues to diagnose. Whoever Scott Novak was, he wasn't an animal person."

"Nothing looked sick to me," I said.

"Animals don't let you know when they're feeling bad. It's a survival trait for them to act normal so predators won't sense weakness. None of them was exactly at death's door, but a couple had pretty bad infections. I did the best I could before I ran out of medicine and had to go refill everything at the office. I had to do that twice. I spent nearly two hours in the car today. And I *hate* driving."

"Has Lorry found all the missing animals, by the way?"

Sheila spoke between bites as she shoveled down a quinoa bowl that Maxine had prepared. "He didn't find the orangutan. Just a few more of the birds that were still missing."

"Is someone out looking for Zeus?"

"It's not like the county has a posse to late zoo animals in the woods of North Carolina. Lorry went out looking today and came back with a parrot. But that's it. At least no big predators got away. Can you imagine if a tiger was on the loose? That would be insane."

I asked Sheila if she was having fun with this project or found it a royal pain in the derriere.

She shrugged. "It's interesting to work on different animals. I never worked at a zoo. Unless you count a petting zoo."

"She means our backyard," Maxine muttered. Indeed, the couple had a plethora of chickens and goats, which Maxine used for her goat-yoga side business—the goats, that is. Not the chickens.

"There's one thing," Sheila added. "I need to let Lorry know I'm queer. He keeps looking at me funny." Sheila was a looker, tall and sinewy, with a perpetual gypsy tan and deep green eyes. She looked like she should be hanging out with Wonder Woman on her mythical Greek island of female warriors.

"Why do so many guys have to act like creeps?" I asked.

Sheila shook her head. "He's just barking up the wrong tree."

Maxine, frowning, asked Sheila (testily, I'd say) if she planned to go back the next day.

"Got to. The serval is limping. Might need to take him in for x-rays. I'll see if Dr. Reynolds will allow me to bring him in."

Maxine, perhaps remembering that I was the one who recommended Sheila for this job, cast a look my way. "And what are *you* going to do tomorrow, Miss Marple?"

"I need to visit RidgeLine Computing and meet with my supervising P.I. But I also hope to look inside Scott Novak's house."

Sheila said, "There was a sheriff's deputy still there this morning looking around the grounds and taking pictures, but he left by lunchtime."

That made me more eager than ever to have a look around the property.

On the half-block walk home, I asked Lydia if she thought Sheila and Maxine might be having problems. "I sensed some tension."

"It's called 'm-m-marriage,' Sherlock." Actually, the pair weren't married, but they had been together for five years. Maxine had yet to tell me how their relationship had turned from therapist-client to something romantic.

Speaking of tension, I asked, "When Karl was alive, did he ever talk about cases with you?"

"Nope," she said, "and I d-d-didn't ask."

Was she not-so-subtly judging me? I still couldn't tell.

When Lydia wished, she could be as inscrutable as her son.

RIDGELINE WAS LOCATED in the famous Research Triangle Park, roughly halfway between the cities of Raleigh and Durham. It's where IBM built their huge regional headquarters in the early 1960s. Other tech firms followed, and today the area was known as the "Silicon Valley of the South."

In contrast to its owner's mansion, RidgeLine's headquarters was nothing fancy. Paul Maroni occupied an office on the first floor. The front desk attendant helped me create a name tag sticker with a bar code. I felt like a box of cereal as I waited for my mentor to fetch me.

I was soon greeted by the distinct smell of Old Spice, which reminded me of my late grandfather. Far as I could tell, Paul was wearing the same get-up as the day before. As we walked past the cafeteria, I apologized that he was having to waste his time with a greenhorn like me.

"We all have to start somewhere," he said. "Want some coffee? Sweet tea?"

"I'm trying to slim down." In some ways, going off sweet tea was harder than dropping the wine habit. I sometimes craved that double jolt of caffeine and sugar.

As I sat down in the chair opposite his desk, I decided to get one thing out of the way.

"I'm not sure I want to be a private investigator, Paul. Three-thousand hours is a lot of time. Even if I devote 10 hours a week, I'm looking at a six-year long slog." This was our first work session, and I was already complaining.

He smiled. "Time flies when you're having fun."

I asked him an obvious question, the one his Yankee accent begged. "Why did you leave New York?"

"Didn't like the winters. So, I moved to Florida—where I

didn't like the *summers*. Then I moved halfway back, to North Carolina. I guess that's why they call us 'halfbacks.'"

"Or 'Floridiots.'" Maroni grinned at that. "Do you like North Carolina?"

"What's not to like? Sammy Patel has got a lot going on. That guy is ridiculous with energy. He never sits still."

"I can't decide if I'm fond of him. He's kind of—"

"—rich?"

"Yes, and," I added, quoting someone, "'the rich are not like you and me.'"

"You're right. They got more money than we do. I think it was Ernest Hemingway who said that."

"Another Floridian."

"Flor-*idiot*," he corrected. "By the way, I've got a question for you. Why are you taking cases? You sure don't need the money."

"Sammy told you I'm wealthy?"

"Actually, I told *him*."

"That's right. You do all his company's background checks."

"I have to earn my keep. But you, on the other hand, could sit at home and eat bon-bons."

"*You* wouldn't do that even if you could."

"Yeah, but I'm a weirdo. I can tell you have your britches on straight. There's no reason for you to step out on a limb like this."

"I've played it safe most of my life. I'm ready for a little adventure." I wanted to get everything in the open. "Are you annoyed by having to work with me?"

"Is your boyfriend annoyed?"

"I don't *think* so. I just think he might be a little hurt that I'm operating in his territory."

"It's county jurisdiction."

"I meant that solving crimes is Darryl's thing."

"And there isn't much left these days for a man to call his

own, right? Used to be he was protecting the family from danger, swinging an axe. Now, we have computerized alarm systems, hydraulic wood choppers."

"But we've got kitchen appliances to do a 'woman's work,' too."

"Meaning a woman can go to the office and compete with men there, too. Look, it just seems to me that most men these days are completely lost. If I was a lot younger I'd probably be mad at the world, ready for a fight."

We women had faced our own uphill battles for so long, I wasn't eager to hear kvetching from the guys.

"That brings us back to my original question," I said. "Does it bother you that I'm involved in this case? I have almost no experience, absolutely no formal training, and I couldn't beat someone up if you brought them to me in a coma."

"Then let's stay out of bar fights, okay?"

"I don't drink anymore anyway."

"Me either," he chuckled. "Aren't we a fun pair?"

"What is your hunch about this case?" I asked.

"The facts don't lie, Ms. Swinson. And, right now, none of them points to murder."

"But you're not going to settle for that, are you?"

"We're not paid to settle."

"And what if—I'm saying 'if'—our boss becomes the main suspect at some point?"

He shrugged. "I may get paid by Sammy, but my ethics dictate that I may neither aid, abet, nor cover up a crime. But tell me, is there some strong reason I ought to suspect Sammy Patel of murder?"

"I think we should be willing to go where the facts lead us. Sammy argued with the deceased, who had talked about walking away from his work—and presumably RidgeLine."

"Fair enough. But there are others to talk to. Who do you want to interview first?"

I said, "While I'm here I'd like to meet Scott's friend and associate, Emerson Cramer."

"I've already talked with him, but you should interview him, too. Who else?"

"Scott's girlfriend, Esther Mills."

"She's all yours."

"You don't want to speak with her?"

"No need to duplicate efforts. And you might have better luck getting information. I don't have the best touch with the ladies." He gave me a bashful shrug.

"What will you do in the meantime?"

"I'd like to try to get cozy with the sheriff's office," he said. "For starters, I'd like to get my hands on a copy of the case file. We might see something they overlooked."

Paul threw me another sly wink, and I wondered: What did Paul Maroni really think? Did he believe his job was to protect his boss? And did he really respect me as a crime investigator, or was he just buttering me up to keep me off the scent?

I would try to keep both eyes on this private eye.

CHAPTER 5

AN EMOTIONAL ENCOUNTER

P aul walked me back to the front desk and asked the receptionist to dial up Emerson Cramer.

Emerson was tall as Scott but built more like a wrestler, somewhere between fat and barrel chested. Irish in looks, his hair was a long, black curly mop, and a goatee covered half his face. He wore loose, faded blue jeans and an oversized yellow t-shirt that said, "Slow Child at Play." His skin was white as a fish's belly, leading me to think he didn't get much sun.

I had already gone online that morning to learn a bit about him. Emerson had worked for Scott even before the pair left Carnegie Mellon University. Emerson started out doing software development but worked his way up to become Novak's chief operations officer, leading his corps of coders on the company's most high-profile products.

They worked together in that capacity for nearly 10 years before Emerson went out on his own to start a new virtual-reality company. That enterprise ran out of capital in less than a year, at which time he came right back to work for Scott.

Emerson instantly struck me as anxious and on guard. I thanked him for agreeing to speak with me and suggested we go to a table in the far corner of the nearly empty cafeteria so we'd have some privacy.

We had no sooner sat down than he started grilling *me*. "You say you're working for Sammy. What are you hoping to learn?"

"I just want to discover what happened to your friend and colleague."

"And if you find out—are you just going to run and tell Sammy?"

"The authorities, too."

"Are you sure?"

"Of course," I said, though I wasn't totally sure. "Now, do you mind if I ask you some questions?"

"Fine, but I've told the sheriff everything I know. No one wants answers more than I do right now. *No one*."

I asked him when he last saw Scott.

"Friday night," he said decisively. "We saw a movie at the Rialto. Something with Natalie Portman. It was pretty good, but we left early. Scott was tired."

"Did he seem off to you? Depressed? Especially after that speech he gave in Kansas City?"

"In other words, had he gone off the deep end? Look, the Novak brain is not like yours or mine. It follows its own logic. That's how Scott has been able to innovate faster than most others. I don't think you're going to find a murderer by blaming the victim."

"You don't believe it was a suicide?"

"I think this has to be treated as a homicide until murder can be firmly ruled out." I knew that most people didn't want to admit that their friend or loved one had died by their own hand.

I tried to redirect.

"What happened after you went to the movie?"

"I drove him home. He was tired, and so was I. I planned to work the next day, and he said he was going to lie low. We'd made plans to touch base again on Sunday, but that never happened, of course."

"I'm trying to retrace Scott's movements in the full week leading up to his death. Could you help me do that?"

He looked at his smartwatch. "I'm pretty swamped..."

"Then give me the quick version."

"Fine. We hung out for a few days after he returned from his talk in Kansas City. He always liked the Natural History and Science museums, so we went there. Went to the art museum, too."

"Did he talk about the bomb he dropped at the convention?"

Emerson took a large gulp of his giant Mello Yello. "Scott is brilliant, but he can be impulsive. He doesn't always think things through." I noted that Emerson still talked about Scott in the present, like a lot of people who have lost friends or family. Was he in denial? "I'm not sure that Scott would have stopped working on AI, but some people hearing that speech might have taken him seriously."

"By 'some people,' do you mean Sammy Patel?"

He raised an eyebrow, looked around him. "You said it, not me."

"Was Scott worried about his safety?"

"No, but maybe he should have been." He glanced around again and leaned forward, whispered, *"I have to be careful what I say in the House of Sammy."*

I remembered what Margaret had said to me, how the surveillance devices at Sammy's house could hear a chipmunk's flatulence. Maybe it was the same at his office.

I provided a nod of understanding and switched topics. "How did you and Scott meet exactly?"

"We were in a business class working on a group project.

Our project won a start-up award. That's when we realized we worked well together."

"Did you ever meet his family?"

His brow narrowed. "I'm not sure what he would be comfortable with me telling you."

"Mr. Novak is dead, Mr. Cramer. He can't be any more uncomfortable than he is."

Emerson frowned. "Scott came from a pretty rough background."

"Abuse?"

"His father was manic depressive. His mother was very OCD. They divorced when Scott was, like, 10, and his dad took his older brother to live with him in California. Then it was just Scott and his mom for about six years. Scott left for college, and she died of cancer while he was there. His dad overdosed soon after that."

Overdosing could be a means of suicide. Maybe Scott had come to mental illness by way of his parents.

I asked, "Did they have money?"

"Not really. His dad was in radio at one point but lost his job and became kind of a vagrant over time. His mom had a regular accounting job."

"What can you tell me about the brother?"

Emerson sighed and got quiet for a moment. "Adam was always an interesting guy. Followed The Dead—or what was left of them—one summer in college. That's when I met him, one time when I was out there visiting an uncle. Anyway, after his dad died, Adam dropped out of college and made his home in the Alaskan wilderness."

"Scott had just the one sibling?"

"Yeah."

"Scott was the oldest?

Emerson shifted uncomfortably.

"Something I said?"

"Adam was a little older, but Scott ended up surpassing him in school by skipping a couple of grades. I think Adam resented that. I think it was one of the reasons they fell out."

"But they reconnected in the past year?"

"Yes. Through letters."

Emerson's watch beeped. He touched it to see the full message.

"Drat! Another problem with the beta. I've got to go."

"May I follow you? I feel like we just got started."

"Suit yourself."

On the way out he refilled his Mello Yello. I struggled to keep up as he shuffled through a secured door which opened onto a long hallway.

I asked, "It sounds like Adam stood to benefit the most from Scott's death. Do you know how I can get in touch with Adam to speak with him?"

He shook his head. "No way Adam killed Scott. The two made up. It was one of the bright spots in Scott's life in the past year."

"People talk about the past year as being very hard for Scott. Tell me about the sale of his company. I don't even know what it was called."

"It was called G4, and, yes, Scott was conflicted about selling. But about a dozen of his earliest hires would become multi-millionaires. He knew that they had been on a long journey with him and wanted to cash-out. They had companies of their own they wanted to start."

"So those employees were happy when he sold."

"Definitely."

"What about you? Did you cash out, too?"

He blushed. "I had sold my stock a couple years earlier to start my own company."

"Why?"

"Scott wasn't as interested in virtual-reality technology as I was, so I left and assembled my own team. I ran out of money pretty quickly, but he let me come back and resume the project. I learned the hard way how hard it is to be the one in charge."

"Seems you're working really hard these days. Even now— when your good friend died just two days ago."

He stopped in the hallway and turned to face me. "Look, I owe a lot to Scott. And I'm going to keep his legacy going, no matter what."

Emerson's watch beeped again. "I have to ... why don't I park you somewhere for a little while. I have to put out a fire. I'll be right back."

I followed him down a different hallway to a small conference room. He left me there, closing the door behind him.

The room had a small window that allowed me to see into a computer lab where two men, one young and one elderly, were working on something. The elderly man, whose back was to me, featured the whitest, most beautiful hair I'd ever seen.

I thought I recognized that fine white hair, that neckline above the flannel shirt collar...

What the heck was my ex-father-in-law doing at RidgeLine headquarters?

I'D ALWAYS LIKED and respected John Swinson; we got along very well. By contrast, Allan had never felt he could impress his dad. Allan's older brother by three years, Nick, had died by suicide at age 16, shooting himself with his father's pistol in his parents' bedroom. Even before that horrendous event, Allan had felt his dad focused most of his attention on Nick.

It wasn't something the family ever talked about, but I

remember a particular moment at my wedding reception when John and I were doing the obligatory bride and father-in-law dance. John seemed preoccupied, so I asked him what he was thinking. I thought he might share something about Allan as a little boy or share a story from his own wedding long ago. Worst case, I figured he was still upset over the rehearsal dinner from the night before, when my sculptor friend, Freddy, who was gay, had given a toast and play-flirted with Allan in front of everyone by saying, "If things don't work out with Rett, give me a call." The crowd had hooted and hollered, but in private after the event, John had let it be known to me that he didn't approve of "Freddy's homosexual lifestyle."

But the reality was none of those things. As the DJ played "What a Wonderful World" and numerous other couples danced around us, John shouted to me over the music, tears streaming, "I'm just thinking about Nick, and the fact that he'll never get to enjoy his own wedding someday."

I hadn't predicted that he'd be thinking of his deceased son in that moment. I stopped dancing. "I am so, so sorry, John."

"Rett," he said after a moment, "do you reckon Nick was one of them queers like Freddy? Do you reckon that's why he—?" His voice caught. To any of the reception crowd sipping their champagne, John was simply having a typical wedding day moment.

I gently lifted John's chin so he would be looking into my eyes while I spoke.

"John, it doesn't matter if he was gay. He was your son, you loved him dearly, and you have every right to miss him."

"I would have loved him still," he said. Then, heartbreak-ingly, he buried his head in my shoulder, sobbing like no one I had ever held before or since, even my own child.

After Nick's death, Allan felt a million miles from his parents. Allan's father became a workaholic, while his mother became a diazepam addict. It all took its toll on Allan. He found ways to make himself happy, anything to convince himself that his brother's death hadn't turned his home life into an emotional tundra.

Though I thought of John often, I hadn't seen him since the divorce. I watched as a RidgeLine worker fit him with a large headset, then scampered over to a laptop connected to a larger machine. Curious, I opened the door that separated the conference room from the lab so I could hear them while I continued to watch.

"Okay, Mr. Swinson," said the worker. "We're going to get started. How do you feel?"

"Ready, I guess."

The young man typed something on his keyboard.

"Dad?" said a boy's voice.

John stood up like a rocket. He reached out an arm. "Oh, my God! Nicky? Nicky?"

"Hi, Dad!"

"I've missed you! Oh, sweet Jesus! I…" John broke down.

I found his reaction alarming. I watched the young man to see how he would help John. He got up and put a hand on John's shoulder. "Do you wish to stop, sir?"

"No, no, it's just—I can't see anything right now. My tears…"

"Okay," said the young man, hunting down some tissue. "Let's pause just for a minute and get everything set up again. Don't worry, Mr. Swinson. You'll see your relative again very soon."

Once his goggles were off, John was able to wipe his eyes. I finally found my voice.

"John!" I said, stepping into the room. "It's Rett. I didn't know you were here!"

"Rett?" I could tell he was still in a state of shock. I turned to the confused technician.

"John is a family member of mine," I explained. "Emerson Cramer wanted me to see your research, and it so happens I know this man." I sat down in the chair next to John and put my arm around him protectively. "What are you doing here, Dad?"

"I saw an ad in the newspaper. Yes, I still read the newspaper. The ad was in the obituary section. It was for people who missed a loved one to be part of research. All we had to do was bring as many pictures and as much video and audio of our loved one as we could. I pulled everything I had of Nick's together. That was maybe two months ago. Then they called and said it was time."

"Time for what?"

John's voice wavered. "Time to see Nicky again."

"We have the glasses ready to go," said the technician. I could see his name badge now. His name was Devon.

"Are you sure you want to keep doing this?" I asked John.

"I'm ready," he said to Devon. "Please hurry." Alex eagerly fit the goggles to John's face.

Standing this close, I could now see something on Devon's computer screen, a two-dimensional version of the image John was probably viewing in his goggles in full 3-D.

"Hi, Dad!" said the figure again.

"Hi, Nicky!" shouted John. "I've missed you, buddy."

"I've missed you, too, Dad!"

John was shaking. He took a couple steps forward—and bumped into a table.

"I can't hug him!" John cried. "I want to hug him!"

"We're still working on that part," said Devon.

"I can't see!" said John. "My tears. Oh, God, this is torture!"

Devon stopped the program and hopped up once more to remove John's goggles. "I'm sorry. That's why we're running these tests. It's still in development."

John stammered, "No, don't apologize." I put my arm around

John again. "Oh, Rett, I just miss him so, even after all this time."

I was speechless. I just held my ex-father-in-law and let him cry into my shoulder, a replay of our wedding dance moment.

Devon said, "I have some ideas for what we can do to improve the experience for you. Would it be okay if we met again in a couple of weeks?"

"Certainly."

I said, "Dad, are you sure? This seems rather painful for you."

"No, it's okay. It's a good thing."

Something caught my eye, a movement in the conference room. Emerson had returned.

I told John that I had to go but I hoped we could visit together soon.

"Of course," he said, in his gentlemanly way. "Love you," he said.

"Love you, too."

"I WASN'T EXPECTING THAT," I told Emerson. I explained to him what had just happened and added, "How can your company exploit people like this? Why would you—?"

"—help people reconnect with their loved ones? Perhaps so they can say things they wish they had said in life. Doesn't it seem like a technology that could help a lot of people?"

"If they're ready." I just wasn't sure John was.

"No one is ever 'ready' for new technology," Emerson said. "But everyone adapts."

I was still reeling from the experience when Emerson and I left the boardroom. He led me to the door of his office, which opened when Emerson put his thumb against a sensor.

It was the most boring office ever. Nothing on the gray walls. If not for a narrow mattress on the floor, one might wonder if he spent any time here at all.

He closed the door behind him and said in a lowered voice, "I'll speak quickly. Sammy is definitely your main suspect. Did you know he had an insurance policy on Scott? But if the death is deemed a suicide, he won't get a payout. That's a cool $100 million."

"Wow. I didn't know that." I thought for a second. "But Sammy did say—and I believe him—that Scott's death reduced the value of his company by billions. Why would Sammy give up billions to gain millions by killing Scott?"

"He might have lost his cool. Look, you can understand why Sammy would be angry. He spent a lot of money betting that our technology could be made into sellable products before other companies do the same. I think Sammy was terrified that Scott wasn't going to be forthcoming with all of his knowledge. Sammy acts like he's in control, but he's kind of paranoid."

"Meanwhile," I said. "Scott vowed to leave AI research and seemed to have isolated himself at his home with his animals."

"Despite what he might have said in Kansas City, Scott was always looking for new mechanisms, new models for computer learning. At some point he began referring to the animals in his zoo as 'prime survivors.' I think he wanted to get into their heads, maybe get inspiration that he could apply to any new intelligences he was devising." He waved his hand. "But not many people know the details about his research. I'm his closest friend, and I don't even know everything he was working on."

"Is there anyone else he may have talked about his research with?"

"Esther, maybe. Have you met her?"

"Not yet. By the way, why did Scott break up with her?"

Emerson shrugged. "I'm not really sure of the details."

But I sensed he was pretty sure of those details.

I asked, "What's this I heard about a party house he used to own in town?"

"Yeah, that place was a magnet for dysfunction. All kinds of crazy found its way in there. I mean, 'All Hail Esther the Queen' for walking in and putting an end to that insanity."

"She stopped it. How?"

"You'll have to ask her." He put his hand on the doorknob. "We've talked long enough. I've helped you as much as I can. Please, don't tell Sammy I suspect him. There's no telling what he might do."

As I left RidgeLine, I couldn't get the image of anxious Emerson Cramer out of my head. The man definitely had issues. And it sounded like Scott Novak had a lot of baggage, too: Dysfunctional parents. Estrangement from his brother. A rocky romance.

All of Scott's problems seemed wound together, like an intricate knot.

And it all ended in his bed with a scarf around his neck.

CHAPTER 6
PLAYING POKER

I returned home mid-afternoon. Lydia was taking her afternoon nap in her room, so I laid down on the couch with the *News & Observer* to see what it had to say about Scott Novak's death, which had only received brief mention in the previous day's paper.

Turns out the reporter knew less than I did, but what was provided was a thorough biography:

Novak was 35 when he died. Though he'd started G4 with seed money raised in Silicon Valley, he brought the company east where the cost of living was lower and he could hire more coders for less. He eventually chose Raleigh because the company's biggest customer was located there; G4's first software product "used artificial intelligence to model medicines and compare them to one another to predict adverse interactions." That client ended up going bankrupt, but G4 was stronger for the partnership and was able to enlist several other pharmaceutical companies as customers.

G4's business took off, which required more coders. "If you're going to attract the best coders, you need to be a fun place to work," he was quoted as saying. Fun in the G4 context meant a playboy mansion where otherwise work-obsessed employees—nearly all of them male—could unwind once a week. The article speculated that the police looked the other way given that Novak represented economic development in the eyes of city leaders.

The story mentioned Emerson Cramer leaving to start his own business, which was based around using virtual reality to simulate meeting dead relatives. When that company ran out of money, Novak brought Cramer and his technology back. "Without Scott's AI know-how, I realized that the product was never going to approach viability," Emerson was quoted as saying.

G4 eventually gained the attention of local billionaire Samarth Patel, who wanted to upgrade his own company's product mix. The $250 million acquisition was hailed by onlookers as "the biggest bargain of the decade" and roundly criticized by Silicon Valley for "devaluing tech." One prominent entrepreneur called Novak "a disgrace" for not knowing his own worth.

Novak had not attempted to defend himself. He merely put his mansion up for sale and moved into the country.

With his death, those same tech luminaries now praised his genius while winking to the possibility of suicide. The reporter wrote, "Many in the tech world are saying, without wanting to be named, that Novak's earlier decision to leave AI research signaled serious mental distress."

The coroner's preliminary report cited "death by asphyxiation." Suicide or accidental death were the likely causes, said Wake County Sheriff Tom Jordan, who added, "There is nothing to indicate foul play."

I took pictures of the story and emailed them to myself.

Then I called Esther Mills. When she didn't answer, I texted. I explained who I was and that I was trying to get to the bottom of Scott's death. She agreed to see me later that afternoon. I texted Paul to let him know.

Once Lydia was up again and back in her flower garden, I headed out.

Esther lived in a tony apartment in Glenwood South, a popular Downtown Raleigh neighborhood with dozens of hip restaurants, coffee shops, and bars. I'd forgotten to ask Emerson how much Esther's stock was worth when Sammy bought G4, but I guess it was enough to live where the rent on a single-bedroom apartment could be upwards of $5,000 a month.

She buzzed me in. As I was approaching her apartment door, a team of housekeepers were in the process of leaving, toting their buckets of cleaning supplies and a vacuum cleaner.

"Hello?" I called.

"Come in," came an expressionless voice.

The apartment was impressive. Stone floors. Track lighting. Tile backsplash in the kitchen. Modern furniture. Esther, a short blonde with a thin face and long, golden hair, greeted me and led me to the living area where we both sat down.

"It's nice to meet you, Esther," I said. "You have a lovely apartment."

"If you don't expect the best, you're never going to get it." She could have pulled that line from any of the magazines on her coffee table: *Fast Company*, *Inc.*, *Forbes*, *Fortune*.

I pegged Esther as a bit younger than Scott. She made me think of a particular female professional poker player I'd seen interviewed on TV once: Cold. Calculating. Gorgeous.

And very hard to read.

I thanked her for letting me visit with her. "How did you and Scott first meet?"

She cocked her head. "Not so fast. You haven't really explained why I should be talking with you."

This put me off balance. I'd assumed that being invited into her apartment meant she'd be forthcoming.

"I'm trying to find out if someone killed Scott," I said. "I assumed you'd be just as curious as Mr. Patel is."

"Scott committed suicide." She reached into a drawer that was part of the coffee table and pulled out a vaping device, took a hit, and blew out a puff of steam. "I'm not going to sit here and let Sammy do a hit job on me."

"I'm not here to do a 'hit job.' I'm just trying to get to the truth."

"But if Sammy is signing your paycheck—"

"I'm already a self-made millionaire," I cut in. Her eyes became wide in reflex surprise. "I don't have to work, but I enjoy criminal investigation. I made my money in real estate. If you don't believe me, call any of the big developers in town. I'd be glad to come back another time once you've had a chance to do a thorough background check." I began to stand.

"No, that's not necessary. Please sit. I can tell when someone is bluffing."

Poker skills.

I sat back down. "Before we talk about Scott," I resumed, "I'd love to know what brought you to Raleigh. You don't sound like you're from here."

"I grew up in Providence, Rhode Island. Went to Brown, majored in sociology. Thought I might want to be a lawyer, so I went to Harvard—but hated it. Left after a year. Then I went to New York thinking I wanted to work in publishing, but that was a nightmare. All they wanted was to sign the next celebrity tell-all. Finally, I saw an article about Big Pharma's growth down here, figured there might be something for me." She abruptly stood and asked, "Would you like something to drink?"

"Water, please." I figured I'd get something tastier than mere tap water. *Expect only the best.*

As she withdrew to the kitchen, I casually moved around the apartment, trying to get a sense of Esther's personality. Very little could be classified as personal. Framed posters advertised French ballet, Italian wine, and Belgian chocolate. Sophistication mass marketed.

One detail did catch my eye: On a bookshelf leaned a framed photo of Esther and Scott. They looked to be riding a roller coaster. Both were wide-eyed and gleeful.

"That was taken about a year ago at Busch Gardens," Esther said, as she handed me a drink of fizzy water with a slice of lime.

"You two look really happy."

"Or scared out of our minds."

"Was that before or after Scott sold his company?"

"Before." We both sat down again with our drinks. I noticed something else on a shelf above the picture: an empty bottle of Clyde Ray's Rye Whiskey. I pointed to it.

"A whiskey you recommend?"

"Scott's favorite. I don't know why I should care now." She took it down and put it in a cabinet. The gesture struck me as cold.

"You were going to tell me how you two met."

"It was an accident," she said. "I had just flown into town that afternoon to interview with another company the next day. A nice, very wealthy older woman I met in first class on the plane invited me to attend a charity gala at her home that night. It was dark when I drove up; from the road I saw a house all lit up and just assumed it was the right place. I parked, walked to the front door—and knew then I was at the wrong house. I could see a few people were very drunk and not well dressed—like a college keg party. But just before I turned to leave, I locked eyes with one of the men there."

"Scott Novak."

She nodded. "He comes running out and begs me to come in, tells me it's his house and his party. I wasn't the least bit impressed, and I think he saw that. I told him I was leaving. He asked where I was going, and, if he were to spiff up a little bit, if he could be my date."

"Were you put off by that?"

"Scott had a sort of goofiness to him that was endearing. I was intrigued by someone who would walk away from his own party, so I agreed. We had a blast at the gala and then stayed out all night, just talking. He was brilliant. Before we said good-bye, he offered me a job to lead G4's human-resource function which they had been outsourcing up till then. I impetuously accepted the job offer and told him, as his new director of HR, the first thing I was doing was shutting down his parties, because they were a lawsuit waiting to happen."

"I imagine that decision disappointed one or two people."

She smirked. "I heard some grumblings about that at the office. In the minds of some of those programmers, I was like Yoko Ono breaking up the Beatles."

"Did they think you prompted Scott to sell the company, too?"

"Actually, I was one who urged him *not* to sell. I told Scott that his company would someday be worth billions if he just showed some patience. But he wouldn't listen."

I could relate. It had been a continual struggle with Allan to save money rather than waste it on luxuries. Thank God I won those battles, or there would have been very little for me to claim in the divorce years later.

"Why do you think Scott sold?"

"The coders were ready for a pay-out. But, also, Sammy charmed him, like Sammy charms everyone."

The look she gave me insinuated that I had been charmed,

too. I didn't think that was true, but my thoughts flew immediately to my friend, Margaret. The idea that she might be the victim of manipulation had crossed my mind. But Margaret was a smart woman who could stand up for herself. At least I hoped she could.

"You made out okay from the sale?"

"Not bad, but I hadn't been there nearly as long as some others. And I was doing HR—not as high-value as software development. My stock was minimal."

"Did his decision to sell G4 drive a wedge in your relationship?"

"Yes and no. I accepted his decision. What was the point of fighting it at that point? But once the company was no longer his, he bought that country house and its zoo—"

"Why?" I asked.

"He needed another obsession, something else to focus on. But he also saw those animals as a lot like him. He didn't come from much, and he didn't have much in the way of family."

"There is the brother."

"I guess you could call him that."

"You have a negative opinion of Adam Novak?"

"I never met him. I just know he's a dropout from life. Not really sure why Scott reconnected. Just kind of a disturbed, aimless guy."

"Did Scott talk about him?"

"Just that they lost touch after the divorce when Scott was in, like, the sixth grade. I know his brother is really into Nietzsche —*Neet-shay, Neet-shuh*—however you say it. He got Scott caught on that weird kick, too."

"He mentioned that philosopher in his Kansas City speech," I said.

"Yeah, someone sent the video link to me."

I suddenly remembered something from one of my college classes. "Isn't Nietzsche the 'God is dead' philosopher?"

"That's what I said back in the spring when Scott mentioned him for the first time. Scott could explain it better, but I guess Nietzsche was all about strength, while religion just seemed weak to him. Nietzsche talked about the 'Will to Power' and turning himself into the Übermensch—Superman, Overman, however you translate the German."

"What does 'Overman' even mean?"

"I never really figured it out. Just a path to becoming powerful, I guess. Anyway, it was just one more thing for Scott to get obsessed over. I think he just felt so diminished by the sale of G4 and so taken advantage of by Sammy's contract that he was grasping at whatever he could find."

"But he had you—and yet he broke up with you. Why?"

She took another vape hit. "He said he needed some time to think. I didn't fight him on it. Truth be told, he was acting quite self-centered, and I've got my own ideas for a company. So, in a way it was mutual."

"Did you think he was depressed?"

"More like distracted. But if he was depressed, I blame Sammy and that ridiculous contract. Scott couldn't go anywhere. For nearly a year he was basically like a prisoner. That would depress anyone, I guess, but I wasn't particularly worried about him, because I was pretty sure he was planning to start another company. Right before we broke up—and not too long before he went off-script in Kansas City—he told me he was working on something new, something he was really excited about and hoped to share with me soon."

I challenged her. "But Scott wouldn't be able to start another company, right? After all, he must have had a noncompete agreement with Sammy."

"I told Scott he could find a way around that non-compete, which was unnecessarily strict and would be thrown out of most any court. That year in law school wasn't a total loss."

"Why do you think Sammy suspects foul play?"

"Sammy took out a lot of life insurance on Scott. A suicide won't pay out. He has to prove it was murder."

"Any reason he should suspect you?"

"Why would I kill Scott?"

"Inheritance?"

"Emerson says Scott didn't even have a will."

So, she and Emerson are close enough to talk about a will. I filed that away for later.

I said, "Just playing Devil's Advocate—perhaps you killed him because you were bitter about the break-up?"

"Like I said, the breakup was basically mutual."

"But if you were broken up, why did you visit Scott the night he died?"

"He texted me. He sounded desperate to meet." She closed her eyes. This time the tears were something she couldn't simply beat back with a hit of nicotine and artificial flavoring. Even when Esther wept, she looked stunning. No wonder Scott had been bedazzled. But looks can wear thin. Maybe she wanted to get back together, and, when he refused, she lashed out.

I gave her some time while she composed herself. Esther used a tissue to wipe her nose and dab her eyes. "His text sounded frantic: 'I need you to come back. I have to set things right. PLEASE come back tonight.' At first I told him no, that I couldn't be jerked around like that. But then I thought about it, and about an hour later I decided I'd go. I let him know I was on my way, but I didn't get confirmation. It takes a good half hour to get there from here. I parked my car. There were no lights on in the house. Even though I had a key, I knocked to be polite. There wasn't an answer, so I used my key and went inside."

"Deadbolt?"

"No. Just the lock on the knob."

"Meaning it can be locked from the inside and just pulled

shut?"

"Yes."

"Go on."

"I had a bad feeling because the house was very quiet. I made my way upstairs. It was totally dark, so I turned on the bedroom light. Scott was lying in his bed. The first thing I noticed was his right hand; it was black and blue. Then I saw the yellow scarf tied around his neck and to the brass rail at the head of the bed. His eyes were open, and he looked ... terrible."

"I'm sorry," I said. "I didn't mean to upset you all over again."

"It's okay."

"Did he leave a note?"

She paused, shook her head. "No."

"But you still think it was a suicide? Why?"

She took a breath. "I just think he was punishing me somehow. I don't know why—and I certainly don't understand why he'd be so cruel as to have me show up and find him like that."

"Did you ever know him to play that choking game during sex?"

"Never."

In Esther I saw a confident, hard-driving individual. Could she have become angry in the moment—angry enough to kill? But if she saw any chance at all of her and Scott getting back together, she would have to know he was worth more to her alive than dead.

I was curious to talk to someone who had been at the wild parties Scott was known to throw, so I got from her the name of one of the programmers—Trey Gamble—who used to attend them.

I wanted to keep a door open for us to talk again in the future.

"Will you be staying in town for a while?" I asked.

"Yes. I'm part of a—" She cut herself off. "That is, I have

some friends who want to start a new company. We've been tossing some ideas around. Once you've been part of one start-up, it's hard to go back to 9-to-5 work. But I don't have much time. I'm about to hit 30."

I glanced at the covers of the business magazines, those young and glamorous entrepreneurs. My thoughts weirdly flew to Baptist Sunday school as a teenager, when our teacher, in his early fifties, announced to the group that he had been diagnosed with cancer and was likely not to live to see his next birthday. A boy asked if he felt sad about his diagnosis, and our teacher shook his head. "Son, I got 20 years on Jesus. You won't hear me complaining." It was conventional wisdom in our church that Jesus died at 33—well before, you might say, he could make his first million.

I said to Esther, "You've got time to make your mark," but I knew she wasn't listening to an old lady in her forties, one who was probably too pudgy to be considered successful no matter how much money she had.

I'd never met someone so completely obsessed with controlling the air around her, and I wondered what might happen if Esther ever lost that control, if only for an instant.

CHAPTER 7

FIGHTING WORDS

I n the time I was meeting with Esther, three texts had arrived on my phone. The first was a note from Paul, asking if I could join him at Sammy's mansion that evening after dinner to discuss the case some more. I texted him that I could.

The second was from Darryl, wondering if he could come eat dinner with his mom and me. Charlie was going to stay at his mom's tonight, freeing up Darryl for the evening.

I texted:

—*I miss you. Already have something cooking that you'll like.*

—*I like it all. ESPECIALLY you.*

I loved this man. I felt optimistic that everything would go smoothly, that we would stop being at odds over this case—if we were even at odds in the first place.

The third text was a mysterious message from my sculptor friend, Freddy:

—*Got time to drop by the studio? Important info you need to hear.*

I looked at my watch.

—*How about now?*

—Now would work.

Freddy lived in my downtown neighborhood where it began to blend into Raleigh's old warehouse district. Only a single walkable block separated Freddy's studio from his home.

I'd never think of just dropping in on Freddy. Though on the one hand he was the quintessential sassy gay friend, he could also be intimidating. His bald head was perpetually aimed at you like some formidable shield.

I found him welding in the center of his unheated studio space, which felt expansive as an aircraft hanger. Some of the raw materials of his work—metal, wire, rubber, glass — were neatly sorted and stacked along the walls. Freddy's life was meticulous in every way, down to each bite of food and wink of sleep.

I caught his eye even through his thick welding mask. The next moment he was giving me a hug and we were sipping cucumber-infused mineral waters on yoga mats.

"My back won't tolerate this for long," I said.

"You won't be sitting after I tell you this, honey."

"Do I really want to hear this?"

"No. But better from me than someone else."

"Tell it."

"KayLeigh is talking some smack about you around town. And it's not good smack."

I rolled my eyes. KayLeigh Rider, my ex-husband's mistress and now wife, had not been happy with me ever since the investor party last November that saw her being upstaged by the connivances of her wily caterer, one of my other good friends, Paige Kirkland.

In that fairly public moment, KayLeigh had seemed—not just like a doe who was caught in the headlights—but as one mangled and embedded in the SUV's grill.

"After your little party that made KayLeigh look like a

doofus, it seems she found herself being excluded from a number of societal gatherings. Rather than just lie low until everyone forgot about it, KayLeigh decided to go on the offensive by insinuating certain, um, alternative realities."

"Spill tea."

"One, that you are and have been a closet alcoholic for years..."

"A *lie*. I only overdrank during my separation, and I stopped altogether before it became a real problem."

"...and that you had been stealing from the company you shared with Allan..."

"Another lie. I *made* that company."

"...and that you cheated on Allan long before he even thought of looking outside the marriage himself..."

"I *wish*."

"...and, finally, that you abused your daughter."

"Stephanie? How exactly did I abuse her?"

"Emotionally. Maybe physically..."

"Are you kidding me?" I shot up and assumed battle position.

"I told you you'd be on your feet. I don't blame you for being pissed."

"Oh, this goes far beyond 'pissed,' Freddy." I then used a few choice words that expressed just *how* far. Freddy didn't try to soothe me. He just allowed me to vent.

"Who are you getting this from?"

"Alice Huffman."

"Art-collecting Alice? One of the biggest patrons of the arts in Raleigh?"

"The one."

"How does Alice know all this?"

"She signed KayLeigh to help sell Alice's family mansion."

"The one on St. Mary's?"

"Yep," he said. I suddenly wondered if Alice Huffman might have been the socialite Esther met on her flight to Raleigh.

"How much is Alice asking?"

"Four-point-five." I gulped. As in *million*. If you did the math, an agent's six-percent commission would equal a cool $270,000. That would just about cover KayLeigh's salon, tanning, and spa treatments for the year.

I stamped my right foot. "And KayLeigh talked shit about me to her?"

"Alice doesn't know you that well, which is why she ran everything by me."

"What did you tell her?"

"I told her none of it was true, and that I didn't appreciate people telling lies about my friends." It had led to Freddy telling Alice the whole story of my divorce and how it had been instigated entirely by Allan and KayLeigh's deception.

"After you told her the truth, did she drop KayLeigh as her agent?"

"She can't. It's a year-long contract."

"But those contracts are normally six months."

"Not if you're KayLeigh Rider and you own the market. Have you seen her billboards? They're *hot*."

"WHY DOES HER HOTNESS MATTER?!"

"Sorry! Anyway, I thought you should know. But when you think about it—I'm not sure you need to do anything."

"Oh, but I'm going to sue her ass!" I was like a redneck female Hulk—skin Scotch-Irish red with Eastern North Carolina vinegar running through her veins. "That wench is gonna be tore up from the floor up!"

"I figured you'd say something like that, but you might want to think again." Freddy proceeded to remind me of his life in the New York arts scene in the late 1990s near the end of the AIDS crisis when rumors still flew—rumors that could ruin an artist's reputation in a New York minute. He'd heard of acquaintances bringing slander cases against one another. Judging from that experience, he said, finding someone to go on the record and attest to KayLeigh's lies was going to be difficult.

"Besides," he added, "you're bullet-proof. Anyone who knows you well knows KayLeigh's spreading a pack of lies. If Alice had known you, there's no way she would have given KayLeigh that listing."

Freddy was right. I shouldn't care. KayLeigh's words couldn't hurt me.

But then I remembered one way that they could.

"Freddy, listen to me. I don't care what KayLeigh thinks about me. And I don't care what she says to her ho-bag friends at the spa when they are getting their butts waxed and their chin hairs laser-beamed. But if she's telling stories to new people she meets—"

"But people are *smart*, they know—"

"They don't *know*. And someday soon I'm going to have an exhibition for my paintings and—did I just say that?"

"You did! It's about time!"

"That's right. *I am going to have an exhibition.* And if I invite Alice Huffman and her other art collector friends, I want them to come. But they won't come to my show if they think I'm low-rent."

"But suing her will do no good. It will just make some lawyers rich."

He was right.

But then an idea rose up in me and announced its arrival in the form of a gross Italian-soda belch.

"You don't say?" Freddy joked. "Well, you can take the girl out of Eastern North Carolina..."

"That's right. And she's got herself a plan."

Freddy begged for me to tell him more, but I shook my head. "You're an artist of sculpture. But I am an artist, too."

"Yeah, I know. A painter."

"No," I said, "an artist currently working in the medium of *REVENGE!*"

He laughed cattily. "Once you're ready for that show, call me. You know I can't wait to see it!"

MY BLOOD BOILED the whole way home. Thank goodness Darryl would be there tonight. His presence always managed to calm me.

And, at first, it did. But then, after dinner, when Lydia retired to the den with Charlie to watch *Jeopardy* and *Wheel of Fortune*, the fireworks started.

After venting about KayLeigh (which he was sympathetic about) I began talking about my interviews with Emerson and Esther. I thought he was focused on the details, but at some point he interrupted me.

"Why did you accept this case? I can understand why you were into solving Wanda Hightower's murder. She was your neighbor. But why this Novak character?"

"Sammy Patel thinks I can help."

"But it's not your job."

"You mean I shouldn't be helping because I'm not a full-time detective like you?"

"No offense, but I've got the experience and training."

"And how will I get the experience if I don't take cases? As for the training, you said once that you can't train someone to be observant, or to ask questions, or to think analytically. Besides, I'm officially working under a certified private investigator."

"You mean Deputy McGoof?"

I did a doubletake. "Who?"

"That's what the guys at the sheriff's office call Paul Maroni. Tom says he's been dropping by the last two days trying to sniff out information, trying to get access to evidence, and so on."

"Wow, name-calling is really mature," I said, sarcasm getting the best of me. "Why would grown men act like they're in middle school?"

"I'm just telling you what they say."

"I think you're being a snob."

He shrugged off the accusation. Yet his hand shook the slightest bit as he took a sip of his evening decaf. Darryl didn't enjoy arguing. That's how I knew that this argument meant something. I couldn't discount his feelings, but I needed to engage him in a way that didn't cause him to run for the door.

"Look," I said, "you've said yourself that asking good questions and running down clues isn't always rocket science. Sometimes it's just spending the time to track down every lead. And we both know that the police—and in this case the sheriff's office—are usually overwhelmed with cases. Are you afraid I'll embarrass myself somehow?"

"I didn't say that."

"Look, I'm testing out a new line of work. I'm having a second act that's different from the first. And so far I *enjoy* it. I'm not particularly good at it yet, but I'm getting better every day. Isn't that the way life should be? Do we give up on something just because we aren't perfect at it?"

"I don't think so."

"Me either." I reached across the table and put a hand on his arm. "I hope you can learn to accept this weird part of me. I've started to work in your field, though on a very different level. I don't think this has to be a competition. It sounds like there is plenty of work to go around."

He nodded. "You're right about that."

"And you're the detective. You'll have a type of power I will never have. You'll always have better access to, well, everything. And I'll be on the periphery. I'll be 'The Skirt on the Outskirts.'"

He smiled at that. "Actually, if you ever decide to wear a skirt, I want you to stand close enough for me to see you."

"There's a reason you haven't seen me in a skirt yet—because I can fill one up in a hot minute." I wasn't shy to say it, for if I thought that Darryl wanted me super skinny like Esther Mills, I would have thrown in the towel months ago. Skinny just wasn't ever going to happen.

He smiled wider. "Now you've got me *really* interested."

"Oh, Lord! Coon Dog's got the scent!" But I was loving the attention.

"Seriously, honey," I said, "moving forward, if you find out anything interesting about the case, will you please let me know? Not for my sake. There are people suffering over this man's death right now." I just didn't know from among Sammy, Emerson, or Esther which ones were mourning him—and which ones might be directly involved in his death.

I had put Darryl on the spot. Darryl wasn't a gossip, and he respected his relationship with Tom Jordan too much to endanger a case.

"How about this," he said. "Even trade. You share details that you and McGoof—"

"Paul," I emphasized.

"—that you and *Paul* find, and I'll do my best to return the favor. That's the best I can offer. You're not a licensed private investigator yet, and loose lips sink ships."

"These lips also do this." I leaned forward and met his. Then we both stood up and put our arms around each other.

"I've got you right where I want you," I said.

"Oh? Who's got who?"

I was trapped in his burly arms. But I didn't have the least interest in escaping.

There was something Darryl and I didn't discuss much, and that was the fact that I really did have a lot of power. I could pursue one hobby or another irrespective of whether it paid me an income. Meanwhile, Darryl could barely afford to live in the same city he protected every day. It was a testament to his manhood that he would date a woman so much wealthier than he was—but it also formed a complicated subtext to many of our interactions.

I didn't see my boyfriend as poor. He was rich in integrity, dignity, and love for his fellow man. Since his own divorce, he had become committed to self-discovery and growth—which is a lot more than I could say for my ex-husband. I didn't want another relationship that skated on the surface of life, that pursued wealth as a distraction or a drug.

Reluctantly, I extricated myself from his grasp. I had to get ready to meet Paul at Sammy's mansion.

"Now I'm disappointed," he said.

I had an idea.

When I came downstairs again, Darryl smiled, his eyes wider than I'd ever seen them. "Oh, yeah!"

I posed with my hands on my hips—smooth and tight in my black skirt.

He said, "It's not quite as short as I would have liked, but—"

"Darryl, you need to *behave*!"

PAUL WAS WAITING for me in front of Sammy's mansion.

"What's the reason for this?" I asked. "Does Sammy want an update? Because I don't have anything to share yet."

"I'm not completely sure." We walked to the front door.

"Kraft Macaroni and Cheese!" he shouted, and the door clicked open.

"Wow, you can really learn a lot about a person from their passwords."

The boardroom in Sammy's home could have been found at the nicest law office in Manhattan. Sammy was there; so was Margaret, though she was looking impatient. "I don't like all this drama," she had admitted to me on the phone the day before. "Besides, I signed the contract to rework the Governor's Mansion, and that's one large house. We're not going to fill it by going to Target a couple of times." She said that Sammy wanted her present at the meeting to witness some big reveal. "You never know with Sammy. It could be something amazing, or just his latest sports car, which I don't give a rat's ass about."

"What did you bring us here for?" Margaret asked Sammy once he waltzed in. "Rett is a busy woman. She's trying to solve this case, you know."

Sammy smiled. "You'll see soon enough. First, Paul has some information pertinent to the case."

We all sat down around the end of the long table. Paul pulled a stack of photocopies from a folder and passed them around.

"What's that, Paul?" I asked.

"Case notes and autopsy," he said matter-of-factly. "It's not pretty. But these things rarely are. Honestly, I don't think they are very revealing, unless you had trouble envisioning how someone could hang from a scarf tied to his bedframe. I saw that more than once when I worked in New York."

He allowed a brief pause as everyone got their bearings with the documents.

"The coroner identified the cause of death as asphyxiation. But! There's a chance Mr. Novak had some drugs in him, too.

There was a plastic syringe cap found under the bed with his fingerprints."

"Heroin?" I asked.

"We won't know until the labs come back. We do know it wouldn't take much to incapacitate him. The deceased weighed only 135 pounds."

"I thought Scott had put drugs behind him," Sammy said. "Maybe someone else drugged him? That would explain why no syringe was found."

"Quite possible," said Paul. "Of course, he might have hidden the syringe somewhere to cover up his habit."

"I'm just thinking about Mr. Sneed," added Sammy. "I wonder if Lorry was Scott's pusher. Scott didn't like to leave his property, and Lorry was always running errands for him."

"We should definitely talk to Lorry again," I said.

"This is really upsetting," Sammy said. "I really believed Scott had become a teetotaler."

"If he was fighting depression by self-medicating, he could easily get hooked," I said. "Most of us have had a friend or family member who has become addicted."

"I've never had patience for addicts," Sammy countered. "Weak in the head, if you ask me."

Margaret said drolly, "Sammy likes to inform the drowned that they should have held their *breaths*."

Everyone giggled—except Sammy. "Now, Margaret—"

"Sammy, don't bother arguing," said Paul. "Just let the lady make you a better man. My ex gave up too early in the process. You don't want to end up like me, do you?"

Sammy gave Margaret a noncommittal look, the ego in a struggle with affection.

I asked, "Did the autopsy say anything about his bruised hand? Maybe he got in a fight with someone?"

Paul said, "Or bruised it while tying his noose?"

"What was the hanging material?"

"'A yellow piece of cloth.' That's all it says."

"Could it have been an accident?" Margaret asked. "You know, that choking game you hear about?"

"I already asked Esther about it," I said. "She wasn't aware of Scott ever doing that."

Paul said, "There was no sign of a break-in, which suggests either a murderer obtained a key somehow—"

"Lorry," muttered Sammy.

"—or was let inside as someone known and trusted."

"If only zoo animals could talk," Margaret muttered.

Paul said, "The only prints found on the front door were Esther's, who had allowed herself to be fingerprinted by the authorities. But in addition to the deceased's prints, yet another person's prints were found throughout the house. Could be unrelated to the murder, but no match has been made to those."

"So, we've narrowed the suspects down to virtually anyone?" Sammy asked, exasperated.

We were all silent for a moment.

"Okay," Sammy said. "We're at a bit of a standstill. Fortunately, we've got another tool at our disposal. I've recruited someone who can help us."

"A witness?" asked Paul. "Because that would be really nice."

"Someone better," Sammy announced.

As if on cue, Emerson Cramer walked into the room. We all looked his way.

"Not *him*," said Sammy. "Everyone, follow me."

CHAPTER 8

A VISIT FROM THE GRAVE

The group made its way up the elevator to the second floor and to a room I hadn't visited—a theater with a stage. There were enough seats for about 30 people. I tried to observe how Emerson and Sammy interacted—which was basically not at all. Emerson was clearly annoyed about having to be here.

We settled into our plush chairs as Sammy pushed a button on a remote. The curtains opened, revealing a partially see-through screen suspended over a wide stage.

"Put on these special glasses," Sammy said handing them out.

The lights went down. The screen lit up. When I put on my glasses, the screen dissolved, and an incredibly realistic image of a chair appeared at center stage. I had to remove my glasses briefly just to verify I wasn't looking at a real chair.

A tall and lanky figure walked onto the stage and sat in the chair.

"Oh!" uttered Margaret.

Once again I had to take off the glasses for a second to

double-check I wasn't looking at Scott Novak. It wasn't. But it was a perfect facsimile.

The ghost clearly looked bewildered.

I looked over at Sammy, but he was looking down the row at Emerson as if to monitor his reaction. Emerson, for his part, seemed unruffled.

"Scott," said Sammy as he redirected his attention to the personality on stage. "Are you doing okay right now?"

Scott looked out into the audience. "'Hello, World,'" he said. He looked at his hands. "You asked if I'm doing okay, but I don't know how to respond."

"You're not alive anymore," said Sammy, his voice cracking. He gathered himself. "But we wanted to meet with you. Do you remember Margaret?"

"Of course. Hello, Margaret."

"Hi," she said softly.

"And this is Harriet Swinson. She goes by Rett."

"Nice to meet you, Rett," said the digital dead guy. "He" looked at me. Did "he" "see" me?

Sammy said, "For the past several years, Scott has been recording his daily experiences with an experimental device he called an Amulet. Think Google Glasses, but less glitchy. Today one of our senior programmers discovered that Scott, while he was still alive, had connected his database of lived experience both to the AfterLifeLine technology Mr. Cramer has been working on *and* to one of the artificial intelligences that Scott himself was developing."

"May I explain?" interjected the Virtual Scott.

Sammy laughed. "Go right ahead. After all, you're the one who invented you."

The 'Scott Bot' stood up. He put his hands behind his back and began slowly pacing on the stage as he talked. "The 'AI brain' as Sammy called it isn't just a way to scan a database of information. It is able to think. What *is* thinking? For one, it's the ability to remember what has happened (that's the database part) but thinking is also about imagining new possibilities and making connections between what *has* happened and what *could* happen.

"My AI brain isn't programmed to invent memories. But it may detect recorded memories whose significance Sammy and his team can't see. As Sammy told you, while I was developing this AI prototype, I was also recording practically everything that happened in my life, a sort of real-time digital journal. I accomplished this by wearing a particular device." He touched something hanging around his neck that I had taken to be a microphone. It was a gray piece of plastic with a lens in the center that resembled the pupil of an eye.

"I wore this Amulet almost continually for over two years. It's no wonder that Sammy wanted to resurrect me."

"Here's the problem," interjected Sammy. "There are nearly eight thousand hours of audio and video that Scott recorded over the course of about 30 months. They are in the system, but encrypted in such a way that we can't access the raw footage. If I could, I'd just hire a hundred people in India to watch it and transcribe what happens. Instead, we can only tease out information through interactions with Scott."

"Okay, Scott," I said, gathering my courage to address this walking computer mind. "If you don't mind me getting too personal too quickly, I'd like to ask: Who the heck killed ya?"

Scott frowned. "Sorry. I have no record of being killed. Sammy just told me I died. But I don't know how."

Sammy said, "The data stopped collecting two and a half weeks before his death. We think Scott turned off his Amulet one day and just didn't turn it back on again."

"Why?" I asked.

"We don't know," said Sammy, "and we don't even know

what happened to Scott's Amulet. It's not mentioned in the case file."

I asked Virtual Scott, "Based on what you do remember, who do you think may have killed you?"

"I can imagine a number of possibilities," he said. "For example, I can imagine that Sammy killed me to control the direction of the company. We had some disagreements, you understand."

Sammy smiled. "Isn't it also true that we worked out most of those disagreements before you died?"

"That's true—the best I can recall."

"And he does recall the best of anyone," Sammy added.

"But it's also possible we had an argument on the day I died. I have no indication we did. I'm just, again, imagining the possibilities."

"It's also possible," said Sammy, "that any number of people could have killed you, correct?"

"Yes," Scott conceded.

"Well, that narrows things down," I muttered. "Scott, tell me. Are all of your stored memories accessible?"

"What do you mean?"

"I mean, are there memories that you might have stored while you were alive that you can't access now?"

"I'm afraid it's not possible for me to know that for sure."

"Sammy," I said, "what are the chances that some of the data Scott saved while he was alive is encrypted and kept from the thingamajig program that's pretending to be Scott?"

Margaret spoke up. "I just want to point out I keep hearing the word 'crypt' and, frankly, it's freaking me out."

Sammy kept things serious. "Scott, tell me, how much data do you have access to, in terms of terabytes?"

"4.68," he said instantly.

"That's a lot of memory," said Sammy.

"But how much memory does a secret take up?" I asked.

"Could be a little," said Sammy. "Could be a lot."

"Are you sure there isn't a way we could access his memories directly, rather than in this roundabout way?"

Sammy shook his head. "I've got people working on it, but Scott was a master at protecting data. And that's just the server rack that powers Virtual Scott. There's another server of information that is so protected we don't even know where to begin." Sammy looked at Emerson. "At least, I'm told no one knows how to get into it."

Emerson said, "I don't have access to Big Cat."

Sammy gave a skeptical grunt.

"'Big Cat?'" I asked.

Paul explained, "That's all we know about this secret server of Scott's, that it's named Big Cat. The hardware is offsite somewhere in the ... what do you call it ... 'the cloud.'"

"Basically at a random server farm run by a no-name data company," Sammy said. "What's interesting is the Big Cat server holds a massive amount of memory. Ten times more than he needs to power his virtual self, for example. And absolutely no one can access it."

"What could Project Big Cat be?" I said. "It sounds ominous."

Sammy shook his head. "I guess the name of the project is fitting, because most servers are stored in actual security cages—but that's usually to keep others out, not to keep the servers in. Again, we don't know where it is. That means it's safe from being physically destroyed, but someone else could try to hack into it from virtually anywhere. A competitor, or just someone intent on mayhem."

"I have no memory of this 'Big Cat,'" added Virtual Scott.

"Maybe Emerson knows," said Sammy. He stared at Emerson. "You were Scott's closest confidant."

"I would tell you if I could get into that server, and I can't."

Sammy turned to the hologram. "Thank you, Scott. You can go now, but before you do..." He struggled to find his voice. "I just want to tell you that I miss you. The real you. I'll never forget you."

Scott bowed while wearing a narrow, closed-lips smile, same as I'd seen him in photographs.

Then he walked off the stage and dissolved into the shadows.

"Wow," I said. "That was something."

Sammy nodded. "That's what I thought, too. And it's exactly why I bought Scott's company. The banks that loaned me the money are plenty nervous now that Scott is dead. So am I."

"Are you?" shouted Emerson, standing. "You were paranoid that Scott wasn't going to reveal his research and was walking away from his projects. You resented him."

The billionaire fumed. "Scott *was* holding back. But I talked to him about it. We were square with each other. He promised to reveal his research, and I believed him."

"Then maybe you just didn't need him anymore. Or maybe you wanted to kill him to remove a future competitor."

"How dare you accuse me in my own home!"

Emerson, not able to summon a comeback, stormed out of the room.

Sammy said, "That man infuriates me!"

"Why don't you fire him?" Paul asked.

Sammy shook his head. "He just lost a friend. I can't do it."

"That's why I love you," said Margaret, standing up and giving Sammy a kiss on the cheek. "I'm tired, honey. I'm going to go to bed and let you all save the world." She left the room.

I turned to Sammy. "Is the fact he was Scott's friend the only reason you won't fire Emerson?"

"Emerson is in charge of the virtual reality segment of the business," Sammy said. "I need him to keep those projects going. But if it ever becomes clear that he's stalling progress, I'll have to let him go. And, I've even wondered if he's the one prowling around RidgeLine's servers looking for things that don't concern him. Any new progress there, Paul?"

"The hacker's activity has revved up lately. Any day now our cybersecurity firm hopes to identify him."

I asked Sammy, "Who do you think—?"

But Sammy cut me off and stood up. "If there are further questions for me, Rett, they will have to wait. I must leave for the airport and fly to the West Coast for a board meeting. Thank you for coming out tonight." Just before he departed, Sammy handed me a piece of paper with a phone number written on it. "That's Virtual Scott's contact information. You can text or phone him anytime. He'll always be ready to take your questions."

Sammy left.

Paul and I made our way outside. My mind reeled. I didn't know what to think about Virtual Scott. I had so many questions about the scope and validity of the information to which the Scott Bot had access.

As we waited for the good-looking valet to bring our cars, I asked Paul if he was comfortable with the technology being created at RidgeLine. "Don't you think this virtual reality stuff is really weird and disturbing?"

"Same old, same old."

That was the last thing I expected him to say. "But this stuff is brand new."

He laughed. "I don't think so."

"You mean you're used to talking to dead people?"

"All the time," he said. "I talk to my grandma, especially in the kitchen. She's always reappearing, telling me not to overdo the spices. 'Taste it, Paulie! Don't be afraid to *taste* it!' I'm like, 'Okay, Gran, okay! I hear you!'"

"But this is different. These techno geniuses want to create entire virtual worlds so we can avoid having to live in this one."

Paul laughed. "If you ask me, we already live in virtual worlds. Heck, we have to. If we didn't, we'd all be totally depressed."

I appreciated Paul's down-to-earth personality. I wondered if a robot could ever emulate that sort of friendliness, and, when it did, if I could bring myself to care.

CHAPTER 9

TRACKING PREY

Darryl was already asleep when I got home. The next morning he was up early and out the door before I awoke. At least I knew we were on good terms. I could focus my energy worrying about the Novak case—and my arch nemesis: KayLeigh Rider.

As I sipped my coffee, I went online to look for a list of the properties KayLeigh represented. Unfortunately, KayLeigh's website was offline. This was not surprising if she was now using the same web company Allan used. Even when I oversaw Swinson Development, the website had issues. Our webmaster, Roger, was always difficult to get in touch with. We called him Roger the Dodger because he was an expert at evading his clients' phone calls. But he was very sharp otherwise and extremely inexpensive, so we decided to keep him.

I always knew where to find Roger; it just required visiting a certain coffee shop where he tended to camp out and do his work. I sped north against morning traffic to Sola's on Lead Mine Road and, sure enough, there was Roger, sitting in the back with his long, stringy blond hair up in a man bun, earbuds, and a grande cappuccino standing guard like one of the statues on Easter Island.

"Hi, Rett," he muttered, pulling out his earbuds. "How's it goin'?"

"Great, Roger. Hey, I need a quick favor." I pulled my chair around to sit right beside him.

"Well, I'm pretty busy, but..." He took a large gulp of his drink. "What is it?"

I wasn't even sure that Roger knew I had divorced Allan, left the company, and experienced a total life change. We were about to find out.

I smiled. "I need access to one of my websites. It seems to be off-line."

"Really?" He typed the website URL into his browser. "You're right. No one told me."

I kind of doubted that.

"I'll put it back up."

"No need to worry about getting that site online just now," I said, imagining the mounting panic on KayLeigh's cover-girl face as one client after another read her the riot act. "I just need to know KayLeigh's current listings, that's all. Could you grab those for me really quick?"

"That data is in a folder on the server." He poked a few keys and a moment later the information appeared on my phone as an email with a zipped attachment.

"Oh, thank you, Roger. I really appreciate it!"

"No problem." He replaced his earbuds and returned to his previous groove.

Back in my car, I looked more closely at KayLeigh's listings, especially the photos that went with them. Several gorgeous homes—all of them a million dollars or more. One of them was Alice Huffman's mansion—spectacular. Inside I growled at how much money KayLeigh would net for minimal effort.

But that wasn't all. KayLeigh was also representing the house next to Alice's. Could this be Scott's old house, the one Esther had mistaken for Alice's on that fateful night? I clicked through the images quickly. The home had some furniture but looked mostly empty, betraying odd and various hooks, cords, and outlets. Not a good look for KayLeigh. I was skeptical that Roger had sent me the most recent photos.

I moved on to her short list of commercial properties. Certainly KayLeigh must be actively working to take on new ones. I just needed to find out which.

A moment later, I had Paul Maroni on the line.

"As your apprentice, am I allowed to follow someone? Like, in my car?"

"Who's the mark?"

"KayLeigh Rider, real estate agent."

"The alleged malfeasance?"

"Slander. I need to see who she's talking to."

"We can't investigate just anyone. Who's the client?"

"Me."

"That's a gray area. What's she saying about you?"

It took a while, but I told him.

"That's a heck of a hatchet job, alright," he said. "When do you want to get started?" I was beginning to appreciate Paul's up-for-anything attitude.

"Immediately."

"Okay. We can use my car because she's not familiar with it. Where are you?"

A half hour later I was riding in Paul's Saab, traveling down memory lane, loving those low riding, bucket seats.

KayLeigh drove a red Mini Cooper with a white stripe, an easy car to spot in traffic. Tooling around near her office, we spotted it parked in front of one of the Cameron Village restaurants where someone like KayLeigh would pay fifteen dollars for a piece of Bibb lettuce dribbled with a teaspoon of olive oil.

"There it is!" I cried.

Paul maneuvered to a lot across the street. It was the perfect stakeout location.

"And now ... we wait," he said.

I should have known a stakeout was going to be the most boring thing ever. "I don't want this chick wasting any more of my time. I want to be *done* with her."

"Do you want to leave?" He put his hand on the key as if to start the car again. It was actually half a key which had broken off in the ignition and required a pair of pliers to turn it. *Darryl: "Deputy McGoof."*

"I'll wait a little while longer, I guess."

"Look, I know it's boring work being a P.I., but people usually do something eventually. Ever been fishing?"

"Of course." I told him how my mom always loved to fish. My dad, on the other hand, never had the patience for it. Maybe I was more like my dad in that way.

"You learn to enjoy the process. Watch people while you wait. It's interesting."

Not *that* interesting. I had almost zoned out when KayLeigh finally emerged from her lunch and sped off in her little English coupe. We followed.

She drove straight to her office a couple blocks away.

"Dang it!" I said.

"Don't sweat. Let's give her 20 minutes."

I was in luck. Five minutes later she emerged and sped off again. As we passed the North Hills outdoor mall with its fashion boutiques, yoga studios, and beauty salons, I held my breath, for I was just certain she was going to stop and spend several hours on self-care.

Fortunately, she passed by the boutiques and turned left on

Six Forks Road. When her car pulled into the Wells-Farley Building drive, Paul turned into the office building's second entrance and parked out of sight.

"Now go inside to see what brought her here," Paul said.

"She'll totally recognize me."

"Then I'll go in instead. What's my cover if someone accosts me?"

"Tell them ... your phone died and you're looking for directions to the North Library."

"I do look bookish," he chuckled, adding, "If I don't come out, will you please tell Mother I love her?"

"Hush!"

I didn't have to wait long. Paul came out just a couple minutes later very much unscathed.

"KayLeigh went into an office on the first floor. 'Stiles Accounting.' Know it?"

"That would be Hank Stiles." I explained how Hank, now in his early seventies, was in the process of winding down his successful accounting firm. "This whole building is Hank's. He probably wants to sell the building and ride off into retirement on a nice nest egg."

Hank and his wife, Katherine, had never had children of their own. Instead, their three beagles—Huey, Dewey, and Louie —were their dependents, and the couple were actively fundraising for a new adoption wing at an animal shelter which, I suspected, would bear the Stiles name (or at least the name of a beagle or two).

"Do you want to get Hank to secretly record KayLeigh talking trash about you?" Paul asked. "That would be my first thought."

"No," I said. "I have a better idea."

"Of course you do."

As Paul started the Saab again, KayLeigh came out of the

building—but she wasn't alone. She was with a pretty blond woman I recognized.

"That's Esther Mills! Why are those two together?"

Paul shrugged, "The beautiful people always seem to find each other. It's like a law of nature."

We watched them chat outside the building and then go their separate ways to their cars.

"That was a very business-like exchange," Paul said. "It wasn't a lovey-dovey, 'soooo glad to see ya, girlfriend,' sort of deal."

"Agreed," I said. But what sort of business might KayLeigh and Esther be engaged in together?

Dropped off again at my car, I pulled out my phone and checked my notes for the name of the coder from the house parties that Esther had given me. I googled Trey Gamble's RidgeLine email address and introduced myself. To my surprise, Mr. Gamble wrote back right away and said he could meet me at five o'clock. I suggested Foundation, a small bar on Fayetteville Street.

There was time to kill. I felt the urge to run home and paint, but as I was heading that way, I remembered the conversation I'd had at Needless Necessities with painting instructor Ken Grimes. His studio was on my way home. Maybe I'd just drop by. I had in my car's trunk the Raleigh cityscape I could show him.

Ken's home studio was not far from Freddy's in the warehouse district. I'd always thought this to be the perfect set-up for a visual artist, allowing one to have a home, studio, and storefront all in the same building.

A "closed" sign hung in the small window of the front door. That was meant for customers, so I walked around back and knocked twice on the studio door before pushing it open and stepping in.

Had I walked into Heaven? Light poured into the room from large windows on every wall. Most of the windows were translucent, painted with a frost that let the light in but obscured what was inside, so no one could peer in from the sidewalk and watch Ken painting.

Much of the hardwood floor was draped in drop-cloth. Actual paintings—some finished, some in process—covered nearly every surface of the walls. The furniture consisted merely of three plush chairs, a couch, a small round stone coffee table. A refrigerator—one of those old-timey white ones from the 1950s with rounded edges, like the one my grandfather always had in his basement to store his fishing worms—hummed away in the corner.

The room transported me. It smelled like the studio at East Carolina University where we students used to do our work. I immediately felt 20 years younger.

I stepped inside and closed the door behind me. Ken acknowledged me with a quick glance but didn't pause his brush. I carried my cityscape over to the sitting area and leaned it against the sofa.

I was about to take a seat and wait him out, but Ken stopped and stepped back to regard his painting, a study in purples, just as he'd talked about. It was abstract and impressionistic—a flurry of seemingly random brushstrokes that made it look like a half dozen paint buckets had exploded onto the canvas.

"That's so beautiful," I said.

"I'm having fun with it," Ken said as he turned and faced me. "What's shaking? Were you at Needless today?"

"No, I've been busy," I said, but I had no interest in talking about the Novak case. It was painting I wanted to discuss. I was dying to show him my cityscape and mention to him my idea of doing an exhibition, just to see what he might say.

Ken walked over to the refrigerator. "What would you like to drink? Glass of wine?"

"I don't drink," I said, though a glass of wine in a studio this lovely would have put the finishing touches on the moment. "Water would be great, thank you, if you have it."

"We have."

He brought me a glass of water. We both sat on the sofa. He didn't bring anything for himself to drink. Instead, he had a small wooden box which he proceeded to open, producing a joint and a lighter.

I felt uncomfortable. Though I'd been around plenty of people smoking pot in college and a few people since, it had always felt like a crutch that was as bad as alcohol—and I knew about that one all too well.

He offered me the joint. "No, thanks," I said. He lit up, toked, and regarded me.

"So, you've been working on landscape," he said.

"Yes," I said, trying to focus on Ken's eyes through the pot smoke. "I've been using it as a way to get out of the house—and out of myself. Life can be so intense."

"If you can redirect those feelings on your work, it's like therapy."

"You just put it right plain."

He grinned at my colloquialism, took another toke, and set the joint on an ashtray.

"Let's see what you've been doing."

I reached for the painting and held it between us. Ken, accommodating, moved his ashtray over to the side table beside him. I let him take the painting in both hands. The painting made me proud, as I felt I'd captured the look of Raleigh from the south as it seemed to rise out of a green, semi-urban oasis.

I explained, "I got the idea of using a lot of colors from that portrait of Abraham Lincoln at the NC Museum of Art. You know, the one that builds his face from a thousand spools of thread?"

"Of course. I love that piece."

I waited for him to say more, but he continued to examine the work. I wondered if it was out of courtesy more than interest. Could he not say anything at all?

I was *dying*.

"I like to really look at a painting," he explained. "Landscape is like a lot of realist painting these days—endangered. Every phone has a camera now. Every person can capture their own sunsets and add a painting filter. And no one has time to look at it. They are too busy scrolling to the next post. But I want to honor a work in the spirit it was created."

"Thank you."

After a few beats, he said, "This is really good."

"Do you really think so?"

"I do."

He leaned forward so he could really see the strokes. "I'm looking at the texture. You have good coverage throughout. Nothing thin about this."

"I had a teacher in college who said, 'Beauty grows in oil the way flowers grow in soil.' She always said to lather it on."

"I'll buy that."

He leaned the painting against the coffee table. Then he extended his hand and took mine, giving it a single shake. "Well done."

I felt myself blushing and nervously took my hand back.

"Just curious," he said with a slight smile. "When did you realize that you were more aware than most people, smarter than most people, deeper than most people?"

"I don't know that I did. I think I've spent a lot of my life feeling inferior."

"How many people do you think are making art? Not many. They are making out shopping lists. Most aren't even doing that. They are going through a drive-thru because they didn't think ahead."

"We all have to eat."

"But what's feeding their souls? My point is that most people are just sleeping. We've got to wake them up. That's why the great ones exist. To wake others up."

I nodded. This guy was thoughtful. Smart. More academic than Darryl, that's for sure. When I was talking to Ken, I felt like I was back in school again, in a good way. *The mind on fire.*

"Would you like to stay and paint something?" he offered suddenly.

I thought about all the things I needed to do that day, beginning with a meeting with Paul.

"I'm afraid I have to go meet someone."

"Your boyfriend?" he asked casually.

"No, a colleague."

"Then come back again soon," he said.

"I will," I said. "I'll come up with another landscape to show you."

"Or paint something here. That would be fun."

"Sure." If I did that, maybe I'd finally find the confidence to share with Ken my dream of a show and get his thoughts.

I snatched up the cityscape as Ken went back to his canvas. Just before I left, I got one last look at that studio's glorious light....

... and immediately a shadow fell across my heart, for I had not accepted the clear opportunity to tell Ken I had a boyfriend.

Why hadn't I?

CHAPTER 10

PAYBACK

"Does *she* have to be here?"

Trey Gamble, the former G4—now RidgeLine—coder, sat at our table under the bar's low light. The short and skinny 20-something with greasy black hair wore a bomber jacket and sunglasses even though we were inside.

He had directed his question to Paul.

The "she" was me. Paul—God bless him—screwed up his face like Trey had just stepped in dog poop. "You mean Ms. Swinson? She's the one you agreed through email to meet with."

"I thought 'Rett' was a dude's name, not a chick's."

I wanted so badly to respond, but Paul placated me with a look that said, "*I hate this little twerp, too—but let's play along.*"

Paul smiled at Trey. "She's learning the trade. You can ignore her if you want." Suddenly magically endowed with the power of invisibility, I could now monitor said twerp's words and body language without feeling self-conscious.

Paul asked Trey, "How did you come to work at G4?"

Trey told how he had come to G4 right out of college, the top of his class from a Michigan school. "Scott Novak was a genius. I wanted to work for the best."

"What was he like?"

"Didn't see him much, actually. I did write his brother a couple times."

"The Alaska brother? Adam?"

"Yeah, Scott said his brother was an expert on Nietzsche, really talked him up, so I thought I'd get his thoughts on Nietzsche's political philosophy. But Adam turned out to be a fraud. He really didn't know much about Nietzsche after all, if you ask me."

"I am asking you."

"Then, no, he didn't know much about Nietzsche. He didn't even speak German."

"And you do?"

"I'm learning it. German is a language of power."

Germany lost two world wars, I wanted to say. *The* only *two.*

"Back to Novak's company," Paul said. "You liked working at G4?"

"It was cool. Everyone was into gaming and sci-fi. Every weekend, Scott threw a party."

"Fun?"

"Heck yeah. Booze, music—legs. It's like all our hard work during the week paid off. Finally, we got to cut loose."

"Get laid, you mean."

"Of course."

I was trying very hard not to throw up.

"Where did the ladies hail from?"

"Local colleges. They were there for the same things we were, except maybe also to land themselves a rich husband."

"Were you gentlemen there to find wives?"

Trey guffawed. "No. Most of us weren't even looking for a steady girlfriend. We just wanted to have fun. Nothing wrong with that, right?"

Paul laughed. "Course not." He was playing his part well. "And then..."

"And then The Bitch shows up." He was clearly capitalizing those words.

"You mean Esther Mills?"

"Yep. Scott meets her, make her our HR director. It was *ree-dic*. I mean, HR doesn't even *build* anything. Scott basically gave his girlfriend-of-one-night a cushy job."

"She made out okay?"

"She got a huge signing bonus paid in stock like the other directors and VPs. She's not hurting."

"Did you and the other front-line programmers get paid in stock?"

"Sure, but some of us who were fairly new are still grinding it out."

"Did you use your winnings to buy that beauty on the curb?" Paul asked. We'd both noted the silver electric self-driving car in front of the bar. Paul had looked up the model and found it sold for a hundred grand.

"Chicks dig it," said Trey smugly.

And you need all the help you can get, Herr Wiener Schnitzel.

Paul said, "Must be nice to have a ride like that. But I wonder if any of you resented Scott Novak just a little bit? I mean, when Yoko broke up the Beatles, there was some anger toward her, sure, but Lennon was the one who ended up dead."

Trey swallowed. "I don't think—"

Paul interrupted, "If we got a warrant to look at the emails and instant messages and what-not between you and the other programmers, do you think we'd see some serious hate directed toward Mr. Novak?"

Trey Gamble was squirming now—and I was loving every second of it.

"Let me put it in a succinct manner for you." Paul shot me a quick look as he leaned forward and lowered his voice. "The authorities are very interested in learning more about who had grudges against Novak. I'd love to help them out, because they might see fit to help *me* out. You get me evidence of what your colleagues were saying—emails, messages, texts, whatever—and maybe they'll come to see you as helpful instead of getting the notion that you had something to do with Novak's death. Do you think you could do that?"

Mr. Gamble was looking less self-assured. He glanced in my direction, briefly, as if in search of some assistance—but he wasn't going to get it from me.

"Sure," he said, finally. "A lot of the older guys resented Scott after he shut down the parties. They were totally desperate in terms of their love lives."

"As in they required a pimp," I cut in, "and Novak had stopped pimping for them."

Trey scoffed. "Whatever."

Now that the woman had a voice at the table, the conversation was over.

"I don't like him," I told Paul after the coder had left.

"An entitled little prick he is. But he's nervous. He'll bring us something—I'd gamble on it."

The conversation troubled me. I was used to sexism, but Trey's brand of misogyny felt like something darker. It's one thing if you don't think women are quite as good as men. It's quite another if you believe women are the *sheisse* on your shoe.

I quickly tried to put Trey Gamble out of my mind.

I hadn't even gotten home when Paul called again. "Sammy says it's important to come by RidgeLine right now."

"Again? Why?"

"He says he's caught the hacker who infiltrated RidgeLine's systems."

THE EXECUTIVE SUITE at RidgeLine wasn't much fancier than any other part of the company offices I'd seen. Sammy waved us in, then picked up his desk's old-fashioned office handset and pushed a button. "Patty, ask Emerson to bring in the girl."

"The hacker is female?" I asked.

"Yes," said Sammy, "and to my chagrin, she works for us. An intern. I thought we did a better job than that of hiring." He cast a stern look at Paul.

Paul held up his palms in protest. "With all due respect, Mr. Patel, I don't run the internship program, and no one has asked me to do background checks on them."

"You will moving forward," Sammy said. "Here's Emerson now with our hacker in tow."

The door to the boardroom slid open. Emerson wasn't the first person my eyes lit upon. When I saw the thin 22-year-old Black woman with close-cropped hair, I had to grab the chair near me so I wouldn't faint.

The woman's eyes widened briefly upon seeing me. I didn't see shame, though. She bore an expression best described as amused.

Augusta Jones and I had met a year ago when her younger cousin was being singled out for the murder of Wanda Hightower. At the time I had encouraged her to go back to college, but Augusta said she found it easier to learn her craft—computer coding—on her own. Whatever family genetics helped guide her grandfather as he created his eye-popping sculptures had also gifted Augusta with an understanding of computer networks—a certain sixth sense. She was a wonder, and I suspected she couldn't yet imagine the power she might be able to wield someday.

But now I was fearful on her behalf.

"Augusta?!" I cried. "What are you doing here?"

Augusta stood her ground. "I *work* here. What are *you* doing here?"

Sammy started to say, "Ms. Swinson is—"

"I asked the lady, thank you," Augusta said curtly. One thing I loved about Augusta was her refusal to take crap from anybody, but it was also the thing that caused me the most concern. She was not much older than my daughter, and I wanted her to see that there was a certain amount of compromise adults had to make to get ahead.

But Augusta was an idealist (a "radical" according to those who didn't share her ideals). Plus, she liked to argue how, being Black, she was often faced with making a double concession: one to a capitalist America which could be predatory; the other to elements of white power who didn't want her to succeed.

Sammy Patel wasn't white, but he was definitely The Man. I felt the need to defuse a fight before it started.

"I'm here to help Mr. Patel solve the mystery of how his star employee, Scott Novak, died. Anything you can share to help us would be really appreciated, Augusta."

Sammy cut in. "This young lady is supposed to be helping to build a website for our global business. I want to know why she is poking around our servers."

"Because you asked me to," Augusta said.

"I certainly did not!"

"I'll show you the email." Augusta pulled out her phone and quickly did a search. "Okay. I just responded to it. Check your account."

Sammy looked at his computer screen. "That's my personal email account. No one in the company has that address." He looked at Augusta suspiciously. "How—?"

"Man, you emailed *me*. Read what you said."

She had copied the email to me, too. Paul looked over my shoulder as everyone read silently:

Ms. Jones,

I am delighted that you chose to conduct your internship at RidgeLine!

If you don't mind, I'd like to provide you with an additional task, should you find yourself with some extra time.

I would like for you to do some penetration testing of our servers. I'm reaching out to you directly because it's important that we test our system. Telling your supervisor would alert him to the testing and allow him to harden defenses. Again, do this only if you have the time. I don't want to detract from your assigned duties and put you over the number of hours you've contracted with us. That said, if you're able to penetrate our company's servers, I'll be glad to compensate you for any extra time you have spent doing so, plus a little extra as a sort of grand prize.

Sincerely,

Samarth Patel

CEO, RidgeLine Computing

"I didn't send that email!" Sammy shouted.

Augusta shrugged. "If you say so."

"That's social engineering. Why didn't you ask someone to verify it was from me?"

Augusta smiled. "I thought about that. But if the email was for real, you wouldn't *want* me to reach out to anyone. And it's not like I can just call you up without tipping off a secretary. Besides, even if it wasn't real, I still figured you would like to know if your systems were leaky."

The logic was solid. "I can see your logic," Sammy said.

"Frankly," I cut in, "I'm pretty impressed that an intern was able to get into some of this company's sensitive data. Aren't you impressed, Mr. Patel?"

Sammy spoke through his teeth. "I don't exactly like it, but, yes, I'm impressed."

Augusta took a second to make a sweet face and frame it with swan-wing hands.

"Fine," said Sammy. "Moving forward, I want Ms. Jones officially on Project Big Cat. You might have gotten this far into RidgeLine's defenses, Augusta, but Big Cat is something else entirely. We need to find out what Scott was working on before he died. It might even help us understand why he was killed."

I said, "What about that grand prize that was mentioned?"

Patel nodded and turned to Augusta. "I'll give you a hundred thousand dollars if you crack Big Cat."

"Say what?" said Augusta.

"Say what?" said I.

"But you have to be the first, Augusta," he continued, "and, you can't look at or copy anything that is there. It's proprietary. I'll give you a different email you can use to let me know when you've succeeded, now that this one is compromised. Your internship is suspended with pay so that you can work exclusively on trying to unlock Big Cat."

Everyone was looking at Augusta.

"I'm not saying no," she said.

LYDIA'S STROKE last year (which had taken place in the passenger seat of my Camry) had made her wary of driving. She'd drive if she had to, but she was still afraid she'd have a medical event and hurt someone. And, she might not admit it, but I think she preferred the company. Lydia's husband and Darryl's father, Karl, had been deceased for a number of years.

Lydia was especially crabby the next morning as I did the driving to her quilting club.

"I need a vacation," she said once we got in my car and started moving. "We could go to Door County, just n-n-north of Milwaukee. It's nice up there in the fall. We could take the whole family. Why don't we do that?"

I didn't know how I could get away, not with the Novak case in full gear. I'd never been a big traveler anyway. When I had the development firm, I was too wrapped up in it to travel. I just never got into the habit.

"Maybe," I said.

"You don't want to g-g-go anywhere?"

"I didn't say that."

"It's okay. You've got lots going on. Good for you."

I felt terrible. "Please don't be angry," I said.

"I'm not angry," she lied.

"This case will be over soon," I added. "Then we can go somewhere. Or maybe you can just go somewhere with Darryl and Charlie."

"M-m-maybe." Clearly, Lydia had wanted to go with me.

"You'll give yourself another stroke if you don't calm down about this," I said. "Try to meditate."

"I haven't meditated *in my life*." She was fibbing about this, too. I'd seen her close her eyes and do deep breathing now and then, if only as a tactic to keep from smoking, a habit the doctors had made her abandon after the stroke.

"Maybe one of the Qrazy Qwilters will want to go on a trip with you."

"They won't."

"Would it hurt to ask?"

"It's okay. I'll be f-f-fine."

Oh, Jeez.

At Needless Necessities we walked past the painting class

(where Brittainy, a young, tattooed artist, was holding court today) and marched into the Double-Qs space. The quilting tabby, Q.T., abandoned her bed in the corner and headed for Lydia's legs. At the last second, Lydia, still steaming at me, stepped around the cat. Q.T., who knew very well that she was worth twice her weight in creature comfort, just stood there looking absolutely confused and maybe a little indignant. *Well!*

Today there were six women at their quilting stations. The air here always felt lighter than in the rest of the world, as if the room were built on top of a layer of bunting, the cottony substance that filled the blankets of the women's creations. I wasn't a quilter, but I liked to hang out with the ladies sometimes. The group never stood on ceremony. Not long after I had purchased the building and assumed control of Needless's board, I'd asked Lydia if the ladies knew about my new role. She set me straight. "Missy, the Qrazies know *everything*."

Of course, they did.

"What's new in Quiltville?" I asked the group as I took a seat in the corner.

Susie, the youngest in the group, took an opportunity to needle the group's leader, Pleasance Miles.

"Pleasance is in a mood," Susie said. "Nothing new there."

Pleasance looked at her and literally growled. "*Grrrr.*"

"We just can't figure out why," Susie added.

"Let me guess, Susie," I said. "It's because you won't stop bothering her about it?"

"Ding, ding, ding!" Pleasance said. "Rett really is a detective. All the rest of y'all need to *hush*."

"Dream on," said Susie.

I couldn't stay long. I had things to do. But even I was curious to know what was bugging Pleasance.

"Pleasance," I said, moving my chair within a couple feet of hers, "what are you working on there?" I could already see she was pulling thread on a colorful, complicated paisley design that bled from one square to the next. The Qrazies pushed the edges of quilting convention. In some ways they were as bold as any painter, even though they were forced to work within stricter parameters.

"I'm making mistakes right and left," Pleasance said, undoing some of her work.

"Am I distracting you?" I asked.

"No. I'm just annoyed with my sister."

There was a collective in-breath in the room as everyone finally understood the source of their leader's gray cloud. Though we had never met Pleasance's only living sister, Charity's reputation was notorious for a persistent grouchiness. It's a shame children received their names before their true personalities became known. Pleasance—who was a nice enough person but could hardly be characterized as *pleasant*—described her younger sister in terms that were a million miles from charitableness. Pleasance's family had tip-toed around Charity their whole lives, tolerating her misanthropic nature, even allowing her to take possession of the coveted family vacation home on Harris Lake.

The rest of the siblings had died, making it Pleasance's regular task to check in on her dysfunctional sister, who had never held a real job and, in fact, seemed totally incompetent in human society.

"What is up with Charity these days?" I asked.

Pleasance explained, "I went to deliver soup to her the other day, and she wouldn't let me inside. Made me leave it on the deck."

"So?" I said.

"So, she usually lets me inside so I can do some cleaning."

There was a moment of silence so that everyone could judge

the fact that Pleasance's sister couldn't be bothered to clean her own home.

"Is that all?" I asked.

"No. What's really odd is she was *nice* about it. That's not like her. She just came up to the door and said through the screen door to 'please put the soup on the porch.' 'Please'! Then she said something else that didn't make sense."

We all waited.

"Well?" said Susie. "What?"

Pleasance frowned. "She said 'thank you.'"

Everyone gasped.

Pleasance shook her head. "In 75 years, Charity has never said thank you for *anything*."

"I can see why you'd be concerned," said Susie.

I asked, "But is this really such a bad thing?"

"I'm worried she's got dementia," Pleasance said.

Lydia could bite her tongue no longer.

"Charity would not have been allowed to act like such a pill in my family. My father would have told her to shape up or ship out!"

Pleasance shook her head. "That's just the way Charity's always been. I don't much enjoy her company either, but she's all I've got in terms of family."

"We're loyal to family even when they do things that annoy us," I said, looking hard at Lydia. "By the way, Lyd, you should tell them about the vacation you want someone in the group to take with you."

"What are you t-t-talking about?" Lydia protested.

Seed successfully planted, I scooted out of there.

~

I HAD a date with Katherine Stiles, the wife of Hank Stiles. I needed to act fast, because if the couple was thinking of doing business with KayLeigh, I would need to step in before her agent representation contract saw ink.

I didn't know Katherine too well, but her grand-daughter, Austin, and my daughter had been friends while they were in high school. I hoped that Stephanie—whose past was littered with battered friendships—hadn't done anything to alienate Austin. Even so, it might not matter. My call had been about providing a donation to the animal rescue nonprofit Katherine chaired.

Katherine had suggested lunch, but I didn't want something as public as that. My idea was that we meet at her family's office building.

"As I mentioned in my message, I'm looking for an animal-related nonprofit to give some dollars to," I stated as we sat across a conference table from each other. "Know one?"

Katherine smiled and put her hand on mine.

"We're in the middle of a capital campaign to expand the shelter," she said. "It will give us room so that we can help more animals and keep them longer so that there's a better chance of them being adopted."

"That's fantastic," I said. "There's just one issue." I got a little teary. It wasn't totally a put on.

"My goodness, Rett. What's wrong?"

I sniffled. "I might not be able to free up the dollars I'd like to give. I might have to invest in a lawsuit. And you know how lengthy and expensive those can get."

"If you don't mind me asking, what sort of lawsuit? Is it related to a real-estate development?"

"Oh, no! Allan and I parted ways on that when we divorced. I walked away with several million dollars—my fair share of the business. No, the lawsuit has to do with his new wife, KayLeigh Rider. Have you met her?"

I watched as a small cloud of danger flitted across Katherine's brain. "I'm sure I *have* met her. She's a real-estate agent, isn't she?"

You know exactly what she is, Katherine.

But I wasn't there to cause Katherine any embarrassment. "That's right," I said. "It's just that—KayLeigh has been saying some awful things about me. Even though she and Allan started their affair while he was still married to me, she's bitter that he didn't receive more in the divorce. She's lucky Allan got what money he did, but to get revenge, she's been telling stories about me."

"'Stories?'"

"That I'm a drunk, that I abused my daughter when she was young, that I embezzled. It's not right."

"No, it's not." Katherine thought for a moment. "Excuse me, Rett. I need to let Hank know he's on his own for dinner tonight. I'll be right back, okay?"

"Okay."

She sped out of there, and I think I knew why. She needed to tell her husband to hold off on signing the agreement with that agent he considered such a nice piece of...

Wasn't I naughty?

She was back a moment later, looking much relieved, for she'd evidently caught Hank in time.

"Now where were we?" she asked. "I think you were talking about a lawsuit. Are you sure that's going to be necessary?"

"I don't really want to do it. But my lawyer is pushing me."

"Sometimes," Katherine said, "bringing a lawsuit just stirs up a bunch of publicity. I have this feeling that 'what goes around comes around.'"

"What do you mean?"

"I mean it's quite possible that the new Mrs. Swinson will come to regret her actions quite on her own. In fact..." Katherine weighed her words carefully. "I aim to tell everyone I know that I do not appreciate anyone dragging the good name of an old friend of mine, someone who was so sweet to Austin when she was young, through the mud."

"You would be willing to do that?"

"I would!"

"Why, if you could do that, then I wouldn't have to rely on the courts to solve my problem!"

"That's right!"

"And I could do something so much better with those dollars!"

"Why, yes, Rett, you could!"

"How fantastic, Katherine! Could you share with me the different giving levels of your capital campaign with me?"

"Of course!"

I went with the Silver Level.

But the feeling I got was worth its weight in gold.

CHAPTER 11
THE PLACE OF DEATH

There was a Saab waiting for me outside.

"What are you doing here?" I asked. "Did you follow me?"

Paul winked. "'Ask me no questions...'"

I quickly told him what I'd done to thwart KayLeigh.

"Congrats on that. I'm going to go search Novak's house. Thought you might want to come along."

We took off in his car. "How did you get permission?" I asked. "Let me guess. You bribed someone."

"'Bribed' is a such an ugly word. I like to think I reduced the incentive for them to stop me from breaking and entering."

"By giving to a first-responders charity, perhaps? Who in the world would do something sneaky like that?"

We both had a good laugh.

"Actually," he said, "they're all but ready to close the case. A judge is allowing Sammy to pay for the care of the animals. I don't think Sheriff Jordan will exactly complain if we discover something interesting."

We had some time to kill on the drive. I asked, "Have you been thinking about that fake email Augusta got from Sammy?"

"Not too much. Sammy has been the target of nonsense like that the whole time I've worked for him. And you can't track that stuff down. It's kind of frustrating."

"Are we positive that Sammy didn't write that email?"

Paul shrugged. "Even if he did, it's his company. I think it's more likely your friend wrote it to cover her tracks."

"Augusta isn't like that," I said. "She sets herself to a high standard." Even as I said it, I wondered if even she might compromise her ethics for the right cause.

We parked between the zoo and the house. Mechanical sounds emanated from beyond the property, drowning out the usual sounds of birds.

I spied Sheila amidst the cages, so I introduced her to Paul and asked about the continued search for the missing animals.

"We've got all the birds now but still can't find the orang-utan," she said. "That guy can't hide forever. And it's going to start getting cold soon."

I'd been following Zeus in the news. There had been alleged sightings of the missing ape. One headline read: "Wake County is the New 'Zeus-Topia'" The tongue-in-cheek story speculated that the Research Triangle had become the landlocked version of the Bermuda Triangle.

People who were missing items from their porches or yards blamed it on Zeus. A meme circulating online showed an ape partying in the forest with a bunch of random items torn from Amazon boxes.

A couple of campers near Jordan Lake reported that they'd seen a Sasquatch-type creature near their tents. Having read a blog post speculating Novak had been murdered by Zeus, they packed up, leaving their gear behind.

Finally, a drunk hunter shot his buddy in the leg, mistaking him for a belligerent ape. "Why bother to wear orange in the woods if it's just gonna get you shot?" asked the victim rhetorically.

All humor aside, I knew Sheila was worried about the missing primate.

Now I noticed Sheila observing the serval with concern.

"How's she doing?" I asked.

"I cleaned out the infection in her paw. She'll be okay."

"What is to become of these animals?" I asked.

She shrugged. "We haven't heard from Adam Novak, who technically owns them. But if they aren't claimed within 30 days, they'll have to be relocated or destroyed. I've already started getting on the phone, trying to find places that will take them. It's not easy."

"If anyone can do it, you can." I looked around. "What's that awful engine noise I'm hearing?"

"Mr. Sneed is getting his septic tank pumped today."

"*Ewww...*"

"Yeah, but not as gross as the fact he's been doing his business outside for the past several weeks. He was waiting until his buddy had time to come and pump it for him for free."

I wished Sheila well and informed her that Paul and I were going to have a look around the Novak house.

First, we looked around the grounds. I noted the easy access to all the windows on the bottom level of the two-story house.

"A killer could have gotten in very easily," I said.

"Yeah, but these windows all have screens. You can't open them from the outside, and none of them appear torn." Paul stepped between some overgrown hedges to get a closer look and make sure he was correct.

We went around back, where a screened-in porch stretched along the entire back of the home. It looked packed with junk, probably inherited from the home's predecessor. Higher up, on the second floor, was another window, inaccessible unless someone used a ladder to reach the porch's roof.

We went around front again and examined the front door closely. It hadn't been forced. We used Paul's key to let ourselves inside.

The ground level featured a living room and kitchen. The floors, as Darryl had reported, sagged in places. I was amazed that someone who could afford most anything had decided to relocate to such an aged dwelling.

Dozens of books of a technical nature were stacked on the kitchen table and the floor. In their titles I noted computer programming terms such as "C++," "Python," and "Non-linear Algebra." I took pictures of their spines, remembering how important books had been to understanding Wanda Hightower after she died. But this material seemed totally inaccessible to me.

"It's hard to know what to look for," I said.

"Notice everything," said Paul. "Decide later what's important."

I took tons of pictures—the beauty of smartphones.

I did find a pair of titles about evolution. Also, there were two slim books by Friedrich Nietzsche: *Beyond Good and Evil*, and *Thus Spoke Zarathustra*.

The kitchen was clean. There was nothing of note in the fridge, not even any leftovers. I got the sense that Scott was an expert bachelor. His pantry was full of canned goods, including boxed milk and juices. No need for a grocery trip into town for at least another month.

The back porch looked mostly unused, except for a clothes washer and dryer.

We went upstairs. The bathroom seemed ordinary. Nothing odd or out of place. I took pictures anyway.

Then we went into the bedroom.

Suddenly things got interesting.

"What a mess," I said.

Paul let out a whistle. "This doesn't match the crime scene photos. Someone else has been here since that night."

We both walked over to wooden desk with every one of its drawers pulled out. Papers were strewn everywhere on top of and around the desk, like a paperwork volcano.

Most of the papers seemed to be board of directors minutes and financial reports.

"What do you think the person was looking for?" I asked.

Paul shrugged.

I quickly went through the papers and snapped more pictures. If there was financial malfeasance, it was unlikely to be found in these official documents.

Besides, one might presume that anything truly interesting had already been taken.

On top of the desk itself were scattered some hand-written letters. They were unsigned but all seemed to be in the same hand. Their return address: Billings, Alaska. I pointed them out to Paul.

"Adam," he grunted. I made sure to collect all the letters that I could find and take pictures of all their pages to read later.

After photographing Adam's letters, I cleared everything off the desk's surface. In the bottom right corner written in black sharpie was what looked like a computer password:

Fe@BEth_gira

Someone had tried unsuccessfully to scribble over the password with a ballpoint pen. I took a photo of it and joined Paul, who had been examining the queen-size bed where the body had been found. The bed had been stripped and all the coverings taken away. There wasn't anything left to look at besides a bare mattress, the brass headboard, and the steel bed frame.

"You said they're testing the fabrics for DNA?" I asked.

"They took them into evidence, but if they aren't calling the death homicide I doubt they are bothering to test."

"Should we report the fact that others were here?"

"We can, not that it will evoke a ton of interest. The authorities already went over this space. It's just a house at this point."

We heard the front door open and a voice shout, "Who's up there?"

I whispered to Paul, "*Lorry Sneed.*"

"Just us chickens!" Paul shouted back. "Paul Maroni P.I., and his more elegant protege, Rett Swinson!"

I followed Paul downstairs.

When Lorry saw me, he relaxed and said, "Oh, it's just you. I saw y'all from the house and worried it was trespassers."

"We told Sheila we were here," I said. "Did you see anybody else enter the home the last couple days? There's evidence that someone was upstairs looking through Mr. Novak's bedroom."

I watched him closely, wondering if it might have been him. Lorry casually spit some tobacco juice into a Mountain Dew bottle he was holding. "I saw a car leaving yesterday when I was coming back from town."

"What kind of car?"

"Light blue Audi, about 10 years old. People get lost down here all the time. I didn't think much of it."

"Are you sure the car didn't run you over?" Paul asked. "Looks like something did."

For the first time I noticed the cuts and bruises on Lorry's face.

"Lorry, what happened to you?"

Reflexively, he touched his face. When he did, I noticed his right hand was wrapped in bandages.

"Just a bar fight," he said. "You should-a seen the other guy. Well, I gotta go tend to my buddy. He's doing me a favor with the septic. Talk later. Bye!"

After Lorry had put some distance between us, I said to Paul, "He really was scraped up. Until you said something I hadn't noticed. He's kind of a scruffy guy anyway."

"He didn't like us taking note of his wounds. Either he lost the fight, or he doesn't want to tell the whole truth about how he got them."

Paul headed for the car and took a call. Seeing that he was on his cell phone, I went over to Sheila again, who was pulling crates of various fruits and meats out of her SUV.

"How is your relationship with Lorry going?" I asked. "Is he being more helpful?"

"Yeah, turns out he knows these animals pretty well. He's even drawn their blood. Said he had to tranquilize them first, but didn't know why Scott wanted him to do it. I'm going to call the North Carolina Zoo and see if they remember running diagnostic tests on the animals."

"You're really invested in these beasts."

"Yes, and it's pissing off Maxine."

"Oh?"

"She's got issues." Sheila didn't sound like she wanted to elaborate.

I changed the subject by mentioning the bruises and cuts on Lorry. "Do you remember when they showed up?"

Sheila shrugged. "I didn't notice them before today."

"Lorry seems like kind of a rough customer."

"He's an alcoholic just like my dad and my ex-husband." I was unaware that Sheila used to be married to a man. "But he is helpful. I convinced Mr. Patel to pay him for his time."

I asked, "What if you can't find homes for all the animals?"

"If it was up to me, I'd just take them all in myself."

"What's stopping you?"

She looked at me like I was on crack. "This isn't just a hummingbird in my sock drawer, Rett. It's a dang menagerie. We don't have room on our property. Just to feed them every day would break our bank."

"Not there. *Here.* You could probably buy this place from Adam Novak. It could be a place where you rehab animals and find them new homes. Raise donations to help with their care. A lot of people would come here from the Triangle and pay a small donation to get an intimate, up-close experience with the animals."

"You're insane, Rett."

"I'm just trying to find a way for you to help these animals. Isn't this exactly what you've been trying to do in town: build your own zoo?"

"But Max wouldn't ... she'd ... I think she would probably—"

"Try her," I said. "What do you have to lose?"

Sheila began to pace like the serval in its cage. "I need time to think about this."

I put my hands on her shoulders to steady her. "Don't freak out. You're starting to resemble that one bird..."

"You mean Alvin the Ostrich?"

"Him."

She closed her eyes and took some breaths. "Okay. I'm not going to freak out. I'll think about this. I'm just not going to mention this terrifically awesome idea to Maxine yet."

"Wait for the right time. This could be the start of something really amazing."

"Or the end of it all," she muttered.

∾

PAUL HAD LEFT. I was about to leave, too, when I thought of something. I looked through my pictures of Scott's bedroom and office. I texted Augusta:

—*Technical question: Do printers "remember" the documents they print?*

A moment later:

—*Depends on the printer, but yeah, usually.*

I sent her a photo of the laser printer from Scott's office. It took forever to upload from here in the country, but it did send. I asked:

—*Might this printer remember?*

—*I'll check.*

A few seconds later.

—*This brand has enough buffer memory for a lot of documents.*

—*Any chance you can do me a BIG favor and come out to Scott Novak's house, like, right now? I can send you the address.*

—*What are you offering?*

—*My undying friendship.*

—*Got anything better?*

—*Nope.*

—*Then I'll take an IOU.*

I GOT comfortable waiting in my car. A half hour later, Augusta rolled up in her Mercury. We stood in the little gravel lot while I explained my dilemma.

"I have all these letters that Scott's brother sent him. But I don't have the letters Scott wrote back. I'm wondering if he might have typed and printed them out to mail."

"Which room is the printer in?" Augusta asked.

"The upstairs bedroom." I pointed.

"Let's try it from here." She sat on the hood of my Camry,

opened her laptop, and got down to work. "Okay. I'm detecting several devices. There's my phone, there's your phone ... and there's the printer. I'm just going to try to guess the IP address, hoping it's standard..."

"And I have no idea what you just said."

"You don't need to ... because I'm already in." A second later, she added, "Okay, there are about 50 documents in the cache from the past several months. Would you like me to send them to you?"

"How did you do that?"

"I didn't do a thing—and if you say I did, I'm going to call you a liar."

"Fair," I said.

"Wait," she said. "*Another* device just popped up."

"Really? What is it?"

"I don't know. It's a very weak signal. Maybe a security camera."

"Scott doesn't have security cameras."

"It's weak, but we can try to follow the signal."

We went on a little walk with Augusta leading the way. She tried various directions in the yard, but steered us closer and closer to the zoo. We ended up at the Bird House. Squawks and other chatter signaled our approach, and the mayhem only got louder when we entered the tent.

"It's probably somewhere in this room," she shouted above the din.

I looked around. I wasn't excited about reaching into bird cages and running my fingers through the various layers of wood shavings and bird poop looking for an electronics device.

But I didn't have to. I saw something on the ground, in the corner of the room, just outside of the owl's cage.

"Scott's Amulet!" I cried, picking it up.

"His what?"

"It's basically a recording device that Scott wore until a couple weeks before his death. It powers the Virtual Scott AI. Looks like someone dropped it. It was almost camouflaged against the gravel."

"Let me try to get into it," she said. A second later. "Unfortunately, it's password protected."

I remembered the password on Scott's desk and pulled it up on my phone — *Fe@BEth_gira*. I read it to her slowly so she could type it in.

"I'm in," she said almost immediately. "There's only one file, dated... September 5, 2018, at 3:23 p.m. Central Time. It's a video file."

"Just one file? Really? Can you play it on your laptop?"

"Sure."

We watched. The video was chaotic, as if the Amulet was being jiggled. The device came to rest on a desk where a lamp was in view. A gigantic wallet plopped within an inch of the camera. In the same instant that the wallet dropped, there was the distant sound of a shower turning on.

Then someone—it sounded like Scott—uttered, "Oops!" The Amulet jiggled again before camera and microphone were turned off.

"Interesting," I said. "Are you sure that's all that is on the device?"

"Yeah."

"Can you tell where that video was taken?"

"Sure. I'll just copy the coordinates from the metadata into Google Maps. Here it is: 894 Howard Road, Kansas City, Missouri. The Imperial Hotel."

The one trip Scott took during his "year of imprisonment" was to Kansas City for the AI conference. This everyone knew.

Now we knew he wasn't there alone, for he couldn't drop his

wallet in one room with one hand and simultaneously turn on the water in the shower with the other.

"Can you send the video clip to me?"

"Sure."

I thanked Augusta profusely. Before she left, I asked her how she felt about the much more difficult task of hacking into the mysterious Big Cat server. "A hundred grand is no joke."

She muttered, "Patel will probably make a million on what's there," she said.

"A million? Could be more like a *hundred* million. We just don't know."

"I don't like being used. Maybe I'll look hard for it. Maybe I won't."

I thought about that old rich man who buried treasure out West and challenged everyone to find it. Several people had already died looking for it.

"Whatever you decide to do," I said, "please, be careful."

"I've got Pops telling me that. I don't need to hear it from you."

"Sorry. I meant: 'Go, Girl!'"

"Better."

WHEN I ARRIVED HOME, a single text showed up on my phone. It was from Darryl:

—*Someone texted me a photograph. Do you know what this is?*

I looked. It was a security camera view—of me, stepping into the studio of Ken Grimes.

—*Yes. I went to talk to Ken Grimes about painting recently.*

—*You didn't mention it to me.*

—*I didn't think you'd care. Who sent this? Why?*

—*I don't know.*

I typed:

—*Ken is just a friend.*

—*Are you sure?*

—*Of course!*

—*Okay.*

—*Can I call you and we can talk about this?*

—*Busy now. Maybe later.*

He was annoyed. And part of me didn't blame him. Why hadn't I talked to him about Ken?

But what was there to talk about?

I immediately called Paul and told him about the security camera photo that someone sent to Darryl.

"That's a pretty low thing to do," he observed. "Who did it, and why?"

"I think I know who. And her name rhymes with 'Daily Hider.'"

"Maybe she knows you tailed her and she's just getting you back."

"I think she wants to make me look like a cheater just to justify her telling everyone in town what a tramp I am."

"Maybe you should confront her."

"You can bet I will." I just needed to figure out the best way to do that.

There was more to tell Paul. I mentioned that I had discovered Scott's letters to Adam. "I'll look at them more closely tonight."

But the bigger find potentially was Scott's Amulet.

"The sheriff will want to see that," Paul said right away.

"Oops."

"What's wrong?"

"I hacked it already."

"Really. You?"

"Yes, using the password on Scott's desk," I said, not wanting to implicate Augusta. "I found a single video on the device. And this is huge: Scott wasn't alone in Kansas City, Paul."

"Maybe he met someone at the conference. He was single at the time, you know."

"Maybe. But whoever it was, we need to find and talk with them."

"We can call the hotel, see if anyone spotted someone."

"Do you really think they're going to share information over the phone? I think we need to go in person."

"Not me!" Paul protested. "I don't fly."

"A big, strong man like you? Afraid to fly?"

"I'll fight dragons all day long," he said, "but I do not do airplanes."

"You expect me to go alone?"

"T-t-take me," cut in a voice at my left elbow.

I told Paul I'd call him back later.

I turned to face Lydia.

"Take you where?"

"To K-K-Kansas, Einstein."

"Why?"

"To find clues...whatever."

"Oh, Lydia, I don't know..."

"Do I have to b-b-beg? THE OLD LADY NEEDS A VACATION!"

"Let me talk with Paul about it later," I said, but it was just a stall tactic. Really, I needed to run the trip by Darryl—but I didn't want Lydia to think that her son had the last word on what she was allowed to do.

When I did call Darryl, he didn't object. "They have doctors in Kansas City, don't they?"

I was out of excuses.

Lydia would come with me to Kansas City.

I WAS ANXIOUS. I was going to be leaving town in the morning not feeling good about where Darryl and I stood. He hadn't wanted to talk about the security pics, and I didn't either—especially now as I was getting ready to leave on a trip.

Lydia didn't have trouble getting to sleep the night before our flight, but I did. I remembered the letters between the Novak brothers. The screen made my eyes hurt, so I printed out the letters and began to read...

PART II

INTO THE WILD

"I sincerely hope ... that these analysts holding a microscope to the soul are actually brave, generous and proud animals, who know how to control their own pleasure and pain and have been taught to sacrifice desirability to truth, every truth, even a plain, bitter, ugly, foul, unchristian, immoral truth . . . Because there are such truths."

—from Aphorism 2, *On the Genealogy of Morality* by Friedrich Nietzsche

CHAPTER 12

MEN OF LETTERS

January 18, 2018

Dear Adam,

This is a difficult letter to write. My God, I don't even know if you're still alive.

About a month after Dad's funeral, I tried reaching out, but you had already left Berkeley. No one knew where you had gone. Then about six months later Rooney called me and said you'd gone to Alaska. He even gave me this address, but I didn't write then. I should have, but I didn't really know what to say. The funeral had been such a cluster, followed by all those hoodlums who knew dad and kept getting in touch asking for money. Then I got super busy for the next 10 years, my head down building a company.

I sold that company last month and made out pretty well. Technically I never have to work again. Now I have time on my hands to think—and to regret all the ways I've avoided you.

I apologize. I really do. I guess I was just self-absorbed and feeling sorry for myself. Mom wasn't as nuts as Dad but she was pretty cuckoo. I remember she'd walk me to the bus stop even when I was in high school and she'd just do all the talking. Each day it was the previous day's list of dangers plus a new one, so by the end of the school year she had to talk a million miles a minute to get everything said before the bus came. It was all I could do not to grab her and flop the both of us in front of that bus.

Later, when Mom begged me to come home from college during Christmas break, I didn't. She had always been a hypochondriac, so I didn't believe her when she said she was sick. She went downhill fast and died alone.

So, I had my own challenges, but I'm sure it was nothing compared to what you had to endure from Dad. I shouldn't have turned my back on you. I guess I thought it would be easier for me to do that than to face your pain.

I'm inviting you to write back and tell me what a bastard I have been.

I'll be right here, just outside of Raleigh. The buyer of my company, Sammy Patel, made sure of that. I didn't really look closely enough at the wording of the sales contract, and it seems I've basically imprisoned myself for the next 12 months. I'm allowed to take one work-related trip out of the state, and I've already used that up by committing to give a talk in Kansas City the first week in September. So I can't even come see you, unless you want to convince the organizers to move their AI conference to the woods of Alaska.

I did manage to find a quiet place in the country where I can be One With My Thoughts. I even have a little zoo on the property that includes an orangutan, a giraffe, a serval, and a couple of kangaroos, to name just a few. It's cool, and it does allow my mind to roam to new places. Also, I met a girl. She's amazing. Her name is Esther. I think you'd like her. (See photo enclosed.) She's the one pushing me to get in touch with my feelings and my past. This letter is the first fruits of that. If you can find it in your heart to write back, please do and we'll keep going. If you don't want to, I'll understand.

I love you, brother. I am very sorry for everything.

Sincerely,

Scott

FEBRUARY 8, 2018

Scott,

Three questions for you:

1. As we were leaving Pennsylvania did you really tell Dad that you never wanted to see me again because I was a "sissy" and you were ashamed to be related to me? Dad swore you told him that.

2. At least once a week did you and Mom laugh at that story of how I shit my pants that one Christmas morning?

3. Did Mom really tell you that it made her sick to see my face?

Tell the truth, goddammit.

Adam

FEBRUARY 16, 2018

Dear Adam,

Thank you for writing back. Here are the honest answers to your questions:

1. I never said that. Joe lied—as usual.

2. Another Dad lie. Mom hated that she couldn't see you and worried about the fact you were living with a maniac—namely, Joe Novak.

3. Also a no. (See Question 2.) It made Mom mentally sick to think of you only because she loved you so much and missed you so much. She knew if she reached out to you that Dad

would just punish you somehow, so for your own sake she thought it best just to "put Adam's future in God's hands" and trust you'd survive.

You were always a survivor.

That's the only way I have ever thought of you, Adam: As my tough big brother. Tough as damn nails. Really, the toughest guy who ever lived.

And I was right. I mean, you survived our dad. And now you're living off the land in freaking Alaska.

All of this is truth.

Love,

Scott

March 3, 2018

Scott,

Man, I don't know what to say. Your two letters just shattered me. I've been a freaking crying zombie the past two days. It's all coming back. I've been going on long walks in the woods and coming back and not even remembering where I went. I've been banging on trees with fallen branches and baying at the fucking moon. Barking and growling and roaring. A Dionysian expurgation.

I was surprised to get your first letter. For a long time, I just looked at it, afraid to open it. It brought back a lot of shit that I had come here to get away from.

I had to blame someone for the divorce and for never being able to see you and Mom all those years. Dad made sure I blamed you two. That's why I didn't go to her funeral, because I was basically brainwashed.

When Dad finally died, something snapped. I just wanted to run, to go very far away, and then die like that Hemingway character sitting with my back against a tree. I came to Alaska to die.

I didn't die. But I probably didn't exactly heal either. For the past many years, you have been the only one alive in my family and so the only one I can blame. Kind of like that Grateful Dead song, "Throwing Stones." Only it's true that we're the last ones standing and it's kind of fucked up to be blaming each other. Dad stoked division for his own twisted ends.

It's not your fault we've been out of touch. I made myself intentionally hard to reach. But I swear I'm less crazy now than I've ever been. Alaska will do that to you. It either kills you or it grounds you. Not a lot of in-between.

I sobbed so hard the past two days that I threw up several times. I think I've purged a lot of that old baggage. There now. Going to try to move forward...

Congratulations on selling your company. You don't sound too delighted really, but all that money has to feel pretty good. I mean, you can do anything you want now.

But, yeah, it sucks you can't travel this year. This Patel dude sounds like a control freak. Sorry he's cramping your style. Glad you found the house and the animals.

Your girl—she looks special, and you look real happy together in that picture. I never really had much luck with the ladies. Maybe you and she can keep the Novak line going. I take it back: I had plenty of ladies in Frisco. But it was all "wham bam thank you ma'am." I don't think that Mom and Dad provided any real example of how to have a relationship.

I don't miss those two. They are what Nietzsche called "bound spirits." I admit, for a long time I was bitter that you were allowed to stay with Mom while I got sent off with Dad. What kind of a divorce settlement is that? Still, I can see why you worked so hard to skip ahead of me and go off to college early. You shouldn't feel guilty that you were not with her when she died. She was an anxious religious nut, worried she wasn't reading the mind of God perfectly. No one told her what Nietzsche tried to tell everyone: that God is dead!

If she had learned that little fact, she might have been a lot happier.

Sincerely,

Adam

MARCH 25, 2018

Adam,

I hate that you got the brunt of dad's garbage. But I'm willing to hear what you want to share. I won't run from your pain again.

Since you mentioned it, I'll deal with the fact of getting promoted past you in school. That was awkward, but, remember, in the beginning you were an extra year ahead of *me*. Now I realize our parents only thought I was slow-witted because I was quiet (that school counselor, who was from the South, told Mom that I was "feeble-minded"). I didn't talk until I was almost four, and by then you were already pegged as a prodigy.

But even back when they thought I was a little slow, I had the better end of the deal. I could be quiet and hide, while you were having to do one circus trick after another for Dad. Gregarious were you, Young Skywalker! It made you an easy target of Dad's wrath. You tried to talk yourself out of his disfavor, but it never worked.

So getting promoted wasn't part of some contest. It's just that once you and Dad had left it felt safe enough to reveal all the thinking I was doing in secret.

I hated that you and I got split up, but I never missed Dad. Or maybe I missed what Dad could have been for both of us.

I remember the day you called me to tell me that he was living in a homeless shelter in San Francisco. How you took him into your dorm and cleaned him up. How he started to berate you again. How he was a broken man, and how you drove him back to the shelter after a few days with a hundred bucks in his pocket. How he threw the money at you as he walked away, and how you just left it on the sidewalk. I remember those details from your phone call. You were inconsolable and didn't stop talking for an hour. I can see how you'd want to destroy yourself after that. Why getting the call from the authorities that he was dead a week later might put you into a strange fugue between sweet relief and utter despair. Why the day after his funeral you'd just disappear into Alaska.

I too am grateful to be free of our parents' dysfunctions. Of course, I miss Mom, but not that constant doting, as if I was her fetish. You got your gift of gab from her, of course. I can still hear her blabbing about our crazy grandparents, about her professors at Julliard (even the ones she didn't sleep with)—and I remember, too, how sometimes she'd SING, and it was lovely but shocking, and too loud, and it would make me cry. Sometimes she'd do it when others were around, and this was especially terrible. Though it was gorgeous, it made me upset. Because I knew she was crazy. I knew she was not of this world.

Oh, God, remembering is so hard.

I survived my own pain by burying myself in tech. I became obsessed about how computers learn. Figuring that out has always felt like looking for the Goose That Lays the Golden Egg. (Funny, there's a company called Yellow Goose that is suing us for a hundred million dollars. Moving right along...) We get closer to an independently thinking computer every day. Yet, the more I think about that, the more I think that the whole enterprise is doomed. The logical end of an independently thinking artificial intelligence is an all-powerful AI that just obliterates everything. It will start with the things it can easily reach, like online data. So, if you have a computer connected to the Internet, make a copy of everything, and print it all out. Hard copies will outlast anything on a hard drive, or even in the cloud.

On that happy note,

Scott

APRIL 7, 2018

Scott,

I'm glad to hear that you've finally come over to the Luddite perspective. Human beings always find a way to sabotage themselves. Money or power or just plain nihilism will motivate an individual, corporation, or cabal to develop the Hitler computer of which you speak. I suggest you find a safe place to hunker down. Like you say, it's just a matter of time.

By the way, I was telling my neighbor Dave about your zoo. Dave is the son of Mike and Emily Nash who really helped me get started out here. You'd love Mike, by the way. I mean, he's an utter jackass who totally warps historical evidence to suit his benefit—that's Nietzsche's Will to Truth in the extreme—but he's the best comic relief I've found out here on the edge of the American wilderness and, better yet, he's got a great bear story and the scars to prove it. His son Dave is a nature guide who probably knows the flora and fauna around here better than anyone. Totally the person you want to guide you if you and your girl ever decide to honeymoon in Alaska. Dave will train you in some basic survival skills then leave you on your own for a weekend and you'll somehow get by and you'll end up feeling like a champ.

Anyway, Dave said something interesting recently: He said that all the animals we see today carry memories of every other survival trait their species owns. I think the actual language he used was, "Animals may not remember what happened a year ago, but their genes remember everything. They are prime survivors."

What do humans remember? Maybe when I dream I'm remembering the shit that went down a million years ago. Maybe I am the wolf, the squid, the wildebeest. And all those beasts are just sleeping inside me, inside you, inside all of us.

I have to chop some wood. I'm trading some pelts next week, so I'll try to mail this with Christopher and Sarah, who run the lake outpost and basically keep us connected to The Greater World. If you ever need to reach me in a hurry, you can even call them. Their satellite phone number is below.

BTW – Do you still hang with that guy Emerson? I liked him. I think he's the only one of your college friends I ever met. One summer he found me in Berkeley when I was still there and we ate burritos together.

Yours,

Adam

AT THE END *of Adam's letter there followed a satellite phone number for Christopher and Sarah Gates.*

After this there seemed to be a missing letter from Scott. I noted that and went to the next letter from Adam:

MAY 2, 2018

Scott,

If you want a real mind trip, you'll have to read some Nietzsche. Nietzsche saved my life. I'll explain:

When I came to Alaska all I had with me was my Nietzsche library and enough blow to kill a moose. That's when I ran into a couple of other survivors—Mike and Emily, I think I mentioned them—and saw that they were just as messed up as I was, but they were not trying to die. They were restless, but able to put that restlessness to good use.

I realized then that I didn't have to float anymore. I could become responsible for my own survival. Funny how that matters, but it really does.

I felt a lot of guilt after Dad died. But Nietzsche calls out guilt as hogwash. It's slave morality, the way of all bound souls.

Nietzsche thought we can be free spirits who choose life at every turn. And, no, he's not talking about dropping acid or doing hedonistic acts. He's talking about becoming an Über-mensch—the Overman, something beyond the beasts and even beyond men, who are themselves just clever beasts. Becoming what you and I want to be. Embracing one's fate, in fact living as if your life were going to repeat itself infinitely, what he called the Eternal Return.

Study on that.

Yeah, like you wrote, after your imprisonment we can try to meet somewhere halfway, but really, I'm not worried about the distance. Outside of Alaska, the distances just aren't very consequential. What's another 1,200 miles? That's just a trip to the nearest restaurant, man. (And if you ever get turned around, just stay put, because some shaggy bear will find you. At least someone will be eating a BBQ lunch!)

And, yes, I totally remember our old pet chameleon. Gem—that wise, old soul—and I always had a blast. "To be able to lick one's own eyeball—the epitome of wisdom." Clear one's outlook. See things anew. Wouldn't that be nice!

Your bro,

Adam

MAY 23, 2018
    Adam,

I have ordered all of Nietzsche's books and have been reading about his Overman. I see that some translators of the German call the Übermensch the "Superman" — which is a little off-putting. A man in a red cape and blue tights.

I wish Nietzsche offered more examples. That said, he writes with great exuberance. Is this what he's talking about the Superman doing: Making great movies? Writing the Great American Novel? Just being a Great Man—like Napoleon(!)? (And not much room for women?) Seems a little vague.

I went out to a movie with Esther. I just felt so down the whole time, then guilty for weighing her down. I'm probably depressed but not even in terms of feeling hopeless, just having no enthusiasm for society. Been going down the rabbit hole of research on something that maybe helps avoid the traps of AI-gone-wrong. It's the only thing that drives me, that keeps me going.

Scott

JUNE 13, 2018

Scott,

There's very little I miss about society. Sitting around and wondering, "What shall I do now? Watch another string of music videos on MTV?" Civilization is such a drag.

What is the Overman? I'll begin by telling you what he's not: He's not a successful human as we typically define him, at least in terms of *money*. I mean, Solzhenitsyn wrote his *Gulag Archipelago* on toilet paper—that dude was amazing—then he finally got out and did his United States tour and observed how anti-intellectual Americans were. Is this what he suffered for, so that someday Russians could eat a Big Mac?

I just feel like all your techie friends are doing is building a better Happy Meal prize. Ask yourself the question: Are you helping humanity to experience LIFE—or simply helping them extend their life spans and distract their addled brains, to become that pitiful creature Nietzsche calls The Last Man.

His hero, Zarathustra, spoke: "Man is something that is to be surpassed."

"Lo, I teach you the Overman: he is that lightning, he is that frenzy!"

"...the lightning out of the dark cloud..."

What people need is a nudge to recognize their own Will to Power—that driving force that Nietzsche says is critical to achieving greatness, a love of life, and their own new values to surpass the hand-me-down morality that enslaves us.

Your brother,

Adam

June 22, 2018

Adam,

I had to laugh: You've been gone so long you weren't aware they don't play music videos anymore on MTV.

But you're right about The Last Man. I can't stand to hear the way Sammy Patel talks about tech. It's all $$$ for him, and if he could have gotten me to sign a contract to have my brain pickled in a jar on his desk, he would have done it. I don't think he's evil —then again, I might be wrong. A person doesn't have to BE evil to DO evil. They can even call themselves "good" while they do it.

I wish you could meet Esther. There's more to her than meets the eye. For all the crap you and I went through, I don't think it holds a candle to the junk that girls and women get thrown at them from Day One in this world.

Esther wants me to share my feelings more often, but what

can you do when you're not even AWARE of HAVING feelings? I'm afraid if I don't figure things out, she's going to move on.

I'm digging the Overman, but I have to say we don't have the luxury of another million years of natural selection. Something has to happen sooner rather than later to get humans ready for our challenging future.

BTW – Did you know that now you can listen to any music ever recorded, whenever you want? That has come about in the past few years. I remember how much you love music—following The Dead and all. Now you can get a number of their concerts from the cloud—anytime you want.

Scott

JULY 2, 2018

Scott,

I'm sorry your feelings are causing consternation. Feelings are a funny thing, man. It's not like every homesteader out here is in touch with his feelings. Not even close! What you see out here is a lot of what you see out *there*: Some people are mystics, but others are just distracted. Some people throw themselves into their work so they won't feel anything. Some still think they are going to find gold and get rich.

I think you get out of Alaska what you want out of Alaska.

I've gotten this much from the experience: *radicality*. I mean, it makes me laugh, all the 'experimentation' me and my friends used to do with drugs, all the 'exploration' we used to do of 'the Mind.' Delusions of grandeur. You ever seen a school of salmon swimming just under the ice as you stand there looking down? That's *real*. THAT's radical.

Sometimes I think I could play Rip Van Winkle for a weekend or two and remind myself what I left behind—if only to remind myself that I don't miss it.

Man, I always wanted to feel real. Out here, I do. I think you'd get something out of it, too.

Yours radically,

Adam

JULY 13, 2018

Dear Adam,

I like the sound of feeling real, because I don't know what real feels like anymore. As a kid I always wanted to feel invincible, like a Transformer, the combination of animal and machine.

Did you know that wombats poop cubes? It's true. Imagine squeezing out crap that has corners! I have two wombats and they put out enough of those little bricks each day to build a little wombat house. That would come in handy for a survivalist in Alaska, eh?

I'm intrigued by the life you are leading and the Overman example you are truly following. I think the hardest thing for me is overcoming our shared past. Sometimes I just want to forget.

By the way, a while back I told one of my coders, Trey Gamble, that my big brother was a total Nietzsche expert. Don't be surprised if he writes to you. Between you and me, the guy could use some guidance.

Best,

Scott

P.S. Our giraffe, Beth, died today. She was an old lady. Old Man Snake who built this zoo before he died must have paid a mint for her, as she was mostly all white. In any case, he saved her life, because she would have been an easy kill for lions or poachers. She was totally my favorite.

JULY 24, 2018

Scott,

My body hurts today. I may not be forty yet, but at times my body feels middle aged. I'll do some tasks and stay in bed the next day—all day. I'd pay big money (if I had it) for a drug that could truly make me stronger, faster, smarter.

You're right, not everyone can forget the past. Christopher and Sarah who run the lake port sure can't. Their teenage daughter died not long after I got here eight years ago. You and I weren't speaking back then, so I never told you about it. It was awful. Her name was Brenda. She was a senior in high school, though she only did correspondence school. She was smart as hell, intrigued with computers but without access to a lot of the Gadgetry of the Civilized Realm. I bragged to her about you and all you had already accomplished in that area. (I'd seen you featured in some magazine I found when I went to the doctor in Anchorage.) She had planned to write to you. I was too embarrassed to tell her you and I weren't on speaking terms.

Anyway, I think because I was so new out here her parents still connect my arrival with her falling off that cliff. I feel for them, I really do. Their only kid. Anyway, I need to ask them about the next float plane so I can go to Anchorage for my annual check-up. If you did the kind of drugs that I did back in the day, you'd be paranoid, too. We can't all be immortal like Keith Richards. I'm watching my liver like a damn hawk.

Soberly,

Adam

P.S. Yes, I heard from your employee Trey a month ago and wrote him back. He's one of those Nazis trying to find credibility for his hate, and he's hoping I'll tell him that Nietzsche was on his side. But Nietzsche would have nothing but contempt for the twerp—and I told him so. Whelp, one less pen pal to worry about!

.   .   .

AUGUST 20, 2018

Adam,

Sorry for the delay in writing back. I just broke up with Esther. Told her I needed some time to think. I've been burying myself in research and just haven't had time to develop any kind of closeness with her. It has made her bitter, and I don't blame her. I did this for her as much as for me.

My research has hit a breakthrough in a way I hadn't quite expected and—it's exciting. I owe it all to what your guide Dave said about animals carrying their survivability in their genes, plus something Nietzsche laid down as well. I'm just not sure if it's the right thing to be doing. I need to step away from it for a little while. I've got that AI conference in just a couple weeks, so maybe that's good timing.

I'm just kind of exhausted and distracted right now and don't have the energy to write any more than this. Sorry.

Yours,

Scott

AUGUST 27, 2018

Brother,

I had a feeling you'd connect with Ol' Fritz! Keep reading. Soon everything will start to make sense.

Do what the Overman inspires you to do. Express your Will to Power. The only value that has value is the value you create.

Look, you're more than halfway through your contract with that Sammy dude.

Be that lightning! Be that frenzy!

Get ready for a new dawn!

I just know you're going to be amazing.

Your brother,

Adam

CHAPTER 13

A CHANGE OF DIRECTION

And here I thought the Raleigh-Durham Airport was small.

The Kansas City Airport felt like a high school from the 1960s with a bunch of 737s parked around it. The airport was in the process of expanding, and certain hallways were closed, meaning everyone had to weave between the chairs at gates to get anywhere.

The city was a good half-hour drive away. I'd researched the various ride-share apps and picked the pink one. We pulled up to The Imperial Hotel and thanked the driver before grabbing our bags from the back and walking in like we owned the place. Lydia was so excited I thought she was going to pee her pants.

I mentioned our reservation to the person at the desk who, after a few clicks on his keyboard, made a relieved sound. "Here it is! I worried for a second there you had made reservations at our other property, in Kansas City, *Kansas*. That happens sometimes."

I had a quick flashback to the time I'd arrived in Portland, Maine, only to realize I'd accidentally booked a hotel in Portland, Oregon.

Lydia announced with feigned sophistication, "I would very much like to p-p-purchase a drink at the bar and take it to our r-r-room."

"Go grab your Southern Comfort," I said. "Meanwhile, let me poke around a little. Certainly someone here remembers meeting Scott."

"You better not g-g-get us thrown out."

"You're the one who's starting a bender."

Lydia winked. She could already taste her naughty alcoholic drink.

I was beginning to think this wasn't a good idea. Mixing sleuthing with vacation might be a cocktail that produced quite the hangover.

While Lydia went in the direction of the restaurant and bar, I finished checking us in. After getting the keys and the spiel about the fitness room—an amenity always lost on me—I showed the gentleman a picture of Scott Novak on my phone, a screenshot from the video of his talk. "Do you remember this individual from the artificial intelligence conference a couple weeks ago?"

The man nodded. "I remember him. He forgot what room he was in and had to ask the front desk."

I guess I wasn't surprised. Sometimes the most intelligent people forget how to tie their own shoes.

"What else?" I asked.

He shrugged. "He was back and forth a lot from the conference. I mean, he was always coming around. Maybe he had a medical condition and only wanted to use the bathroom that was in his room? I thought about that."

"Or maybe there was a girl in that room he was seeing?"

"None that I saw, but I really wouldn't know."

"Would you have camera footage?"

He smiled. "Sorry, but I can't show it to you without a warrant."

"What if I told you this was a homicide investigation?"

"Are you an officer of the law?"

"I'm just a private investigator in training."

"Then I cannot. Sorry."

"Okay. Do you mind if I talk to the housekeeping staff at least?"

"Sure. I'll buzz the head of housekeeping. I can send her to your room. It may be a while, as we are full today. "

"That's fine. Thanks!" I waved to Lydia over at the bar that the room was ready. She joined me, drink in hand.

The room wasn't nearly as fancy as the foyer might suggest, but it was spotlessly clean. I noted that the bathroom was at least 10 feet from the desk; the shower, five feet beyond that. When Lydia hopped into the shower ("I feel so g-g-gross whenever I'm in airports!") I stood near the desk. Since I could hear the shower, it was likely Scott's Amulet mic would have heard it, too. Without question during that brief recording there must have been a second person in the room.

There was a knock at the door. I opened the door to a short, middle-aged Hispanic woman wearing a housekeeping uniform.

"I'm Julia." She pronounced it *HOO-lee-uh*. "I'm head of housekeeping."

"Thanks for coming by, Julia. Quick question. Do you know who might have cleaned a specific room on a specific day?"

"Of course. Maids have to sign off on the rooms they clean. We do random inspections."

I wrote Scott's name on a piece of paper, his room number (which the front desk guy had given me) and the days he was here.

"I'll look it up," she said, "but it's going to be a little while. It's super busy. It might be the morning before I can get you the information."

"That's fine. Thank you."

THERE WAS nothing else to do for now, so while Lydia lounged in the room's plush complimentary robe, worked on a crossword puzzle, and sipped on her drink ("This is Heaven. HEAVEN!") I took a nap. I slept over an hour, waking up to the sound of water running in the shower again.

"Lydia," I shouted, "are you taking *another* shower?"

"The water pressure is just so m-m-much better than at the h-h-house!"

There was a knock at the door. I answered it and found an exhausted-looking maid. I asked if she had been the one to clean Scott Novak's room. She nodded. "I remember him because I saw him once, and he made me feel uncomfortable. He looked at me like a *wolf*. I told my boss. She went with me to make sure he was gone whenever I cleaned his room. She stayed close by. I have never cleaned a room so fast!"

"Did you see anyone else? Maybe another woman?"

She shook her head. "No."

"Anything strange at all?"

"I think he slept on the floor."

"Not in the bed?"

"There was a pallet on the floor he made from blankets. It happens more often than you'd think. Some people find our beds too soft."

I remembered the pallet in Emerson's office.

"Please describe Mr. Novak to me," I said on a hunch. "Was he really skinny or fairly stout?"

"Oh, very skinny." She described Scott to a tee, right down to the beard he had grown in the weeks before his death.

"What else? Did you see him outside of his room?"

"In fact, I saw him the last night of the conference, at The Green Lady."

"Is that a bar?"

"It's a jazz club. It's open every night of the year, in fact."

"I didn't know a lot of people liked jazz anymore."

"You'd be surprised. My dad took me when I was a kid. He played clarinet professionally. He's deceased now, but every now and then I go there to remember him."

"When you saw Mr. Novak at the club that night, did he give you the same feeling as before?"

"I kept my distance, but he didn't look as aggressive. Maybe it's like one of those fairy tales. You know, music taming the beast. But I stayed clear of him. They have multiple stages at the Green Lady. I went to the basement stage. I think he stayed on the main floor."

"Was he by himself?"

"I think so."

I thanked her and sent her on her way, but not before getting her cell number in case I had other questions. Lydia, toweling off, had heard the whole thing.

"Sounds like we're going to a j-j-jazz club!" she said.

WE NEEDED to eat dinner first, so we found a barbecue restaurant. It was tasty, but the sweet, tangy style. Not the vinegar style I like best.

Lydia ordered an Old Fashioned with dinner.

"You might want to slow down," I said.

"The night is y-y-young!"

Afterwards, we headed for the jazz club. I didn't know what we expected to find here. Besides, how could a gal get any sleuthing done when her ears were ringing?

I never did like jazz. That said, it was pretty incredible for a music hall to be packed with people on a Tuesday night.

We sat at a table right near the front by the main stage. The room was quite narrow, the stage barely a foot off the floor. I could have stepped onto it and kicked the bass drum or tinkled the piano keys.

A young waitress came to serve us.

"What will you pretty girls have?"

"Just a club soda for me," I said.

"What do you recommend?" Lydia asked the waitress.

"Some people like our pink lady," she said.

"A pink lady at The Green Lady?" Lydia said. "I w-w-want that."

"Don't you want to know what's in it?" I asked as the waitress dashed off to fill our order.

"I'm sure it's d-d-delicious," she said, still slurring her words a little from the bourbon drink earlier.

Our drinks came, and we did a toast.

"To c-c-criminal investigation!" she said. After her sip, she said, "Oh, it's fizzy!"

We listened to the jazz. Lydia downed her drink quickly, then gestured to the waitress for another.

When the waitress came back with the drink, I was ready. I showed her a photo of Novak from my phone. "Were you working here when this man came to the club? He sat up front here, we think."

She looked at me strangely. "Actually, I do remember him. Is he in trouble?"

"He's dead, honey," Lydia slurred, as she made progress on her second pink drink.

The waitress put her hand over her mouth. "Oh, my God, I had a bad feeling about him."

"Why?"

Her face went pale.

"He made me sign his will," she said. Then she excused herself and raced away, as if she were going to be sick.

SHE WASN'T the only one feeling queasy. The girl's reaction seemed to trigger Lydia's gag reflex. "Bathroom! Now!" my friend cried. I helped her to a stall in the ladies' room, where she paid homage to the porcelain god.

"Better," she rasped afterwards.

"I sure hope that it wasn't the barbecue, because I had the same thing you did." My stomach, however, felt fine.

"I wonder what was in that drink," Lydia mused.

"We need to track down that waitress again anyway."

We found her talking to her manager.

I said, "I made you upset. I didn't mean to. I'm sorry." I looked at her manager. "Did you meet Scott Novak, too?"

He nodded. "We both signed his will as witnesses. He had hand-written it. It was the weirdest thing. I've never had a patron do that, and I've been in this business for 30 years."

"Did he explain why?"

The manager nodded. "He said he was flying in the morning and wanted to make sure that he was covered in case anything happened."

"Did he seem distraught?"

"Tired, maybe," said the waitress. "A little anxious."

"What happened to the copy you signed?"

"No clue," said the manager. "He left the club right after we signed it."

The waitress excused herself and went back to waiting tables. The manager asked, "What happened to the gentleman? Did his plane crash? I don't remember hearing about it."

"No," I said. "It was an accident at home." I didn't want to say any more than that.

After a glance at Lydia—who was still looking green—I asked the manager, "What's in your pink-lady drink, by the way?"

"Gin, grenadine, and egg white."

Lydia cried out, "Raw egg-whites make me sick and always have!" Off my told-you-so look, she added, "Don't judge," and made a beeline for the bathroom again.

"THERE'S A WILL," I told Darryl on the phone as soon as we got back to the hotel and showered off.

Lydia was already asleep. She wasn't drunk so much as depleted. The front desk kept Gatorade and ibuprofen, thank goodness. It wasn't good for an elderly woman—and former stroke victim—to become dehydrated.

"I wonder why he was so secretive about it," Darryl said. "He could have drawn up a will in Raleigh with his attorney there."

"Maybe he didn't want his beneficiaries to know who they were. Might give them a motive for murder."

"With heirs like that, who needs enemies?" Darryl mused. "I mean, it's weird, don't you think?"

"I'd like to get my hands on that will," I said. "He'd want people to be able to find it in the case of his death, right?"

"If no one finds it, who is set to inherit?" Darryl asked.

"The next of kin would be his brother, Adam."

"So, Adam probably thinks he's going to inherit everything?"

I grumbled, "Who knows what Adam thinks, because no one has talked to him. He's just this mysterious dude lurking in the woods of Alaska."

After exchanging a perfunctory good night with Darryl—

things still weren't on an even keel between us—I hung up and called Paul, filling him in.

"You need to go to Alaska," Paul said.

"Me? Why?"

"Because you're already halfway there."

I wasn't sure that Kansas was halfway to Alaska. But I was more concerned about something else: my wardrobe. "I'll freeze to death."

"No, you won't. Book a flight with a long layover in Denver. Buy one of those Eskimo suits at the airport. Skiers arrive there all the time forgetting their long underwear. Seriously. This ain't rocket science. And it's still September. How cold can it really be?"

"You don't sound very intimidated, Paul. So maybe you should go."

"I *still* don't fly!"

In the morning I broke the news to Lydia. "You're going home alone. I already talked with Darryl about it. He'll be waiting for you at RDU."

Home girl was in no shape to protest.

DARRYL DIDN'T HAVE a problem with his mom flying home alone, but he made plain his feelings about my own impending adventure. Adam lived in the mountains to the north and east of Anchorage. There were no roads to Billings. I'd be flying into Anchorage, then taking a float plane to a mountain lake.

A literal puddle jumper.

Darryl said he worried about me on such a small plane, and he challenged me on why I wanted to go so far to investigate a case that the sheriff's office had concluded did not involve foul play.

"I still don't think we have the whole picture," I said. "A lot of people had it out for Scott. There's more to this case, I just feel it."

"There you go *feeling* again."

"Darryl, I turned off my feelings for nearly 20 years. Do you blame me for going into overdrive now?"

"I just don't get it."

"Are you sure you're not just annoyed that I'm working as an investigator?"

"This fight again."

"It doesn't have to be a fight. It can just be a discussion."

"It's graduated from discussion to full-out conflict. I'm tired of talking about it."

"We were talking about Alaska."

"And I wish you wouldn't go."

"I know it's a long shot. But I'm missing at least one letter from Scott to his brother that might explain what he was thinking around the time of his death. It might hold a clue. You know, your deputy friend could have made this trip unnecessary by asking law enforcement in Alaska to interview Adam."

"Law enforcement can't be sending short-staffed Alaskan sheriff departments on wild snowmobile chases."

"They might use sled dogs," I said. "Looks like I'm going to find out."

"You're not going to change your mind, are you?"

"No. Besides, I can get some small landscapes done while I'm there. I haven't told you this but—I think I'd like to prepare over the next year for an exhibition. I know it will be a lot of work, and I might fall flat on my face. But I need a goal to shoot for."

"That sounds awesome."

"You don't think I'm being silly?"

"No, but don't put too much pressure on yourself. You just started painting again less than a year ago."

"Ken saw my cityscape and really admired it. He said I needed to take myself seriously as a painter."

"Well, Ken would know what's good for you."

I pretended I didn't hear that. I knew he was jealous of Ken, but it just seemed too ridiculous.

Darryl could really use a break from me, I told myself.

I hardly wanted to admit it, but I could probably use a break from him, too.

CHAPTER 14

THE EDGE OF THE WORLD

L anding on an Alaskan lake was a real thrill. I am inept at water skiing, so I'm glad the landing didn't depend on me keeping my balance.

We pulled up to a dock, where a lumberjack type—flannel shirt, boots, and denim jeans—was waiting. The mountain man, who looked to be in his fifties, waited for the propellers to stop spinning before he grabbed a long pole to hook one of the pontoons and pull us in. After securing us to the dock, he proceeded to help us off. The pilot handed him my luggage before climbing down.

"You must be Christopher Gates," I said.

He smiled through a thick red beard. "Yep. My wife Sarah and I run this port. It's everything from an airport to the county hospital to the general store. We get a few flights a month that pick up and drop off supplies for this area. There's about a dozen homesteaders who hike in to get their mail and other things they need."

Now on the dock, I looked around. Snow-packed mountains overlooked the lovely lake ringed by a green scarf of fir trees.

"What a view! This is gorgeous!"

"It's our life. So, you're going to go sight-seeing with Dave today?"

"Sort of." I had decided to keep my real reason for visiting the area secret, lest it scare off Adam Novak somehow. I had told Chris in a call to his satellite phone that I had been a friend of Scott's who he had encouraged to seek out his brother if I ever wanted to paint Alaska.

"Okay. If you're ready, I'll take you to your guide."

"I'm ready."

Chris and Sarah Gates's house was a shack that stood about 20 feet from a warehouse, around which various equipment used to move supplies to and from the dock were scattered.

Sarah came out to greet me. Her hair was entirely gray, but the closer we got the more youthful she looked to be.

"Welcome to the metropolis of Billings," she said, taking my bag. "You're staying in the guest cabin. It's a real five-star affair. Dave is cleaning it now."

"I'll only be staying two nights," I said. "I hope it's not a bother."

"Of course not. It's nice to have the company. Let's tell Dave you're here."

Dave Nash would be my guide to Adam's homestead. He was the son of Mike and Emily Nash who were mentioned in Adam Novak's letters as being so essential in helping Adam to get settled in Alaska.

Paul had spoken over the phone with Dave about Scott Novak's death and my role in investigating it, extracting a promise that the real reason for my visit be kept hidden so as not to scare Adam off.

I immediately found Dave to be a pleasant and confident creature of Alaska. He was in his mid-20s, of average height and rugged good looks, with brown hair and brown eyes, sporting a bowl haircut that looked homemade. His hiking boots, jeans, and flannel shirt were all well-worn.

"We're not used to seeing many ladies up here," he said with a twinkle in his eye. "Be careful, or we might just insist you take us with you when you leave."

"Or I might decide to stay here."

"That would be great!"

I was offered all kinds of coffee and food, but I wasn't hungry. I was anxious to talk with Adam. When Dave and I were alone, I asked him when we could set out.

"It's too late to hike to Adam's place today. In the dead of winter, it would be no trouble, because we would just snowmobile it and it would take forty-five minutes to get there. But on foot it's a good four hours in one direction. If we left now, we'd get stuck in the woods tonight, and that wouldn't be smart. There are bears in these parts, and even if you hang up your trash and ring the camp with rope and bells you can't totally protect yourself from bears when tent camping. I suggest this afternoon you do a little sightseeing close to the lake and we'll set out in the morning for Adam's camp."

I relished the opportunity to paint a vista of the lake and surrounding mountains. But I worried that this trip might prove fruitless. I asked, "Are you sure Adam's going to be near his place tomorrow?"

"My guess is he'll be around the camp fixing things, but you never know. He could wake up in the morning and decide to go trapping. Best thing to do is just try our luck. It's good you didn't give him any warning, because he's just as likely to avoid you than meet with you."

"Do you think he saw my plane?"

"You can bet he saw or heard the plane, but this is Alaska. Bush planes are everywhere. I call it the Alaskan subway."

"Have you seen Adam since his brother died?"

He nodded. "Actually, I'm the one who took the message to him."

"You did? I thought Chris or Sarah told him."

He shook his head. "I'd just gotten back from taking a group on a canoe and camping trip down the Susitna River. I stay with my parents when I'm here, and Adam's place is on the way to their house."

"How did he take it?"

Dave frowned. "He didn't say much. I think he was just really surprised. Just thanked me and said he wanted to be alone."

"Did that reaction surprise you?"

"Yeah. A little bit. I mean, he wasn't close to his brother. He didn't even like him, if you want to know the truth. Talked about how spoiled he'd been by their mom, for example. But he was his brother, so I guess at the end of the day he'd be upset."

I nodded. The letters from Adam to Scott pointed to a reconciliation, but there were plenty of years of bad blood to be overcome. I began mentally preparing myself for just about anything I might encounter in the person of Adam Novak.

The rest of the afternoon I spent alone wandering the banks of the lake, exploring the reedy marshes as well as the vistas. I didn't see elk, but I did see black-tailed deer. I also spied a pair of beavers, several leaping fish, and a dozen different species of birds. I painted three of my six small canvases. At dusk the mosquitoes drove me back to the Gates's guest cabin. It was rustic and felt a lot like summer camp, but it was clean and comfortable.

The next morning, Sarah served me a bowl of oatmeal that I was able to improve with all sorts of wholesome nuts and fruits. "Eat two bowls," she urged.

I noticed a photo of a pretty girl on her wall.

"Is that your daughter? She's lovely."

"That's Bren," she said. "She died seven years ago, not long after Adam arrived here, actually." *Did she connect the two things in her mind?*

"I'm so sorry."

"We miss her so. She had an accident. Fell off the edge of a cliff where she liked to study. I don't mind talking about her. She was a spitfire."

"She was in high school?"

"We homeschooled. Mostly correspondence courses. Really smart. She wanted to go to college. In fact, Adam told her that his brother might help her get a scholarship. Brenda thought maybe because she was a girl who was interested in computer science that she would stand out. She was so excited. But then the accident happened."

"I'm so sorry."

"It was very difficult. Still is. But people came together in such a good way. Mike Nash, Dave's father, reached out to his world-wide network. You have never seen so many float planes arrive in this lake, just good people coming to aid in the search for her. I'll show you."

She pulled a scrapbook off a shelf and turned to some newspaper clippings. One of the most impressive photos was of a flotilla of planes of all shapes and sizes. A craft in the foreground looked more like a spaceship than an airplane.

Most of the clippings featured Brenda's picture: a smiling brunette, favoring her mother's dimples.

I read one of the headlines aloud.

"'Accomplished Teen Was Headed for Great Things.'"

Sarah smiled.

"Bren would have succeeded at anything she put her mind to. She was tough—Alaska tough."

~

DAVE SLEPT in the spare bedroom in the Gates's cabin and got up at the crack of dawn to walk over and greet me. I had put my backpack together the night before. "I'm ready," I told him.

The journey was like nothing I had ever experienced. This was not an excursion so much as an ordeal. Even though we were taking a path that snowmobiles used in the winter, the way was precarious. Rocks, branches and mud threatened to turn my ankle any moment. I felt so slow! Fortunately, Dave didn't seem to be in a hurry. He spent time clearing the path of whatever branches and rocks he could.

Thank God I'd listened to the store manager when buying my gear in the Denver airport. My pack was light, and my shoes were snug. When I did feel the start of a blister, I asked my guide to stop so I could cover it with a band-aid.

After a couple hours of trekking, Dave suggested we stop and have a rest and snack of GORP (Good Ol' Raisins and Peanuts). He told me how this area used to be a popular place for cross-country skiing in the 1950s and 60s because loggers had basically cleaned the place out. But the trees grew back, and now no one wanted to assume the responsibility of keeping the paths clear of the naturally accumulating debris.

"Sometimes nature wins," Dave smiled, "takes back what's hers."

I told him I agreed (though what would I know about Alaskan landscapes?) I took out my lightweight travel easel and one of the three remaining 8-inch square canvases I'd packed. I wanted to capture the path we'd just taken, but I kept getting distracted by the sky.

"Why is the sky so blue here?" I asked.

"No moisture in the air to cloud it."

"No humidity? We really are a long way from the South."

I sketched in pencil, then took a few pictures of the scene

with my phone. That would do for now. I didn't feel the need to delay our journey any longer.

The second half was harder than the first. One, because I was already pooped. Two, because this leg was even more up-hill. We still weren't high enough for the atmosphere to present a problem, thankfully, and with every step in increasing eleva-tion I knew that the way back would be that much easier.

I tried to distract myself with conversation. I pummeled Dave with questions about growing up in Alaska. He talked about learning to live off the land by hunting, trapping, and fish-ing. How to make a fire with flint and without. He told me about some near-death experiences along the way, too, most involving rock climbing or bears.

"You're lucky. Not many young people learn to do those sorts of things," I said.

"That's what Adam always says. How lucky I am. How so many men these days have missed out on learning these kind of survival skills. That got me to thinking. A while back I decided I wanted to start a sort of business out here, where people can come and learn different wilderness skills. Sure would be easier than leading them on excursions."

"That sounds like a great idea," I said. "What's stopping you?"

Dave laughed. "It's a lot of work."

"I started a business a while ago. It's just one foot in front of the other. Like this difficult hike."

"I suppose you're right."

It was just past 10 in the morning when we made it to Adam's camp. I sensed right away that no one was home, even before we got close enough to the front door to read the hand-lettered sign:

YOU'LL SEE ME IN 2.

Dave knocked on the door. When there was no answer, he opened it.

"He isn't here," Dave said.

"Rats!" I cried. I hadn't heard Dave cuss yet and didn't know how he'd respond to my potty mouth. "What does '2' mean? Two hours? Two *days*?"

"Maybe two weeks," muttered my guide.

"I sure hope not." I told Dave I wanted to sit down to rest and eat our lunches.

"He wouldn't mind you coming inside," Dave said. "It's the unwritten law of homesteaders. If you need something, use it. Just compensate the person the best you can." He excused himself to use the bathroom. "Adam has an outhouse around back if you need it. It's clean."

Alone in the cabin, I looked around. The cabin was small, but neat. A dining table and two chairs. A narrow bed. Wood-burning stove in the corner. Another, smaller table was pushed against the wall in the way of a desk, with a few books. Most were technical, having to do with survival in the wild. One book stood out: *Thus Spoke Zarathustra* by Friedrich Nietzsche.

Open on the desk was a thick notebook, its paper identical to the handwritten letters mailed to Scott. A letter had been started, undated:

SCOTT,

Not sure I'll get this letter finished before I head to the doctor in Anchorage. I was just thinking about something I hadn't remembered in a while, when we built that two-person go-cart with dad's old lawn-mower engine. We got going but the choke stuck, and we couldn't stop. To save our lives going down that hill you ended up crashing into the curb and turning the thing into splinters. Ouch! Dad beat us senseless, and I blamed you. But it wasn't your fault. I'm sorry, Brother. That might have been the last time we really did a project together. I still remember the thrill of that go-cart ride. Maybe we could try to build something together again someday?

THE MEMORY MADE ME SAD. It didn't seem right to invite Dave to read the note, as it hadn't been my place to read it in the first place.

I stopped reading the journal, for something near the back cover caught my eye. It was another letter poking out, this one from Scott and dated in April—right in the middle of the time window of the missing letter.

This letter was unusual in that it was handwritten rather than typed. Whereas Adam's handwriting was very small, almost reclusive in its own right, Scott's was tall and flowery:

APRIL 15, 2018

 Adam,

 That's pretty interesting about what your friend Dave said. His observation begs the question: What are the qualities of a creature that allow it to adapt and endure? Just thinking about the memory of genes combined with Nietzsche's concept of Will to Power has caused a bit of a brainstorm inside me. I might be on to something very big! Please tell Dave thanks for the insight.

 Like you, my way of dealing with things is to escape—but in a different way. You escaped to Alaska; I escaped into my research.

 Remember Gem, our pet chameleon? Gem and I would play together for what felt like days at a time. Strangely enough I have a serval and a monkey but don't have a chameleon. But I'd love one, if only for old times' sake.

 It would be great to get together. I still have to give that talk on September 6, but just flying in the day before and then flying out the day after. You could come to Raleigh sometime, I guess, but rather than coming all that way maybe we could meet in Twin Cities, Minnesota—keeping so many of the miles out of your journey (1200 according to Google)?

Seriously. Think about it.

I'm glad you're going to see the doctor. Maybe you'll get that brain transplant you've been needing (ha ha) like when Gilligan and the Professor switched brains. Remember all those old shows we'd watch on Saturdays? We'd watch like 12 of them in one sitting and during the commercials run together to the bathroom to pee in the toilet ("Don't cross the streams!") so we wouldn't miss anything. If we had Netflix back then, I bet we could have spent a full month just bingeing on shows.

You asked about Emerson. Yeah, he's still my right-hand man. He left for a little bit but then he came back and he's working hard for the merged company. I'm including his mailing address, email, and phone number below if you ever want to reach out to him.

Thanks again for writing back after all these years and meeting me halfway.

Yours,

Scott

I NOTICED Dave coming up the front path, so I quickly took a photo of the letter with my phone before putting the journal back where I'd found it. I knew I didn't have a right to poke around in Adam's belongings, but I justified it because I'd come all this way.

Dave and I ate lunch slowly. We waited for "2"—hours, that is. If we waited much longer, we'd get stuck in the dark on the way back to the lake port. My legs were eager to get back—but not eager to get moving. I told Dave as much.

"I've got an idea," he said. "Why don't we leave Adam a note.

We can walk to my parents' house, stay there tonight, then come back here tomorrow. It's a bit of a haul, but I think we'll both be more comfortable at my parents' than here. Now, my dad is—" he paused, considering his words carefully "—a bit of a character, but most people survive his company. They have a private room you can use."

I quickly surveyed Adam's spartan quarters and agreed that the two of us staying here tonight was not a comfortable option.

My legs and feet weren't happy about it, but we hit the trail again.

CHAPTER 15

THE PATRIOT

Mike and Emily Nash lived even further from the lake, a bit higher on the mountain and about an hour's hike from Adam's cabin. As we were getting close, I asked Dave to tell me more about his parents.

He took a deep breath. "My mom is super nice. You'll like her. She's quiet. On the other hand, my dad is not quiet. First of all, he goes by 'Patriot Mike.' He's got a video blog, *Zero Dark Alaska*, where he blabs about his politics. He talks like the government is out to get him. Like, there are over three-hundred million Americans, and he thinks the government is out to get *him*. And he's so free of the government that he hides in his little prison of a home, with all these security cameras everywhere. It gets a little annoying, to tell you the truth. But I'm used to it."

"I heard something about a bear story. What's that all about?"

"Oh, he'll tell you all about that. Don't let me steal his thunder."

"Are he and Adam Novak good friends? I know Adam credits him with helping him get established out here."

"Yeah, they are pretty friendly."

His voice trailed off. Dave's upbeat demeanor grew more subdued the further we walked, until we came to a metal gate crossing the path, the first sign of human presence since we'd left Adam's cabin. Dave unhooked a keychain from his belt and found the small key that uncoupled the lock from the gate's rusty chain. After we'd both moved through, he pulled the gate closed again and locked it behind us.

We kept going on the trail, which rounded a curve and revealed an amazing view of the valley.

His parents' house was a mansion compared to Adam's. It looked like it had been added onto over the years. After working in real estate for so long, I'd learned how to measure a home's integrity; the work here had been expertly done.

The one thing that surprised me was the large tank positioned on the hillside above the house. I asked Dave about it.

"Dad has a generator that pumps water from a well in the valley. That's the only way they're able to live so high up. Most homesteaders live in the valleys so they can access water. When that thing is full, they can live out here for months without leaving—assuming they've got enough food. The same generator can keep the tank and the water lines heated in the winter so they don't freeze up."

"It's like they live in a castle," I said.

"Dad's the King alright. Do you mind if I tell him the real reason we're here? He's a skeptical guy. He's not going to buy the whole painting thing, I promise you that."

"Okay," I said. "I want to ask him some questions about Adam anyway."

Dave went up to the narrow porch. The door opened for him, as if he'd been anticipated (those cameras) and he stepped inside.

A moment later the door opened again, and Dave came out accompanied by his parents. Mike Nash, very tall, brunette, with dark, movie-star looks, utilized a cane. While he remained on the porch, his wife came down the three steps and walked right up to me. Emily Nash had ultra-long black hair like someone 20 years younger.

She seemed excited in a nervous way. She probably didn't get many social calls here at the edge of the world.

"Welcome to our home! So, your name is Rett?"

Mike shouted from the porch. "Dammit, Emily, she didn't come here to gab and socialize! She's looking for Adam! The law always comes calling eventually! A man must be up to no good if he's living the way he wants!"

"Can I get you something to drink?" Emily asked softly.

"Sure. Some water would be wonderful."

"Okay. Come."

She left me on the porch with the men. Mike waited until Dave and I had sat in our chairs before seating himself. I noticed (I think it had been meant for noticing) a pistol dangling from Mike's belt and made a vow not to make any sudden moves.

Mike said, "Not many people have been up here. Good thing you're with David, or you wouldn't have gotten very close. This is private property. Does that mean anything to you? I suppose it don't, given you're with the authorities."

"She's a private investigator," Dave said. "She doesn't deserve your scorn, Dad."

"Is that right?" he said. "Are you a P.I.?"

"Not even," I said. "I'm only helping a P.I. investigate a case."

Mike laughed. "It's a long walk to Alaska from ... where did you say you were from?"

"Raleigh, North Carolina."

"What else don't I know about you?"

Emily re-emerged from the house, handed me a coffee mug filled with water. Probably from that tank. I'd always found mountain water to be the tastiest around.

There wasn't another chair for Emily, so Dave stood up and offered his. "I'm going to freshen up a little," Dave said, then followed the porch to the end of the house and disappeared around back. Emily turned her chair more in my direction. I was hyperconscious of her beside me and felt that if I put my hand out, she would grab it in an instant.

I said to Mike, "I'm not here to investigate Adam Novak. I'm just hoping he can tell me more about his brother, Scott, who was killed last week. The investigation has stalled there. Adam and Scott had a relationship through letters and we just wonder if Adam might have learned something that could help the investigation." I didn't mention that I had already read all their letters.

"Who hired you?" Mike asked.

"Scott's boss. Though the death was ruled a suicide, he suspects foul play. Scott didn't strike many people as suicidal, though it's certainly possible." I didn't mention the possibility of a sex game gone wrong.

"His boss, huh? Just curious: Did Scott Novak carry?"

"Excuse me?"

"Did he carry a *gun*?"

"It's possible. But I don't believe so."

"If he did, maybe he'd still be alive today." I got the impression I was slowing being introduced to Patriot Mike's religion.

"Maybe not if the killer was someone he knew well," I said. "Sometimes people who act friendly aren't so friendly after all."

He chuckled. "There's always a catch, ain't there?"

Emily remained silent, but I could sense her looking at me. I didn't feel threatened by her in the least. Though we sat in separate chairs, she was like a cat curled by my side.

I took another sip of my water. Mike had yet to betray a single opinion about Adam. I didn't think asking the same question would do anything but make me seem desperate.

I turned to Emily.

"You sure live in a beautiful place."

"We—" she started to say.

"We like it," Mike interrupted. "It's peaceful. We have the right not to be bothered."

Is freedom of speech part of those rights? Because I'm trying to ask Emily a question and you won't let her answer.

"If you don't mind me asking," I said to Mike, "what happened to your leg? I noticed you walk with a limp."

He didn't hesitate. Perhaps by way of shock value, he extended the leg out and yanked up the pant leg, revealing a spindly ankle adjacent to a truncated calf.

"She-bear surprised me one evening when I was coming back from the bathroom. She must have smelled our food, she was lurking in the shadows outside the kitchen. I made noise but she must have felt trapped and come after me. I fell down and started kicking. Emily heard the ruckus and came out shooting. The bear ran but took part of my leg with her. You can bet I carry this with me *everywhere* now," he said, tapping his pistol. "Even to the bathroom."

He released his jean leg. Story over, I grunted acknowledgment. But it didn't seem to beg for any more than that.

I took another sip of my water, gathered my courage. "I won't waste much more of your time. I'm just trying to find Adam, that's all. I think he'd want to help find anyone who might have killed his brother. If you don't want to help, I understand. It's a free country."

Oh, Rett! *Wrong. Thing. To. Say.*

"Used to be," Mike replied, and he started on a hard-to-follow monologue about gun rights, Waco, and Ruby Ridge that made it sound like government agents were ready to descend in helicopters any second. About halfway through his droning, I put out my hand for Emily, who took it and squeezed hard.

I don't think Mike even noticed. He kept on about tyrannical leaders and the Revolutionary War and the First World Order and the Illuminati—painting an apocalyptic picture of imminent war and destruction.

When Dave arrived again, I stood up in the middle of one of his dad's growls, letting go of Emily's hand and facing Dave, and in the process turning my full back toward Mike. I was doing the thing I bet few dared to do.

I was ignoring him.

I asked to use the bathroom and was directed to the outhouse, its reek causing me to hold my breath. I had my tampon pouch kit with me, but I didn't need it, thank goodness. I said a prayer of thanks that I wasn't on my period and could get out of there quickly.

I rejoined the couple on the porch.

Mike said, "I've got a theory about Scott Novak. Want to hear it?"

I took and released a deep breath as I sat down. "Sure."

He nodded. "Adam has told me all about his brother. Smart dude. Grows up in a small town in Pennsylvania, goes to college, makes something of himself. That's the American Dream, right? But let's break it down a little bit...

"*Grows up in a small town.* A small Pennsylvania town that raised him, nurtured him. He goes to college, starts a company. Creates jobs—but they aren't jobs in the small town or even the rural state that invested in him originally. So far in the story, Scott Novak is somewhat of a traitor to the people in his home state. But let's keep going.

"What kind of a company does he build? Is it one where good ol' Americans can work with their hands? I mean, we've already seen coal mining go down the tubes—it's 'just not good for the environment.' Furniture-making, that's gone over to Vietnam, which historically did so much for America, right? And textiles, same deal; we didn't like breathing cotton fibers in the air anyway. Steel—well, bad trade deals. But that was a loud, hot, messy industry. It made us perspire quite a lot. Hard to replenish the electrolytes...

"But we'll win the next industry: 'The Information Age'! 'Clean' jobs. No one is going to get black streaks on their face or cotton fibers in their lungs or cut off their fingers at the saw or melt their hands in molten iron. These will be climate controlled. And we'll keep the industry here because we have the smartest people! When we don't have the smartest people, we'll import them. They can work here and help us build our magnificent economy." He put his hands out, as if he were lifting a boulder, or raising a skyscraper. Then he smiled idiotically, turned his hands upside-down, and started miming typing on a keyboard.

"Tap-tap-tap, tap-tap-tap. Look! I'm a little pansy-ass, yellow-bellied nerd, never getting outside, never doing a lick of manual work in my life, just watch me type. Folks"—he might as well have been addressing his Web-video audience now—"that's not building anything. No self-respecting American male is going to aspire to that kind of work.

"'Oh, but all those *jobs*.' Last I saw, ain't none of those hi-tech jobs locating right here. Last I saw, Detroit was still rusting. Last I saw, the good people in coal country are sitting on the side of the road, getting high on meth, while a precious few namby-pamby nerds leave the state to go hi-tech.

"And, let's talk about what Novak's company made. 'Robots?' That sounds pretty cool. Robots can help us make cars and such. Might be better if they were people helping other people to make the cars, but, okay, robots are something we can *touch*. But, no, these are *invisible* 'bots.' Bots that pretend to be people when they answer the phone. Bots that analyze data and decide if you're cheating on your taxes and take you to task. Bots that, well, who the hell knows what all they do. They don't make anything—except money for the people who own them.

"All that help from a small town, all that investment by good people who work with their hands, all that hope placed into the person of Scott Novak, Hero of the Information Age, who left his hometown and rural state to build invisible robots that put good ol' Americans out of work—and made a killing doing it. Maybe Scott Novak wasn't murdered. Maybe Scott Novak experienced a tremendous tidal wave of guilt, put himself on trial, and dealt himself the appropriate punishment. Maybe Scott Novak had a sense of justice in the end. If that's the case, God rest his soul. He saved a patriot a bullet."

There was a beat of silence as everyone realized Mike had finished.

"Did anyone get that on camera?" he added with a chuckle.

Mike's argument held a kind of power. He was good looking and a good speaker, so it was easy to see why he had built up such a following online. But I also knew how rhetoric could win arguments while leaving out some important details. I could sympathize with the observation that so many talented people left their rural upbringings for the big city, sometimes in another state, never to return. But I wasn't going to allow myself to be persuaded that Scott Novak had been a "traitor."

The Scott Novaks of the world (wherever they had grown up) were merely meeting the needs of a market, which was the whole point of capitalism, something I knew a thing or two about. Maybe it wasn't the kind of work that Patriot Mike and his friends respected, but a Scott Novak burying his talents in the sand wasn't going to bring back all the industries Mike had nostalgia for.

Patriot Mike, sitting in his bunker in Alaska recording videos on his computer—*tap-tap-tap!*—wasn't getting his hands dirty creating a company that could compete. It was always easier to sit on the sidelines and criticize than to get in the middle of things and do something to change the status quo.

Mike was a smart guy, but a little-too-cute-by-half. I wasn't going to fall for the click bait, and I certainly wasn't going to become one of his vlog fans. Mike's spiteful rant about Scott Novak said more about him than it said about Scott.

As far as I was concerned, it made him a suspect.

Not that he, personally, could carry out such a crime with that injured leg. But didn't he have that network of go-to buddies around the country, the ones who had responded to his call-in force when Brenda Gates went missing?

What if one of them had watched his videos and gotten it in his head one day to take out an elite, 'namby-pamby nerd traitor?'

THE EXTRA ROOM that Dave had talked about was his own. I tried to protest, but he ended up letting me have the room and its bed, while he chivalrously slept on a pallet near the wood-burning stove in the home's den-slash-kitchen.

The sleep was restorative. In the morning, we ate an oatmeal breakfast and said quick good-byes to his parents.

"I'll walk you to the gate," said Emily. I walked quickly, not wanting to give her husband the opportunity to intervene.

But Mike shouted from the front porch, "Has Dave told you about Adam and the skunk yet?"

Dave didn't slow his stride, didn't turn his head toward his dad, just shouted back, "Yeah, thanks. Got it."

He waved a hand in the air in token politeness and sped ahead of us toward the gate.

Emily grabbed my hand with both of hers and forced a piece of paper into my palm.

"Don't look," she whispered.

"Okay," I said softly, keeping my hand neutral.

"Come back and see me some time," she added in a normal voice.

I smiled and nodded. "I will."

Emily let go and left to walk slowly up the path, looking to me like the loneliest woman in the world. I casually put the note in my pocket.

When we were through the gate again, Dave said, "So, you had the pleasure of meeting my father. That must have been the fucking highlight of your life."

"He's really something," I said, noting the curse word.

"A piece of work is what he is." It seemed like he was going to say more, then thought better of it.

We had gotten about an eighth of a mile when I realized something. Embarrassingly, I had left my toiletry kit in the outhouse—including the only toilet paper I'd brought for wiping my privates after peeing. If I started my period on this trip, I needed that kit. I regretfully told Dave we'd need to go back.

"I have a better idea," he said with a gleam in his eye. "Follow me."

We went off the path, scaling rocks until we were skirting the bluff through dense woods. I followed him step for step. The growth was thick, but we got through it. In a short time, we were on the top of the steep but minor bluff looking down on his parents' house.

"There aren't any cameras trained on this part of the property," he said. "Sort of a blind spot. I'll just sneak down, grab your toilet supplies, and come right back."

"Are you sure?" I said. "I'm sorry for the trouble."

But he seemed energized by the challenge. I watched him

slide down the hillside and walk nonchalantly to the far side of the home.

Remembering the note that Emily had handed to me, I pulled it from my pocket. It was old newsprint, but I could still make out what Emily had scrawled in pencil lead: "It was so nice to meet you. I'm so glad you came to visit us! O X – Love, Emily."

A totally generic message, something I might have received from a friend in the fourth grade. Feeling too sorry for her to throw it away, I placed the note back into my pocket.

Just in time, for Dave was scrambling back up the bluff with my kit.

"Good thing I wasn't the Big Bad Government," he said with a smile, "or Patriot Mike would be toast."

We retraced our steps and rejoined the mountain path.

"What was that about Adam and the skunk?" I asked.

Dave chuckled. "He was reminding me of a time one summer when Adam went hunting. A skunk made it into his tent in the middle of the night. Adam freaked out, and it set the skunk to spraying. Not a good look for a man of the wild."

"Why do you suppose your father mentioned that?"

He shrugged. "To make another man look bad? Who the heck knows. You grow up under a man like that, you stop hearing him after a while. Just white noise, know what I mean?"

"I understand," I said, but I had a thought. "Do you remember where Adam met the skunk? I wonder if your father was telling us where to look for Adam."

Dave cocked his head. "I believe that was down in the cedars, in the valley. We can go back that way if you want. It's off the beaten path, but not too far out of our way. Will only add about an hour to our hike."

"Can we still get back to Adam's and then the lake station before dark?"

"I believe so. Unless Adam is there. You think my dad can

talk? Oh, my God. Adam is a dang fire hose where that's concerned."

But that's what I wanted. A brother who would talk.

We took the diversion into the valley. Unfortunately, there was still no sign of Adam. "Maybe we'll get lucky and he's back at his cabin," Dave said.

But when we returned to the cabin we found it just as we had left it.

Could Adam be lost? I shared this worry with Dave, who shook his head. "Adam is the smartest person I've ever met. He's not lost. Just busy doing his thing."

We made the mostly downhill trip to the lake in just a couple of hours.

I shared my worries with Chris.

"Will you contact me if you see Adam?" I asked him. "And, not only that, I wonder if you'd ever consider going to look for him?"

Chris shrugged. "I don't think I can leave long enough to do that. Have you asked Dave to look?"

"I haven't. But I will."

The next morning, I asked Dave just that, promising to compensate him for his time. "And when you see him, please ask him to contact me. Here's my phone number and address." I gave him my card.

"I sure will," Dave said. "I need to get in touch with him as well. I want to tell him I may have just found an investor."

"An investor?"

He smiled wide. "One of the businessmen I led on my last trek wrote me. His postcard came on the same plane that brought you. His name is Ralph Neeley and he wants to learn more about Alaskan Survival Camp."

He handed me the postcard, which read: "*Dave, It felt so cool to rely on our own devices on our trip. I love the idea of Alaskan*

Survival Camp. *Let's find a way to make it happen. I'll be in touch soon. —Sincerely, Ralph.*"

"Wow, that's fantastic!" I said.

"I know. I can hardly believe it. It was nice to meet you, Rett Swinson." We shook hands.

There was still some time to wait for the plane, so I brought out the last of my blank canvases to work with. I could have left it blank, symbolic of the great waste of time that constituted my trip to Alaska. Instead, I went through the motions of rendering the lake. By the end, I was feeling hopeful again.

As the engine of a plane announced its arrival, I quickly gathered up my paints. Chris and Sarah both came out to the dock to see me off.

"I can see why you live out here," I said. "It's beautiful."

Chris nodded. "We've thought about leaving, because sometimes it's painful. So many memories of our girl. But we feel like we'd abandon her if we left. Brenda's spirit is strong in this nature."

Sarah added, "And the nature out here is very big."

CHAPTER 16

A DASHING OF HOPES

I called Paul from the Denver airport to talk to him about my dud of an adventure, the only real highlight being my conversation with Patriot Mike that showed his disdain for Scott Novak. I mentioned the pitiful note Emily Nash had slipped to me, which I had kept out of a sort of respect for her, as she seemed to get so little respect in life. "Her husband acts like some sort of movie star because of his Internet audience."

"Sounds like an interesting guy."

"Not interesting enough. The one person I wanted to meet wasn't to be found."

"Do you think Adam was actively avoiding you?"

"I don't know. He does have to hunt for his food. At least I found what I think is the last of Scott's letters. Esther was right: Scott thought he had hit on some new discovery and seemed really excited. But it's also possible that the project didn't bear fruit. Maybe that's why he announced later that he was quitting the field. I'd still like to find out what that research was."

"So would Sammy. But your pal Augusta hasn't cracked that code yet. Are you sure she knows what she's doing?"

"If she wants it bad enough, she'll succeed."

ON THE FLIGHTS home my thoughts had dwelled mainly on the Gates family and their immense loss. Maybe it was because I was so worried about my own daughter, who I hadn't heard from in weeks. As mothers and daughters went, Stephanie and I weren't close. The last time we did speak, about a month earlier, I sensed she was struggling with something. Even though her infatuation with KayLeigh had crashed and burned a while back, it did not result in any new closeness between us.

I flew into Raleigh expecting a chilly reception from Darryl. But the truth is we had both missed one another. He took me out to eat at Outback, our old stand-by.

"We make a good team," I said over dinner. "I'd much rather be working on this case with you than Paul Maroni."

He blushed. I needed him to know that he was the main target of my affection.

MY BODY CLOCK was all off, and the next morning I slept until 11. At noon I got in my car and headed for Greenville.

Stephanie was a member of the Epsilon Beta sorority, which hadn't been around when I was a co-ed at East Carolina University. I had hoped that college would cause something to take root in her, some kind of intellectual passion. She was in her junior year, and I was still waiting for her to have that eureka moment. The topic of law school had come up once or twice, though she'd never shown any actual interest in the law; I think it just served as something impressive for her to say when people asked about her future.

The sorority's front door was partially open, so I went right in. I found myself in a commons room where a soap opera blared on the television. Two sorority members were talking about the episode loudly while textbooks lay open on their laps:

"Is she going to tell Harold he's being set up?"

"No way! He did her wrong. She's going to watch it all unfold."

"But he's her baby daddy."

"What if it turns out he had an evil twin?"

I cleared my throat.

"Hi! Has anyone seen Stephanie Swinson? I'm her mother."

The girls' heads turned to look at me.

"Um," said one, "I haven't seen Stephanie today."

"I haven't seen her either," said the other. "She's probably with Alex."

"Alex?" I asked.

"Her boyfriend."

My heart clinched, but I tried to downplay the moment. "Do you expect her in today?"

"She'll be here for dinner. She always cooks."

"She's the best cook in the sorority. Did you teach her how?"

I felt a small surge of pride. "A bit, though her father is the better cook, I have to admit."

"A lot of girls hang out near the kitchen when she's cooking, hoping for a free meal."

"I'll be back later," I said. "Maybe I'll get a free meal, too."

I smiled and showed myself to the door. I hoped they would report back to Stephanie that I'd dropped by—and that I didn't look too upset when they'd mentioned her boyfriend. But my heart was racing.

Alex was more than likely Alex Kelly, Stephanie's high school flame—as in incendiary, all-consuming. The two would fight like cat and dog, get back together, then fight again—a destructive dance that had practically killed me with worry. Athletic, boisterous, and gregarious, Alex was perhaps no worse than the average man, but Stephanie brought out the worst in him—and he in her. Warrantless jealousy followed by vindictive cheating on both sides was followed by rollercoasters of contrition and tears.

It took Alex finding a different girlfriend and Stephanie going to a different college for the two to finally make their last break-up stick.

Now it seemed they were together for a sequel.

No wonder she had been so evasive—because she knew I wouldn't approve.

I was loathe to do it, but I needed to call the only person who would truly understand the gravity of the situation.

I called my ex-husband.

"Stephanie is seeing Alex again," I said.

He muttered, "I know."

"You knew? Then why didn't you tell me?"

"Because I knew it would upset you."

Typical Allan. "Allan, she's my daughter, too. I need to know these things."

"We can't tell her what to do. Stephanie is an adult now."

I said, "We can counsel her."

"Are we talking about the same daughter? When was the last time Stephanie asked for our advice? She's stubborn as all get-out. She comes by it naturally."

"Are you saying she got her stubbornness from me? Wait, don't answer that. We both know it's true."

"You said it, not me."

I said, "I'm in Greenville now. I'm going to try to see her later tonight. Maybe she'll talk about it. Maybe I'll *make* her talk about it." Allan had never liked being direct. I, on the other hand, was stubborn enough to try.

"By the way," I said, "I saw your dad last week in a very strange situation." I told him about John's experiment with the virtual version of Nick. Allan listened, but I could almost hear his anxiety rising, his desire to flee the conversation.

"Thanks for letting me know," he said.

"Does it bother you that your dad is doing this?" I asked.

"Bother me? No. Dad can do what he wants. It's his thing."

I could have asked more probing questions, like whether Allan ever thought much about Nick, or whether it still bothered him that his dad didn't call to ask about Allan's life, or whether he had thought again about staging an addiction intervention with his mom, something he had briefly considered over a decade ago.

But my questions would have received the usual pushback, and I didn't have the energy to deal with Allan's evasiveness today.

"Okay," I said. "Just thought you'd want to know."

We ended the call cordially, which was worth something, I suppose.

I had a little time to kill and wondered if I should drop in on the art department and try to catch at least one of my former professors in the studio. But I didn't really feel like explaining my 20-year hiatus from painting. So, I took a walk instead.

I was passing by one of the science buildings when I was accosted by two students, a boy and a girl, handing out flyers.

"Do you believe in animal rights?" one of the students asked. "We're having a meeting right now if you'd like to join us."

I glanced at the flyer, which showed a cartoon cow looking sad in a cage. The text beneath the picture asked, "Does she deserve to suffer?" I remembered the animals that were released the night Scott Novak died.

"Sure," I said. "I have a little time."

I followed them into the building to a classroom where a conversation was already taking place. I listened to the banter, in which members of the group were debating whether to conduct a sit-in over the shortage of vegetarian options at campus eateries or join a statewide march against cruel farm practices. They decided in the end to do the sit-in and start a letter-writing campaign about farming policy.

When there seemed to be a break in the conversation, I asked, "What about zoos? Does anyone here have a problem with zoos?"

"Hell to the yeah," said one boy. "But what are you going to do, let the animals out of their cages? The animals would die. You have to stop zoos from opening in the first place."

"I don't know," said a girl. "I think zoos do serve a purpose. They help people start to appreciate animals and all the diversity in the world."

"Then it's okay for some animals to suffer as long as it helps other animals to survive?" the boy challenged. "That's using some animals as means rather than as ends. Not cool."

There was more back and forth, with no consensus.

Someone asked me why I had an interest in zoos. I told them about Scott's little zoo and how someone had let the animals out and possibly even killed the zoo's owner. I asked, "Are there any groups in the state that engage in that sort of hard-core activism?"

"You mean animal liberators? There are raids on research labs every now and then," the group's apparent leader said. "But your example doesn't have the fingerprints of a hard-core liberator. And you don't see them kill *people*. Probably more likely that someone killed the guy, then opened some cage doors to make it look like an animal liberator did it."

"I see." He made a good point. But I had one more question. "Has your work made a difference?"

They looked at one another. "A couple years ago we joined a national movement to close circuses," said the girl who had handed me the flier. "It worked! Even Barnum and Bailey shut down. That was huge."

"Yeah," cut in someone else, "but I'd argue that it was just a marketing problem. Kids want to play video games these days. Circuses are old-school."

"And it helped that that tiger attacked what's-his-name in Vegas."

"Yeah. That was the beginning of the end. Good riddance."

When the meeting was over, I thanked the group and walked a few laps around the main quad. Squirrels cavorted in the grass and up and down the giant oaks.

Like a flash, a watching hawk swooped down and grabbed a squirrel in its talons. Perhaps not a big believer in the rights of all animals, the hawk used its beak to dispense of the squirrel's life, then took off with the corpse.

I SMELLED her before I saw her.

Sweet scents led me to the sorority kitchen, from which a parade of girls carried bowls of steaming deliciousness. Somewhere inside was my girl, cooking up a storm.

"What's for supper?" I asked.

Without turning to look at me, she said, "Shrimp and grits. What are you doing here?"

"Visiting my daughter. Seeing if she's doing okay."

"I'm fine."

I wanted so badly to ask about Alex, but I didn't want to risk having her shut down.

"Are classes going okay?"

"My professors are all idiots. Now, can we talk about something else?"

"Well," I said, "we could talk about all the things that KayLeigh is saying about me around town that aren't true."

"If it makes you feel any better, she's still on my shit list, too." I had to admire Stephanie for taking my side the last time KayLeigh went too far in trashing me.

"Am I on that list, too? Because I haven't heard from you in a long time. I've been worried about you."

"You don't have to worry about me."

"Someone said you're dating Alex again." *There, Rett. You went and did it.*

"Who told you that?"

"Does it matter? Is it true?"

"Don't judge."

"I just remember how turbulent that was for you." *For all of us.*

"Please don't make an issue of it."

"It's not about me. It's about you and your happiness. But I'm not going to push."

"Good."

Even without the steam from the boiling shrimp, the room's air could be sliced with a knife.

I decided to pivot.

"You say your professors aren't very good. But have you been going to class?"

"Sometimes."

"'Sometimes?' Why don't you switch classes then?"

"I'm just not that into school right now, Mom."

I didn't respond. My face was probably as red as the shrimp she was drawing out of the hot water.

A moment later Stephanie put two heaping plates on the table and sat down. "Are you going to eat?" She poured pinot gris into two glasses.

"No wine for me, thanks," I said.

Without a beat she emptied the wine from my glass into hers.

This was going to be some dinner.

I took my first bite. Divine. Something she'd done to the grits.

"I'm working on another case," I said. "A young man was murdered—or might have been murdered. He was very wealthy. A tech mogul."

"What was his name?"

"Scott Novak."

Stephanie raised an eyebrow. "Jess knew that guy — like in the Biblical sense knew him."

"Who is Jess?"

"One of my sorority sisters. I didn't know her in high school, but she's from Raleigh, too. Anyway, she partied at Robot Boy's house the summer after high school. Lots of drugs. She was kind of into him."

"'Robot Boy?'"

"Yeah, that's what she called him. I don't think she's seen him in quite a while. He got himself a steady girlfriend and moved out of the party house. Moved somewhere in the country, she said."

"I met the girlfriend," I said. "Her name is Esther. Impressive woman."

"You mean, 'not a redneck ECU girl.'"

"I didn't mean that. You're looking at one, remember."

Stephanie continued. "I guess after he met 'Esther' that was the end of the party. Sounds like Novak was quite the playboy."

"Is Jess around? I might like to speak with her."

"Are you going to play detective with my sisters?"

Stephanie took a huge gulp of wine. She ate like a lot of the chefs I knew, as if she didn't really savor the meals she had so expertly thrown together.

"Why don't you work in a restaurant, Stephanie? You're super comfortable in a kitchen."

"No, thanks. I'm not interested in being one of the help."

"It's honest work. And you might learn something."

"Are you dissin' on my dinner?"

"It's delicious. You've got a talent. What if you became a real chef, like Paige Kirkland?"

"Mom, everyone I know in the restaurant business is a drug addict."

"Just how many drug addicts do you know?"

She sighed. "When did you say you were planning on leaving?"

"Right after I talk to your friend Jess."

She took a final swig of her wine, picked up her phone, and texted. The next second, an in-person voice said, "I'm right here, Steph."

We looked up and saw a short blond in the entryway. I had to look twice because Jess looked a lot like Esther. It seemed Scott had a type.

Steph let out a shriek. "Jess, you freaked me out! Sit yo' fanny down and get you some shrimp-n-grits."

To me she said, "Jess is always eating, but she's always working out, too. It's disgusting."

Jess looked fit, but not anorexic.

Stephanie added, "She's on the gymnastics team."

"It's just a club sport here, but she's right," Jess said.

I introduced myself. Jess responded pleasantly, "So nice to meet you." The girl had better manners than my own daughter.

Jess sat down at the table. "I can never resist your cooking, Stephanie."

I didn't waste time.

"Stephanie says you used to be acquainted with Scott Novak.

We don't know if foul play might be involved. I've been hired to help find out what happened."

Jess looked at Stephanie. "Do you have some water, please?"

I could tell my questioning had taken her by surprise, but I continued. "I'm curious to learn how you knew Scott. He wasn't someone a lot of people knew very well."

Jess drank some water and cleared her throat. "I had just graduated from high school. I had a bad injury from the state championships and had to give up my gymnastics scholarship to Arkansas, so I was super bummed. A friend of mine talked about this house that had nonstop parties all weekend. The place, she said, was called 'Silicon Dreams.' She said all the tech millionaires in town hung out there. Free drugs, free alcohol, and great food. I kind of got sucked in."

Sounds like a recipe for date rape, I thought. But I didn't have to say it. We were all thinking the same thing.

"Turns out it was just a place for rich nerds who had never been successful in romance. I mean, they were all super annoying. Total know-it-alls, with no ability to talk about anything other than their own work and hobbies, which no one could understand anyway. You had to be totally inebriated to sleep with any of them. Except for Scott. He was geeky but nice." She fell quiet.

"How many girls joined the parties?"

"A dozen or so, I guess. But you had to be a guest of one of the boys—men, officially, but they seemed like boys to me. They all wore Hüsker Dü and They Might Be Giants t-shirts."

"Hüsker who?" asked Steph.

"An 80's band," I said. I turned again to Jess. "Were you even of age when you started in with Scott's group?"

"I was eighteen, but it was still so wrong."

"And Esther Mills put a stop to it?"

She nodded. "I was there that night. Esther walked in and

everyone noticed her. She was gorgeous. She just looked around, saw right away what was going on, and walked out. Scott ran out to chase her down. We thought he was going to bless her out for judging his party. But he ended up leaving with her.

"I don't know what Esther said to Scott exactly, but when he came back early in the morning, he wasn't the same. That was the last party that was ever held at Silicon Dreams. I tried to talk with him after that, but he was never home, and he wouldn't answer his cell. The house went on the market a little while later. Still for sale, I think."

"What did you do?"

"I realized that none of those people I had partied with cared about me as a person. And, to be honest, I didn't really care about them either."

"But you did care. You cared about Scott."

She frowned. "I guess I did. Even though it was his house, I didn't think he was evil or anything. I think he was just searching for, like, a connection. Scott was in his head all the time. I think he thought he could liberate himself with the drugs and the women."

"I have to ask you: Did you meet anyone there who would have wanted to see him dead?"

"Besides me? Because I was really angry at first when he wouldn't return my calls. I mean, really angry. Of course, I was also coming down from the drugs and felt absolutely wretched."

"Preach," said Stephanie. I hoped Jess wouldn't sense my embarrassment.

I asked, "Who else might have had it out for him? Any of the men?"

"Well, there was one. A coder named Trey Gamble."

"I've met him," I said.

"Trey was really pissed that the parties stopped. We talked a couple times, and once he told me he wanted to kill Scott. I didn't think much of it at the time, but I've thought about it since."

"Thanks for letting me know."

Jess had finished her dinner and took off to study. I was alone once more with Stephanie.

"Look," I said, "I'm not going to bug you about Alex. But will you promise me you'll stand up for yourself? Not let him get inside your head this time?"

"I can take care of myself, Mom." She looked past me to the conversation in the commons room.

"I'm just remembering how—"

"Can you just stop? This is embarrassing."

"Is that all I am to you: 'Embarrassing?'"

I was angry, and I was done eating what Stephanie was dishing out. I pushed my plate away, took a deep breath, and then let out my fire:

"You don't have to tell me anything about your personal life, Stephanie Jane. You don't even have to like me. But I do deserve some measure of respect. Maybe I didn't ask for it enough when you were growing up. You were the center of my world, and I indulged you. Now you've turned out spoiled and just plain exasperating. What I see right now is a deeply unhappy young woman who is intolerable to be around."

She pretended I wasn't there and started cleaning up. Shaking, but trying to hold myself together, I grabbed my purse. A dozen pairs of eyes watched me as I marched across the commons room, past Pat Sajak and Vanna White and out the front door. I didn't even pause to buy a vowel.

I walked to my car slowly, allowing plenty of time for my daughter to chase me down and say something like, "Wait, Mom, don't leave like that." But she didn't. And I felt crushed the entire way back to Raleigh.

CHAPTER 17

COINCIDENCES

I returned home to a strange sight in my living room.

Ten-year-old Charlie was hopping around like a chicken with his head cut off. Actually, his head was intact, but it was outfitted with a green helmet that made me think he had begun training as a welder. In each hand he was holding a small sphere with buttons.

"What in God's name…"

"It's an Optimus Link!" he cried. "I'm killing Goons from Planet V! Die! Die! DIE!"

You never met a kid so happy to be attacked by aliens.

Darryl came down the stairs looking guilty.

"Mom called when it showed up this afternoon," he said. "Seems to be a gift from your friend Margaret?"

Suddenly it all made sense.

"It's really from Sammy Patel," I replied. "Are we okay with this?"

Darryl shrugged. "He seems to be having a good time."

"We should monitor it. How long has he been plugged in?"

"About two hours."

"That strikes me as about ninety minutes too long."

Darryl said, "Charlie, five more minutes, okay?"

"Yes, sir."

I looked at the system box plugged into the wall. It didn't look much more sophisticated than the Nintendo my little brother played when he was Charlie's age.

Darryl frowned. "I looked it up. That thing costs almost two thousand dollars."

"That's an absurd amount of money for a gaming system."

"Want to try it, Rett?" Charlie offered.

"I might hurt myself. Maybe some other time."

Though it was a school night, I convinced the pair to stay for dinner.

At the table, Charlie seemed agitated. It was like he was still seeing Goons coming from the wings.

"It comes with a deer hunting game, too," he announced.

I knew Darryl had been excited to take Charlie on his first deer hunt at the end of the month.

"That sounds like good practice for the real thing," I said.

"I don't want to kill a real deer," Charlie said.

Darryl cut in, "We've discussed this, son. It's a rite of passage. My dad took me hunting in the Wisconsin Northwoods when I was 10."

"I know. But I just don't want to kill a deer."

I watched Darryl try to hold his tongue, but he soon gave up. "If you're going to eat meat, you need to know where it comes from."

"I don't have to eat deer meat."

"That's not the point, son."

His voice had grown stern. I worked to change the subject by asking Lydia to talk about her day.

She asked me why I didn't take her to Alaska.

"The air is too thin there," I said. "Your head would have exploded."

"That's how it felt after Kansas City," she said. "Why did you make me drink all that a-a-alcohol!"

What ensued was an absurd debate over whether I had corrupted the most scandalous woman in the room.

Once Charlie had retired to do his homework and Lydia was in front of the TV to watch her game shows, I had some time with Darryl.

He was hot.

"What's wrong with boys these days? It's like they don't want to do anything manly at all, just sit in their living rooms playing games."

"Well, it does keep them out of trouble," I said. "That seems worth something."

"Some of them use the games for target practice. Remember Sandy Hook? That kid played games all the time. So did that nut job in Norway. Or maybe it was Finland."

I knew this wasn't the only thing bothering Darryl. We still hadn't fully talked through the photograph of me outside Ken's studio, its dark insinuation.

I said, "It's important to you that Charlie take part in this rite of passage, isn't it?"

"I don't think it's asking that much. It's not like when he was born I bought him a lifetime hunting license and a camouflage stroller like some of my coworkers did for their kids. But if he can't kill *one* animal intentionally even though he eats meat, then he's just living as a hypocrite."

But he wasn't done.

"I'm sorry, it's just messed up. I mean, there's this aversion to hunting, and then all this gender bending. I just feel like our society is turning all our boys into weaklings."

He was upset, and I was trying to understand. To a point, I did. But I had never been a fan of machismo. Maybe at one point the swagger served some sort of purpose, but it seemed silly now. It's not like we lacked for food. It's not like hand-to-hand combat was necessary for survival.

That said, I admired Darryl's quiet strength and, yes, his protective presence. He was worried that the ideals he strove toward—to be a man, whatever that meant to him—would be lost on his son. There was something in him that was rattled to the core, that made him as stressed as I'd ever seen him.

We wanted our children to be a certain way. Was it so that they'd be successful, or so that we could live out our own ideal selves through them?

I wanted to put him at ease, so I changed the subject. "I'm sorry someone sent you that photo of me at Ken's. I'm pretty sure that's the work of KayLeigh Rider. It's just another way that she's trying to get my goat, to paint me as a cheater so she can justify the rumors she's spreading about me."

"I figured it was something like that," he said.

"It's nothing more than that. Ken is a terrific artist I can learn from, but I have no interest in him romantically—at all."

"I believe you."

"Good," I said. We ended the evening with a kiss goodnight as he took Charlie to their home. But the whole evening left me feeling unsettled.

THE NEXT MORNING I was awakened by a call from Paul, who had made it into my favorite contacts.

"Lorry was arrested last night," Paul said.

"What? Why?"

"Remember those cuts and bruises on his face? Bad as they were, I think he really did make the other guy look worse. He was arrested for battery and released on $5,000 bail."

That was curious to me. "I got the impression Lorry didn't have two nickels to rub together."

Paul said, "Maybe someone loaned him the dough." I loved that Paul said "dough." He added, "Let's go to his house and see if we can talk to him."

"I'll drive this time."

On the way, I shared details of the conversation I'd with Jess Bennett.

"Sounds like someone we should keep our eye on," he said.

"And she said that Trey Gamble had threatened Scott's life. Have you heard anything from him? I thought he was going to get you something you can use?"

"Not yet. But now I have reason to call him again. If you'll dial, I'll do the talking."

A moment later we had Trey Gamble on speaker.

"Hello," answered Trey's flat voice.

"Mr. Gamble, this is Paul Maroni P.I. What's this I'm hearing that you once threatened Mr. Novak's life?"

"That's a total lie."

"Is it? Well, I haven't seen any other data telling me that someone else wanted him gone. You said you had record of that sort of thing. Where is it?"

"Still looking through old emails," Trey said.

"I'm still waiting." Paul hung up before the coder could respond.

"I think you like messing with his mind," I told Paul.

"It does float my boat a little," he said.

WHEN WE GOT to Lorry's house, his rusty pickup was missing.

I knocked. No answer.

Paul tested the door. It was unlocked.

"Let's go in," he said.

"Isn't that illegal?"

"He invited you, remember?"

"He did?"

Paul winked. "When we saw him earlier, Lorry said we could 'talk later.' Remember? Oh, I think I just heard him call us inside, so I'm going in. Whether you follow me is up to you."

I can be such a follower sometimes.

We both stepped inside. I was immediately transported into the small house my mom's mother used to keep. Like that home, this one was filled with the touches of a Southern country woman, including a million framed cross-stitches with sayings such as, "Home is Where My Heart Is" and "Kiss the Cook."

"This isn't the kind of place I would have pegged Lorry to live," I said.

"This was the house he grew up in. His parents are long dead. He was married for several years and they lived here. His wife and young daughter left after the divorce more than 10 years ago. He has no contact with either of them."

"You tracked all this information down?"

"It's what I do."

The kitchen was exceptionally tidy. I remembered Lorry telling me he had served in the Navy.

"What are we looking for?" I asked.

"Remember, we were invited in. We're just making ourselves comfortable while we wait. Why don't you go check the bathrooms, see if he's there. Announce yourself first. Take the long way, through the master bedroom. Make sure he's not unconscious somewhere."

I took "the long way." I passed a guest bath and stepped into a side bedroom that looked to be a little girl's, presumably his daughter's. It was mostly devoid of toys. I imagined a scene of

Mom hastily throwing stuffed animals into a garbage bag. The room still featured a pink comforter on a single twin bed.

I moved to the only other bedroom, the master. I saw a half roll of Rolaids and some change on the dresser. I wasn't going to go snooping in his sock drawer.

The bathroom was tidy but for a number of shaving implements on the sink.

I retraced my steps and found Paul on the far end of the den where I'd left him. The computer's screensaver had stopped.

"Did you—?" I began, but I was interrupted by Lorry bursting through the front door.

"What's going on here?" he shouted.

I practically swallowed my tongue, but Paul kept his cool. "Just looking for you, Mr. Sneed. We understand you were arrested yesterday. What for?"

"Nothin'," he said, as he quickly retreated to the kitchen.

Paul followed him. "I looked up the report." He pulled out a small notebook, "What did your friend Buster Crenshaw do to warrant you assaulting him?"

"Buster's no friend of mine," Lorry muttered, pouring himself two fingers of Canadian whiskey from one of those *big* plastic bottles.

"He was supposedly a friend," Paul said, "before you beat the snot out of him."

"We had a disagreement. He owes me some money. Things got heated."

"Did you get your money?"

"Maybe," he said. "What business is it of your'un?"

"None of my business. But I wonder if he threatened to tell the police about something that would implicate you in Mr. Novak's murder."

Lorry looked at both of us and shook his head. "I don't know nothin' about that."

"Okay," Paul said, "then maybe we need to go talk to Mr. Crenshaw. He might not be talking to the police right now about the exact reasons for the fight, but we're friendlier than the police. Catch more flies with honey than vinegar, as they say down here."

Lorry downed his drink.

"Fine. I'll tell you what that scoundrel done. He lied and said he saw a friend of mine visit Mr. Novak's house at the time he was kilt. I know he's lying, because I would of seen them myself if they was. But they wasn't. And he's threatening my friend saying he's gonna tell on her—" He stopped himself too late, the liquor already betraying the accused friend's gender.

I asked, "Was Buster here with you that night?"

"Here drinking. And three sheets to the wind. He couldn't see crap."

I looked through the kitchen window toward Scott's house. Due to the contours of the land, one could only see the roof from here. I asked how Buster could have claimed to see anything at all.

"Bathroom was out, so he walked out back to relieve his-self. You can see a little better back there, but not much. Go see for yourself. Just watch where you step."

Paul and I did so. And, yes, we watched where we stepped.

Lorry was right. No matter where one stood, they could see at most the second floor of the home.

"Who did Buster say he witnessed?" Paul asked pointedly when we'd returned to the kitchen.

Lorry shook his head. "I'm not repeating his nonsense. You can talk to him if you want, but I'm telling you, he's just a scoundrel. I don't know why I even ever bothered with him. I cheer for the Wolfpack. Should have known better than to trust a Carolina fan."

Back in my car again, I asked Paul what he had found on Lorry's computer.

"'Computer?'"

"Come on, Paul."

"Give me a second. I copied his browsing history and emailed it to myself."

"'Browsing history?' You're a techie as well as a snoop!"

"I saw it on one of those *CSI* shows once. Here."

He handed me his phone. I opened the file and called aloud what I saw: "Some Internet porn... A couple of fishing videos... A bunch of political videos, right-wing stuff... Hmmm. Nothing about 'How to Strangle Someone.' Isn't that the kind of thing that the sidekicks of detectives say?"

"You're learning."

"Just a second," I said, looking more closely at the list of URLs. "Okay, I'm looking at his YouTube history. One channel he's visited a lot is called *Zero Dark Alaska*. Hey, that's Mike Nash's channel!"

"The patriot guy you met?"

"Yep. According to this Lorry has watched several dozen of his videos."

"Any chance that those two were in touch somehow?"

"I think we need to consider the possibility. Wow. Maybe going to Alaska was a good move after all."

SPEAKING OF COINCIDENCES, a question had been nagging me for a while:

How did Esther and KayLeigh know one another?

I could ask Esther and hope she told me the truth. I could try to be a tough interviewer. But that just made me nervous.

Or, as I'd had a lesson in following people, I could put that newfound skill to the test.

I parked outside Esther's apartment complex. I decided to give it an hour.

I didn't know what she drove, so I'd have to recognize her at a glance when her car came out of the underground parking lot.

Only that's not what happened. She came out walking, wearing active wear and sneakers but with a stylish throw-over top that was a little warmer.

I got out of my car and followed on foot. This wasn't part of my surveillance training from Paul, and I felt extremely exposed. Wasn't I supposed to have a newspaper that I could duck my face behind whenever my quarry stopped and looked around? To say I felt stupid was an understatement.

After just two blocks, things got even stupider.

That is: KayLeigh appeared.

I spotted her in a parked car's driver-side mirror, walking about 20 feet behind me. I could walk faster, but I was sandwiched between both women and didn't want to get too close to Esther who was still walking in front of me.

I had no choice but to duck into the nearest building.

"Can I help you?" asked the receptionist.

I had no idea where I was.

"I'm a little lost," I said. "Which direction is the State Capitol Building?" I looked over at the front window, hoping to see KayLeigh pass by. *Please pass by...*

She did so, but now I didn't have much time, or I'd lose her.

"Okay, ma'am," the woman began, "if you go—"

"You know what?" I said, "I think I know which way to go. Thanks!"

I returned to the sidewalk, resuming my previous stalking position.

Esther was gone, but KayLeigh remained in my frontal view.

(I hated how good she looked in a skirt.) I expected her to turn the corner, but she ducked into the last building on the block. I rushed to get there, but there was nothing I could do; I had to wait until I suspected she was no longer in the building's lobby. I counted to 10 before poking my head inside.

The lobby was empty. The building was one of those co-working deals they have where companies rent rooms on the cheap. No way was I going to go searching for her. I'd been to one of those places in the past and remembered every room as having glass walls.

I walked back to my car. On the way I received a text from Paul:

—*You might want to come to Sammy's house right away...*

...He says he's got a video that shows Novak being murdered!

CHAPTER 18

DUBIOUS EVIDENCE

I rushed to Sammy's mansion. Paul met me at the front door and led me inside, waving off my questions. "All will be revealed in time," he said. The elevator took us to Sammy's theater, where the mogul himself was waiting.

"A video was sent to us today," he said. "I think you better take a look at this."

He hit a button on his smart phone. On the theater's screen, the picture started out dark and murky. It was a shaky video like something submitted to Funniest Home Videos.

But this video wasn't funny.

The video showed Scott Novak sitting in his living room, reading a book. Scott seems to hear a noise. He lowers his book and looks up just in time to see a masked intruder entering the room. Scott stands as if to challenge him and is immediately grabbed around the throat by the intruder, who is taller and stronger, and who proceeds to choke him.

"Oh, my!" I gasped.

My heart thumped faster as I watched the intruder continue to choke Scott until the computer genius's legs collapsed. He landed back in the chair, clearly unconscious, likely dead. Then the intruder, winded, takes off his mask to give himself some air. Here the video freezes. The face is unmistakable.

It is the face of Samarth Patel.

"What the...!?" I screamed. Here it was, undeniable proof of who killed Scott Novak—and that very person was standing right in front of me.

"How could you?!"

"I couldn't," Sammy said. "And I didn't."

"It's fake."

It was the voice of Emerson Cramer, who entered the theater wearing his usual yellow t-shirt and faded blue jeans.

"But...?" I didn't know what to say. I felt the need to take cover somehow. "I just watched—"

"You just saw the latest in deep fake technology," Emerson said. "The video is staged with actors and uses sophisticated algorithms combined with video of Sammy and Scott readily found on the Web from their public interviews to create semblances of the two of them superimposed on the bodies of no-name actors."

"Why would someone do this?"

Sammy said, "Because they can. Whoever made this charade would like nothing better than to see me arrested for the murder."

I said, "It must be terrifying to see something like that."

"If you saw the stuff that's online, this is nothing." He looked at Emerson. "Do I have your word that you had nothing to do with this, Emerson?"

"I swear."

"Then I think I have an idea who did: The Hubers."

Emerson nodded. "Could be."

Paul addressed my confused look. "He means Gustaf and Daniella Huber of Yellow Goose, the company suing RidgeLine. I've been looking for an excuse to question them."

"I don't think it would hurt," Sammy said.

"We'll pay a surprise visit tomorrow," Paul said. "Rett, can you make it?"

"Sure. But can I ask everyone a question? Whoever invented the Internet, are they having second thoughts by now? Because I sure am."

Sammy thanked everyone for coming and disappeared through a door in the back of the room.

As the rest of us left the meeting through the main door I turned to Emerson and asked, "How did you know that the video was fake? I mean, it looked real to me."

"Oh, the lighting is off. You can just tell."

Driving home, I thought about the deep-fake tape. It was a red herring, and everyone knew it. Then why did Sammy insist on everyone dropping everything to come and watch it in person? Did he want to create the impression that he was being targeted, even framed?

What if Sammy had commissioned that tape? But, if so, it didn't make sense to investigate its origins. And that's exactly what we planned to do in the morning.

DURING THE MEETING with Sammy my phone had received a text message. I waited until I was home to read it:

—*I just heard what you've been SAYING about me!!! How dare you SABOTAGE my business and POISON my clients against me!!!*

This was no deep fake. This was all too real. And there was only one person this message could be from.

It had been nearly a week since I'd met with Katherine Stiles and given to her animal shelter cause. Now Kayleigh was barking like a spoiled pedigree poodle whose favorite chew toy had been stolen.

I considered what my response to KayLeigh would be. I could ignore the message. I could feign ignorance of what she was talking about. Or I could apologize profusely. But all three of these approaches seemed cowardly.

I typed:

—*I take your accusation very seriously, KayLeigh, as SLANDER is a very serious offense. Don't you agree? Or is the lying you've been doing at my expense been acceptable in your eyes? Perhaps agents of glass houses shouldn't throw stones.*

I could have added, but didn't: *And why did you have one of your minions take my picture in front of Ken Grimes's studio?* Unfortunately, I had no proof she was behind that one.

The three rippling dots showed up. It took her a while to get it out, but she was to the point:

—*I have never LIED about you!!! You ruined your marriage AND alienated your daughter!!!! Those things are true!!!*

She was leaving out the parts about me being a drunk and an embezzler. But I figured I'd gotten the closest thing to an admission of guilt I would ever receive.

The question was where to go from here.

I typed:

—*I aim to share MY side of the story wherever I go and with whomever I choose. That is my prerogative. If you want to try to end this feud, meet me so we can discuss this like adults, instead of like 8th-grade girls on Snapchat.*

(I didn't know if Snapchat was where middle-schoolers blessed one another out, but it sounded good.)

The dots rippled:

—*Fine. Where and when?*

—*Tonight.* I didn't want her to have second thoughts. And I didn't want to lie awake in bed worrying about the meeting. I continued:

—*8 p.m. at Whiskey Kitchen. I'll have a table in the back. It's a loud enough place that no one will be bothered if you decide to start using a lot of ALL CAPS and unnecessary exclamation points!!!!*

Silence. I know I shouldn't have made a dig about her childish use of punctuation, but I just couldn't help myself. She deserved it.

At last the dots reappeared, with a brief note:

—*Fine. See you THERE!!!!!!!*

THE DOWNTOWN RESTAURANT opened to a huge patio that formed the corner of Martin and McDowell. Rather than a small, dark, and cozy spot like Foundation, Whiskey Kitchen was roomy and bright. It wouldn't intimidate KayLeigh for a second. But it did have a bit of an Old West saloon feel which felt suited for the occasion.

KayLeigh showed up right on time. She wore sunglasses, black boots and belt, red pants, and a red tank top. She looked like something of a superhero, one of the sexy ones that Marvel Comics would give some kooky power, like telepathy to summon dive-bombing fly squirrels.

She stopped a few feet from my table holding on to her Kate Spade purse as if she'd fall to her death if she let go.

"Please, sit down," I said.

She plopped down in the chair across from me. This wasn't the closest proximity we'd ever enjoyed, but it was certainly the most public. Woman to woman, face to face. She wasn't looking like a superhero anymore.

She looked a little scared.

"Do you want to order something to drink?" I asked.

"No, thank you," she said, followed by the brief flash of a fake smile.

"How's Allan?" I asked.

"He's fine." KayLeigh was looking for a way to start a conversation she didn't want to have—and so was I.

"I might as well jump in," I said. "I need you to know that I don't have hate in my heart for you, KayLeigh. Allan Swinson is an adult. He can show discipline when he wants, but he chose to betray me and our marriage. If it wasn't going to be with you, it was going to be with someone else."

Did KayLeigh hear the subtext—that she wasn't Allan's soulmate so much as a crime of opportunity?

I continued. "I'll have to deal with Allan for the sake of Stephanie—and I can handle him. You see, I understand Allan. And, to some extent, I still care about him, but I'm not grieving my marriage anymore. I'm ready to put all that behind me. But you, KayLeigh Rider, are making it really difficult."

"Me? I'm making things difficult? How about telling Katherine Stiles that I'm a gold digger who ruined your perfect marriage—when you and I both know that you and Allan had irreconcilable differences, that you drank too much, that you neglected your daughter—"

"How dare you—?!"

"Now who's using too many exclamation points? Get off your high horse, Harriet!"

"My *what*?!" I guess this really was a saloon.

She didn't pause. "You think you're so much better than everyone, just because you're a lot older and have had time to make more friends in town."

Now she was calling me old. I tried to assume the gaze of one of those Disney villainesses cornering the cartoon's sweet young thing.

"Look," I said, "I know I made mistakes in my marriage. And there were many ways Allan and I weren't well matched from the start. But you know what? If Allan had wanted to work on our problems, I would have been delighted to do so. I waited a long time for him to share what was in his heart. Perhaps you've already figured out that Allan is a classic avoider. Now you get to deal with Allan's baggage, because I can guarantee you that *he* won't."

"I don't know what you're talking about." I had a feeling she'd already seen Allan's way of brushing off the important conversations. And it didn't amuse her. In fact, I suspected it had begun to worry her.

"It's okay," I said. "I'm not here to dispense marital advice, and you're not here to receive it. What we need to do is come to an understanding before our feud starts to make news on its own."

"I can agree to that," she said.

"So here is the deal I'm putting on the table. I won't approach any more of your clients or potential clients with my side of the story. And, if I do have to interact with one of your clients, I'll steer clear of the subject of Allan. That I promise. And I, Rett Swinson, keep my promises."

She narrowed her eyes. "Go on."

"I need two things from you. First, never slander me again. You helped Allan end my marriage, KayLeigh, but you will not tarnish my reputation in the process of trying to rehabilitate yours."

"I never did in the first place—but okay. What's the second thing?"

I settled back in my chair. "Second, I need to know how you know Esther Mills. And what you two do together on Tuesdays."

She looked surprised. "Why do you want to know that?"

"Esther is a suspect in the death of—"

"—Scott Novak. Yeah, everybody knows about that. Esther said someone tried to blackmail her about it."

"Blackmail?" It clicked. Lorry's friend, Buster, must have

thought he'd seen Esther at the time of the murder. "Did Esther pay off the blackmailer?" I asked.

"Of course not," said KayLeigh.

"I know who's doing that—and I also know who sent my boyfriend a photo of me suggesting that I'm cheating on him."

"Your boyfriend? What are you talking about?"

"Never mind." There was no sense in pushing it. Besides, she actually acted surprised. Maybe she wasn't involved. But, if KayLeigh hadn't sent Darryl that pic, who had?

I brought the conversation back to Esther.

"I'm investigating the Novak case. Esther keeps popping up. What can you tell me about her?"

KayLeigh leaned back in her chair.

"She's terrific. I met her about a year ago. She was helping Scott find a seller's agent for his mansion and a buyer's agent for a new home. But before I could even sign a buyer's agent agreement he'd already bought that icky zoo house in the country. Esther didn't like it, but she loved Scott, so she tolerated it."

"You became good friends?" I asked.

She shrugged. "Good enough friends. I didn't see her much. She was kind of into everything Scott. Then when he died, I reached out. She was devastated, but also angry at him. They had broken up by then, but she kind of took his suicide personally, you might say."

"It's not necessarily a suicide. But go on."

KayLeigh continued. "I invited her to a ... well, it's an investment group. It's very exclusive. There's a waiting list of women wanting to get in."

"Women?"

"It's women only. It's a V.C. fund. Do you know what that is?" (i.e. "...*you old person who is certainly very stupid.*")

"As a matter of fact, I do know." Venture Capital was big money, often eight or nine figures. Taking the biggest risk, V.C.

investors often got the biggest payout—but more often lost their shirts. Only about 1 company in 10 ever became viable. But sometimes the profit was so large it more than made up for the other bad bets.

She smiled. "Then you know the stakes. You should come sometime. After all, you've got money." Translation: *You stole money from Allan that should have been mine.*

"But that waiting list..."

"Oh, I can get around that. In fact, we have a special meeting called for tomorrow at 10 a.m."

"Are you asking me to be your guest?"

"Sure! Won't that be fun?" She looked around the room quickly, as if trying to make sure she wasn't being seen at the cafeteria with the fat girl. "Are we done now? Great. See you tomorrow. I'll text you details in advance." And she marched out of there like someone carrying a load of kryptonite in her purse.

I had made my point—and gotten the information that I wanted.

So why did I feel like KayLeigh had won this bar fight?

CHAPTER 19

YELLOW GOOSE

The next morning, Paul and I drove together to the offices of Yellow Goose, the software company owned by Gustaf and Daniella Huber, plaintiffs to the lawsuit that had been dogging Scott Novak's company—and now its parent company, RidgeLine.

The office park had seen better days. Parked in front of Yellow Goose were four cars.

One of them stood out: A light blue Audi. Paul and I both saw it at the same time and exchanged a look. This could be the car Lorry said he saw leaving Scott's property before we found his bedroom ransacked.

"Even if the Hubers are here, we probably won't be allowed inside," muttered Paul, as he rang the office doorbell. "But you can't kick a mule if you keep both feet on the ground."

"Did you just make that up?" I asked. "Because it sounds like you just made that up."

"'Ask me no questions...'"

A man's German accent came over the intercom. "*Ja?*"

Paul shouted, "Paul Maroni and Harriet Swinson. We're here on behalf of our client, Samarth Patel of RidgeLine Computing."

"*Ach!*" the voice growled. "Did you come to settle that lawsuit?"

"Probably not," said Paul.

The sound on the intercom went dead. I got myself prepared to be kicked off the premises. Paul just looked amused.

Then a buzzing sound. I grabbed the door before it locked again.

"Well, well, well," said Paul. "Our lucky day."

The space was basic. There was no lobby, just a single large room where a young man and woman wearing headphones typed at their terminals. Three small offices lined the back.

A tall man, balding and wearing a thick mustache, came out of the middle office to greet us. "If you're here to steal more of our intellectual property, you won't get far. I've got cameras everywhere. We can talk in my office. Daniella will join us."

A moment later we stood with the middle-aged couple in one of the small offices. Their overall bearing suggested they had tried many times to jump on the success train and each time barely missed.

I was worried. I had always found geese to be mean.

Gustaf said, "So tell us why you're here, Mr. Maroni? Did you come to harass us?"

"You heard about Scott Novak, I take it."

"Couldn't have happened to a nicer *thief!*"

"Now, Gus," said Daniella, in a German accent of her own, "be kind of the dead."

But her husband only became more vehement. "He went to his grave knowing what he did, Daniella!"

"What did he do?" I asked. "I'm new to the company. I don't know any of the details."

Gustaf scowled. "Novak poached several of our programmers, milked from them our secret sauce."

"The programmers' noncompete agreements had expired," Paul said.

"*Ja,* but not their nondisclosure agreements. How else did Novak come up with the algorithms we were using? Algorithms are gold."

"Isn't it possible that Scott came up with those independently?"

"It was a little too coincidental for our taste," Daniella said.

"Why did the programmers leave in the first place?" I asked.

"Novak lured them with his debauched parties. Disgusting!" Gustaf spat.

I looked at Paul. "Should we ask him about the—"

"—the video? Sure!" Paul activated his phone, pushed some buttons. "I just emailed you two something interesting. Care to take a look?"

Both went to their screens and pushed play on the deep-fake video. I watched Daniella, and Paul kept an eye on Gustaf.

"Hooray!" said Gustaf once the video was finished. "Now you've got your killer! Sammy Patel will live behind bars where he belongs!"

"You know it's fake," said Paul.

"Of course. It's obvious. What's your point?"

"I just wondered if maybe you produced the video as a sort of prank—or threat."

"Daniella's coders would do a much better job than that. Look, Maroni, I'm glad you came by, because we need you take a message back to Samarth. Tell him if he talks to our lawyers, we'll go easy on him. I think we all want this to be over."

"In other words, you're running out of money for the lawyers?"

Gustaf turned red. "I assure you that our investors are prepared to go all the way."

"I'll let him know," said Paul, "but we're really here to find out who might know something about Scott's death. Did you see him the day he died?"

"No. We were right here. I've got camera footage to prove it."

And deep-fake technology that could fool us?

Paul continued, "What about *after* Novak died?"

"What do you mean?"

"Scott's house was ransacked a few days ago. Someone was looking for something. Tell me you don't drive a light blue Audi that was spotted driving from the scene."

Gustaf shouted, "We do not break the law! We are not cheaters and liars! Get out, Maroni! Get out!"

Daniella said, "Gus, *bitte...*"

But Gus was screaming. "I can't bear the indignity, Daniella! I can't bear it!"

"WHAT A HOTHEAD!" I said, after the door practically slapped us on our rears. I didn't even care if the Hubers heard me through their intercom system.

"We definitely hit a nerve in there," Paul said. "I'm certain it was their Audi that Lorry saw. What were they looking for?"

"What if they were there to find something outside the home? We haven't really looked to the animals for clues to this case."

Paul looked confused. "If they wanted to see a real zoo, they could go to Asheboro and get some cotton candy, too. What's to see?"

But I had a thought. As Paul drove, I went online and googled: *old man snake nc small zoo*. Several headlines came up, all speaking to the controversial saga over the menagerie's original owner, Russell O'Leary, a.k.a. Old Man Snake.

Paul hummed a little tune as I sat in silence reading through the articles. It turns out O'Leary had several run-ins with various state and county agencies due to animals escaping. Near the end of his life, there were several animal rights groups protesting his zoo and claiming the animals were suffering from neglect.

Mentioned within the list of animals that were allegedly being starved: Beth the Giraffe, an albino animal who ended up surviving but finally passed away of old age not long after Scott moved in.

I looked on my phone and found again the photo of the password on Scott's desk that had unlocked the Amulet: Fe@BEth_gira.

I shared my finding with Paul.

"Scott created a password from his pet giraffe's name. Fascinating."

"You don't have to be so sarcastic about it."

"I'm sorry. I come from a long line of smart alecks. I used to be taller—until I got pounded down on the playground."

"I'm not surprised."

That reminded me of something else. The day I'd seen the books on evolution in Scott's apartment, I'd done a little reading on the subject—just enough to remember how terrible I'd been at biology in school. In fact, my high school biology teacher had been a Creationist; she always skipped the chapter on evolution. Because evolution equated to forbidden fruit, I suspected it was the most-read chapter in the textbook.

Either from my reading the other night or from way back in biology class, I remembered something about giraffes. I googled *evolution and giraffes* and came across the reference: At least one early evolutionary theorist proposed that giraffe necks got longer from one generation to the next simply because each giraffe stretched its neck a little more than its parent to reach the leaves on a tree.

That scientist's name was Jean-Baptiste Lamarck, and what I had read in my high school textbook stated adamantly that Lamarck was wrong: Giraffe necks did not get long in this way, any more than the child of a right-handed blacksmith would be born with one arm stronger than the other.

I wasn't sure whether any of this business about giraffes and Lamarck was important at all. Maybe Paul was right to mock me.

I called Virtual Scott and asked him if there was some significance that Scott attached to Lamarck and giraffes—specifically, his albino giraffe named Beth.

Virtual Scott corrected me. "Beth was leucitic — she lacked melatonin for many but not all of her tissues. Would you like to hear a poem about her?"

"Go right ahead."

"Okay. I give you, 'A Lamarckian Limerick':

> Standing hungry beneath a tall tree,
> The giraffe wished her neck was lengthy:
> "Instead of kvetching
> I'll get on with stretching—
> So my kids will be taller than me!"

"Clever," I said.

"Thank you."

"Now, is there any particular reason that Scott—you, that is —may have directed attention to Beth in that password written on your desk?"

He didn't answer. In the background played a cacophony of jungle animals: lions roaring, baboons screaming.

"Scott? Are you there?"

"Sorry," he said. "I sense something is wrong. I think someone may be trying to ... hack me? Is this what hacking 'looks' like to an artificial intelligence?"

I exchanged alarmed looks with Paul.

Could this be a memory of an attacker?

"Who is trying to hack you, Scott? Can you see them?"

"I can't 'see' them…" A beat. "Okay. I think they are gone. I feel I should share with you another poem."

"Go ahead," I said.

Scott Bot recited:

> *"In a historic and not-so-distant land,*
> *The Big Cat encircles his band.*
> *Dragon sparkles with rules.*
> *Lion roars at the fool.*
> *And the Child finds the key in his hand."*

I had him repeat the limerick twice more until I was able to remember it by heart.

"What does it mean, Scott?"

"I'm actually not sure. But the poem seems to bear a resemblance to a parable in *Thus Spoke Zarathustra*, in which a Lion overthrows a Dragon that represents handed-down rules. Then the Child, who can create his own values from scratch, takes over the kingdom from the Lion."

"Great," I said. "Another esoteric riddle from that very odd book. I don't even know where to begin."

"I have to go now," said Scott.

"What—?"

"I'm sorry. Someone's knocking at the door. Someone—*Who are you?! STOP!*"

Suddenly the call dropped. I tried calling him back as well as texting, with no luck each time.

I turned to Paul.

"This is crazy. What just happened?"

"Maybe it's just a glitch with the program. I'll let Sammy

know when I see him later today."

But the rest of our drive was spent in tense silence.

DROPPED OFF AT MY CAR, I received a text.

—Do you still need me to get you into our investment club meeting today?

I repressed my reflex pride and responded:

—Yes, please.

KayLeigh texted the address. The meeting would be held at the same co-working space I'd followed her and Esther to a couple days earlier.

The fourth-floor room was guarded by a woman who was checking ID. I tested whether KayLeigh had put me on the guest list. "Is there a Harriet or a Rett on there?"

"Yes. I see here you're a guest of Mrs. Swinson," she said. I actually hadn't expected to hear my ex-husband's name attached to KayLeigh, who went by her maiden name on all her advertising. Another subtle dig at me.

At least 20 other women were in attendance, milling about and talking. It was a mixed age group. A few looked to be professional women, while others were the unemployed wives of doctors and attorneys I recognized from various galas and investor gatherings over the years.

I saw KayLeigh chatting with someone near the front and waited for her to become available. I was still waiting when Esther walked in.

She kept her sunglasses on and didn't look at anyone else. She hadn't seen me. Without talking to a soul, she took a seat in the middle of the back row.

The meeting was about to start. As the women found their seats, KayLeigh waved at me to come toward the front. No doubt someone in the crowd was already texting to their network how Rett and KayLeigh had become "frenemies."

"I want you to meet a friend of mine," said KayLeigh. She presented me to a stern but attractive woman of around 60, well accessorized with lots of gold and wearing an ivory-colored jacket, blouse, and skirt. "G.T., this is Harriet, who I told you about. She used to be in business with Allan. Harriet, this is G. T."

"My given name is Gertrude, but I've chosen to go by G.T.," she said as she shook my hand.

"And I go by Rett," I said.

"So nice to meet you, Rett," said G.T. "I hope you'll contribute to our fund *soon*. We're going to make a big play this month. You'll learn all about it."

KayLeigh led us to seats she'd saved in the front row. Along the way I cast a glance toward Esther, who was looking down, but I'd be shocked if she hadn't seen me by now.

"Did you tell Esther I was coming?" I whispered to KayLeigh.

"Of course not," she said.

Of course, she had.

G.T. welcomed everyone and began her presentation:

"For those of you here for the first time, my name is G.T. Lamb, and I represent a unique venture capital opportunity. What is venture capital? It's the most risk-taking, the most *aggressive* money. And guess what? It's usually *male* money. That is to say, it's a little reckless. It's money that sees big boobs and turns its brain off. But, at the same time, it's the kind of investment that creates billionaires, not just millionaires. It's money that is *unafraid*.

"Before I give an update about the first play we're going to make, for the sake of those who are first-time here I want to share a little bit about what started me down the VC path.

"About 20 years ago, I was like a lot of you. A homemaker.

Whoever decides these things to make us feel better about the fact that women are not in the fray, that women are not in the inner circle, that we are not actually *making* houses or building wealth—please, spare us women the condescension. Do not patronize us." There was a spattering of applause that grew boisterous as most everyone joined in.

I clapped to be nice. It's what we women did. Perhaps G.T. counted on that, too.

She continued. "I decided after 15 years of marriage that I was quite fatigued from making my lovely husband successful and that I wanted to make myself successful, too. I started a flooring business. I started small, but I had the patience to make it work.

"But we weren't growing very fast. So, I asked my life coach, a man, what was wrong? Why was I just puttering along? And he said, 'Gertie, what do you expect? You risk so little. Do you expect people to shower you with riches just because you're *nice*? You're never going to be successful if you're afraid your success will hurt people's feelings.'

"And my coach was right. 'Nice' doesn't get it. I decided if being nice meant staying small, I was going to have to be bold. I wanted 50 percent growth. Do you know that when I decided that, I felt guilty? I felt greedy. And I didn't like that feeling. But I was more angry that society had made me into someone who would feel guilty just for chasing the American Dream.

"Fifty-percent growth. That's what I saw my company do each of the next five years. That's really good. But I looked around. And I saw others getting 10 times richer. And they weren't working nearly as hard as I was. They were investing in tech. They were *men* investing in tech. That's when I sold my company and became a full-time angel investor. That's when I started *doubling* every year.

"But it was tedious. An investment of a million here, a

quarter million there. It was big money, but it wasn't the biggest money. I was still on the outskirts." She looked down at her skirt in a surprised way and lifted it a tad. There was a titter of play-along laughter at this joke of mine she'd magically stolen.

"Ladies, what I'm doing isn't anything that a thousand men out there aren't already doing. We won't ever achieve equality by living in the margins. We can be just as bold, just as successful as the men. And we don't hate men. We love men—a lot of them, anyway. We just need to stop thinking that being successful is going to cause them to dislike us."

She talked about the company that she wanted to invest in, something having to do with algorithms and e-commerce. I wasn't here to invest, so I didn't listen very closely. She wanted the group to invest $10 million to obtain a one-percent stake. "Those shares will be worth 20 times that in three years," she said. "That's when we'll get out, when second round funding comes in, long before the IPO and all that craziness.

"Are you going to enter the arena with me? We're going to do the deal next week. I need the funds by this Friday. We have already raised 10 mil in this group—give yourselves a hand. (*Boisterous applause.*) I'm matching your 10 million with my own 10 million. Twenty is quite good, but 25 would make us key play-ers. Twenty-five will put us on equal footing with the men in the room."

I listened as other women spoke in support of the fund, while still others asked hard questions. "There are no guaran-tees," said G.T. at some point. "Is this a sure thing? Hell no! There is considerable risk. If it was a sure thing, everyone would be bringing their money and fighting to get at the table. But I'm betting big. That's why I'm prepared to bring another five million of my own dollars if I *need* to. We don't need you to invest any more than you have already. It's just if you want to. If you're feeling truly bold—and not so *nice*."

WHEN THE MEETING WAS OVER, I stood up and looked around.

Esther was gone.

I would have liked to catch up to her, but I had to say nice things to KayLeigh first.

In the end, I could only shrug at the investor meeting. I'd wondered if there might be some secret here that Esther was hiding. But it's no crime to seek a place to invest one's money.

Unless it was more than money that she was planning to invest.

What if she was bringing some intellectual property to the deal? What if it was some secret research that Scott had developed—like Big Cat?

CHAPTER 20

BIRDS OF A FEATHER

Back at home, I found myself frustrated. I wasn't any closer to solving the case of Scott Novak.

Sammy seemed more concerned about digging up Scott's AI research than anything else.

Emerson acted anxious to find out more about the would-be killer, but at the same time seemed to have forgotten to grieve for his friend.

I needed to go deeper.

I pulled out my smartphone. Wasn't this thing handy? My first instinct when I needed something was to reach for it. When I was bored. When I was anxious. When I thought I might need to talk with someone or just needed to pass the time. A crossword, or a sports score. To look up a word. It was the go-to, the be-all. The end-all.

I looked again at Scott's letters. One name popped out: "Rooney," someone in Berkeley who reached out to Scott when he was trying to locate Adam after their father died. Might this Rooney be able to shed some more light on the man who was due to inherit Scott Novak's immense fortune?

I googled around and found an email for University of California, Berkeley, Associate Professor of Philosophy Angus Rooney. I sent him an email that included my phone number and asked if he knew Scott or Adam Novak. Almost immediately I received a call. He was very upset to learn about Scott's death. "I knew both brothers at a very young age," he said. "My God, I babysat for them."

"You're the first person I've talked to who knew them when they were young."

"I met their father when I was a doctoral student at Pitt. Joe was hired to help run the student radio station. Meanwhile, I was doing some part-time deejaying, just for fun, and we hit it off. Amanda, Joe's wife, was giving private piano lessons. After about a year or so they started asking me to babysit the boys sometimes, which was great because it gave me a cheap way to do my laundry. The boys and I would play board games and have sock wars and just goof around. The kids were fun. They liked to laugh—though for some reason I always kind of thought the joke was on me when we were together, like they are laughing at me behind my back."

"What were Scott and Adam like?"

"Joe and Amanda moved into town when the boys were little, maybe when Adam was four and Scott must have been around three. I know Adam seemed way more than a year older than Scott, because Adam was already reading and Scott was practically non-verbal, even though he should have been talking a lot more by then. These days I'd probably wonder if he was on the autism spectrum — though no one back then really thought much about that. Joe didn't want to get him tested. He just waved it off as Scott being younger, a late bloomer. It worried me at the time, but now we know Scott was just fine. I guess it was just latent genius after all. Both parents were absolutely off the charts smart."

"What happened to the family?"

"For a few years there I think everything was going okay, but I know Joe's mental health started to deteriorate. He began missing work, had an argument with the station manager and threatened him. He was fired, and then the couple divorced. We lost touch. More years passed. Eventually I was teaching at Cal, and then in the late 1990s, out of the blue, Joe gets in touch with me, says Adam is a genius, loves philosophy, and can he go to Berkeley? I'm like, well, I don't know, he'll have to apply.

"Joe says Adam's schoolwork and test scores are spotty, yada yada, but insists he's definitely a DaVinci. I say, let me meet with him. And, yes, he is an actual genius. He's read most of the philosophers. He's an autodidact — self-taught — and I'm able to pull some strings and get him in, but he only lasts a little over two years. He was just too messed up on drugs, too disturbed by his dad, and felt so much animosity to his brother and mom."

"You said he had read a lot of philosophy. What is up with his love of Nietzsche?"

I heard Rooney take a deep breath.

"Nietzsche is one of the philosophers he studied in my intro class. Nietzsche doesn't write like other philosophers. He sort of engages in rant. But he's incredibly important. He's the first atheistic philosopher of note in the West. He isn't compelled to believe in a world beyond this one and thought the only philosophy worth having was one that affirmed life in the here and now. He saw Christianity as denying this world, denying life, denying the body, and believed it was the ultimate betrayal a human being could make to life."

"In other words, 'God is dead.'"

"Yes, but Nietzsche is different from your typical materialist atheist, in that he thinks human beings can achieve something beyond themselves, what he called the Übermensch, or Overman, sometimes referred to as the Superman."

"What about this Superman?" I asked. "It seemed like both Novak brothers were pretty obsessed with the concept."

"The Superman is an ideal for Nietzsche. He's not like the comic book character, of course, but a sort of heroic figure who embraces the world and life in such a way that he surpasses humanity. Young people today throw around the word 'epic' a lot, but Nietzsche wished for people to lead truly epic lives. He didn't think that people should act depraved, like animals, nor did he think they should live according to hand-me-down moralities, which he thought were dependent on one's culture and time—not given to us by some otherworldly god."

"He really seems to hate God."

"It's not that he hates God, he just doesn't think it's possible in the modern age to believe in God. He thinks most people will come to realize that God cannot possibly exist. And more than a hundred years later he seems to be correct in that more and more people identify as non-believers. The church in continental Europe is almost entirely extinct; meanwhile, the fastest growing answer to survey questions about personal religion in America is 'None.' Nietzsche thinks the Christian religion, which started with a crucifixion, is literally a dead religion."

"Do you believe that? Because I don't."

"I've been an agnostic my whole life, so I'm not the one to ask."

"Was Nietzsche a Nazi? I've read that a lot of people think so."

"It would be hard for him to be a Nazi, because he died more than 30 years before Hitler came to power. But there was an abundance of anti-Semitism back then, too, and it's notable that Nietzsche condemned anti-Semites, even as he sometimes talked about Jews in prejudiced ways. He also was adamant that German culture was completely decadent. Nonetheless, his rhetoric was later co-opted by the Nazis in their propaganda. While he wasn't an anti-Semite, he was a snob and a chauvinist."

"A chauvinist?"

"On some level he didn't respect women. His mom and sister treated him badly, and, though he's very sweet to them and other women in his letters, he generally refers to women in his books as conniving, shallow, weak—you name it. It's hard to read."

The first atheist philosopher? "He sounds like the first *incel* philosopher," I said.

Rooney gave a gloomy chuckle. "It's possible he resented women because he saw himself unfit physically for marriage. He had a chronic condition from childhood that produced debilitating migraines. So, you're right, it's not unreasonable to believe that Nietzsche died a virgin."

"And this is someone Adam worships?"

"He wrote me a couple times early on, but I haven't stayed in touch. I'm not that into Nietzsche, and there are a lot of other alumni who correspond with me."

"Adam and Scott seemed to patch things up. Does that surprise you?"

"I think when Joe died, Adam went a little crazy. I always hoped he would get his head straight. Sounds like, despite everything, he has."

"Because of Nietzsche?"

"Just a theory, but I feel like Adam felt so helpless in his life for so long that maybe Nietzsche was inspiring in that regard. Nietzsche suffered terribly in his life, too, yet Nietzsche himself preaches—there is no better verb than that—that we embrace our lives and even work to overcome them. And he thought that greatness was available to people, though realistically he believed few could ever attain it."

I said, "Scott seemed to have been involved in research

inspired by Nietzsche. Maybe he was hoping to become great, too?"

"There is quite a lot of ego involved in all this. It's not clear to me—and that's why ultimately I'm not a huge fan of Nietzsche —what 'greatness' consists of. I mean, he thinks that compassion and mercy can only come from self-assured, secure, powerful people, because such people don't feel threatened by anyone. But not everyone can be a millionaire—in fact, most of us will not be. In other words, I can get behind some of Nietzsche's thinking, but I don't see how most of it works in a middle-class society. Again, Nietzsche was a snob. I just don't see his philosophy ultimately as ever being democratic enough to be useful to a very large number of people."

Rooney was right: Not everyone can be a millionaire, yet I was one. And how did that inform my choices, my outlook?

I thanked the professor for his time, and we hung up. My mind swirled. I felt like I'd just been through a college lecture, one I barely understood.

It was all very interesting, but I needed to get my hands on a clue that I could touch and feel.

~

I CALLED Paul and told him about my conversation with the professor. "Do you have anything you can report?"

"Just a theory. I wonder if maybe Huber tried to work a deal with Scott but Scott refused and Gustaf went into a rage and killed him. Then Huber went back a few days later to look for any evidence he might have left behind. He or maybe his wife are the only people besides Lorry and Esther that we can sort of put at the scene."

"Where do we go from here with that theory?"

"I'd like to put a tracking device on Huber's car, see if he tries to make any more trips out to Scott Novak's neck of the woods. Other than that, it's just wait and see if Herr Huber shows his hand."

I WAS FEELING secure enough in my relationship with Darryl that I thought it might be okay to pay another visit to Ken Grimes's studio, to share the landscapes I had done in Alaska and to get his feedback.

Ken loved them.

"These are extraordinary," he said.

"Are you sure?"

"I'm sure. Has no one told you how amazing you are? Why don't you schedule a show?"

I loved that he came up with the idea on his own. But coming from his mouth, it also somehow intimidated me.

"I don't know if I can do that."

"Why?"

"I might not be good enough."

"I say you're good enough."

"But I don't have enough pieces yet."

"Schedule a date and work toward it. Each day, just stand in front of the canvas whether you're inspired or not. And see what happens. Don't you find that something always happens?"

"So far it does."

"Then it will continue to happen. We're birds of a feather, you and me. We have this latent power, these amazing abilities, but we've barely scratched the surface. Here's a crazy thought: What if we combined forces and did a show together?"

"The two of us?"

"Why not?"

I shrugged. "Maybe. I'll think about it."

I did think about it, all the way home. Charlie was there, but Darryl had gone out to a retirement dinner for a colleague. It was a quiet supper without him. We let Charlie play a round of Optimus before Lydia made him go to bed.

Darryl came in around 11. He was tipsy. One of his detective buddies had driven him home.

"You're drunk, Darryl."

"Maybe I am," he said. "Maybe I AM."

"You definitely are."

"Congrad-u-lations for noticing!"

"Why are you acting like this?"

"A man can't get his drink on?"

"It's just not like you."

"Then maybe you'll like me better this way."

"Why would you say that? Is this about Ken?"

"You can't stop saying his name, can you? Or visiting his place."

Swaying in place, he took out his phone and showed me yet another photo of me stepping into Ken's studio—this one from just a few hours earlier. It had probably popped up during the dinner. Seeing it, he decided to tie one on.

Why was KayLeigh still doing this?

"He's someone I *paint* with," I said. "If you painted, I'd paint with *you*."

"But I don't paint."

"I know. And that's okay! We don't have to do the same things."

"But we do-do-do the same thing. We both catch *crin-i-mals!*"

"Actually, you catch *crin-i-mals*—plural. I've only caught one *crin-i-mal*—singular."

"I don't do grammar when I've been drinking."

"It doesn't matter, because we're not going to run out of criminals. Or don't you agree?"

"Who cares what I think? My son wants to shoot imaginary deer. Maybe I'm better off being imaginary, too! Maybe I'll be like Gene Wilder in that movie and just crawl into a whiskey bottle and disappear. Who cares?"

"I care."

"Well, maybe you could start acting like it." He stumbled up the stairs and disappeared into our bedroom.

I sat on the sofa, partially in shock, partially sick to my stomach. I'd done this. From start to finish, I'd made my own bed—which tonight was going to be a couch.

But I also resented the stunt Darryl had just pulled. Could I not have a boyfriend *and* develop my art? Could I not be mentored by someone willing to take a chance on an old beginner?

I picked up my paper copy of *Zarathustra* and turned to the middle of it. I'd been trying to read it off and on. Here at last was a passage that spoke to me, from a section called, "Before Sunrise" in which Nietzsche's hermit hero had something normal to say for a change:

> And all that traveling and mountain climbing were
> mere necessities, not wants — the only thing my
> will desires is to blast off and fly into you!

All my will wanted right now was to get close to my man. But Darryl, up in our bedroom, seemed a million miles away.

CHAPTER 21

HIDDEN WILLS

Darryl was up and out of the house before I awoke. I'd slept fitfully and went about my day with a knot in my stomach.

Ever since I'd gotten back from Alaska, Emerson had been texting me, begging me to meet somewhere secret. I had ignored him, because he was never very forthcoming when we met. It was all about what he could learn from me—and not the other way around.

Finally, I couldn't avoid him. I had left a meeting with Paul (a quite useless meeting, just going over the same evidence) and had turned out of the RidgeLine campus when a car cut me off, forcing me onto the road's shoulder.

"What the fudgesicle!" I shouted (more or less). Emerson Cramer got out of the other sedan. He made a quick show of looking at my vehicle to make sure there wasn't any damage.

I rolled down my window.

"You did that on purpose!"

"Please calm down. I need to talk to you." He looked at my chest. I turned red.

"What are you looking at?"

"Just making sure you aren't wearing an Amulet."

"I'm not. Now could you please stop staring at me there?"

He looked around him, then did something else strange: He started walking around my car and bending down to feel underneath.

I got out of the car. "What are you doing?"

When he stood up again, he was holding up some sort of device.

"Your movements are being tracked." He reached across the hood of the car and handed me a piece of round metal.

"Are you serious?" My mind was racing. At least this tracker explained how someone could know when I was visiting Ken Grimes's studio. "Why—?"

"It's how Sammy and Paul operate. Look, I really don't want Sammy to know we're talking, and we don't have a lot of time. Were you able to speak with Adam? What did he say to you?"

"I wasn't able to meet with him. He was out foraging or something. And why don't you answer some questions for a change? Where were *you* when Scott was killed?"

His face reddened. "I was with someone who can vouch for me, but I'm not going to embarrass them unnecessarily. You're supposed to be finding out who might have wanted Scott dead."

He was trying to turn the tables. But it was a strange way to act. If you're guilty, why would you promote an investigation so hard?

"Emerson, if you don't tell me what you know, I can't help solve this murder."

He scratched his head, closed his eyes. "Okay," he said. "Scott said he was working on something outside the lines of law and ethics. He'd been reading Nietzsche and began thinking a lot of those lines were arbitrary. But he said he didn't want to make me or anyone else culpable, and that's why he refused to get more specific about his research."

"Look," I said, "you knew Scott better than anyone. If he was murdered, who do you think killed him?"

"I don't know!" he screamed above the traffic. "But we've got to find out. *You've* got to find out. And you've especially got to see if Sammy was involved. Just hurry up about it, okay? Time is running out."

Before I could argue, a cop parked behind us. After confirming there was no damage and no one was hurt, he told us to get a move on because we were slowing down traffic.

Once he had left, Emerson assured me he'd be in touch.

"Fine," I told him, "but don't try to run over me next time, okay?"

WHEN I GOT HOME, I reached for my cell phone in order to call Paul about my conversation with Emerson—but then I paused.

Emerson had acted as if he was being spied on by Sammy.

What if there was something to it? Paul had discussed putting a tracker on Gustaf's car. Next thing I knew, Emerson found a tracker on my car.

There was no law that said I had to call Paul. Not yet anyway.

I needed a breakthrough. I needed to act like that old computer advertisement and "Think Different."

I took a drive into the country in order to think. Almost without trying I found myself at Scott's country house. I gave myself a walking tour of the zoo. Lorry wasn't there; neither was Sheila.

If only these creatures could talk.

I thought about it:

Scott comes back from Kansas City. He has a new will in his possession. He doesn't share it with his attorney. It has to be somewhere. Where?

I wanted back inside that farmhouse.

I called Esther. She didn't pick up, so I texted her:

—*I think you still have a key to Scott's house. I have a hunch about something. Can you come let me in?*

There was a long pause. Eventually she wrote back:

—*What were you doing at the investor party? Have you been following me?*

Busted.

I wrote:

—*Sort of. I was just suspicious because I'd seen you talking with my ex's new wife, KayLeigh Rider. Please don't take it personally. It's hard for me to be neutral where she is concerned.*

A moment passed. Then:

—*Okay. I'll come. Give me an hour.*

I had some time to kill. I walked over to Lorry's house and knocked. When he came to the door it was clear I had roused him from a snooze—a drunken snooze, judging by the smell of him.

I told him I was waiting for Esther, who would be there any minute. "You've been protecting her, haven't you? You beat up your friend Buster because he threatened to tell the police about seeing Esther earlier than she originally said. Then, after he went to the police, you bribed him to keep quiet about her. Where did you get the money to do that and also bail yourself out? Did you get it from Patriot Mike? I'm asking you, Lorry Sneed, 'Did Patriot Mike hire you to kill Scott Novak?'"

Lorry looked at me. He was struggling to process what I had said.

"'Kill Scott Novak?' That's, uh, the craziest thing I think I've ever heard."

"Then please explain where you got the money. Did Esther give you the money because she really was at Scott's house twice and needed you to cover it up?"

He shook his head. "No one give me any money. Old Man Snake was always burying money around his land. When I dug my septic, I dug a little in his backyard. Hit pay dirt."

It took a moment for Lorry's bizarre confession to soak in. He added, "So now you know I took money that wasn't mine. It was less than 10 thousand dollars, but are you going to rat on me? Are you a rat, like Buster?"

"It depends. Do you believe Buster did see Esther earlier?"

"I don't know. He said he saw her climbing down the drainpipe from the top floor. But why would she do that? Besides, when he tried to blackmail her, she just told him to get lost. Didn't give him a dime. If she was guilty, she would have paid him *something*, don't you think? I think he was hallucinatin'."

I admitted I didn't have an answer either. But maybe Esther would. I let Lorry get back to his snooze, and I was waiting in front of Scott's house when Esther finally arrived. She wore blue jeans and a t-shirt. Sunglasses hid half her face. Still mourning —or still maintaining a poker face?

"I'm going to let you in," she said, "but if you don't mind, I'm not going to stick around."

Rumors of trouble showed in her expression.

"Is something wrong?" I asked.

"I can't stay here. Bad karma."

She handed me the key. I unlocked the front door with it, then walked the key back to her.

Before she could leave, I asked, "The night Scott died, did you leave by way of the bathroom window and climb down the drainpipe? You're athletic enough to do it."

She held out her hands, showed me her nails. "Are these the nails of someone who climbs drainpipes?"

Her manicure was impeccable, but I knew she could have tidied them up.

"I'm leaving now," she said. She got into her black Lexus and drove away.

I'D THINK MORE about Esther's involvement in the murder later. I entered the home with one question on my mind:

What good is a will if you don't tell anyone where you put it?

Maybe the will was found by whoever ransacked the house. If not, there was a chance it was still here.

I put myself in Scott's shoes. If I had just returned from Kansas City, what's the first thing I would do?

I went to the closet and discovered a single suitcase.

It felt empty. I checked the main front pocket and the smaller one, too. Both compartments were empty.

Ah, but there was always that back pocket that no one ever used. I unzipped it; it, too, was empty.

But something was off. The feel of the fabric inside the pocket was different from the rest of the suitcase. It wasn't the feel of fabric.

It was duct tape. I used my fingernails to find the edges of the tape and peel it off.

Bingo.

Behind the tape, handwritten on a single piece of Imperial Hotel stationery, was "The Last Will and Testament of Scott Novak."

I scanned it quickly. According to this simple document, witnessed and signed by two employees of the Green Lady Jazz Club in Kansas City, Missouri, Adam Novak was no longer the sole heir to all of Scott Novak's wealth. The new will split the vast majority of Scott's assets between just two people: Emerson Cramer and Esther Mills. From what I already knew about the sale of Scott's company and the stock payouts to all the various parties, that would equal at least a hundred million dollars in cash for each of them.

One million dollars was earmarked, "with sincere apologies" to his brother, Adam Novak.

And the country house and zoo? Those were left to neighbor Lorry Sneed.

So much additionally given to three people. So much to be lost by one in particular: Adam Novak.

Who besides me knew about this will? If Adam knew about it (though I didn't know how he could) you'd think he'd want it destroyed, for it equated to a major financial loss. Was it possible he persuaded the Hubers to find and destroy it, offering to pay them once he received his massive inheritance?

That wasn't the weirdest thing about the will. It would be in the best interest of Emerson, Esther, and even Lorry to bring this will to light. Maybe they were the ones searching the home for it. Lorry especially would have easy access to the home.

I needed to tread very carefully around these people moving forward.

I texted Esther and told her it was urgent she call me. Maybe I could trick her into revealing something about Scott's research and see how she reacted to my accusation that she was going to sell his innovation to that investment guru.

I hopped in my car. I also wanted to visit Needless Necessities, where I hadn't gone since returning from my trip.

When I had gotten about a mile from Scott's, my phone rang. I glanced and saw the call was from Darryl.

I answered immediately. "I'm so sorry," I said. "I didn't mean to hurt you last night. I love you so much."

"I'm the idiot. Never was a very good drinker. Can we forget last night?"

"Yes, let's."

"Thank you." He sounded very relieved. "That's not why I

called, actually. You know that woman you told me about who was raising money from those female investors?"

"Yeah. 'G.T. Lamb.' What about her?"

"She flew the coop with over $20 million in investor money."

"You're kidding! When?"

"Yesterday, right after that meeting you attended. I guess someone had researched her background and confronted her. She got scared and fled."

I thought about KayLeigh — no sadness there on my part if she lost a bucket of money.

But Esther? Come to think of it, she had seemed preoccupied just a moment ago at Scott's house.

"Are you sure G.T. didn't take *10* million?" I asked. "G.T. said she was matching investor dollars with her own."

"Yeah, apparently that's what she told the group of investors in Charlotte who likewise gave her 10 million dollars."

"Do the police have any leads?"

"They think she's in South America somewhere with a false identity."

In that moment I was coming upon a bridge to Harris Lake and saw a black car parked that sure looked a lot like Esther's Lexus.

"Darryl, please hang on. Something is weird."

I was halfway over the bridge when I saw Esther on the right side of the bridge sitting on the railing. She was dangerously positioned, I thought.

Darryl asked me, "What's going on, Rett? Are you okay?"

"I'm fine. Promise. But let me call you back if I need you. Love you."

～

THE SHOULDER on the bridge was narrow, but I was still able to park on it. Traffic was light out here in the country.

I got out of the car and began running toward Esther, shouting: "Esther! Are you okay? What are you doing?"

When I reached her, I could see she had been crying behind her sunglasses. But she didn't acknowledge me, even when I stopped a couple of feet from her.

"I just now heard about Gertrude running off with investor money. Did you invest a lot?"

"Yes," she said. "Pretty much all of it."

"I'm so sorry," I said.

"I'm not," she said after a moment. "I thought the whole thing was fishy from the start. I think part of me hoped she would take it from me. Because I felt guilty having it. I didn't feel I deserved it. It was never appropriate for me to run HR while dating the CEO. Trey Gamble and his buddy coders were right. I was born with a silver spoon in my mouth, and then I effectively slept my way into a C-suite job."

"You shouldn't feel that way," I said. "It sure sounded to me like Scott really respected and admired you."

She reached into the back pocket of her blue jeans. "I found this when I found Scott's body. He must have written it with his left hand after he hurt it."

She handed me the note, written in a sloppy, left-leaning scrawl:

> Dear Brother,
> I let my weakness get the best of me. I didn't
>   mean to hurt Esther. I guess I'm all too human
>   after all. That's why I'm doing this.
> I cannot resist: I'm going to step over the
>   abyss now.
> Love you, Man. Whatever happens, no regrets!

I recognized some of the wording from Nietzsche's work. "Human, all too human" was even a title of one of his books. "The abyss," too, was a common theme, a famous quote from *Zarathustra*: *"Sometimes if you stare into the abyss, the abyss will stare back into you."* Scott could be certain that Adam would recognize the reference.

"The sheriff will want to see this," I said. "Why did you take this from the scene?"

"I was so angry—too angry to show it to anybody."

"Angry?"

"Think about it. Scott says in that letter he killed himself because of our relationship. But he didn't address the suicide note to me. No. He wrote it to his *brother*, who he hadn't seen in over a decade."

"They had buried the hatchet," I said, somewhat lamely.

I quickly read the letter again, trying to put myself in Esther's position.

"I can see now how this letter must have hurt you. What if I told you, though, that you really did mean a lot to Scott? I mean, a whole heck of a lot?"

"What do you mean?"

I told her about the letters of Scott's that I'd read and the way he agonized over not being able to connect with her.

Then I told her about the will I'd just found—how Scott had made her heir to nearly half his fortune.

She took off her glasses and stared at me. "Are you kidding me?"

I shook my head. "I'm not kidding."

She looked at the water. "That asshole. That fucking asshole!"

I reached out and grabbed her arm. "Esther, don't—"

She tore her arm away. "I DON'T WANT IT! I can make my own way! I am done with Scott Novak—forever."

She descended from the railing and began marching in the direction of her car.

But she wasn't getting away from me.

"Esther Mills, stop right now!"

She stopped walking and turned.

"You're in no state to drive back alone. You're riding with me."

"I'm not leaving my car on this bridge," she said. "Besides, I'm not a danger to myself. You're not taking me to the psych ward."

"Okay, but I'm going to lead you to the next best thing. Get in your car and follow me."

ESTHER HAD SEEMED LEGITIMATELY SURPRISED, tortured even, by her inheritance. It was weird, and I was worried about her. If I had known any of her family, I would have given them a call, but I didn't. Instead, I was going to introduce her to the most generous, helpful person I knew—assuming she was working today.

I pulled into Needless Necessities where I was relieved to find Jasmine working. While Esther waited at a table, I walked Jasmine to the kitchen and explained the situation. "She needs a friend," I said. "She's confused and doesn't know which way is up."

Jazz didn't miss a beat. "I'm glad to keep an eye on her. Who knows? Maybe she can figure out how to keep us fully staffed."

"Jazz, you don't even know Esther. And yet you're willing to help her. Why?"

"It's who I am, Rett. And we've got to be who we are. 'Bee Yourself,' remember?"

I NEEDED to confront Emerson next, to get his reaction to the will. But something told me to tread carefully. Emerson had seemed really interested in finding Scott's killer, but maybe he'd actually been keen to locate Scott's *will*. I didn't want to give him what he wanted. If he was the killer, this piece of paper was the only leverage I had to get more information out of him.

That said, I was pretty sure that it was a crime to hide a valid will. I'd already told a few people about it. How much longer could I get away without sharing it? I called the best person I knew who could tell me that sort of thing: Paul Maroni.

"That's an interesting find, Ms. Swinson. You're really impressing me. The state might have to give you your license early."

My heart swelled. Why did I respond to the praise of men so readily? Was I that easy to manipulate?

I told him about Esther's angry response to being named in the will—a response partly informed by the suicide note that had made her feel so small.

I added, "I'd like to see how the others in the will react as well. Starting with Emerson."

"That guy is so mysterious. He still doesn't act like someone who lost his best friend."

"He says that someone can vouch for him, but he won't say who."

"I wish I knew more about that guy."

"What is there to know? He practically lives at the office. He literally has a *bed* in his office."

"It's the weekend. Maybe he'll go home on a Friday night."

"Are you thinking another stakeout? Because I don't have time for that."

"I'll follow him when he gets off work. Maybe I'll learn a bit more about the mysterious Emerson Cramer."

AUGUSTA TEXTED, wanting to talk. It was a nice day, so I recommended we meet in a park somewhere. "How about Pullen Park? Just park near the pool and wait for me."

We arrived at the same time, found a path, and began walking. Just two girlfriends getting their exercise and talking about high profile computer hacking.

After getting the update on her sculptor grandfather ("He's incorrigible, as always," she reported) I asked if she was still trying to meet Samarth Patel's challenge to break into the server for Project Big Cat.

She sighed. "I've been working it. It's crazy protected, so I haven't made much headway—but I noticed a couple others poking around, too. I traced one to a software company called 'Yellow Goose.' Heard of it?"

"I have!" I told her all about Gustaf and Daniella Huber.

"Right. 'Gus.' I think that's the character who has been trying to track my hacking efforts, while some other troll named 'Trey81' has been trying to bait me with a Trojan horse."

"I'll bet that's Trey Gamble," I said. "What's a trojan horse?"

"It's a way to spy so he doesn't have to do any work himself."

"Are they working together that you can tell?"

"Absolutely. And they have been pissing me off. Anyway, I got frustrated with them both, so I took a little break from Big Cat, spent some time on the RidgeLine servers, and found some other things that looked interesting."

"What did you find?"

"I'm not sure exactly, but it's financial documents with a lot of zeros."

"How do you know they're important?"

"Because someone tried real hard to hide them."

"Sammy, maybe?"

Augusta said, "I'm not sure. What should I do with them?"

Paul would want to know. *But I'm not sure I wanted him to know. Not yet, anyway.*

"Is there a way you could share the documents with me? I could show them to my accountant, and then we could decide whether they implicate anyone."

"I saved copies to my own cloud storage. I can use my phone to send you a link. I'll do that now."

While she did, I looked around. My eye caught sight of the Pullen Park Circus Animal Carousel. Raleigh's own historical treasure, it had been refurbished a few years ago and was protected from the elements inside a large room. Through its windows I could see children have a blast going in circles on their animal of choice.

Encircled...

"Augusta," I said, "I'd like to ride the carousel."

"Why?"

"Because ... I just have to see something."

We stepped inside as the current ride was winding down. Just inside the door a wooden placard of a glittered dragon demonstrated how tall a child had to be to ride. *Dragon sparkles with rules...*

After the riders stepped off, we were allowed to get on. The lion, just like Virtual Scott's limerick poem suggested, stood on the outer ring of animals and definitely "encircled his band." A coincidence? I went straight for the lion and began examining it closely.

"What are you up to?" Augusta asked.

"I'm looking for a key. The poem stated that a child would receive it."

"What poem?"

Like a child, I dropped to all fours.

"Ma'am, you're going to have to find a seat," said the young worker making his rounds outside of the ride.

I realized that Augusta and I were the only ones on the ride.

"Could you wait a moment before starting the ride?" I asked the worker. "I dropped a contact and I'm looking for it."

"Sure," he said. "Five minutes."

But a moment later as I searched the paws of the lion for anything unusual, pipe organ grinder music started (a cheerful Sousa march) and the carousel started moving in its counter-clockwise fashion.

BUZZ!

A loud sound began emanating from the motor of the carousel. At the same time, the music that had been accompanying the ride changed to a more ominous tune, the famous *Flight of the Valkyries*. It took a moment to realize the music wasn't the only thing becoming more intense.

The carousel was rapidly speeding up.

"Whoa!" Augusta shouted, as she reached and grabbed an ostrich's neck.

We went yet faster.

"I don't like this!" I cried out, as we began to hit Mach speed and the music became louder. "This is getting dangerous!" It was too fast to try to get off.

Still on all fours, I held onto a lion's leg for dear life, as we sped faster and faster—

CHAPTER 22

ROUND AND ROUND

Augusta began screaming, "Make it stop! Make it stop!"

But all the controls for the ride were in the center. The young man who had let us on the carousel could be seen trying to get on the carousel to make his way to the controls. But it was going too fast for him, too.

Augusta crawled her way to the carousel's inner edge.

"I need something kind of heavy that I can throw at the emergency-off button!" she yelled over the music.

I looked around me. All I could think to toss her was one of my tennis shoes. She threw it and hit the target, but it didn't do anything.

The worker saw what we were doing. "Take mine!" he shouted, and he managed to toss her one of his own, much heavier, shoes.

We were going faster still, but this time Augusta finally managed to time and aim the man's shoe properly at the emergency button.

The ride ground to a halt.

Woozy and rattled, Augusta and I found each other and hugged tightly.

I screamed at the young man as he ran over to see if we were hurt, "This thing was trying to kill us!"

"I've never seen it do that, ma'am," he said. "It was like it had a mind of its own. Maintenance gets a status report automatically when things like this happen. I'll bet they are on their way." After making sure an ambulance wouldn't be necessary, he proceeded to turn off the music and literally unplug the engine entirely.

Augusta finally stepped off. When, instead, I began making my way to the other side of the carousel, Augusta saw me and shouted:

"Lady, are you crazy? Get off that demon ride!"

"It's okay. I need to see something." Holding onto the various animals' poles I stumbled but stayed upright until I found my way past the lion to a certain other animal.

The giraffe.

Once again I plopped to the carousel's surface (partly because I was still swaying) and began giving the giraffe a closer look.

Augusta, remaining on firm ground, had followed my orbit. "What are you doing?"

"Looking at the metal that's holding this thing down," I said.

"Why?"

"Remember that password that got us into the Scott's Amulet? 'Gira' can mean 'turn'—like a gyroscope or a carousel. And 'Fe' means iron in chemistry, doesn't it? What we thought of as a password might really be a clue to something bigger. Aha! I think I found something!"

Beneath the giraffe, attached to the metal by a sort of magnet, was a thin plastic box that had blended in perfectly with the ornate metal.

"What is it?" asked Augusta, joining me on the ride.

I held the box in my hand and slid its lid off.

We both gasped.

"Now that's a strange place to hide a key," I said.

On the side of the key was etched a name: OLIVIA.

AUGUSTA USHERED me from the carousel house into the open air. She led me to a bench, where we both anchored ourselves. The world was still spinning a little.

I looked up and noticed Augusta watching someone in the distance who was running. It looked to be a thin, young white man—but that's all I could tell before he hopped a fence and disappeared down Pullen Avenue toward Western, which skirted the edge of NC State's main campus.

"Who was that?" I asked.

"I thought I saw him when we were first getting on the merry-go-round," said Augusta. "He was just getting off as we were getting on. Now he's trying to get lost."

"Should we tail him?" I asked. "I know how to do that now —sort of."

"You're too wobbly right now to tail anybody. You'd probably fall into the pond with them ducks."

It's true that Augusta was not a generally trusting person. But just because you're paranoid doesn't mean you're not being followed.

After all, I had carried a tracker on my car for who knows how long.

"Let's go back to our cars," I suggested. "I want to check something."

When we got there, I grabbed my purse from my Camry and fished out the tracking device Emerson had found on my vehicle.

"We're going to look for one of these under your car, too," I said.

"Let me do it." It was kind of her not to add, *"because you might have trouble getting back up."*

Almost immediately she hopped back up, holding between two fingers an identical magnetic tracker.

"This is disturbing," I said. "Who is having us followed? And who just tried to scare us?"

"'Scare' us? How about *kill* us?"

She was right. We easily could have died. The reality was just now sinking in.

"Augusta, the worker said that Maintenance gets notified automatically by the carousel system when something goes wrong. That means it's connected to the Internet, right?"

"That's not unusual these days."

And whoever can track a car can certainly make an amusement park ride go haywire.

Augusta continued: "Maybe someone else wanted to find that key before we did."

"Or maybe they knew about those documents you found," I said.

"Should I get rid of them? I'm not willing to die for some stupid documents."

"No, I still want to have a look at them," I said resolutely. "If those are the reason we were targeted, I want to know exactly what they are."

I'M PRETTY good with balance sheets and P&L statements, but I couldn't make out a single thing from these documents, which were complex and internal to RidgeLine. I enlisted the best CPA

I knew. I paid him extra to drop everything and spend a Friday afternoon to look at them.

It took him just two hours.

"It's tax evasion," he said on the phone, "at least, just based on these papers. The company made a lot of money three years ago—money it would normally have to pay taxes on. But it concocted a way to pretend-spend on precious-metal futures. I'll refer you to page—"

"No need, Frank. I trust what you found. What would you do if you found this out about, say, a friend's company?"

"I'd inform him right away."

"And what if he was the one directing the fraud?"

"Maybe I would give him a chance to fix it before I went to the IRS. It depends how much culpability I had. Where did you get these papers, by the way?"

Um, from a friendly hacker.

"If I told you, then I'd have to kill you."

"No, thanks," he said.

I texted Augusta and asked if she could meet me at Needless Necessities right away. We met over coffee, where I filled her in on my CPA's analysis.

"I need to know if Scott knew about the tax fraud," I said. "Is there a way to find that out?"

"Oh, he knew about it," Augusta said confidently. "His bots left a footprint."

I'm sure my face went pale. "That's a motive for Sammy. I've been hired by a potential killer!"

"What does Sammy get from killing Novak?"

"Keeps Novak from turning him in on tax fraud, of course."

"Yeah, well, he sure waited long enough. Novak knew about this stuff nearly a year *before* he sold his company to Sammy."

"Was Sammy's buying Novak's company just a way to keep him quiet?"

"I doubt it. How much tax money did Sammy save by cooking his books?"

"About 10 million dollars."

"So, Sammy pays $250 million for Scott's company to save 10 million? Doesn't make a lot of sense."

She was right. It didn't.

But it still bothered me.

Paul had been trying to get in touch with me, and I had been avoiding him. I needed to confront this issue. I went to his office and skipped the small talk.

"I need to know: Have you been tracking me and Augusta? Be honest."

He closed his eyes. "Well..."

"How could you?!"

"To know where you are, so I can help to keep you safe. That's the only reason."

"Guess what? It didn't work, because I think someone sabotaged the Pullen Park carousel to try to kill us. Are you sure you're not involved in that?"

"I don't know what you're talking about."

I looked at him hard.

"Honestly," he said, "I don't."

I wasn't sure I believed him. But right now, I needed allies.

"I need to talk to Sammy about something," I said.

"Okay, but could you give me a hint at what it is before you talk to him? Because if it pisses him off, he's going to blame me. I'm his whipping boy on all this stuff."

"You can wait for it," I said, "but, trust me, this isn't something you could be blamed for. It involves high-level mathematics."

"I suck at math."

"Surprise, surprise."

I got my audience with Sammy in his office. Paul looked on

nervously as I got ready to accuse Sammy of a crime, but our billionaire asked the first question.

"Why is this investigation stagnating?" It was a legitimate concern.

"I've admittedly been going in circles," I quipped.

I dropped on his desk the report my CPA friend produced with his bullet points listing the steps of the tax evasion scheme.

Sammy picked them up to get a better look. He laughed and handed the papers back. "That's old news."

"So, it's true?"

"Yes—and Scott was the one who brought it to light."

"Okay.... So you *did* have a motive to kill him."

"Actually, no, but it did give me motive to buy his company. I had been looking for AI technology that could find financial malfeasance. Scott's company was one of 10 we were looking at. We were doing due diligence on him as part of that, but, at the same time, he was doing due diligence on *us*. He—his AI technology, to be exact—found something in our accounting even I had not been aware of.

"When this was uncovered, two things happened: We fired our chief financial officer—you can look it up—and we stopped looking at the other nine other AI firms we were considering. Fortunately, the scheme was found before it was put into action. Our CFO swore he was just creating a hypothetical, but I don't appreciate such games."

"But you kept the paperwork."

"We keep everything—but we never used it to build our actual tax return. You can double-check that, too. By the way, how did you find these papers? Did someone give it to you to try to make me look bad—another deep-fake moment?"

I shrugged. "It was sent to me anonymously." There was no use in implicating Augusta again.

~

I CALLED Augusta and reported everything that Sammy had said. She hung up saying she wanted to verify some things and got right back to me. "Okay. There are emails between Sammy and that CFO about the matter. Sammy acts surprised and angry about the scheme. Back to the drawing board."

"Augusta, this stuff is insane. You've even hacked into Sammy's old emails? By the way, are you still looking for a way into Big Cat?"

"I found some chatter between that Yellow Goose guy and his friend, Trey. They were on a Reddit board. Trey was asking Gus to translate some German for him."

I explained, "Trey is really into that German philosopher, Nietzsche, same as Scott Novak and especially his brother, Adam. Trey actually wrote Adam to try to learn if Nietzsche was a Nazi—as in *hoping* he was a Nazi—and Adam called him out, made him angry."

"Don't know much about all that," she said. "Now, I did see that movie where Tom Cruz played a Nazi with an eye patch. What was the name of that movie? It was pretty good."

Ten seconds later, my movie database app had the answer. "*Valkyrie*. As in that devilish tune that played when we were on the carousel: *The Ride of the Valkyries*."

"We played that song in community orchestra when I was in high school. I never liked that song. Wagner, right?"

"Right. And for a long time Nietzsche idolized Wagner." I pulled up the Wikipedia page that talked about *The Ride of the Valkyries*. It included a drawing of Viking women riding horses which carried the bodies of fallen soldiers to Valhalla.

Augusta said, "Wait a minute. No wonder..."

"'No wonder what?"

"What was the name on that key again?"

" 'OLIVIA.' But what does that—"

"I've got to go."

She hung up before I could respond.

It was Friday night, and Darryl wanted to go out. I think he still felt guilty about his drunken scene from the night before.

When we sat down to dinner, he could probably detect there was something weighing on my mind. I deflected from telling the whole truth by sharing only about the tax evasion scheme Scott had found at RidgeLine, one which Sammy claimed he had not acted upon.

"Do you believe your client on that one?" he asked.

"Augusta corroborated everything Sammy told us. I think I've got to look elsewhere. I guess—"

"You seem frustrated."

More like "concerned for my life."

I just said, "I don't think I'm up for this case after all."

"Don't worry. You'll get to the truth."

"I'm not sure it's worth it." *Especially if I end up dead.*

Darryl asked, "So you don't think Scott Novak was murdered?"

"I've had my doubts—until today."

Darryl looked confused. "What happened today to suggest he was killed?"

I fell silent. I just couldn't tell him. He'd worry too much.

My phone on the table blew up. Both Darryl and I could see it was Paul calling.

I looked at Darryl, who provided an understanding grin.

"Go ahead and answer."

So I did.

"I've got some news," Paul said. "You sitting down?"

"Yes."

"You won't believe it: Gustaf was just found dead in his garage, apparently electrocuted by his garage-door opener while he was trying to repair it."

"What?"

"Weird, huh?"

Immediately my other line lit up. It was the number I recognized as Virtual Scott's.

"Let me get back to you later, Paul. I've got another call." I switched lines. "Scott! It's good to hear from you. Are you okay?"

"*Gute nacht*," said a voice much deeper than Scott's. Sounds of orchestral music boomed in the background. Beethoven? Wagner?

"Excuse me?" I demanded. "Who is this? Is it Gustaf? But I just heard you're—"

"This is not Herr Huber," the voice said in a thick German accent, "but I have a limerick for you that immortalizes him. Please, allow me to recite:

> *"Could it have been an electric eel*
> *That buzzed at Herr Huber's heel?*
> *Did it spring from the wires*
> *Like lightning a-fire*
> *Resulting in a murder concealed?"*

The voice gave a guttural laugh.

"Who is this?" I shouted, my hand shaking. "Where is Scott?"

"My name is Friedrich Nietzsche," the voice intoned, "and haven't you heard...

"Scott Novak is dead!"

PART III

OVERCOMING

"It doesn't happen all at once," said the Skin Horse. "You become. It takes a long time...."

The Rabbit sighed. He thought it would be a long time before this magic called Real happened to him. He longed to become Real, to know what it felt like; and yet the idea of growing shabby and losing his eyes and whiskers was rather sad. He wished that he could become it without these uncomfortable things happening to him.

—*The Velveteen Rabbit*

CHAPTER 23

NEVER SAY DIE

I cut the call short in the middle of the laughter.

"I think I just talked to a ghost," I said, putting my right hand over my galloping heart.

"What are you talking about?"

Darryl was totally confused, so I backed up and started by telling him about the crazed carousel and its Wagnerian soundtrack. He took my left hand in his. "That sounds terrifying. Rett, why didn't you tell me?"

"I didn't want you to worry."

"You should file an official report."

"But it will just be judged to be a mechanical malfunction. Besides, if Augusta can't trace who did it, no one will."

"That's disturbing," Darryl said. "Are you suggesting some evil computer program might have caused the malfunction at Huber's home, too?"

"That's what I'm starting to wonder," I said. "Can you at least find out from whoever is working Huber's death if Gustaf's system was connected to the Internet?"

"I can try."

I BARELY SLEPT a wink all night. The next morning, I decided I needed to visit Needless Necessities as a way to calm myself. Lydia rode with me.

"Something's b-b-bothering you. What's up?"

"I'm okay." Darryl had honored my wish to keep Lydia in the dark about the Pullen Park scare and the threatening call. We couldn't risk raising her blood pressure.

At Needless, QT the quilting tabby practically tackled my ankles.

"Something is eating up Rett this m-m-morning," Lydia announced.

Every lady in the room looked up from their stitching at me.

I was surrounded. No sense in hiding now.

"It's just that I about died yesterday on the carousel at Pullen Park," I confessed, without going into the details.

"I've always hated rides," Pleasance said. "Don't know what anyone sees in them."

"It was all for the sake of a case," I said, "but I think I'm going to quit now."

"You can't," Lydia said. "L-l-losers quit."

"But I didn't even know the man who died—and aren't you the least bit concerned for my life?"

"Someone's just trying to s-s-scare you."

"Well, they've succeeded! And there's a second body now." I mentioned the "accidental" death of Gus Huber.

The Qrazies urged me to leave the case behind. Everyone except Lydia. Sometimes I think her life's lack of adventure made her want to live vicariously through me. On the way home, she tried to argue with me some more to stay in the game.

But I had made up my mind. Maybe it was a cop-out to break

up by text, but, nonetheless, I sent Paul a message to let him know I was going to resign.

He immediately called me. "You're going to let a little near-fatal incident stop you from getting to the truth?"

"This is life and death, Paul!"

"What are you—yella'? You could have died just driving to the park. Living is dangerous."

"It's not just that. I keep making a fool of myself, like when my first instinct was to believe that deep-fake video, and then when I accused Sammy of tax evasion."

"Sammy can handle it. He's a tough cookie."

"But maybe I'm not."

"I think you are."

"You're just saying that."

"It doesn't mean I'm wrong. Hold on a second. Emerson Cramer just stopped by my office. I'll put you on speaker. He's not going to be happy you're dropping this case either."

There were muffled sounds of Paul talking, then the phone being passed.

"Rett?" said Emerson. "What are you doing? You can't drop this case."

"Yes, I can." I mentioned how, on top of the carousel incident, Virtual Scott had been taken over by an evil AI. "I can't explain how it happened, but I just know this has gotten too big for me."

"But..." But Emerson didn't have a retort. He handed the phone back to Paul, who signed off.

It was a Saturday, so I decided to write an actual letter of resignation and take it by RidgeLine on Monday. Knowing Paul, though, he was already on the phone to Sammy about it.

At least this would put Darryl's mind at ease—or that's what I told myself.

I needed to paint. On a hunch that he would be there, I went by Ken's studio. The artist was in, and he was perfectly happy to let me set up an easel and canvas without much in the way of small talk. Maybe he noticed I was trying to work out something internally. I painted furiously, and he didn't intrude. I sensed he was in his own sort of zone, so I left after about an hour with a mere wave and "thanks." I didn't even take the canvas with me, as it was merely an abstract venting of color.

I sat in my car for a little while. At some point the phone rang. The number wasn't recognizable, but I decided to answer it.

"Hello?"

"Hi, Rett."

I was relieved to hear a familiar voice: Virtual Scott.

"Why are you calling me on a different number?" I asked.

"Because that one has been taken over by a certain German philosopher."

"I thought you had been killed—or whatever that means in robot terms—by that Nietzsche AI."

"Let him think that. I ran to a different server. But he could accost me again at any moment."

In the background this time I heard birds. I was used to odd nature soundtracks to Virtual Novak's voice, but this one was less exotic than the ones that had come before. From amidst the different tweets I could easily pick out the call of a blue jay.

Something in me reflexively stiffened. Of any bird, I despised blue jays. Not that their call was unpleasant, but I'd learned as a very little girl that blue jays invaded the nests of other birds. *"Blue jays think they are better than other birds and that they make the rules,"* my grandmother once told me. *"Some people are like blue jays. They act like their kind can do no wrong. Watch out for blue-jay people, Harriet. And don't ever become one, you hear?"*

"Yes, ma'am."

"So, why are you getting in touch?" I asked Scott. "I just quit the case, you know."

"Yes, that's what Paul just told Sammy. And Sammy immediately ordered his programmers to shut me down. It seemed odd to my algorithms that Sammy wanted to shut me down so quickly upon learning you were off the case."

"He probably thinks I'm incompetent," I said. "He might be right."

"It is also possible that he is afraid of you. This case needs you. I don't think you should quit."

I couldn't believe I was being pressured by a computer.

"Look, Scott," I said, "I didn't know you when you were alive, and now you're just a machine. So why should I even care about this case?"

"Maybe because your friend, Margaret Strand, may end up marrying someone you have yet to exclude as a suspect in my death."

I thought about that. The blue jay, declaring its supremacy, sounded in the background, as if to say, "*I, Sammy Patel, will do what I wish—and no one can stop me.*"

"Are you trying to scare me?" I asked.

"I think you are already afraid that your friend may be making a serious error of judgment."

"But how can I assure her—assure anyone—that Sammy didn't have anything to do with your death?"

"Perhaps you can get a look at his phone. To see if he was communicating with anyone around the time I died. Just a suggestion."

"How can I do that?"

"However you can manage," said Virtual Scott. "I'm sorry. I better go before Sammy's programmers—or a certain philosopher—catch on to my location."

And he hung up.

The phone call had rattled me.

But Scott Bot was right. The stakes were high. I had to rule out Sammy's involvement.

I sent a text to Paul:

—*Update: I'm returning to the case. But don't tell Sammy that just yet. Give me some time to prove my worth. I'm going to follow-up on a couple of leads.*

Speaking of leads, I still had Scott's will in my possession. I would take it to Tom Jordan on Monday. That would still buy Paul a little time to look into Emerson's enigmatic life.

I needed to confront Lorry about his part of the inheritance.

I found him feeding the animals.

"How would you like to own this zoo?" I asked, "plus this land and the farmhouse?"

He shrugged. "More to take care of. Don't see how I could afford to keep it up."

This I hadn't thought of. But he was right.

"I could help you," I said. "More importantly, Sheila could help."

"Sheila's a wonderful person," he said. "She reminds me so much of my daughter, Delia. Been trying to get in touch with her lately, but she's still angry about a lot of things. I don't blame her."

"What happened? Was it your drinking?"

"The drinking didn't much start until after they left. It was mainly the fighting over money. I wasn't bringing much in. The old lady thought that I was lazy. But there weren't any work worth a darn. God knows I tried a lot of things. *Before* the problem was I was never at home, back when I was in the Navy. Then the problem was I was home too much. Some women don't know what they want, no offense."

"None taken."

"She said I wasn't a man. She said a real man would know

how to take care of his family. She poisoned our daughter's mind. It was terrible. And, yes, I'd get angry. And, yes, I'd get violent at times. I guess there wasn't a day that I didn't screw up in some way." He asked me, "How do you get by without grabbing a drink now and then?"

"I find other things to do, other feelings to focus on."

"Like what?"

"Love. Passion. Hope. A hobby."

"Everything I had, I've lost. Everything good was taken away from me."

"So you're a victim?"

"I'm not a victim. No, ma'am! I'm fighting. I'm fighting every day. And sometimes a soldier needs a drink, to brace himself."

"What are you fighting against, Lorry?"

"All the things that are messed up. The government, if that's what it takes."

Oh, Lorry, how can you expect to fix modern problems with such rusty weapons? When will you stop scapegoating and take responsibility for your own life?

I remembered Lorry's affinity for Patriot Mike's videos. Lorry had denied being involved with Mike once already, so I didn't bring it up again.

But I still wondered.

~

WHILE I HAD BEEN VISITING Lorry, I looked long and hard at the back of Novak's house. Fit as Esther was, I couldn't imagine her climbing the side of a building—not when she had a key. Maybe Buster had been so drunk he imagined the whole thing.

Or maybe he had seen somebody else.

There was a famous section of *Thus Spoke Zarathustra* in which a tightrope artist is performing for a crowd. The acrobat falls, and Zarathustra praises the performer just before he dies for living a brave life on the edge.

That made me think of something.

I went on my phone to the photos and other web files that Roger, KayLeigh's webmaster, had shared with me about her listings. I hadn't realized at the time that KayLeigh was the selling agent for Scott's mansion, but there I found them again: the photos of the house, not yet staged. I zoomed in on one photo in particular: the master bedroom.

I went online to my old website — now KayLeigh's website. Somehow, she'd gotten Roger to put her listings back online. Some of the photos for Scott's listing had been updated, including photos of the bedroom.

I needed to get inside, to get a closer look.

I texted my favorite nemesis with yet another favor to ask. She didn't respond right away. But that evening, a full six hours later, she did:

—*I can help you with that. Here is the combination to the key box...*

After dinner, I hoofed it over to Novak's former home on St. Mary's Street and pulled onto its long, stately, winding driveway. I would have liked to approach it during the day, but I had only two things in mind: to get a better look at something in Novak's old bedroom, and to sample something for fingerprint dusting to help identify whoever's prints were found all over Scott's country house: Were they those of someone new, or of an old acquaintance?

The fingerprint thing would be difficult. I hadn't exactly taken a course on fingerprinting, and Paul couldn't join me on this excursion. "Just grab a couple things that won't be missed," Paul advised. "You can put 'em back later. Just make sure to wear your gloves."

I put on a pair of Darryl's golfing gloves and opened the key box. The key worked—KayLeigh could have set me up, but I was grateful when I was able to let myself in. The door's closing behind me echoed throughout the great foyer. I found a light switch.

Wow.

Did I feel poor.

Even with minimal furniture, the house was amazing. It didn't seem like a bachelor pad at all. There was a traditional sense to everything.

But I wasn't here to gawk at the carved, wooden banister, the impressive chandelier, the marble-floor foyer with its grandfather clock. I needed clues.

I should have asked KayLeigh where the master bedroom was. I guessed on the second floor somewhere. I used my phone to find the light switches along the way. How eerie it felt to be the only person in this giant home.

At the end of a short hallway, I spied a door flanked by coats of armor that had "rich dude's bedroom" written all over it.

The bedroom was bigger than Lydia's living room. It was round, as it was located inside a turret. The turret's ceiling was at least 30 feet high, though two large beams made an X about halfway up. A large fern hung from one of the beams.

This is what I had come to see.

The original photo from KayLeigh's (broken) website had not shown a plant. The fern was new, part of the home's staging.

There was no electrical running to where the plant hung. If there had been a chandelier at one time, there certainly had not been for a while. The room had sufficient track lighting coming from the walls plus a ring of six canned lights in the high ceiling.

The plant looked silly and out of place. It wasn't KayLeigh's fault (at what other time had I said that?) it's just that no plant could possibly look big enough for the space. Plus, the hook it hung on was off center.

Taking off my shoes first, I stood on the king-size bed and zoomed in on the heavy metal hook with my phone's camera. It wasn't a perfect angle, but it got the job done. Before I stepped down, I reached and was able to give the plant a good turn. Round and round it went, a full revolution and then some.

I could have poked around a little more, but I didn't feel comfortable sticking around. It was fully dark now, and it gave me the creeps to be in a house alone.

Then I remembered the "souvenirs" that I was supposed to find so Paul could dust for fingerprints. I found my way to the home's stunning kitchen and had to pause. Where to begin in describing it? The 10-foot-long island with its lovely granite countertop? The wrought-iron rack from which hung the most amazing bronze cook-wear I'd ever seen? There wasn't room for a tenth of this in Scott's country home, so it made sense he'd keep much of it here to help stage the home for selling.

A liquor cabinet larger than an entertainment center beckoned. I opened it and clanked around until I spied a couple of bottles of Clyde Ray's in the back that were practically empty. Thinking they might contain prints going back a long time, I moved around several bottles until I was able to grab them.

I had turned to go when a voice stopped me cold.

"Excuse me. Exactly what are you doing?"

I turned and recognized "Art-Collecting Alice" Huffman, neighbor and queen of the Raleigh art scene. She was the one who had inadvertently brought Esther into Scott's life. How might she change my life someday if I held my own show?

"Oh, hi, Alice! I'm Rett Swinson. Freddy Lane is our mutual friend. Did KayLeigh tell you I'd be coming by?"

"No."

Maybe KayLeigh had set me up after all.

She went on, "Besides, I didn't think you two were on speaking terms."

"It's complicated."

"I saw a car. Then I saw lights in Scott's bedroom. I thought if it was a burglar they were being awfully obvious." She looked at the two bottles in my hands. "Thirsty?"

"I just want the bottles. Dusting for prints."

"And that's why you are wearing golfing gloves?"

"Yes. I'm investigating the death of Scott Novak." *And I'm also a landscape painter, eager to do my first show! I look forward to working with you on that someday!*

Alice said, not so convincingly, "I see."

"I better be going," I said. "Sorry to waste your time, Alice."

"It's okay. I was just ... concerned."

"By the way," I said, as we both walked through the foyer. "I meant to ask you: What made you decide to invite Esther Mills to your charity gala when you had only just met her on the plane?"

"I liked her. You see, I consider myself a good judge of character."

Gulp. "Were you not put off when she brought your rowdy neighbor as a date?"

"I was a little concerned, yes—but I was absolutely *delighted* later when she tamed Mr. Novak and helped him turn over a new leaf. I'm right next door, and I would get all kinds of riffraff ringing the gate doorbell at all hours."

Maybe we should dust that doorbell for fingerprints, too.

Did she see my wheels turning? Did she realize I was just as sober as she was?

I couldn't really wave, so I gestured like a sailor with one of the nearly empty bottles and said, "Thank you for being understanding, Alice. You know, sleuthing isn't my only hobby. I also like to paint. I—"

"I'm sure your paintings are very lovely."

She raised an eyebrow and disappeared into the night.

DEPRESSED AS ALL HECK, I slumped behind the wheel of my Camry. An hour later I was in Greenville, where I pulled up to Stephanie's sorority house. I had called her numerous times on my way there, but she never picked up.

In the commons room I found the usual pair of couch potatoes watching TV.

"Have you two seen Stephanie today?" I asked.

They looked at one another. "Umm...," began one.

Said the other off-handedly, "Oh, Stephanie withdrew from ECU."

I did a double-take. "'Withdrew?'"

"Yeah. Like, last week."

My heart plummeted. I had to sit down in the chair across from them.

"What happened?" I asked. "Did she go off and join the circus or something?"

"No, that was *Jess*," said the first girl. "Wait..."

"Silly!" scolded the second. "Jess was offered a job at the circus but turned it down because of those poor tigers, remember?"

"That's right! Jess did NOT skip college to join the circus."

"She came to ECU and joined our sorority!"

"That's right!"

These two ditzes—while they could be counted on to share vital information—were on my last nerve. I pressed, "Do either of you know where Stephanie went?"

"Stephanie went..."

Finally realizing they had already said too much, they both exchanged a look and officially clammed up.

"Okay," I said, "if you won't tell me where to find Stephanie, at least tell me how I can find Jess. Do you know how I can get in touch with her?"

"Sure," one of them said. "I'll text you her number."

This was known as passing the buck.

BACK IN MY car I dialed Stephanie's cell and prayed she would answer—no such luck. The third call I left a long message telling her I loved her and would she please call me back to explain what was going on.

I called Allan, but he didn't pick up either. Was it too much to ask the people you had loved the longest to answer your phone calls?

I said the Serenity Prayer and gathered my composure. I texted Jess, just saying I was in town and worried about Stephanie. Would she meet with me? She texted back to say she was at work, a place called "The Aerial Mermaid." It sounded like a Disney-type store for kids, but when I got there, I realized it was exactly what I had suspected.

Several girls and women were hanging from the ceiling on long, lush extensions of colorful cloth. They were following the lead of Jess, their instructor, who was pacing them through various moves. I had seen something like this years ago on one of those music award nights. It looked difficult as heck—perfect for a musician like Pink who was in the shape of her life—but a means of death for someone as clumsy as me.

As her students practiced the aerial dance move she had just demonstrated, Jess was able to break away to talk with me.

"Stephanie's just fine," she said immediately. "She's with her boyfriend at the coast."

"Where exactly?"

"I'm not supposed to tell you."

"I know you're not. I'm not going to make you."

I reached out and touched one of the long practice cloths that was hanging from a metal hook near the ceiling.

"What are these called?"

She shrugged. "Silks. Why?"

I pulled on it, testing its strength.

"You could absolutely strangle someone with this material," I said. "I see your students have blue, pink, purple, and teal. Do silks come in the color yellow, too?"

Her eyes widened. "I need to get back to my class."

"Young lady, you were spotted leaving Scott Novak's house the night he died."

She started to shake. "That's a lie."

"No, it's not. You have some splainin' to do."

Her breathing accelerated. "I'll tell you where Stephanie is living if that's what you want."

I crossed my arms. "Okay, where is she?"

"She's in Beaufort, just off Front Street. Her boyfriend's family has a house there. Alex Kelly is his name."

"Thanks for the info," I said, "but I didn't come here to extort you. I need to know what you were doing at Scott Novak's, and did you kill him?"

She looked indignant. "I didn't kill him."

"Then what were you doing there?"

"Which time?"

Okay, this was going to be more than a quick conversation. I said, "Can we go somewhere right now and talk in-depth? Because if you can't, it's my duty to call the police."

Jess nodded. She went and told a colleague she needed to leave. On our way out, she got on a chair and pulled down the red silk she had been using, untying it from its metal clasp and putting both items in a small duffle that she carried with her.

We sat in my parked car. Almost immediately she began to sob. I gave her a moment before pressing her.

"You have to be honest with me," I finally said.

"I knew I'd have to talk about it eventually."

"What happened that night? Start from the beginning."

She took a deep breath and wiped her eyes. "I dropped in on him around seven. For a long time I had been missing him—like, for months. I just couldn't stop thinking about him, so finally after class one day I just drove out there, hoping I'd find him. I got the address from Trey."

"Trey Gamble?"

She nodded. "That very asshole. He's another story. Anyway, I just kept knocking until Scott came to the door. He looked terrible, not even much like himself. Skinnier than I remembered him. His eyes got wide when he saw me. Then he started in with the game."

"The game?"

"Pretending I was Esther. 'Esther! You're back!' And I'm like, 'Of course, Scott! I missed you so much!' And that's what we did. We played The Esther Game. If he wanted to fantasize, I'd give him his fantasy. Anyway. Scott and 'Esther' made love."

"Even though he and Esther were officially broken up."

"Yeah, when he let me in the house, he said, 'It was stupid to break up with you. You're so amazing.' Gag me!"

Gag who...?

I asked, "And you came in through the front door?"

"Yes."

"Did you two do some drugs?"

"I brought some, but we didn't touch them. I kept them in my duffle."

"What sort of drugs did you bring?"

"Oxycodone, for one. I've had a number of injuries over the

years and didn't use all the pills. I don't think it's technically illegal."

"Is that all you brought?"

"A couple of syringes. Heroin that I'd gotten at his mansion. Don't look at me like that. Scott and I were both built the same way. Neither one of us has an addictive personality."

I always considered it amusing how some people thought they couldn't get addicted to substances that were inherently addictive.

"You had sex?"

"Yeah, and afterwards he got all moody, muttering he 'shouldn't have done that, shouldn't have done that.' Okay, so he felt guilty he'd betrayed Esther. That was super annoying."

"At some point did you do one of your aerial dances for him?"

"After we slept together, yeah. It's an old house, and one of the ceiling struts is exposed."

"Did you bring an aerial swivel? Because I noticed there was one in Scott's mansion bedroom with a plant hanging from it."

"You've done your homework."

"It's called the Internet. I'm not that knowledgeable."

"To answer your question, yes, I danced for him that night, but it was clear he wasn't paying much attention. He was getting really agitated. He asked me to leave. Then I got mad, said some things, and stormed out. I never broke character though. I kept the game going."

"Before you left, did you let some of the animals out of their cages?"

"Yeah. How did you guess that?"

"Two of your sorority sisters let it slip that you'd been offered a job at the circus after high school but turned it down. I figured it was because of your views on animals."

"I was angry, and I knew he loved those animals. Pretty cruel to keep them caged, I thought."

"And that's where you dropped the Amulet you'd stolen."

"So that's where I lost it! Yeah, I saw that thing and grabbed it when Scott wasn't looking. He had worn it in the past when we were—together, you know—and I didn't want him to have the satisfaction, even though I figured he put the video on a computer at some point. That's why I stole it."

"And, after letting some animals out of their cages, you left."

"I got down the road a few miles. It was dark by then. I was just getting madder and madder. And then I realized, dammit, I'd left my silk and also my duffle which had the drugs in it. I wanted them back, so I turned around."

"How long had you been gone before you came back?"

"Seven or eight minutes."

"Safe to say you were gone from the house about 20 minutes in all?"

"Sounds right. When I got back the door was locked. I knocked and knocked, but he wouldn't answer. Now I was really pissed. I tried the back porch door, but everything was locked. Then I realized the top floor window in the back was open a bit and I could get up there by climbing the drainpipe."

"That's insane."

"Maybe I *was* feeling little crazy. But climbing is easy for me."

She continued, quieter now. "I crawled up and got inside, yelled Scott's name. He didn't answer. I went over to the bed, thought he was just passed out, but—he had part of my silk around his neck. I figured he'd been playing another sort of game."

"Had he ever played the choking game?"

"No, but I had, with other guys."

You sure do like a dangerous thrill, Jess.

I asked, "Had he taken some of your drugs?" The authorities had found a plastic syringe cap at the scene, so I was curious to see how Jess answered.

"At first I thought he had, because I found a used syringe on the side table. I thought, 'Shit! He OD'd on the drugs I brought!' I threw the syringe in the bag, but later when I was cleaning out my bag at home I realized the syringe must have been his because I still had my original two syringes, too."

"What had he injected?"

"I don't have any idea. All I knew is that when I found him, he was dead. I work in the summers as a medic. I took his pulse. He wasn't breathing. Calling 911 was not going to work—we were too far from help."

"You could have tried CPR."

"CPR works less than five percent of the time. And I just knew he was gone. If you'd seen his face, his eyes bulging out..." She covered her face.

"And you must have known you were going to be blamed for the murder."

She nodded. "Yeah. So I grabbed the drugs and the rest of my silk that was still hanging from the ceiling, the part that wasn't around his neck."

"How did you carry the leftover silk? Did you put it in your bag?"

"I think I just draped it around my neck and my back while I lowered myself down."

And the itsy-bitsy spider went down the spout again. The only way Lorry's friend would be able to see a person in the pitch dark of the country was if that person's "hair" was actually a bright yellow aerial silk hanging down her back.

"You lied about something else," I said. "You told me Trey had threatened Scott."

She nodded. "You're right. I hoped you might zero in on Trey.

He tried to rape me once while his magic car drove us around, and I just— Are you going to call the police now?"

"I don't want to," I said, "but my P.I. code of ethics says I must, unless you turn yourself in first." I wasn't positive there was a code of ethics—Paul never mentioned or seemed to observe such a code—but I wanted something to cause her to surrender on her own.

"Okay," she said. "I'll turn myself in. But will you take me there? My mom is deceased, and my dad's an asshole."

"I will. If you're lucky, they might not keep you overnight."

"Even if they do, I have nothing left to hide anymore. And anywhere is cleaner than that sorority house."

On the way to the sheriff's, I asked her again about the syringe she found.

"Do you still have that?"

"No, I just threw all the drugs away in some random dumpster."

That was a shame, because the syringe could have helped confirm her story.

I asked her more about Stephanie, what she knew of her state of mind. "She was just tired of school. That's why her grades were falling. And she was tired of getting shit about it from the other girls. So, she left."

"After swearing you to secrecy."

"She doesn't appreciate the fact she has a caring mom. Are you going to go kick her ass now?"

"Maybe." Now I was the one who had to fight back tears.

SHERIFF TOM JORDAN debriefed Jess alone before talking with me. It was my first time to speak with him. I knew I'd like him, given his friendship with Darryl.

"The young lady has quite a story," he said. "Do you think she killed a man?"

I shrugged. "No, but I can't say why not. The cloth that choked him was cut from her own silk."

"We'd been wondering what type of cloth that was. It had too much stretch to be part of a bed sheet."

"And she might have been the last one to see him alive," I said.

"And she hid things from us."

"To be fair, you didn't approach her until I did. Besides…"

I pulled Scott's handwritten will from my pocket.

"There's this. I found it in Scott's old closet. Esther had let me inside."

Tom Jordan took the document, looked it over carefully, and smiled. "Darryl said he was dating a genius detective. I guess he was right."

"He used the word 'genius?' No way."

"He did. That's why some of us are wondering why you're working with Deputy McGoof."

"Paul's great."

"I know you have to work under a P.I. to become a P.I. But I'm here to tell you—P.I. work is for the birds. You'd do better to go through the Academy. Become an actual officer of the law."

"Are you trying to recruit me?"

He smiled. "I have a feeling that Darryl will do that on his own."

"I do find him persuasive." But I wanted to get the attention off me. "Do you think you'll hold Jess?"

"We'll charge her for withholding evidence, in hopes it helps her remember other things. But we won't keep her. The problem is it's still not clear that Scott Novak was murdered. He could have been playing that choking game on his own. The coroner thinks that the fabric was unsuited for such a game—and it binded up on him." He shook his head. "What's wrong with people? Is just being normal too boring for folks, that they have to spice things up with these deadly activities?"

"Like, investigating mysterious deaths, you mean?"

He laughed. "It was nice to meet you, Rett. Stay in touch. If you see or hear anything, please let us know."

"Sure," I said. Which wasn't a yes. And wasn't a no.

CHAPTER 24

MASQUERADE

I had texted Paul to let him know about the Jess situation. He arrived at the sheriff's office just as I was about to leave.

"Good job, sister," he said. "You may have cracked this case."

"Thanks," I said. What I didn't tell him was that I still wasn't sure that Jess was the killer, that I still suspected others— including our boss. And that I still didn't totally trust him—Paul —either.

This I decided finally to let on about.

"You said you were just trying to protect us, Paul, but why didn't you tell me and Augusta that you were tracking our movements?"

"Because you're independent women. I knew you wouldn't like it."

"I'm not sure I want to work for Big Brother anymore."

"Look," Paul said. "You're making headway. For all we know, you've found the killer. Jess sounds like she had means, motive, and opportunity."

I shook my head. "True, but she wasn't very smart about it. She used a piece of cloth that could easily be traced to her. She crawled up and down the house like Spider Woman in plain sight. And she wasted time letting animals out of their cages when she could have been getting clear of the crime scene."

"You make a good point. There is one other person we haven't looked at thoroughly. And this new will gives him motive: Emerson."

"Though I don't think he knew about the will," I said.

"Still, we need to try to exclude him from suspicion. When I followed him last night, he ended up going to one of those dress-up conventions downtown."

"You mean cos-play?"

"Yeah, where everyone dresses up as their favorite cartoon character or superhero. I couldn't tell you what Emerson went as. An ogre? Anyway, I think it might be a cover so he can meet someone. Tomorrow night's the last night of the convention. Which means you'll need to dress up. I heard you like a good costume."

Clearly, Paul had learned from someone about the elderly lady costume I'd worn to a travel agency to solve Wanda Hightower's murder. I blushed. "That case happened over Halloween, so a disguise was appropriate. But, if dressing up again will help us to the bottom of Emerson's strange behavior, I'm up for it. There's just one thing."

"What?"

"I'm still a little scared."

"Close your eyes," Paul said. "Now, hold out your hand." He placed something onto my palm.

"What's this?" I said, opening my eyes.

It was an Amulet attached to a thin, silver necklace.

"It's to make you feel safe when you're out and about. It will record what's happening around you. Plus, if you run into trouble, there's a button on the bottom you can push. Do that and the cavalry will come running."

With a strange mixture of relief and trepidation, I removed the Christian cross Maxine had given me several months earlier, put that in my pocket, and replaced it with the all-seeing Amulet.

PAUL'S PLAN for the next day was that I would shadow Emerson at the convention while Paul did a more thorough search of his office. But I didn't want to follow Emerson by myself, and I didn't trust Lydia to keep cool enough for this sort of operation. Instead, I reached out to Freddy, who looked like a mean body-guard. No one was going to mess with us while we were together.

"I need a favor," I told him. "You need to dress up."

"I have to wear a suit?"

"Sort of..."

I had him meet me at a costume shop at noon when it opened. "I'm not sure what passes for cos-play in Raleigh," I said, "but I really think it's up to you. Monster, space man, cartoon—it's fluid."

"How about 'Queer Sculptor Who Really Hates Drag Parties'? Would that work?"

"Come on, Freddy. I need your help. You're my BFF, remember? You owe me one."

"Oh, so today I'm your BFF? I don't remember a call on my birthday."

"I don't have a good head for dates. Besides, who wants to be reminded of their birthday? I sure don't."

"I'll guess I'll return *your* present then."

"What did you buy me? Tell me, and I'll tell you if you need to take it back."

Freddy rolled his eyes. He disappeared among the racks and quickly emerged with a red and yellow Flash-type get-up.

"You're literally flaming," I said.

"I'll take that as a compliment."

I ended up wearing one of the few costumes that fit my short, plumpish stature: a raccoon, tail and all. I grabbed some brown, black, and white face paints off the shelf. I was annoyed, because I could have gotten some at Needless Necessities for a tenth of the price.

The convention was being held in a large hotel downtown. Wearing the costume made me feel less out of place. It was freeing, in a way. I shared this observation with Freddy, the most depressed-looking comic-book hero ever.

"Speak for yourself. I feel like I fell asleep and some fraternity brothers decided to embarrass me."

We hung out in the lobby until Emerson arrived. I recognized his character instantly from movies I'd watched with Charlie: He was Hagrid from *Harry Potter*. The character fit his imposing shape.

Except for the modern backpack, he looked totally authentic.

I wanted to text Paul, but it was impossible to do so in the mittens I was wearing. I couldn't even get to my cell phone under my costume. Why hadn't I thought of this? I asked Freddy to do the texting.

"I'm going to tail Emerson now," I said.

Freddy playfully yanked my raccoon tail. "'Tail...'?"

"Stop it! You keep me in view in case I get accosted. Some of these people scare me. Their weapons look real."

"If you need help, I'll be there in a flash," he winked.

We watched Emerson exchange pleasantries with a few people before he disappeared down a hallway. It was some sort of service hallway—and super gloomy. I always hated raccoons, slinking through the night, messing with our garbage cans. But here I was, one of them.

I could hear Emerson ahead of me, a steady cadence of footfall from his large leather boots. I followed and watched him turn a corner. This was followed by some sort of argument, a woman's voice:

"Go away, you stinkin' cur!"

There was the sound of scuffling, then a cry, and a clanging of metal.

"And don't try that ever again!"

A short man dressed as a knight came scampering down my hallway. As he ran past me breathing hard, he muttered offhand, "You might want to find a weapon before you go much further!" Not wanting to make my presence known to Emerson, I didn't respond.

Up ahead, a conversation:

"What's your poison, Big Boy?"

"I come from Dumbledore. To gain a horcrux."

"You found the first part of that. Did you bring payment? You better have—or I will tell the Ministry all that you've done."

I had eased myself right up to the corner. I peeked around it now and watched the pair facing off. A black-haired woman was clad head to toe in black leather. Emerson took off his backpack and handed it to her. Leather Goddess yanked him inside the room and shut the door.

I was curious, to say the least. What was in Hagrid's backpack?

I waited a few minutes, then began to get anxious.

Was their interaction what it seemed—or something else?

Dang it, there was only one way to find out.

I put my ear to their hotel room's door. My raccoon ear, that is. I had to take off my hood to really listen. In doing so, I realized the door had been closed but had not been pushed all the way to make it lock.

"Ouch! ... Ow! ... Ouch!" came the male voice within. Here was my probable cause.

"Is someone in trouble?" I cried as I barged into the room.

The scene wasn't pretty.

Emerson was lying face-down on the bed while the woman straddled his bare back. She had affixed a large piece of duct tape to one of his shoulder blades and was about to yank the tape off again.

Behind me appeared another figure.

The Flash.

"You okay?" asked Freddie, huffing and puffing.

"I'm fine."

"What are you doing here?" Emerson growled.

I shot back. "What are you doing here? What did you bring from the office? Are you sharing trade secrets?"

I lunged for the backpack. The woman, a sort of Elvira of the Night figure, cried, "Who are these creatures? Do they wish to be dominated, too?"

Hagrid said, "I don't know the red guy, but the other is familiar to me."

"A 'familiar?' This could be fun!"

"I am a raccoon," I said meekly—four words that strongly competed to be the most ridiculous ever spoken.

"Now you know where I was the night Scott was killed," Emerson sighed. "I was here, with Morgana."

I looked at the dominatrix, who echoed, "That's right. He was with me. Under me, that is." She gave his bare, half-hairy back a cringeworthy slap.

"You'd tell that to the authorities?" I asked her.

"Of course," she said.

But was she playacting? I really didn't know how to deal with these people with their adult make-believe worlds.

I needed to know something. I opened the backpack.

Inside was a stuffed dragon. I pulled it out.

"Oh, you brought Cuddly!" said Morgana. "I suppose you want to hold Cuddly now, Little Emmy? But you can't have him!"

Emerson went red. No wonder he hadn't wanted to talk about his alibi. If legit, it was just plain embarrassing.

Freddy spoke up. "Can I please go now? I've got to pee, and that's going to be really hard wearing this thing."

"I have one more question to ask Emerson," I said. "But first I'll need Morgana to leave the room."

Emerson turned on his side and nodded to her. She complied. Maybe he really was the one in charge. I gave Freddy a look, which he interpreted correctly as, *"Follow the sexy dominatrix and make sure she doesn't listen outside the door."*

Once Emerson and I were alone, I asked him if he was aware that Scott had made out another will—and had left half his fortune to him. I watched his face closely, but I didn't see the least bit of excitement play across his expression.

He shrugged. "I wasn't aware. But ... does it really matter?"

"What do you mean? We're talking tens of millions of dollars. It's a crazy amount of wealth. And it's yours beginning today."

He shook his head. "It doesn't make a damn bit of difference."

"Why?"

He looked at me hopelessly. "Because I'm a dead man."

THAT WASN'T the end of my day with Emerson.

He said he had something to give to me. So, after returning Freddy to his house (where we were both able to change) I headed to Cary to meet Emerson in his apartment. On the way I called Paul to update him on Emerson and asked if he'd found anything in the man's office. He had not, but he was excited that I was being invited to his domicile. "Turn on your Amulet and move around a lot."

"He'll notice the Amulet on my chest," I said.

"Then hide it in your pocket. It should still pick up audio. Remember, if you get into trouble, press the button. You can also stream the audio to me while you two are talking. I'll tell you how."

By the time I got to his place, Emerson had cleaned up and dressed in pajamas. He looked exhausted, anxious.

"Morgana's interesting," I said. "Someone you pay to dominate you?"

"It's complicated," he said. "Look, not everyone is built the same. Someday we'll all be plugged into the Matrix and we can lead the sex lives that suit us. In the meantime, we'll just have to make do."

I wanted to be sympathetic, but I was at my wit's end with this guy. It was time to stop playing nice.

"What's the deal, Emerson? You lose your best friend, your closest colleague, and you don't seem to grieve. You run around accusing everyone of being his killer, but you act so strangely, you stand out as the most likely suspect of all." I knew that Paul was listening to all of this through the Amulet, which I had slipped just under my shirt.

Emerson sat at the kitchen table, his shoulders slumped forward, unspeaking. Men and their uncanny ability to resemble uncommunicative rocks.

"I suppose you heard about Gustaf," I said.

Emerson frustratedly ran his fingers through his curly black hair.

"Do you think he had something to do with Scott's death?" he asked.

"I don't know. But I'm wondering if maybe Scott had something to do with Gustaf's death." I told him about the disturbing limerick about electrocution and its creator, Virtual Nietzsche. I reminded him, too, about Scott's Kansas-City talk and his fears of an AI taking over the Internet. I told him about Virtual Scott feeling he was in danger and calling me from a different number. "Do you think a rogue AI is on the loose?"

Emerson swallowed hard. "I don't know. Honestly, I can't keep up with all of Scott's shit. This is all his fault. I'm so pissed off at him right now!"

He went over to the kitchen counter and grabbed a tall container. Sugar? Flour? He set it in front of me.

"His ashes," he said. "They need to be delivered to his brother. I haven't been able to get in touch with him, though I've tried really hard. I'm hoping you'll take them to Alaska. Find the guy. Have him contact me. Tell him I'm afraid for my life and he needs to come here now and help."

"But I just got back from Alaska," I protested. "I couldn't get in touch with Adam then. What makes you think—?"

"It's important you try again! One more time. Please." He put a hand on the urn. "It's important."

"Then why don't you go?"

He shook his head. "The company. I signed the same agreement that Scott did."

"That's convenient."

"You don't understand. I don't trust Sammy for a second not to destroy AfterLifeLine—which he has never cared about—or somehow screw-up the Big Cat project, whatever that turns out to be."

"Emerson," I said, "I need to ask you something else. I believe Scott was with someone in Kansas City. I suspect it was a woman, but I can't prove it. I found a key—don't ask me how I found it. But it's got a name written on it: 'OLIVIA.' Who's Olivia?"

"She's not a girlfriend, if that's what you're thinking."

"Then who was she?"

"You've heard of Siri and Alexa? Olivia was just another one of those virtual personalities Scott was developing."

It was plausible enough. But it seemed like a too-tidy explanation. Maybe Emerson really didn't know what the Big Cat project was all about and was trying to find out, just like everyone else.

I left there with the ashes, feeling more burdened than enlightened.

I STILL NEEDED to talk with Margaret. There was no avoiding it. Virtual Scott had dropped the hint that Sammy's phone records could implicate him in the murder. And there was only one person close enough who could check his phone. Knowing her weekdays were chock full of Governor's Mansion redecorating, I texted her and asked if she was up for breakfast in the morning. She responded right away:

—*Working out in the morning.*

—*But I miss just hanging out like friends. And you're always busy.*

—*How about you exercise with me?*

"Exercise" wasn't in my vocabulary. I had naturally thick legs, and working out just made them thicker:

—*Fine. For you, I'll do it.*

—*Meet me at Rex Gym. We'll have a smoothie together.*

We settled on 7:30 in the morning.

I tried not to think about all the ways that I might be about to destroy our friendship.

CHAPTER 25

THE SEQUENCE

When I got home, I found Lydia still up. I was glad to see her.

"I'm whipped," I said. I told her about Stephanie withdrawing from college—and my deep fear and disappointment.

"That girl is confused. She needs to f-f-find her way."

"Does she have to find it with Alex Kelly? What if she gets pregnant, or she gets married to him, or—"

"What can you do? Karl used to have a saying, 'Wish in one hand and spit in the other—then see in which hand you have the most.'"

"Wise man."

"What else is on your mind?"

"This case. And I think I'm stumped."

She nodded. She'd seen me like this before, back when I was cutting my teeth on the Wanda Hightower murder.

"How about some Sequence?" she asked, meaning the board game. I readily agreed to the distraction.

We were well into the game when it was clear to me she was being a little too quiet.

"What are *you* thinking about?" I asked.

"Darryl was here for dinner. He looked d-d-droopy. What are you two fighting about?"

"I'm not having a fight with Darryl," I said. "We just haven't had enough time together lately due to this case."

"I see."

"No, really, everything is fine from my perspective."

"But maybe not from *his*."

"I think a lot of things are stressing out Darryl right now. Charlie going hunting, for example."

"Sheriff Tom c-c-called him. Said you m-m-made some progress on the case."

"Jess didn't kill Scott Novak."

"Darryl said she was c-c-capable and put herself at the scene."

"Just not enough motive for me," I said.

"He thinks you're becoming obsessive. His first wife had another love, too: shopping. He doesn't want to lose you, too."

"How am I becoming obsessive?"

"Alaska. The Pullen Carousel."

"I was only in Alaska a few days. And after the carousel disaster I tried to quit this case, but *some* people argued me out of it." I looked at her pointedly.

"What's in the bag?" she deflected, nodding toward the thing I'd placed on the counter.

"Oh, just some corpse ashes. Maybe I am obsessed?"

"You want so much independence. What are you afraid of? That Darryl will t-t-trap you somehow?"

"Look, I'm like everyone else. I've got my stuff."

"Then you two make a fine pair."

She placed a chip in the middle of one of my potential sequences. I'd nearly had seven chips in a row—you only needed five for a proper sequence, but our house rules were that seven allowed a person to go first the next round.

Lydia had put a stop to either by separating two of my chips from my other four, and I didn't even have a one-eyed Jack to undo her move.

"'Hiawatha Style!'" she announced. Lydia had a female cousin named Hiawatha—no relation to the little brave in that famous poem—who had always played defense (and never offense) in every game they used to play.

Lydia had put me on the defensive in more ways than one.

I put my head in my hands. "Why can't we get over our crap sooner? Why is everything so *hard*?"

"Don't get nervous in a service," she scolded. "You need to do something to s-s-simplify your life."

"Then help me solve this crime."

"Try me."

Not remembering how much she already knew, I went over the details. "I feel like the biggest key to everything is this one computer project Scott had going. The Big Cat Project."

"Did Scott have any b-b-big cats in his zoo?"

"No, just a little cat. A serval."

"What do you think the project is about?"

"No clue. We can't get into the computer files."

She pulled out her sketch pad which she used to plan out her quilting patterns. In the middle of the page she wrote:

Big Cat

"Actually," I said, "Augusta said when she tries to log into the server she gets a message in which it's spelled like this..." I rewrote it:

biGCAT

We both stared at it.

"What are you th-thinking?" she asked.

"Maybe take the 'A' and the 'i' out of it, for AI? That leaves BGCT." I googled the heck out of every permutation and combination of that. No luck.

We both stared at the full words some more until she said, "Maybe we rearrange CAT to ACT and get, 'Big Act.'"

I shrugged. "That's something." But I looked at it some more. "Maybe ... no."

"What?"

"I was thinking of some of those tests you take to get into college or graduate school: ACT. GMAT. MCAT. I was just thinking of those. But that doesn't make any sense. Now why aren't we thinking this is a big fat cat waste of time?"

"Because you said Novak was a smart cookie. The goofy poems, for example."

"Right. The limericks." I pulled out my phone. I didn't feel like hearing that creepy German voice, so I texted it instead:

—*Hey, Fritz. Know any 'Big Cat' limericks?*

There was a short pause before something came back. I read the limerick out loud for Lydia (trying to use a German accent in the process):

> *Even a cat needs a little T and A.*
> *They just want to extend their DNA*
> *So sometimes they get frisky*
> *With some catnip or whiskey*
> *As they hunt for a lioness like Beyonce!*

"Beyonce was the voice of the girl lioness in the new *Lion King*," I explained. "I watched that with Charlie not too long ago."

"'A and T.' And 'DNA,'" rasped Lydia. "More l-l-letters to p-p-play with."

"I know. It's an endless, twisted puzzle." I looked at her. "Okay. Here's something."

I had googled *DNA*, which prompted the definition of *double helix* to appear. "'A sequence of an endlessly repeating code.' I hadn't thought of that! DNA is made up of code!"

"So?"

"So, we've been wondering why Scott was obsessed with his animals. We also know he drew their blood at some point. Maybe it wasn't to get their health checked. Maybe it was for their DNA—their *code*. Scott was first and foremost a coder."

I looked at the entry on DNA, then back at Lydia's sketch pad.

At our board game with Lydia's defensive Hiawatha move that broke up my sequence.

I needed to break this thing down.

"'Bi' means two," I said. "Computers are binary. So is DNA. It's a *double* helix, remember? That leaves GCAT — it says here on my screen that these letters are shorthand for the four chemicals that make up DNA: guanine, cytosine, adenine, and thymine. The first two—the G and C— go together, and so do the last two: the A and T—or 'T and A.'"

"'T and A' can mean something else, you know."

"Limericks are often on the naughty side, but that's not the point. Somehow the Big Cat project definitely has something to do with DNA, biology, and genetics. Scott planted a clue in his virtual program. And now we're unraveling it."

I reached for my computer again. Where could I go from here? What was the key to this clue?

Now that I thought about it, I did have in my possession an actual key.

"I'm going to google 'genetics' and 'Olivia,'" I said.

"Who was Olivia?" Lydia asked, as I scrolled through a million google results.

"Someone Scott knew, I guess," I said off-handedly.

"Where does she l-l-live?"

"Scott wasn't allowed to travel much. If he was dating someone else, there's a chance she lives around here." I remembered the prevalence of another person's fingerprints in Scott's house. Perhaps they were those of a secret girlfriend.

I googled *genetics, Olivia,* and *Research Triangle NC.*

It was just the sequence I needed.

"'Genetics Researcher Olivia Porter Loses University Position for Unauthorized Research,'" I read aloud. The article was from two years earlier. Nothing more recent appeared in the search. "This Dr. Olivia Porter seems to have dropped off the map."

I looked at Lydia.

"I've got to find Olivia Porter. She might be the final key to Big Cat."

I CALLED to let Paul know about my discovery. We agreed to meet in the morning, right after my meeting with Margaret.

Ugh. Margaret. It turns out there is no good way to say, "I think your boyfriend could be a murderer. Can you help me find out for sure?"

I couldn't soft-peddle it—even as we were next to one another on exercise bikes and I was literally softly pedaling.

"I need you to do something for me," I said, uttering the words between gasps for air.

"Uh-oh. You're not going to ask me to take you shopping again, are you?"

"No. Nothing that difficult." I asked her if she would be willing, for the sake of the case, to look at Sammy's phone and see if there were any calls for the evening of the murder. "I need to be able to rule out Sammy as being involved."

"You can rule him out. Trust me, he's not involved."

"Margaret, he had motive. And I'm not saying he committed the murder himself—he was with you that night, after all, but he might have been working with someone else."

"Darlin', if he was guilty, why would he hire you?"

"As a show. Let's be realistic. It's not like I'm some Interpol professional. If he wanted someone to bungle a case, he could probably do worse than to hire Rett Swinson."

"I talked you up. Why? Because I have good taste. I know quality. Sammy knows that."

"I just need to make sure he wasn't working with someone else."

"Someone doing his murderous work for him, you mean."

"Yes."

She stopped pedaling, grabbed her phone and keys, and strode away.

I'm not very fast, so it's a good thing she wasn't running.

At least I was able to block her from leaving the spin room.

"Margaret, listen to me."

"I don't want to hear this." She tried to move past me, but I blocked her again. I'm not taller than Margaret, but I am definitely wider.

"Listen," I said, "I don't suspect Sammy. I really don't! I'm just trying to cover all my bases. I'm trying to do a good job."

"But you work *for* Sammy."

"Margaret, I refuse to be a blue-jay person."

"A what?"

"What I'm saying is, yes, Sammy's paying me, but I'm *working* for what we agreed I would work for: finding the truth. And I can't find the truth if I don't track down every lead. Sammy had motive—maybe not the clearest motive, but still motive. And, remember, it was Sammy—not the police, and not me—who was convinced Scott Novak was murdered.

"Besides," I added. "You're important to me. And I need to know that you're marrying a good guy."

"Sammy is a good guy."

"I believe he is. But I want to *know* that he is. Don't you?"

Her voice quivered. "This is the first man who hasn't disappointed me, Rett. And I'm not going to betray Sammy."

I let that soak in. How could I argue? "I was wrong to ask you to do this, Maggie. I'm sorry. I hope you won't hold it against me."

"Fine. We'll just forget this ever happened."

"Okay. Should we go finish our exercise routine now?"

"Honey, let's forget that, too."

"Thank you!"

PAUL HAD HAD no trouble digging up Olivia Porter's address. We met at RidgeLine, and he drove us to a neighborhood in Cary. We got there around 8:30 in the morning and waited.

Paul looked thoughtful.

"Why the troubled expression?" I asked.

"I heard from the sheriff's office last night. Those nearly empty bottles of Clyde Ray's you got from Novak's old house? They contained fingerprints from our mystery person, but they weren't Jess's prints and they weren't Esther's either. This doesn't eliminate either one as a suspect, but Sheriff Jordan is trying to track down others who were at those parties to see why they were spending so much time at the farmhouse — and what they might know. Tedious work. Going to take a long time. Some of those programmers have left with their sale of stock and started companies in California."

He snapped to attention. "We're cookin'."

An older woman came out of the house and got into her car. We followed her several miles into the country, eventually to what looked like a small warehouse.

We pulled up just after she'd gone inside. She had locked the door behind her, but I had brought with me the key that I'd found on the carousel.

The key unlocked the door.

We stepped inside where we found a laboratory, industrial white, with dozens of large machines, all humming. Adjacent to the machines were several propane tanks and a huge generator. Out here in the country, such back-ups were nice to have.

"Olivia Porter?" I asked.

The woman must have been in her seventies but looked super sharp, serious. She considered us as she looked over her dropped-down, close-work glasses.

"I thought I locked that door. Who, may I ask, is inquiring?"

"We're here about Scott Novak," I said. "He led us to this."

I held up the key to her lab.

She turned back to her work. "There's nothing to say. Scott Novak is deceased."

"We're pretty sure you know something about his death. How did you meet Scott in the first place?"

"Oh, I think we met years ago at some Chamber of Commerce gathering of entrepreneurs and researchers."

I looked around her lab. "What was Scott Novak working on? What is Project Big Cat?"

"I'm not going to talk about my research with you." She had turned toward us and assumed a defiant stance. "This is a private lab, and I'm beholden to no one. Now, if you'll please leave, I have work to do."

Paul said, "You were kicked out of your last job for doing

illegal human cloning research. Why is your lab out here in the middle of nowhere? What are you trying to hide, lady?"

"If I answer some of your questions, will you both leave?"

"We think whatever happened to Scott might have been connected to your research with him. You were creating something that could change a person's DNA, weren't you?"

Olivia Porter didn't respond.

"We can report you—and this secret lab—to the Ethics Board of Gene Therapy," Paul said. "I learned that's a thing."

A beat.

"Fine. I'll tell you what you want to know, and then you'll leave. Scott wanted to ... evolve."

"As in Charles Darwin evolve?" I asked.

"No. Darwin's version of evolution is too slow. Scott was looking for a faster way."

"Let me guess: Lamarck's way."

She seemed impressed. "In a way. It's called epigenetics. It's all about changing the way genes express themselves in the body. A relatively new field of study. We know that stress can change the way our genes operate, that we can even pass down negative effects of stress from one generation to the next. Scott wanted to evolve positive attributes in a similar way. With this gene therapy, he hoped to become better than he was."

"In what ways?"

"You'll think it sounds naive, but he said he wanted to 'learn how to love.'"

I nodded. It was as I had thought:

Scott wasn't fixated on Beth *the Giraffe.*

Scott wanted to Be *the Giraffe. Stretch himself. Make himself extraordinary.*

I took a step closer. "How was he hoping to pull this off?"

"He brought his machine-learning prowess and worked with me to apply it to genetic code. He included all the animals in his zoo because of their diversity. Each was a survivor, and each brought unique traits to the table. It was his goal to create a therapy that helped a person to change who they were—to 'overcome' themselves, as he put it."

"Like Nietzsche talked about," I said.

She nodded. "Remember, Scott knew how to create self-learning. Combine that with epigenetics and the intelligence of myriad animals—"

"—and you create a superior being."

"No more being stuck in one's blind spots. An ability to achieve one's potential. If I had something like that 20, 30 years ago, I could have gotten to where I am today so much faster."

"That would be quite the innovation," I said.

"He'd make a killing!" Paul said.

"Scott wasn't interested in money," Olivia added. "He had plenty of that."

"How far along did you get with this therapy?" I asked.

"It was ready for its first trial."

"Through the FDA?"

"No. That would require revealing the technology behind it —a technology that at least for now is forbidden. Scott aimed to see on his own how it worked."

"He decided to test it on his animals? Maybe on Zeus?"

"Scott was too ethical for that. No, he was going to try it on himself. I produced the first serum three weeks ago and dropped it off at his home. Just a few days later I read about his death."

Paul asked, "Do you know if he took the serum?"

"I don't know for sure, but I do know he aimed to test it."

"Was it something he would take intravenously?" I asked. She nodded. This would explain the syringe cap. It corroborated Jess's story of finding an empty syringe near his body.

"Why wouldn't he do it in a controlled environment, in case something went wrong?"

"He didn't want to implicate anyone, including me." Her eyes grew moist.

"Wouldn't the autopsy tell us if he took it—and what it might have done to him? What if it made him despondent and caused him to take his life?"

"You'd have to do intensive DNA tests to even know something was different about him. A brain scan could show a difference, but it's not like we have a 'before' picture of Scott's brain to compare it to."

I wasn't convinced. What if Scott had been testing it on one of the animals in his zoo? A really smart ape, made smarter by such a therapy, could escape its cage, shimmy up a drainpipe, and get into a house the same way as Jess. It might even have the dexterity to tie a cravat and the strength to choke a man.

"Could he have given the serum to someone—or something —else?"

"That serum was designed specifically for Scott's DNA. We would have to create a different formula for someone else's genetic code. And no one else knows how. I don't have access anymore to the computer code that helped me develop the serum. Every week he had to unlock it for me. The technology died with him."

"Actually, it probably still exists," I said. "It's just on a protected computer server."

Her eyes brightened. "You know where it lives?"

"Yes, but we can't get into it. Do you think you could?"

Her expression deflated. "I don't see how."

"You might be in a lot of trouble, lady," said Paul. "If the lab tests done on Scott show your serum killed him—"

"They won't find a thing," she said. "Even if you tell them to look for it, they won't be able to find it and pin it on me. That's just a scientific fact."

Paul and I traded a look.

"Don't you feel guilty that you helped Scott with this?" I asked her.

"My conscience is clean. Though I worked hard on this research, Scott was driving the bus."

"What was in it for you?"

"If it worked on him, we were going to see if we could work on reversing the aging process. I was willing to be the guinea pig for that. What good is success when you're too old to enjoy its fruits?"

Knowing Scott was doing this type of research raised some questions. How many others knew about it? Might they want to stop him—or steal the technology for themselves?

Not to mention: Did Scott Novak's own research kill him?

LEAVING THE LAB, Paul and I argued. He thought that the discovery was a very big deal. I told him he was wrong. "Knowing that what is on the Big Cat server is a bunch of genetic code of himself and his animals doesn't get us closer to figuring out how he died," I said. "It just gives us one more possibility—which Olivia Porter happens to think can't be proven."

"Then what should we do next, smarty pants?"

"Talk to the person who aims to gain the most from Scott's death. His brother, Adam."

"And how are you going to do that?"

"There's only one way. I have to go back to Alaska. But this time I aim to get my questions answered."

CHAPTER 26

BREAKTHROUGH

Darryl was furious.

"Why would you go all that way again?"

I mentioned the ashes. He was unimpressed.

"You can ship those. I've seen families do it a thousand times." *In his job, he's seen that much death.*

I dug in my heels. "Adam Novak is avoiding me. I can't help but think he's the key to this whole puzzle."

"The sheriff just opened a murder investigation after you brought him that college student. Why not give Tom more time to follow up? He might end up charging Jess."

"Are you just trying to say that you'll miss me?" *Please say yes.*

"Stop joking around." Darryl wasn't kidding around, but damn this man's pride! I wasn't his possession. I was determined to show I was independent of him. *An Überwoman.* Whether he liked it or not.

The next morning he drove me to the airport, but it felt like pure duty.

We kissed, but that, too, was just checking a box.

This wasn't the relationship I wanted. And what would be waiting for me when I returned?

And what did I *want* to be waiting for me?

I HAD a lot more to think about on this trip. Instead of running around in the Denver Airport looking for boots that fit, I paused to make a few phone calls and use the free airport Wi-Fi. One breakthrough: A voicemail said that a sheriff would meet me at the Gates's floatplane station in Billings; Tom Jordan had asked them to interview Adam Novak—and they wanted to interview me as well.

I crossed fingers that I'd be able to ask my questions of Adam before he was spooked by the authorities.

When I arrived, it was like a reunion. I was delighted to see Christopher and Sarah again. Dave was there, too, along with the sheriff and two of his deputies.

Sheriff Crawford wanted my time right away. There was more of a chill in the air—it was October now—so we sat inside the Gates's cabin where Crawford debriefed me of everything I knew about the case, making it clear in the process that he already knew quite a few new details thanks to Sheriff Tom Jordan who he'd talked to earlier that day.

"What do you know about Novak's longtime friend and business partner, Emerson Cramer?" Crawford asked.

"I know they have been friends and have worked together since college."

"You're aware that Cramer was named in Novak's will?"

"Yes," I said, "but I'm not sure that Emerson knew there even *was* a will at the time Novak died."

The sheriff smiled. "Your sheriff was able to get a warrant to look at Mr. Novak's phone this morning. They found a text from Scott Novak to Emerson Cramer a week before his death on where to find the will. Said it was hidden in his suitcase."

So, Emerson had known about the will. Then why had he made no attempt to recover it after Novak's death? He need only tell the sheriff, and Tom would have retrieved it for him.

But I still had questions. "I'm not entirely comfortable about the focus on Emerson. What else makes him suspect?"

"Scott Novak's boss—an Indian guy, Patel—found a few odd purchases on Mr. Cramer's business credit card."

"What type of purchases?"

"Satellite phones. Three of them. They would work even where cell phones wouldn't pick up a good signal—like in the woods near Mr. Novak's home."

I frowned. "Emerson was doing a lot of technical research. Isn't it possible he bought the phones for his lab?"

"When he was confronted about the satellite phones, he didn't really have an answer. He just clammed up and insisted on having a lawyer."

I turned red. This case was being solved in my absence. I should be happy, I guess, but it only showed that my involvement was now, and always had been, extraneous.

I asked, "If you suspect Mr. Cramer, why did you come out here today?"

"Just before he lawyered up, Emerson kept insisting that Adam Novak could clear his name. Wake County's sheriff thinks those two may be in cahoots somehow."

"The last time I was here, he wasn't even at his cabin," I said. "We might come up empty again."

"The fact he's been unreachable since his brother's death is itself suspicious. We've got a warrant to search Adam Novak's property today."

Clearly my presence here was a waste of time. But I couldn't just turn around and go home.

"Since I've come all this way, with your permission, Sheriff, I'd still like to come along."

"That's fine," he said. "We just reserve the right to question Adam first."

"Deal," I said.

"We'll head to Adam's cabin in a few."

He left the cabin. I didn't have time to feel sorry myself, as Dave Nash appeared in the doorway. He looked to be in a really good mood.

"You sure seem excited," I said, trying not to show my own disappointment.

"I heard from that businessman again. His friends love my idea of the Alaskan Survival Camp! With any luck, we'll be breaking ground next spring. We're going to have a reality show associated with it, too. It's really going to happen."

I congratulated him, and Dave did a little dance in the dirt outside the doorway. It always struck me as cute when a tough guy danced with joy.

After I arranged my things and put together my pack, Dave and I began following the sheriff to Adam's along the familiar route. After a couple of hours, the whole party paused to eat a snack.

"No painting on this trip?" Dave asked me.

"I guess I'm too preoccupied this time. Long story, but it seems law enforcement has already figured everything out. I was worried that I wouldn't find Adam and it would be another wasted trip. But I guess it is already a waste."

"Modern man can't stand to waste time, that's for sure. Out here we've got nothing but time. Time is your only friend. It's only when the bad weather is coming on fast that you start to question that."

"You take your cues from the weather. It reminds me of my friend Paige. She's a restauranteur and she believes in farm-to-table cooking. She serves what is in season. 'Why present last year's play in front of this year's set,' she likes to say."

"That's some pretty deep snow you've waded into, Ms. Swinson," he chuckled.

Everyone got back on the path. Time seemed to go quickly once you got in a steady gait. I felt my anxiety leave me as I built up body heat. I realized that I was in far better shape this time around compared to the first.

The sky began to cloud up.

"It will feel warmer thanks to the clouds," Dave explained. "Clouds hold in the heat from the Earth. In the winter, I'm always glad to see a cloudy day."

I knew that Dave had been all over Alaska. "What part of the state do you most like to explore?" I asked.

He thought a moment. "I prefer exploring near rivers. Canoeing is my favorite way to travel."

"That's right. You've guided river tours. Didn't you say you recently took a group to the Sustina...?

"Susitna. Yeah. That was a good one. I took another group down the Porcupine a few years ago. That's way up past Fairbanks. Quite a trek, but worth it.

"I was thinking of getting a group of my friends together and coming up here."

"They'd be most welcome."

"Would the Susitna be a good trip for us? Were that businessman investor and his friends all experienced campers?"

"Not really. And they did terrific. I'm sure your friends would do fine."

We arrived at Adam's cabin. My heart sank. It looked just as we'd left it. Where the hell was Adam Novak?

The sheriff said, "I guess it's time to go to work."

The deputies swung into gear. They were meticulous. It didn't take long before they announced to the sheriff they had found something under one of the floorboards. They brought to him something that looked like a small, black, plastic brick.

"How about that," said the sheriff. "A satellite phone. Is it still live, Steele?"

"Naw, it's dead," said the deputy.

"Chris Gates never told me Adam had a satellite phone," I said. "You'd think he would have known." Imagine, I could have been calling Adam all this time instead of making the trip in person! It really burned me up.

"He probably kept it secret," said the sheriff.

"I've got a battery charger," said the other deputy, who pulled out one of those portable batteries meant to charge anything from cellphones to tablets. "Give it a few minutes and we'll be able to take a look at its call record."

I stepped outside and found Dave sitting on the front porch. I asked him if he was aware that Adam had owned a satellite phone.

He shook his head emphatically. "Adam wouldn't have wanted a phone. He came out here to get away from all that. Must be some mistake. Ain't there any other suspects back in North Carolina? What about Scott Novak's girlfriend? Who was the last to see him alive?"

"Probably not Esther. It was likely a former girlfriend, Jess Bennett, who saw him alive last."

"Really?"

"The pair had sex, then she left. When she came back to retrieve some belongings, she found him dead."

He looked momentarily shocked. Then he just shook his head. "Sad."

We bided our time.

After a few moments, the deputy came outside to complain. "This battery is defective. It's not taking a charge."

Another deputy looked at it. "I think mine is the same model. I'll grab its battery." He fished his phone from his pack. Immediately, they were able to boot up the phone.

"Sheriff, we've got some text messages stored in here," the first deputy said.

He handed the phone to Crawford.

"The texts are all to and from the same 919 number."

Crawford read the digits aloud.

"That's Emerson Cramer's number," I said. "What do the texts say?"

The sheriff began scrolling the data on the phone and reading aloud: "From Mr. Cramer on September 15: *'Thanks for taking my call. Important: Disappear. Not safe for you right now. Let no one talk to you. Lose this phone. SP can trace anything. He'll put you in danger.'* Who's SP?"

"Samarth Patel," I said.

The sheriff nodded, then continued:

"The next day on September 16, also from Mr. Cramer's number: *Update: SP has hired another PI. I'll talk with her but I won't give anything away. Give me time.*

"I'm sure he's talking about me," I said.

"On September 17, from this phone: *Will get lost. But can't hide forever. Three weeks tops.*

"Later on September 17, also from this phone: *I'm losing this phone in case traceable. As of NOW.*"

"Is that all?" I asked.

"It's enough to establish a conspiracy," said the sheriff.

Crawford announced, "It looks like a manhunt is officially on for Adam Novak." He got on his walky-talky and started calling in back-up. He turned to me. "Here's where we part ways, ma'am. Thanks for your help. We'll take it from here."

DAVE WAS STILL SITTING on the front porch of the shack, shaking his head. He looked deeply concerned.

"I can't believe they suspect Adam. He's totally being framed. That is not his phone. I've never seen him with one." He was stewing. "We should tell my dad what those turkeys just did."

"They had a warrant."

"But you can't just look for stuff in general. You've got to look for something in *particular*. I've seen that episode of Patriot Mike's."

"But they knew about the satellite phones Emerson bought, so I bet that was listed on the warrant. What should we do now? Just go back to the lake?"

Dave shrugged. "I guess," he said. "Or we could try to find Adam before they do, so we can warn him."

"You said you didn't know where he was."

"True, I don't. But the only place we haven't looked is down by the river. He might be there doing some fishing."

"Won't the search party find him?

"There's all kinds of rock formations along the river's edge one can hide among. It's slow to explore on foot, and you wouldn't be able to see him from the air using a helicopter or drone, not if he's among those rocks or the trees along the edge of the river."

I wasn't interested in warning someone who was wanted by the authorities. But the thought of coming all this way a second time without connecting with Adam made me sick to my stomach. I wanted answers as badly as the sheriff did. And I had invested a lot more time in this case than he had.

I asked, "If we go all the way to the river, won't we have to camp the night?"

"Yeah, but it's fine. I'll take some of Adam's gear."

As he got the gear together, I looked over the cabin one more time. The well-worn copy of *Thus Spoke Zarathustra*. The home-made sign, "YOU'LL SEE ME IN 2."

I knew I shouldn't, but I took the book with me.

We walked down into the valley, an effortless walk that made it easy to think.

I thought about why Adam Novak would be involved with Emerson Cramer in a murder. True, *before* the will was found, Adam had a strong motive: he'd be the sole heir to Scott's fortune.

Of course, even with the new will, one could argue there was plenty of profit to be had. A million dollars is no joke. But he'd be incentivized never to let that will be found. Perhaps he'd sent someone to Scott's house to find and destroy it. Maybe Emerson knew about the terms of the will and wanted it not to be found —at least immediately. He'd keep quiet about it for a while to keep the spotlight off him as a suspect.

Adam's so-called reconciliation with his brother could have been just an act, a way to deflect blame. Deep down, he may have still nursed a deep resentment toward Scott for staying with their mother while Adam was forced to endure the abuse of their dad.

Before the finding of the will, Adam could have reached out to Emerson and hired him to kill Scott. Who would suspect a hermit thousands of miles away to be behind a murder for hire? He'd pay off Emerson with some ungodly amount—perhaps even half of Scott's fortune.

This deal, of course, would make the new will pointless from Emerson's perspective, since Adam had already promised to share half of Scott's estate.

So, it did make a kind of sense. Besides, the evidence of the phones and conversations was clear that there was some sort of collusion.

But Dave raised the possibility that Adam was being framed. He didn't suggest who might be the framer, but there weren't too many possibilities, now were there?

Again I asked Dave about his father's relationship with Adam.

"Adam comes and visits all the time. He's the only one who can get a word in edgewise with my dad."

"How does Mike react to that?"

He chuckled. "I don't think he likes it, but it's good for him. The old blowhard. Adam is a lot smarter than my dad. He's been around the block, read a lot of books. My dad hasn't. If he thinks something ought to be true, then his mind makes it true."

"Any chance your dad is jealous of Adam somehow?"

He shrugged. "I don't think many people impress my dad."

There was bitterness there, and the bitterness ran deep.

I meditated on Patriot Mike. We knew he had no love for Scott Novak, that's for sure. And he had that huge, online audience of political acolytes who could provide all manner of help if needed.

"Mike got a lot of his friends to help with the search for our daughter. He came through for us. This lake never saw so many float planes as the week after she disappeared."

It was nice to have friends who would do anything for you, no questions asked.

Blue-jay people.

Wasn't it possible that Mike would make a trip to North Carolina himself? Unknown to Christopher and Sarah, a pilot lands in the night at the far end of the lake. It doesn't bother with refueling. It picks up a single passenger—Mike Nash.

Or a slightly different possibility: Chris and Sarah Gates, still grateful for all that Mike had done for their family, keep Mike's quiet trip to North Carolina a secret.

But I shook my head. Mike had a bum leg. Even if he got himself to North Carolina and the lake near Scott's house, how could he effectively traipse through the woods to make his approach, commit the crime, and then get away? Unlikely. Better to be working with someone on the ground—someone like

Lorry Sneed, one of his Internet fans. The pair do their crime of mutual spite, then work together to frame Emerson and Adam.

Improbable—but still *possible*.

We were nearer the river now. A small creek stretched out before us. It was lovely, water so clear you almost couldn't see the water at all.

"Look up there," said Dave.

I squinted at a speck in the sky.

"Here." He handed me his binoculars. I put the strap around my neck so as not to drop them and trained the lenses at the sky.

"A bald eagle!" I said. "He's huge. And he's carrying a fish!"

"Not a fish. A snake."

"Gross."

"Tons of eagles around here," Dave said.

We set about crossing the creek on rocks. The water was deep in places and swift. We were halfway across when he told me to stop and pointed far downstream.

"What's that?" I lifted the binoculars again.

"I think it's a bear."

"I can't tell," I said.

"Hand me the binoculars. I'll look."

I did so, but in the process of removing the strap, it got tangled somehow. Something plopped in the water; immediately I realized what it was.

"The Amulet!" I cried. "Oh, crap, it's—"

"Was it important?"

"Maybe, but it's gone now. Gone down the river."

"You sure? I can—"

"It's okay. It was probably more trouble than it was worth."

By then the bear—or whatever it was—was gone.

We pushed on. Occasionally a helicopter whirred by. The authorities were serious about finding Adam. But I felt like we were on a nature hike now.

I heard a bird. Nothing exotic like an eagle or an owl. Just a dastardly blue jay. I mentioned it to Dave.

"We don't have blue jays in Alaska," he said. "Jays of different kinds, but not blue jays." He stopped to listen.

"Weird," I said, "because that sounds just like one."

Dave put a finger to his lips and beckoned me to follow him. Together we moved cautiously through the marshy bushes until he pulled up short and gestured for me to come closer.

The bird's call was louder than ever. But now I saw that it wasn't a bird. It was a mammal about three feet tall on wobbly legs.

"What is it?" I asked in a whisper.

"Baby moose. Just a couple weeks old. Odd that it would be born this time of year, but it does happen. I have a feeling its mother is near, so we should skedaddle. I don't want to get on a mama moose's bad side."

We backtracked until he was able to talk in a normal voice again. "We might want to take that as a sign and start to head back."

"Oh, I'm really enjoying the nature walk. Do we have to head back just yet?"

"It's just we'll run out of daylight," he said. "And if you did see a bear, we probably don't want to camp here."

"Okay," I said, grudgingly, and we began the long walk back.

We were low enough in elevation that it was possible to see the mountain from which we'd hiked. From this angle, compared to the angle from the lake, the mountain appeared double, like twin peaks. I remembered the show *Twin Peaks* from the early 1990s. It had been too scary for me, and all my high school friends made fun of me for the fact. Now I wish I had watched the show, because I think it dealt with at least one murder investigation. I might have learned a thing or two, maybe even something to apply to this case.

We spent the next hour walking, me lost in my thoughts. The weather was just lovely. I tried to put the Novaks behind me; the case was in the hands of the authorities now.

Margaret could rest easy that her boyfriend was not a psychopath, and I could rest easy knowing my friend might finally live happily ever after.

We again entered the forest, from which there were no views of the mountain. If I wanted to paint that view someday, I'd have to visit it in my mind. I closed my eyes. It was as if the mountain was speaking to me: *You'll see me in 2.*

"You're awfully quiet," Dave said. "Everything okay back there?"

"When you saw Adam and gave him the message of Scott dying, did he act odd to you?"

"Like I said, he was pretty quiet."

"Anything else unusual or strange? What was he *doing* when you saw him?"

"Reading that book. His favorite one by Nietzsche. He would read from it and quote it all the time."

I opened my backpack and pulled out my copy of *Zarathustra*. I flipped to the table of contents and confirmed what I'd remembered. The book was in four parts.

YOU'LL SEE ME IN 2.

Part Two was super long. How was I supposed to find anything important there?

But he'd used a *numeral* 2. The second aphorism—listed as the numeral 2—was perhaps the book's most famous. That's where Zarathustra encounters a Christian hermit, and, later, marvels to himself that the saint is unaware God is dead.

I read aloud the beginning line to Dave, "'Zarathustra came down off the mountain and into the woods ...' Maybe that's what we're supposed to believe: Adam is telling us that he came into the valley."

"That is where we've been exploring."

"Yeah," I said. I put the book away. Maybe it really wasn't much of a clue after all.

But my mind wouldn't stop ruminating.

"You still thinking about that book?" he asked a while later. Before I could answer, he added: "Mike thinks Adam is an atheist because of that book, but Adam says that *everyone* is an atheist, because even the people who *say* they believe in God don't *act* like it, that the only Christian who ever lived was Jesus Christ himself.

"He says there's only one way that people live, and that's through their will. You want to *believe* something, you find a way to believe it. You want to *do* something, you find an excuse to do it. That's how people are. That's how *all* people are. Even so-called saints.

"I'll say this—a lot of people want to do things for themselves," he went on. "That's what the Alaskan Survival Camp is all about. Helping people to do for themselves. Getting back to where we all belong. It's all *right here*." He gestured around him. "Everything you need is right here. No need to live in a city and have other people doing things for you. This is how we humans were built. For *this*. That's why Adam came here to stay. He's lived in the city, and he came here, and he stayed."

"But I wonder if part of him was restless," I said. "Like Zarathustra, he wondered if he should bring what he had learned back to the world of people. And maybe he was a little bit lonely, too."

"Maybe he sometimes thought about going back to the lower 48," Dave said, "but I swear that Adam is right here walking around in these woods. He didn't leave for San Francisco or anything crazy like that."

I stopped walking. "Dave, I'm pretty sure that Adam isn't hiding. In fact, I have a very strong feeling that Adam is dead."

Dave stopped walking and looked at me. "That's nuts. Adam is the smartest survivor I know." He seemed so upset, I knew I needed to back down. Dave was still my guide in the Alaskan wilderness. I needed to make sure he kept his wits about him.

"You're right. I might be crazy," I said. "The police will find him one way or another. Maybe he'll even turn himself in."

Dave shook his head. "No, he'll outsmart them. But I think I know where he is. Remember how my dad mentioned that skunk that crawled into Adam's tent that one time? I was wrong earlier. I think that was when Adam was camping closer to the lake, not the river. My dad knows things—don't ask me how he knows, but he does."

Dave took a deep breath. "We've got a fair piece to go. We're out of that bear's territory. Let's just camp here after all."

But I didn't want to spend the night. I told Dave I was ready to go home—as in Carolina home.

"Earlier you wanted to take your time and camp," he said. "Why are you changing your mind?"

"I guess I realized how tired I am of this case. I'm just ready to get back to Raleigh."

"You women and your crazy ... you can't make up your minds." He shook his head. "Just like Bren."

"Whatever happened with Brenda, Dave?"

He shot me a hurt, angry look. "Brenda died. That's what happened."

"I know. It devastated her parents."

"It devastated me, too—not that it's a competition or anything."

I stood and waited. For what? We were just standing there, going nowhere.

"We should head back now," I said.

He glanced up at the sun and shook his head. "It's too late. We'll have to camp here." *Here* was near an outcropping—sloped, rocky ground that would make for an uncomfortable night's sleep.

"We can make it back if we leave now," I said.

"No. I'm tired." The passive aggression was instantly recognizable. My daughter had helped me become an expert spotter of it.

"That's fine," I said. "I think I can make it alone. I remember the way. It's uphill until I hit the main path, then I just hang a right. I could do it in the dark. I'll just tell Chris and Sarah that you and I had conflicting plans. Thank you for your help, David."

I leaned in as if to hug him, but he turned away, so I drew my arms back in and began to leave. For a moment I thought he was going to let me go alone. He didn't try to stop me.

All of a sudden, there was a loud *thwonk*. I pulled up. A massive knife was buried to the hilt in the center of the aspen next to me.

More than *hearing* the blade penetrate the trunk, I had *felt* it.

I swung around. "What was that for?"

"I think I'm going to need you to take off your pack and get comfortable, Ms. Swinson," he said firmly. "This is your guide speaking."

CHAPTER 27
FLIGHT

I considered my chances of pulling that knife from the tree. As if reading my thoughts, Dave laughed. "You won't be able to get it out. Besides, there are others where that came from."

"You're threatening me."

"Because you've pissed me off."

My mind raced.

"If you try to run," he said calmly, "my next toss won't end up in a tree. Come over here and sit on this log. Make yourself comfortable."

I did as I was told. All of a sudden, I noticed how cold it was getting. I needed to move, to heat up my core. The sun was nearing the horizon. How had it gotten so late so quickly?

"Is that the same knife you used to cut a length of Jess's aerial silk?" I asked. *The blade would be clean, but an analysis of the knife's sheath might reveal microscopic yellow fibers.*

"You don't waste time, do you?" he said with an amused tone. "But there will be time."

A helicopter quickly grew louder and raced by to our east. In such thick woods, we both knew there was no way for me to signal it. Besides, it was looking for someone else. As quickly as it had arrived, it disappeared.

I started to shiver some more. I didn't know if it was the chill teasing my skin or the worry growing inside my bones.

"You're pretty sharp, Ms. Swinson," Dave said. "Too smart for your own good."

But, no, I wasn't smart. I had done my thinking out loud and said too much too soon. At least there was no reason to hold back my cards at this point.

I said, "I thought you were smart, too. So why did you decide to do such an odd and risky thing as kill Scott Novak?"

He didn't answer me. I watched him slowly walk over to his knife and pull it from the tree with a brief, furious shake.

"Let me guess," I continued, "you thought if Adam inherited a lot of money, he would fund your Alaskan Survival Camp."

He shrugged. "The thought did occur to me."

"Did Adam put you up to it?"

He laughed. "Adam didn't have a damn thing to do with it. I don't know who is trying to frame him. I'm starting to wonder if maybe you are."

"Me?"

"Just to cause trouble. Just to stir the pot."

Another chill went up my back. I crossed my arms, shivered harder.

He said, "It doesn't matter what you do. Adam has an alibi. He was here."

"But *you* don't have an alibi, Dave. That party you were with way out in the wilderness? It's easy enough to talk to them and learn that you left them alone for nearly three days.

"It's all part and parcel of your particular training method, to help people gain confidence in their own powers. I saw it on your website when I hired you, but I didn't remember until I looked at it again when I was killing time in the airport. That's why that one businessman felt so proud having survived on his own. You helped the group set off on their own little weekend excursion, paddled to meet a float plane pilot who was one of your dad's friends, and flew to North Carolina. After the murder, you raced back there and got in place again, making it appear like you'd never left your camp."

"No one saw me. And the pilot will never talk. He'll die before he betrays Patriot Mike."

"Your dad was in on this?"

"Didn't need him. I emailed his friend from his own address and asked him to help me. I used Mike's own way of writing."

I briefly thought to myself: *I'm recording a confession.* Then I remembered the loss of the Amulet and despaired again.

But I pressed on.

"You landed after dark in Harris Lake. Then you walked through the woods—no big deal for you—and made your way to Scott Novak's house. What happened then? Let me guess: The front door was unlocked, allowing you to sneak inside and upstairs. But before you could attack, Jess arrived. You hid—and waited—with your knife. Because of their game, you thought that Jess was Esther—now it makes sense why you seemed kind of surprised earlier when I said it was Jess who Scott had slept with.

"You hid in a closet while they had sex. Then, when Jess left, you decided to frame her with her own silk."

He laughed. "That's right. Scott had said he was so crazy about Esther. That guy wasn't even loyal. But he knew he'd done wrong. He carried on like a baby afterwards."

"What do you mean?"

"He got pissed off at himself and punched a wall. Yelled about how 'human, all too human' he was. Adam used to say that, too. His hand hurt so he wrote out a letter with his left hand—I read it after he was dead. It looked like a suicide note, so I left it behind. Anyway, the druggie shot up with something and lay down in his bed. I waited a little while to see if he'd die on his own, but he wasn't dying, and time was wasting."

"Did you two talk before you strangled him?"

"Oh, I had quite a bit to say to Mr. Scott Novak! For example, I reminded him how he tried to steal my ideas for his own profit."

"You mean when you told Adam that animals remembered their species' survival traits? That idea?"

"Exactly!"

"But no one owns an idea, Dave. You can't expect—"

"He used it in his research. So where was my piece of the pie? Mike is right. Scott was just a user."

"Did he say anything?"

"Now that you mention it, he did. Right before I tossed the knife and wrapped that cloth around his neck, he said, 'We must always be our brother's keeper.' Something from the Bible, I guess. He didn't even fight me."

"Didn't you worry that killing Scott would devastate Adam?"

"Weren't no love between those two."

"But you said you saw a very sad man when you told him his brother was dead."

"'Sad?' No. *Surprised* maybe. He'll get over it."

"Like I said, Dave, I'm pretty sure Adam Novak is dead."

"You keep saying that. Why?"

"Because I'm pretty sure you killed him."

He laughed. "You are one crazy bitch! You probably think I killed Brenda Gates, too!"

"The thought had crossed my mind."

"Well, I didn't. It was an *accident*. I've never told anyone about it, but it was. You can go on accusing me of all kinds of things, but that doesn't make them true."

"What happened with Brenda?" *Her parents would like to*

know.

Dave fell silent and seemed to grow more agitated. He looked at the sky. "Take your clothes off, please."

"What?"

"I'm not going to hurt you. Promise. I'm going to give you a humane death. See, you went off to take a photo of the sunset for your painting and wandered off the trail. Got lost. I couldn't find you in the dark. By the time I found you the next morning, you'd died of hypothermia. It doesn't take that long this time of year, and it's getting cold already. Take your clothes off." He waved his knife. "I mean it."

"Are you going to rape me?"

He laughed again (as if the notion of rape were funny). "No. It's just I don't aim to wait out here all night. Don't worry. They won't find you naked. I'll put your clothes back on you."

"You're an animal."

"Why, yes, I am. Humans are animals—like that ape I passed in the woods near Scott Novak's house. Most surreal moment of my life that was!" He shook his head. "But I'm not heartless. You'll just go to sleep. It's the best death there is. In fact, near the end, you won't even feel cold. It's weird."

He waved the knife again. I started to undress.

"Wait," he said. "Let's both go over there, by the rocks. I'll have a place to sit down."

We went closer to the outcropping, which was big enough to hide a small cave. I briefly fantasized that a bear would come out and overwhelm my captor. Poetic justice. I actually tried to will it.

He saw me pause. "You don't have to look at me when you undress. Just turn around, face the other way. I won't see your privates. Just pile up your clothes there."

I did as I was told.

The light was dimming but I could see my breath clearly, a

white exhaust.

"Okay, now. Sit." *Like a dog.*

I tried to sit still and endure, not panic, just survive till the next minute, the next second. But it was no use. If I wasn't freezing before, now I was. I had to do something. Should I beg for my life?

I stood and faced him.

"Sit *down.*" But I think he liked looking at my breasts, the hair between my legs. When had this young man ever seen a woman naked in the moonlight? I wondered if I could seduce him, get him to let down his guard. Maybe I could sneak the knife away from him, put him on the defensive.

The thought of kissing this scoundrel disgusted me. But I had to think of something to buy more time.

The cold was teasing my body and starting to sting.

"I'm not going to die like this," I said, almost in a whisper. "I'm going to go down fighting."

He heard me. "And just how are you going to fight me?" He seemed amused, if not aroused, by my anger and nudity.

I was no Wonder Woman. What the hell was I going to do?

Standing there, desperate, I put my face in my hands and started to weep.

He shook his head, "You're just making this harder, Woman. Calm down."

Then I started to scream at him. "What the hell is wrong with you? How can you do this to a person? Have you no sense of honor? Look at what you're doing!"

He shouted right back: "YOU POKED INTO MY BUSINESS! YOU COULDN'T LEAVE WELL ENOUGH ALONE! THE FIGHT WAS BETWEEN ME AND SCOTT NOVAK! LET MEN FIGHT THEIR DUELS!"

"What about the law, Dave? What about that?"

"YOUR LAW MEANS NOTHING TO ME! LET MEN

FIGHT THEIR BATTLES ACCORDING TO THE ANCIENT CODE!"

I sighed. If I didn't die first, all these various types of code were going to drive me completely insane.

"Please, sit down," he said more quietly. "Because if you don't, a bear is going to kill you." Now he pulled from his left boot a different type of knife, one with a claw-like blade. "Believe me, I've seen a bear's kill. And I've got bear scent to make it look legit. This ground is liquid right now. Ain't no one going to be able to tell what really happened."

I didn't put it past him, so I sat back down.

"If I'm going to die anyway," I said, "at least tell me about Brenda."

He didn't respond right away. I couldn't see his face too well in the waning light, but I sensed he was nervous, biting his fingernails. *In Scott Novak's house, in the closet where Dave hid, I wonder if bits of fingernail peppered the floor.*

Then he began:

"I'd been out checking traps. I got home mid-afternoon. Mom said Brenda had come by wanting to see me to tell me something, so I went to find her. I went to a place she went sometimes to look over the valley and the river, not far from our house. She was down there on the ledge where she liked to study. She was looking for her backpack, but it wasn't there. She seemed really mad. I asked her why.

"She said it was because in the backpack was an important essay she had written. She was going to submit it so she could get a scholarship to go to college in Pennsylvania, where Adam's brother was a big shot. Scott Novak was a technology genius, she said.

"'You're going to leave here?' I said. 'Why?'

"She said, 'Because I'm tired of this place. I need to spread my wings. DO something with my life.' That really hurt, you know? Like our life in Billings was just garbage or something, a waste of her time.

"I told her to come on up, I'd help her look for the backpack. I reached out my hand to pull her up. She grabbed my hand, and I pulled her up a little, but then I let go—just as a joke. We did that all the time—I figured she'd just land on her butt. But she kind of lost her footing and fell against a rock and hit her head, pretty hard I guess. Then she got up, kind of groggy, and— she just walked off the ledge!" His voice keened. "It all happened so fast! I was like, 'No, no, no! Bren! What have you done?! Why oh why did you do that?! Oh no, no, no!'"

His breathing was rapid. He was right there again. Watching her stagger. Watching her fall.

He was telling someone, me, for the first time.

"Did you try to help her?" I asked.

He wiped his eyes and nose. "That fall is hundreds of feet. There wasn't nothing to do."

"Except to pretend it didn't happen," I said.

"What else could I do? They would blame me. She was the golden child. And what kind of sorry guide loses his best friend, especially when she's a girl?"

"It wasn't entirely your fault," I said. "Your mother knew where the backpack was the whole time."

"What?"

It was hard to speak clearly now. I was shivering uncontrollably. "Last time I was here, your mom snuck me a note. It was just a regular note thanking me for visiting. But it was written on a piece of *newspaper*. I didn't really think much of that detail at the time, but you can see the publication date. It's the same week that Brenda died. I think that your mom pulled that bit of newspaper from Brenda's backpack. I think she was trying in her own way to come clean."

"You're lying."

"The note is in my jeans. I double-checked just an hour ago to make sure I was right about the date."

"You're just trying to pull a fast one. My mom wouldn't lie about Brenda missing her backpack. Why would she do that?"

I had my notions. Now Dave was wondering, too.

He stood to walk to my pile of clothes and look for the note, but he was cut short.

"David!"

My guide spoke rapidly to me in a harsh whisper. *"It's Mike. Put your damn clothes on quickly. And don't say a word about any of this or I'll cut your throat in an instant, I swear to God I will!"*

"Not the best time of year for hanky-panky," said the limping hulk as he slowly came into view.

I had never gotten dressed faster. I was still lacing my shoes when Mike joined us.

"Oh, nothing like that," Dave said cheerfully. "We're going to camp out here." He had sheathed his knife.

Mike was breathing hard, laboring on the leg, leaning on his cane. "Got an email from Sheriff Crawford that they are looking for Adam. Someone's got to warn him the jackboots are on the march."

"Mike, your son is trying to kill me," I said as soon as I'd finished dressing and before Dave could interrupt. "He used one of your friends to fly to North Carolina to kill Scott Novak. Now he's trying to cover it up. Please, help me."

"She's lying!" Dave reached toward his belt as if to grab for a knife, but Mike had reached him at last and put out a hand.

"Don't, son."

I was saved! Patriot Mike was going to save me!

Dave protested. "But she's trying to ruin my life, Dad! She's got this ridiculous theory, and she plans to go to the police when she gets back to North Carolina."

"Is that right?" Mike asked, looking at me. "And those jack-boots are so stupid, they'd just believe such a story, wouldn't they?"

"It's all true, Mike," I insisted. "He used your computer to get in touch with your network and had one of the pilots pick him up in the wild while his party was doing their survival thing—"

Dave cut in, "Shut up! Just shut up!"

"Calm down, son." Mike's voice was steady, measured. "Son, what's your plan?"

"He plans to have me freeze to death out here," I said. "Mike, this is *wrong*. Tell him that he can't do this."

"Tell my own son that he can't protect himself?"

Of course not. For evidently the Nashes are a blue-jay people.

I screamed at Mike, "How can you do this to me and live with yourself? Aren't you worried about your soul?"

"As in God?" he asked.

"As in Jesus," I said.

Mike laughed. "That Jew snowflake? Heck, it's time we brought an *American* Messiah to power. Someone with the strength to get shit done."

My heart sank. The strongest demons aren't scary at all. In fact, they look like angels. This man, so good-looking with thousands of followers—they would never hear the words he was speaking now. But would they even blink if they did?

I turned to the son. "Please, don't do this, Dave."

"I'll do what I have to do to protect myself," Dave said. "That's called self-defense. Right, Dad? She's trying to have me put in a cage for the rest of my life. That's evil." He turned to me and shouted, "You're evil!"

"I'm not the one who killed Brenda Gates," I said. "You are."

"IT WAS AN ACCIDENT!" He pulled out his knife and

turned to his father. "Dad, Bren fell, trying to get off the ledge. She hit her head—"

"Son, let's—"

"We've got to stop her, Dad!"

"I know. But not with that knife. Put it away. Put it away!" I watched Dave reluctantly sheath the knife. *Maybe Mike had just been playing along all this time. Now he was going to find a way to put a stop to this madness.*

The elder Nash put down his backpack and removed something. They were gloves, but they had razor sharp claws protruding from the fingers. He donned both gloves, a literal grizzly cos-play.

"What are you doing, Mike?" I asked.

"Only two things women are good for," he said, smirking, "and one of them is cooking."

"Is that why you had an affair with Brenda Gates—because she couldn't cook?"

Mike didn't answer, didn't flinch. Dave, though, stared at me, confused for a second, then looked at his father, who continued to adjust the deadly mittens on his massive hands.

"What's she talking about?" Dave asked.

"Oh, she's just jabbering."

I persisted. "You were so handsome, Mike, so confident, and you made out as if you had money. For a long time, Brenda saw you as her ticket to college. Until she realized she might be able to get a scholarship through Adam's connection to Scott. Then she broke off your relationship."

"I didn't give a shit," Mike said. "'Pussy comes, pussy goes.'"

"You?" Dave looked more closely at his dad. "You slept with Bren?"

Mike shrugged. "I'm a red-blooded male, and she was willing. Where's the controversy?"

I said, "She was seventeen. Or did it start when she was

sixteen?"

Mike chuckled. "'Old enough to bleed, old enough to breed.' You take what you can get out here. They all have the same plumbing anyway." He turned to Dave, who had not stopped staring at his father. "Calm down, son. There's nothing to get excited about."

Dave began to pace. "I'm not calming down! I'm not fucking calming down!"

"Don't take it personally. Just get over it. Be a man. Move on."

But David Nash wasn't moving on. The memory of what happened on that ledge had ruined his life. And he'd spent the past seven years trying to put the event in a context that made someone else the villain. He hadn't meant to kill Brenda, but he still felt guilty about it, because he'd been acting like a passive-aggressive little shit. He needed a scapegoat: Scott Novak, the rich nerd who, in the boy's mind, was going to lure Brenda away from Alaska in the first place, the one who, it was later revealed, was stealing Dave's unique insights about animal evolution. It was easy for him to believe that Scott really was all the things his father would say he was: a degenerate and a traitor, deserving of death.

But now a third murder was pending. How would he absolve himself of this? Dave Nash knew himself to be a doomed man. And, in this moment, a fool, too. For right under his nose Dave's own father had been bedding the only woman Dave had ever loved.

I could see Dave's anguish, even in the gloaming. Anger, yes, but also despair. He had loved Brenda. That was clear. But he'd been shy, totally inexperienced with girls, and a couple years younger than she. Always judged by his dad as never tough enough, never the acclaimed tracker, the freedom fighter, the Internet star.

Mike, still totally calm in the face of his son's seething, said,

"Let's do this. Take the scent out of my pack. We'll need to make this look like a legit bear attack. You hold her down. I'll—"

But Mike didn't get the next step of the plan past his lips. Dave lunged and got his hands around the big man's neck. A surprised sound came from Mike as he reached out with the deadly gloves to defend himself against the smaller man.

I couldn't believe what I was seeing. I was frozen.

Until I wasn't frozen. Until I was running.

Even as I began to put distance between myself and the men, I could hear the struggle behind me. I prayed it wouldn't end, that they would fight until dawn. But after only a few seconds I heard a terrible scream, a rapid-fire crying out:

"Mama! Mama! Mama! Mama!"

And then a groan from one of the men, followed by the sound of my own breath.

Panic fueled my steps. Was one of them already gaining on me, about to strike? I was running from such a great danger, the fact I was stumbling in dark, wild woods didn't even register. I went to a world beyond this one. I wasn't back there, for to be *there* would be too terrifying…

And, for a moment, I even felt invigorated. Like maybe this was something I wanted to be doing. My Own Personal Alaskan Survival Camp!

I don't know when it occurred to me that I was probably going to run out of energy before I reached safety, that soon I wouldn't be able to take another step.

"God, please help me!" I cried out. "I'm so sorry!"

Was there a God alive to hear me?

And what was I sorry for?

For getting myself into this mess? For thinking I could be a competent sleuth? For not being a better daughter, mother, and girlfriend? For not respecting the power of forces I could neither understand nor control?

For wasting so much time in my precious life on ... nothings? For choosing to live in my own sort of matrix, an ego suspended in self-delusion, disconnected from those I desperately needed?

I could barely see the ground. I fell, but got up again.

I looked up at a rising moon. Through my tears, the moon appeared as double.

YOU'LL SEE ME IN 2.

And I finally did see the world in two: There was the world I'd imagined, and the world as it really was, delivering to me its harsh reality. I tried to squelch my tears, mad at myself that my life was going to end this way.

I tripped on a log or rock yet again. I got up and did it again. And again. By the fifth or sixth time I didn't see the point of getting up again.

But in the dappled shadow of moonlit leaves appeared the image of my own little girl.

I couldn't leave her alone, my lovely, troubled Stephanie.

This child in your arms. She needs you still.

I realized I was hugging something soft: my backpack.

Shoving down the regret and horror at what this whole long journey of illusion had cost me, I stood up.

"This is my body."

I felt emptied, like someone new, someone beyond myself.

I put the backpack on my shoulders and began once again to run.

I began to pray, I guess. Promised that, if I lived, I would become someone better. Someone who loved generously and gratuitously.

Open to new answers, new understandings. Not a resentful ego protecting itself through fear and bitterness disguised as a blind self-righteousness. For it is fear that commands we control reality, even to the point of murder.

At last, the valley's floor began to rise, and I found myself scrambling upslope. I didn't know how much farther I could go, and if I would even reach the path. But, at last, I came to the mountain's sheer rock, removed my pack, and collapsed onto the flat, narrow ribbon of the main path.

I lay there spent. Here against the mountain, a cold wind blew, chilling me. I thanked the Lord for a long life—*"I got 10 years on Jesus, kids!"*—and requested care for Stephanie, Darryl, and Lydia. I hoped they would think of me fondly from time to time.

I prayed I would be forgiven all my misdeeds and short-comings.

Then I curled up in the cold and waited for death.

I believe I was nearly there when a figure appeared above me. Half silhouetted, half revealed in the moonlight, he was a tall, thin figure with long hair and beard.

Zarathustra?

"Hello, Rett."

The Lord knows your name, child, has always known it.

He continued, "I know you're in pain. Quick. Did you bring something for me?"

I must have motioned to my pack, for the man unzipped it and pulled out the urn of ashes. He examined it for a moment in the moonlight, then took off its top and fished inside, removing the plastic bag that held the ashes themselves.

Setting the bag of ashes down, he reached inside the urn again and pulled out something else that, in the dim light, I could only make out as a heavy piece of plastic which he clicked into a device he was carrying.

The phone lit up, and he held it high in the air, like Luke Skywalker in that old movie poster.

"Thank you, Rett," he muttered.

"You're welcome, Scott."

And that is precisely the moment that I passed out.

CHAPTER 28

"SAVIOR, I LOOK TO THEE"

I awoke to the sound of a machine, was lifted up. The engine was terrifyingly loud, but I converted the sound into part of my dream. I was in Needless Necessities, drinking a hot cup of coffee made from the loudest espresso machine ever.

But mostly I dreamed I was running.

Eventually I awoke to the smell of coffee. I stirred beneath heavy, warm, glorious blankets.

Sarah's voice: "She's awake, Christopher!"

"That's a good sign."

I didn't know which way was up. Somehow, I sat up anyway.

I asked what had happened.

"You about froze to death last night, that's what," said Christopher.

Sarah said, "I'll go tell him that she's awake."

"Him." Great. I would have to talk to that sheriff again.

Christopher handed me the cup of coffee. My hands hardly worked, but I managed to grip that mug like it was a life preserver.

A second later I almost dropped it. The person Sarah

brought back with her was not the sheriff, was instead the last person I expected to see in Alaska.

"Darryl!" I cried out.

"Don't be mad at me," he said.

"Someone take this coffee away." Sarah complied, and I tried to stand. "My muscles... Oh, Darryl! It was awful!" Now I was sobbing, but my man came down to where I was, sat beside me on the little bed and put an arm around my middle.

"What happened?" he asked when I was able to talk again.

"Dave Nash was the killer the whole time. And when he realized I was figuring it out, he turned on me out there in the woods. Then his father showed up, and—"

"Did you see the bear?" Christopher asked.

I looked at him, confused. "Bear?"

"The bear that killed Dave Nash."

They all looked at me.

"There wasn't any bear," I said.

Christopher looked at Darryl. "The law went onto the scene early this morning and verified Dave died in a bear attack. Mike led them to the scene, and they confirmed it."

"That's not what happened," I said. "Dave attacked Mike, but his dad had these odd mittens with sharp claws—"

"'Mittens?'" said Christopher. "This is a really odd story."

"You don't believe me?" I looked at Darryl. "I'm not making this up. Maybe Scott saw something. Ask him."

Darryl blinked. "Scott Novak?"

"Yes, Scott is alive. He was the one who found me and called for help."

Christopher looked at me with pitying eyes. "I got a text from *Mike* saying he'd watched you running from the scene of the attack and that you fell and hit your head hard on some rocks. I found you all alone on the path. I carried you back here on my Gator."

"No! That was..." *I almost said, "That was your daughter who hit her head."* But now I was second-guessing myself. Maybe I really had injured my brain.

I would be quiet. I would play nice.

Christopher said, "I'm going to radio the law and let them know you're conscious. They will probably want to interview you." *Said with an air of "even though you're completely insane."*

Sarah left, too, to do whatever chores needed to be done, leaving me and Darryl alone. "I'm telling the truth," I insisted. "Scott Novak is alive, and I can prove it."

"Maybe you need to rest some more," Darryl said.

I looked at the clock: It was a quarter past one in the afternoon. "To hell with resting," I said. The coffee had kicked in. "I'm not crippled." I stood up and found I was able to walk with some effort. "And I'm not crazy, Darryl." He looked at me so lovingly, I nearly started to cry again.

I took a deep breath and decided something. "You and I are going to take a walk."

"To where?"

"To see a friend. For now, just tell Christopher and Sarah that I need to be in nature to get my head on straight."

"Okay. But are you sure you can do this?"

I nodded. "It's something I have to do."

WE WALKED MOSTLY IN SILENCE. When we did talk, it wasn't about the case. I couldn't bear to have even one ounce of Darryl wondering if I really was crazy. I needed evidence.

The sun was well into its descent when we arrived at Adam's cabin. There we used the bathroom and took in some supper that Sarah had packed for us.

Light was fading, and I made us push on. I started to get anxious, as this was just how the light had been when Dave had decided to terrorize me. I told Darryl that his breathing made me feel safe.

He turned on a flashlight, but I asked him to turn it off. Several yards later, I stopped. "Here's where we go off the path." I pointed into some trees on higher ground.

"Up there? How?"

"I'll talk you through it. Please go first and pull me up." I thought about Dave reaching for Brenda, that petty betrayal with such disastrous consequence.

I directed Darryl the best I remembered. The going was very slow, especially in the near dark. I talked Darryl through the thick overgrowth—it was a tighter squeeze between trees for him than for me—until we reached the little bluff overlooking the home of Mike and Emily Nash.

I gave Darryl a quick summary of my earlier visit with the couple, and how Dave had brought me this way to retrieve my toiletry kit.

"That looks precarious going down," Darryl said.

"It's not that hard. I can do it." My whole body already hurt; at this point more pain just didn't matter.

Darryl asked, "What if Mike sees you?"

"He won't. There's a gap in his camera angles here."

"What if he *hears* you?"

"Then he'll shoot me. I know too much. And he'll get away with it, because I will be trespassing on his land."

"I'm not letting you do this alone. I'm going with you." Darryl reminded me he had his gun with him.

"It will be better if I go alone. Trust me. I'm going to be careful."

"I don't know about this."

"It's something I have to do, Darryl."

He took a deep breath. "Okay. Ten minutes," he said. "Then I'm coming after you."

I gave him a kiss, then made my way down the bluff. Muscles I didn't know existed ached like the dickens from the night before.

I moved stealthily to the kitchen end of the house. By stealthily I mean slow as an Alaskan glacier, not even as ninja-like as a missing orangutan named Zeus.

I could see in a window that Emily Nash was washing dishes. I suspected she'd have to come outside at some point, and I was right. She was holding a pan of dirty dishwater for dumping. I was just a few yards away, and I was able to whisper yet still be heard:

"Emily, it's me, Rett Swinson. I need to talk with you."

She froze for a second, then quietly closed the door behind her. "Where are you?"

I stepped out of the bushes and into the glow of her kitchen window. "You can't see me that well in this light, but I'm pretty banged up. Look, a lot happened last night, but I want to say I am very sorry that your son was killed. Where is Mike? I don't want him to catch me here."

"Mike is drugged up. It's the only way he could sleep. I haven't seen him this way since — well, since the Gates girl died."

"Tell me what Mike told you about last night," I said.

"He came in looking rough and bloody. Said he and Davie fought off a bear. Said that Davie ... got killed and he needed to contact the sheriff. That was odd to me. Since when does Mike call the law about *anything*? But I wasn't thinking about all that at the time. I was just thinking about the fact David was dead."

I told her everything I'd learned from her son. Halfway through my words, she put her head in her hands. At the part about the affair, she lifted her head again and nodded.

"Mike would send me out to pick berries, check traps, or

whatever. But I wasn't blind. I knew Brenda was visiting him in his 'sound studio.'"

She continued to speak quickly, but now her voice lowered to a dark place.

"I blamed her for the affair. She didn't know that I knew. One day I came back early and they were in his studio, talking. That's when I found her backpack and hid it. I just put it in the pantry and covered it with some potatoes, and I left again. When I came back, Brenda was running around the house, looking all over the place for it. She pretended to be just dropping by to ask if we'd seen it. She decided she must have left it on the trail somewhere.

"It was just a prank, really. I would have let her find the backpack eventually. I know it had her correspondence course homework and everything. Her parents wouldn't want her to lose that. They had such high hopes for her going to college and all.

"When Dave came home, I told him that Brenda had come by looking for him. His face lit up. I knew that he was sweet on her. I guess I wanted him to feel good about himself for a change. Dave was so gloomy. His dad didn't build him up. I just wanted him to have a little hope for something. Maybe he'd work up the courage to make a pass on her and she'd go for him and stop bothering Mike. I know it's silly, but this was all in the moment...

"I never exactly knew what happened after that. Dave came back a while later and said that he hadn't been able to find Brenda. But he looked so sad."

I looked at my watch. I had two more minutes before Darryl came looking for me, gun blazing.

"Thank you, Emily. I've got to go now. But first I need you to give me something—something significant—so that I can prove to the world I'm not crazy, some proof of what really happened."

She nodded and withdrew. A moment later she came back

holding a school backpack.

"Everything is still inside. Even the journal, with all the bad things she said about me. I was so 'frumpy' and 'meek' and 'not a fitting wife for someone so vital.' She said I didn't have a backbone and wouldn't stand up for myself. She was right about those things, but she was stupid for falling under Mike's spell— just like I was. I've got to find some way to forgive her, and some way for her spirit to forgive me. Maybe this is how."

She handed me the pack.

"The authorities may come back," I said. "They are going to want to interview you and your husband."

Emily nodded. "Tell them the secret way and asl them to wait on the hill. Tomorrow night when he's asleep again, I'll signal them with a flashlight. Three blinks."

I thanked her. I turned to leave but decided first to ask, "What turned the tide for you? When did you realize you wouldn't play your man's games anymore?"

She took a deep breath. "When I saw the blood on his shirt. 'Tweren't no bear that Mike fought off. That was my son's blood. I'd recognize it anywhere."

I HURRIED OUT OF THERE. Darryl helped me up the incline, reaching for me and pulling me to safely as if I were a soldier escaping an ambush. No sniper bullet rang out. I had survived.

We made our way back to the lake. No way we were going to rest at Adam's cabin and give Patriot Mike a chance to catch up to us.

When we got to the Gateses, Christopher was still up. I wondered if he ever slept well since his daughter died. When he spotted us walking up, he turned on the lights to the minicamp and met us at the door.

"I've rarely met travelers this late."

"There's something you need to see, sir," said Darryl.

Christopher made a puzzled expression. When I took the backpack off my shoulders and held it out to him, he said excitedly, "That's Bren's backpack! Where did you get that?"

"I'll explain," I said, "but let's wake up Sarah first. She'll want to hear this, too." Not only would Sarah want to know the story, she would also be a moderating force in case Christopher wanted to grab a gun and go after Mike.

At their kitchen table I told them both everything, but in reverse order, starting with Emily Nash's version of the previous night, then picking up with what Dave had told me about Brenda's last moments.

I said, "That's why the two fought. Dave was enraged to hear Mike admit his affair with Brenda. I think that Dave really did have a deep crush on her."

"But Dave killed her," Christopher said. "Even if it was an accident, he didn't protect my darling..." His voice cracked.

Sarah was silent, too. I knew what she was thinking. She was still processing how her young daughter had been sleeping with an adult she and Christopher had admired for so long.

I said, "Mike is a sleaze, but he's a charismatic sleaze."

"Yes, quite the Lovable Rogue," said Sarah. "A real Indiana Jones." She took a deep breath. "Brenda was too big for Alaska. I know that sounds conceited, but she had such a free spirit. She was looking for a way out of here. At one point she must have thought that Mike had the power to help her."

"On that last day, she broke up with him," I said. "She had a vision of going to college and getting there on a scholarship."

"I should have been able to give her what she needed," Christopher said. "She didn't have to..." He let the thought fade. "I should kill that jerk. He made himself out to be so altruistic in helping to find her. What a bunch of malarky. And he's got an Internet army who would defend him to the death."

"We need to call the sheriff," said Darryl. "That backpack is evidence of a crime. Depending on when the affair started, Mike could be charged with rape."

Sarah put her hand on the pack. "Sorry, but I'm not giving this up for another second. It's too precious." She looked at her husband, reached for his hand. "Mike knows what he did. And now his son is dead. We don't need another Ruby Ridge around here. He can hole himself up in that damn fortress of his and spit out YouTube videos to his dark heart's content. God knows what he's done. He'll have Hell to pay one day."

Christopher nodded. "I support Sarah. Let him look in the mirror. Let him enjoy his precious *freedom*." The still-grieving father almost spat the word.

Sarah turned to me. "Now I'd like to go through what Bren left behind. But I think I want it to be just me and her father, if you don't mind."

"Of course," I said.

Darryl and I left the couple alone to their tender, solemn task.

CHAPTER 29

LETTING IN LIGHT

Darryl and I lay down in the guest cabin's narrow bed and held each other for the longest time.

"I was so worried about you," he said finally.

"I was worried about me, too," I said. "What made you decide to come out here?"

"A couple things. Remember that 'incel' guy you talked to?"

"Trey Gamble?"

"Yeah. His self-driving car crashed into a tree and exploded. What a way to go."

"Oh, my."

"By itself maybe it wasn't a big deal. But I just didn't like the fact that bodies were piling up. I grabbed the next flight out. I'm not even sure you had landed here yet. I hope you can forgive me for being paternalistic. You're the toughest person I know." He added, "By the way, how the heck did you figure out that Scott and Adam had switched places in Kansas City?"

"You mean how did I put two and two together and get ... twins? It wasn't any one thing. But several clues pointed to it:

"First, both brothers were brilliant from a young age, but Scott was exceptionally quiet. His parents worried he might be intellectually challenged. I thought: What if the boys were twins but the parents told people that Scott was years younger to cover for the fact he was 'slow'? Adam, being more talkative and rambunctious, might not resemble his brother at all, not if you didn't already know they were identical.

"But the boys knew, and they played tricks on adults when they were young. That would explain why Professor Rooney, their babysitter while he was in grad school, always felt they were sharing a laugh at his expense. I suspect they were switching identities whenever he babysat them.

"In one of their letters, the only one that wasn't typed, Scott referred to himself and his alleged pet chameleon: 'Gem and I' — or Gemini—the classic Zodiac sign for twins. And in that same letter he referred to an episode of *Gilligan's Island* in which two of the characters switched brains. There was a mention of Twin Cities, Minnesota—but that's not the only pair of twin cities. There's Kansas City, Missouri, and Kansas City, Kansas, too.

"They stayed in the same hotel room. No wonder the front desk staffer seemed to see Scott again and again—there were two of them. Scott had grown his beard so he could match Adam's look, and Adam traveled back to Raleigh with Scott's ticket and ID. Emerson picked him up at the airport and did a bunch of touristy things with him — the city's various museum, an art-house movie at the Rialto."

"Is that the only reason the brothers went through all that trouble? For them each to have a vacation?"

"No. Scott was at a junction in his life. He was struggling with his past, with giving up the business, and with his relationship. He needed a significant change of scenery to navel gaze, and he wasn't going to get that opportunity under his current contract. He thought that some time in Big Alaska would jolt him out of whatever fog he was in."

"And Adam? Do you think he wanted to preach about that philosopher?"

"That, but I think it also had something to do with that photograph of Esther. In other words, it was plain old lust. He holed himself up at the farmhouse, but then Jess shows up and he mistakes her for Esther. Maybe he thought he was helping Scott to get her back—but then once he had slept with her, he felt incredible guilt.

"Up till now this was all just a theory of mine. Nothing that really spelled it out. Certainly nothing I would call proof. But there were other things, too.

"'You Will See Me in 2.' Yes, it might have been a clue from Scott that he'd gone into the valley like Zarathustra. But he might also have been trying to tell me that I needed to look at the case in a different light, that the Brothers Novak were one and the same.

"And, after Nietzsche chased away the Scott Bot, I got a call from a different number—a call from the *real* Scott Novak. I later figured out that blue jay I thought I had heard in the background was in actuality a baby moose.

"Later, the more I thought about it, the more was explained by the twin theory. Why would Scott have played that game with Jess, pretending she was Esther? Well, maybe because he thought she *was* Esther. They have a similar look. Then, after he had sex with her, he got mad at himself and punched the wall and hurt his hand, which is why he wrote that final note with his left hand, making it impossible to compare handwritings—even if Esther had not concealed the letter.

"Adam texted 'Esther' to come back, but initially she refused, so he became despondent. He wanted to do something to make up for his betrayal—so he decided to test the Big Cat formula, which Dr. Olivia had delivered to Scott's house not knowing he was gone. The formula was something Scott had stayed up all night telling him about in Kansas City—one ingenious effort to achieve Overman status using epigenetics, a sort of Lamarckian evolution. The way of the giraffe.

"Adam had reason to think it might work. After all, he had the same genetic make-up as Scott. This way, Adam would take the risk on behalf of his brother. He wanted to see if he could bridge the abyss, go beyond humanity."

Darryl cut in. "The shot must not have worked, at least not right away. I mean, if that serum was meant to give him super-human strength, he could have fought off Dave Nash, right?"

"Good point. I want to talk with Scott about that."

"Where is he, by the way? Where did he go?

"If I were a betting girl, I would wager he's close—and that we'll see him tomorrow on our way out of here."

SURE ENOUGH, we did see Scott. But we almost didn't.

We had said our goodbyes to the Gateses, had even climbed onto the seaplane and were pulling away when we looked and saw someone run out of the woods, run the length of the pier, jump, and then start *swimming* toward us.

"Slow down, pilot," Darryl said.

"It's my brother," I told the pilot. "I've got his fare."

"That's all I need to know," said the pilot. "That's all I *want* to know."

"That water is cold!" said Scott as we pulled him up and into the plane. "Thankfully I've got some dry clothes in my water bag." Indeed, everything he had with him was snug inside a thick, black plastic bag.

As Darryl and I helped pull him into the plane, his breath nearly knocked us both over. "What's that smell?" I asked.

"Sardines," he said. "I've been living off nothing but sardines for the past four weeks."

Scott changed into dry clothes in the plane's tiny bathroom and then joined us in the back of the plane. We wanted to be able to talk without the pilot hearing our conversation.

"Are you going to get in trouble for helping me?" he asked.

Darryl said, "There is an APB out for 'Adam Novak.' I don't see Adam Novak, do you?"

"We've got a lot of questions for you," I said. "Are you up for them?"

"I've got questions, too. First, how is Esther?"

"She's ... actually... I'm not sure." I told him about the venture capital investment scam, the revelation that Adam had slept with Jess while assuming Scott's identity—and Adam's seemingly belittling "suicide" note that Esther had found.

I said, "To answer your question, I don't think she's doing very well at all."

"She's going to kill me," he said. "I really screwed up."

"I'm sorry for the loss of your brother," I said. "It was Dave Nash who killed Adam, thinking it was you."

"I know. You told me last night, but you were delirious, so you might not remember. I let you wear my coat until Christopher showed up."

"Thank you," I said.

He was quiet for a moment. "Our parents really messed us up, especially our dad. It's a miracle Adam made it as long as he did. It's all just so improbable."

"Improbability is the name of this case," I said. "First, a technical question," I said. "While Emerson had one satellite phone, you had not one, but two. So why did you need me to bring you a new battery?"

"Someone hacked the phones from a distance. Ever hear of the Stuxnet worm? Long story short, some government—probably the U.S. or Israel—hacked several of Iran's nuclear plants and destroyed their ability to function. In a similar way, someone hacked both my phones' batteries. I thought the first phone was just a dud, so I ditched it at the cabin. But then the other one crapped out on me right after I called you that one time. When Emerson couldn't get in touch with me any longer, he sent you here with a new battery embedded with anti-virus software."

I nodded. That settled, I had so many larger questions.

"Tell me about Big Cat," I said. "I think I deserve to know, because it almost got me killed."

Scott went into a long explanation, most of it highly technical, about how he drew blood from all the animals in his menagerie and got Olivia to map out specific sections of their genomes. He then tasked his AI to look for patterns and contrast what it found with aspects of his own genome.

"I wanted to find what was essential to survival and also what was completely unique. I wanted to target genes that were ripe for mutation and, well, improvement. But mainly I hoped to become more like those animals."

"How?"

"Animals don't question so much. They don't worry. They don't—agonize. For lack of a better term, they do what comes naturally. I wanted to become more like that. I wanted to be in better touch with my nature.

"That's one thing in Nietzsche's philosophy that I could really get behind—that we need to be grounded in this world, not some artificial, virtual one."

"Like Charlie's Optimus Link," I said to Darryl, who nodded agreement.

"Right," Scott continued. "I've just seen humanity spinning out of control, getting all caught up in the new technologies. I helped it along. But I wanted to make up for it. So, I worked with

Olivia to create an evolutionary shortcut. I'm going to test it out whenever she has it ready."

I touched his arm. "Scott, your brother already tested it. On himself."

"Really? Did it make him sick or anything?"

"We don't know what would have happened, because just a few minutes after taking the serum he was strangled by Dave Nash. Just speculating, but I think Adam probably felt bad that he'd meddled in your love life, and he thought he could make it up to you by serving as the guinea pig for your Big Cat experiment."

"That serum would not have taken effect immediately. At least, I don't think it would have."

"He said something interesting just before he was killed. He told Dave that we should all be our brother's keeper. Did he ever say that to you? I don't remember him quoting the Bible in his letters. In fact, Nietzsche was extremely anti-Christian. Any idea what might have been going through Adam's mind?"

Scott shook his head. "I can't imagine. What do you think?"

I considered the question. "Adam was a smart guy. Really smart. But he was 'human, all too human,' too. He thought that he'd slept with Esther—and he felt terrible about it. Shame wasn't an emotion that Nietzsche respected. He thought it constituted self-hate and that it was something imposed by society.

"In that moment, Adam felt like he'd failed you. But even more than that he felt like he'd failed himself. He had betrayed his own will—and that's why he reached for the serum. He wanted to 'step into the abyss,' become a bridge between beast and Overman.

"Like you said, it wasn't designed to work instantly, yet when he was awakened by Dave attacking him he must have gone to a very strange place in his brain. Here was his friend from Alaska trying to kill him. He must have thought he was in some virtual reality, a dream, or some philosophical thought experiment.

"But he kept his head. And he realized very quickly that he had a choice: reveal to Dave that Dave had the wrong guy, or allow Dave to continue thinking he had Scott Novak in his grasp.

"I think your brother was smart enough to know that if he told Dave who he really was, he *might* prevent his own death, but he might not—while increasing the probability you would be killed. On the other hand, if he allowed Dave to think he had killed you, then it might buy you some time, and maybe even save your life. Which is exactly what happened."

Scott looked dumbfounded.

"Don't you see?" I said. "Adam gave his life *because he loved you.*"

Scott thought about that for a moment. "We were both after the same thing, some way to tear down the walls our parents forced us to build, to finally allow ourselves to be impacted by other people and discover ourselves. It's so freaking hard! I don't even know if someone as brilliant as Nietzsche ever figured out how to do it."

We three sat in silence for a while. I thought about all the ways that people hurt one another, the defenses we put up as victims of trauma. The way the ego works so hard to protect itself. The yearning of humans—mostly men—who turn to anger as a means of feeling powerful in the face of helplessness and resentment.

It was difficult to feel sympathy when someone's way of coping was to deliver pain upon other people. Eliciting sympathy through the limp and the gash of the bear seemed to be a vital part of their manipulation and control. If only they would do the bravest thing: do battle with their egos. Be real and acknowledge their original pain. Not to cover it up for fear of becoming prey, but to recognize it in a first step toward healing.

I asked Scott if he could explain a few more things, starting with that will he made out in Kansas City."

He smiled sadly. "I thought about the fact I was going to Alaska and kind of freaked out, thought I might not survive living on my own out here. I told Adam that I needed to make a will, that I wanted to split my estate three ways: Between him, Esther, and Emerson. He argued that it would corrupt him, that if I gave him a dime he'd resent me forever. But I ended up leaving him a little bit of money anyway. I knew it might make him angry, but I apologized for it in the will."

"And why did you put together that complicated brain puzzle for finding the key to Olivia's lab?"

"If something did happen to me, I didn't want that research to be lost. Olivia would never tell anyone about it—it was too risky for her. But I told Adam in Kansas City that if something did happen to me, that he should track down the serum. I figured Adam could unravel the various clues. To be honest, I thought the serum would take months to formulate. I really didn't imagine Olivia would just deliver it to the house like that while I was gone."

"It seems the AI you applied to the problem worked faster than you imagined."

He asked about the animals. I told him they were well taken care of. "Except for Zeus. He was let out by Jess the night of the murder and still hasn't been found. My friend Sheila thinks he's probably deceased. I'm so sorry."

Scott just shook his head. "It's my fault. I made a lot of enemies at that old mansion. In typical fashion I thought I could just leave it all behind without dealing with it."

"Speaking of leaving things behind," I said, "I'm worried that the Virtual Scott AI you created has been hijacked and gone on a killing spree." I told him about the freak deaths of Gustaf

Huber and Trey Gamble. I also told him about the near calamity at Pullen Park involving yours-truly.

"There's no way that particular AI did those things," he said.

"Are you sure? You had all of Nietzsche's books imported into the program." I recited the German philosopher's limericks, including the one about the electric eel, which still chilled my spine when I thought about it.

"Virtual Scott—or Virtual Nietzsche—were both very weak AIs. Probably the death of Gustaf just triggered some glitch— like an earworm that gets stuck in your brain. Those limericks? One of the first things I did when developing each of my AIs was teach them how to create funny poems. It's harder than you might think. But it's related to other modes of thinking, so it seemed worth doing."

"But what about the deaths of Trey and Gustaf? What about the carousel?"

He shrugged. "Coincidence? I mean, things break. Machines go haywire."

I wasn't convinced.

The ghost in the machine.

There was something called the Turing Test, in which an AI might prove itself indistinguishable from a human intelligence.

But what test could help us tell an AI from random chance?

WHEN WE GOT BACK to Raleigh, no television cameras awaited us, suggesting a lack of information leaks from the two sheriff departments. Scott and Darryl decided to head straight for the Wake County Sheriff's office. Before they left, Darryl told me, "Tom is going to want to talk with you, too."

"Give me a couple hours," I said. Though exhausted, I felt drawn to visit Needless Necessities before it closed.

I went to find Esther at Bee Yourself. A college student named Joseph said she was in the back of the kitchen, cleaning. "Esther's filling in for Jasmine some days while she tends to her mama. Jazz's mama fell and broke her hip."

"Oh, no! I'm sorry to hear that. How is Esther doing in her place?"

"Fine. She's nice."

I hurried back into the coffee shop to locate Esther. Before I could get a word out, she blurted out to me, "This place is nuts!"

She looked frazzled—but also invigorated.

After she put Joseph in charge, we found our way to a table in the front.

"I'm impressed you took this job," I said.

"I like managing people. There's something about getting the best out of everybody that—well, it's a rush. And something else..."

She studied me, as if wondering if she could trust me with something.

"I've been visiting Jasmine at her home the last couple of days, bringing her things that she needs from the grocery or drugstore while she takes care of her mom. I've been watching her, but I still don't know how she does it. If a company could learn how to bottle that kind of compassion, it could change their bottom line and transform the world."

"You seem so energized right now." *No more poker face.* Maybe for the first time, Esther had come into her own skin.

She smiled. "What was it you came to tell me?"

"You're wanted at the sheriff's office. I'll go with you, because they want to talk to me, too."

Esther's eyes widened. I measured my next words carefully.

"There has been a breakthrough in the case. It involves Scott's brother, Adam. I'm not allowed to say anything more. But it's important that you and I go to the station right now. I promise you're going to experience a great sense of relief when you do."

WE HAD to wait over an hour in the waiting room while Darryl and Scott were still inside being debriefed. I learned later that Scott had to prove who he was by his dental records; the sheriff was not making the same mistake twice. Darryl later told me that Scott's prints matched the prints of the "mystery person." Twins don't share prints. The authorities had mistakenly matched Adam's prints in the farmhouse to the prints of the deceased and just assumed they were Scott's. *Oops.*

Darryl was Tom's star witness. Though the Alaskan authorities were irritated at having a Novak evade their search, they corroborated on the phone all the details that Darryl presented. I'd be able to elaborate further later. But in that interrogation room right now, Darryl's story would be enough.

And now there needed to be a reunion. As the two of us sat outside the interrogation room, I offered to hold Esther's hand. She acted puzzled as to why I was being so doting, but she accepted it nonetheless.

The door opened, and Darryl waved us in. He immediately closed the door behind us for the sake of privacy.

Scott was sitting at the far end of the table. He stood up, looking like a scarecrow.

"Esther! I'm so sorry—"

"Who is this?" Esther insisted. "Adam Novak?" The beard definitely made Scott look like a mountain man.

"No. It's me. Scott."

Esther cried out, "Is this some sort of joke?"

Darryl intervened. "Adam and Scott switched places. The only one who knew it was Emerson Cramer. Adam was then killed by Dave Nash, a friend of his from Alaska, who thought he was murdering this man, Scott Novak."

"Esther, I couldn't come back until they found the killer," Scott began. "I couldn't put you in danger. I wanted to tell you, but—"

But Esther had fainted. Darryl adeptly caught her and moved her to the ground, propping up her legs to move blood to her brain.

She came-to after just a few seconds. Scott helped her up and the two embraced.

"Why?" asked a dazed Esther. "How?"

"I'm so sorry I didn't tell you I was leaving," said Scott. "I didn't want you to worry about me. And I didn't want to risk Sammy finding out I was leaving the state for a full month."

"Miss Mills," said Tom Jordan, "if Scott hadn't done what he did, the man in your arms would certainly be dead right now."

"I see," said Esther. "I think."

"Let's give them a moment," said the sheriff.

The rest of us filed out. While we were in pause mode, Emerson was led to us from the jail area, appearing very weary from a couple of nights in jail but relieved.

"Where's Scott?" he asked.

"Inside the interrogation room with Esther," I said. We gave him a quick rundown of everything that had happened in Alaska.

"Tell me," I said to Emerson, "did it ever occur to you to let someone know where Scott really was?"

"I worried you'd feel a duty to tell Sammy. But I also thought you'd figure everything out on your own. I was right. You did."

"It almost got her killed," said Darryl, none too friendly.

Emerson reddened. "I'm sorry about that. But I really didn't think the killer was in Alaska. I thought the killer was right here."

I said, "No wonder you didn't care about the will I found. Scott was alive, so it was meaningless."

Emerson nodded.

The door to the interrogation room opened.

"Scott!" said Emerson, who rushed forward to embrace his old friend.

CHAPTER 30

HERO

Exhausted as I was, I still slept terribly. A number of things were still bothering me about the case.

The deaths of Gustaf and Trey weren't the only things. It seemed like something vital was missing, some thread to explain a number of the small things that had happened along the way.

I wanted to compare notes with Paul. But he wasn't returning my calls. That wasn't like him.

I took Lydia to meet her quilting club. Astonishingly, we met the Qrazy Qwilters as they were on their way to the parking lot.

"Where's everyone going?" I asked.

"To conduct an intervention," Pleasance said.

Explained Susie: "Charity told Pleasance 'thank you' again."

Pleasance said, "Something is definitely wrong. I need to confront my sister!"

Thirty minutes later a half dozen of us were on the back deck/porch of Charity's Harris Lake house as Pleasance nervously knocked.

Charity came to the door. She was shorter than average and had a round, pale, pleasant face. "Please, come on in!"

We had expected a struggle. Charity withdrew into the home, fully expecting us to follow.

"She said, 'Please,'" Pleasance said in a sort of daze.

"She said, 'Come on in,'" added Susie.

We all filed into Charity's mud room.

Charity stood blocking the passage to the rest of the house.

Something reeked, though it wasn't unpleasant. The whole house smelled like something I couldn't quite place.

"I smell cloves and oranges," Pleasance said. Of course! The house smelled like those air fresheners one made in pre-school, oranges stabbed all over with cloves, to be hung in closets as air fresheners until they turned green with mold.

"Charity," said Pleasance softly, "I have been very worried about you."

"I know you have. I've been worried about you being worried about me. But I'm okay."

"You seem ... *happy*. What happened?"

"Oh, life is grand—ever since the Malthusians paid me a visit." She giggled.

"Uh, 'The Malthusians?'"

"Yes! They came on their spaceship. They visited Earth. It's incredible!" She did a little dance in a circle, reaching out her arms and clapping.

We all looked at one another.

"Am I in La La L-L-Land?" stuttered Lydia behind me.

"Charity, what exactly are you talking about?" demanded Pleasance.

Charity put her hands on her heart. "All my life I've just known that there are beings more intelligent than humans. I mean, humans are just so pathetically stupid, aren't they? So brutish. Such unevolved cave people. But I could never prove it. Now I can. I've come to know a Malthusian!" She did another twirl.

"This is really—" Pleasance began. But she was interrupted by a sound—a crash—coming from deep in the home. "Charity, what was that?"

"That's Simon Wellington—my Malthusian friend!"

We all looked at one another.

Charity added, "Would you like to meet him?"

Dumb nods all around. We followed her down the hallway to the kitchen. The whole way we listened out for the next loud crash.

When we turned the corner, Pleasance shrieked.

Lydia said, "Oh, my God!"

Susie said, "Gracious!"

I said something that should never be repeated in mixed company.

Here before us was Simon Wellington—the Malthusian.

Also known as Zeus—the Orangutan.

The ape was going ape. He was tossing various knick-knacks around while also eating grapes, bananas—all manner of fruit.

He was happy as a clam here in Charity's house.

"Simon," explained Charity, "is a very advanced extraterrestrial. He is studying us. He's studying each and every one of you *right now*."

Pleasance stammered, "Charity, he's a—"

"—a real discovery," I interrupted. "How did you come to meet Simon Wellington, Charity?"

"His spacecraft landed almost three weeks ago. But it left without him. It abandoned him! Poor, poor Simon Wellington!"

Of course. An odd-looking floater plane—perhaps that very same plane I'd seen in the photo of pilots arriving to search for Brenda Gates—would have been something very odd to see at night in Harris Lake.

And then this creature, arriving on her porch, after the "spacecraft" had left.

The two events were connected by a murder. Dave Nash had passed Zeus in the woods, man and beast switching places.

In Charity's very unusual mind, the events were connected in a different way.

"You know you can't keep him," Pleasance said.

"Oh, I'd never try to *keep* him," said Charity. "He's free to come and go. He's an advanced being!"

I said, "Did you ever think that he might want to live in a zoo, with other Malthusians, so that people can visit and learn from them?"

"The thought had occurred to me, yes." On some level, Charity knew what was up, that what she was doing was play. But, according to Pleasance, Charity had never done play. *A dour, tragic child.* Zeus had unlocked something in Charity that had made her feel free—even *charitable*—for the first time.

Maybe he also made her feel competent, that she could show some of her own inner feeling and not be judged or rejected.

Zeus had moved to the sofa where he was trying to play with one of the cats.

While everyone else watched him in a kind of shock and awe, Pleasance cornered me and whispered:

"What the Hades are we going to do? He can't stay here. He'll trash the place. We've got to get others involved."

I whispered, "I'll call Sheila."

A half hour later, Sheila rolled in. She opened the cab of her SUV. Zeus could ride up front with her.

Zeus loped toward the vehicle and climbed inside.

We all watched Charity to see how she would react. She began shouting through tears, "Good-bye, Simon Wellington! It was an honor to make your acquaintance! You are an incredible creature! You're just perfect the way you are! Just ... perfect!"

Then she reached out for Pleasance and cried into her shoulder.

How could an animal touch a person so deeply and unlock such feeling? Maybe we could all learn from animals how to live better in our own skin.

I DIDN'T RIDE BACK to Needless with the others. I stood on the edge of the lake looking out. Part of me felt disquiet, anxious, scared. I imagined Paul's voice in my head:

"What are you thinking, Toots?"

"I'm not thinking of anything. I just feel anxious. I'm quite sure I've experienced trauma."

"Don't be yella'."

"'Yella'?"

"You know, 'Scared.'"

"But I'm not—!" I began to shout, scaring one of the lake's blue herons into flight.

"Of course!"

I ran to my car.

When I had driven into cell-tower range again, I called Darryl.

"Hi," he said, "everything okay?"

"Darryl, can you meet me at the Barnes & Noble in Cary? I can navigate us from there. I'll explain then."

"On my way. I'm leaving now."

DARRYL ISN'T afraid to use his police siren. He met me in no time. I quickly filled him in:

How I had accidentally discovered the origins of the Yellow Goose company name: Dan*iella* provided the "yella" to *Gus*taf's "goose."

Of the two, Daniella was the technical one. The coder.
The hacker.

"It was Daniella all along," I said. "She was frustrated with her husband for spending all their money on the court case. Meanwhile, she was doing everything she could to make life miserable for RidgeLine. That deep-fake video was her doing, as was the original email to Augusta posing as Sammy. Daniella, not Gus, was the hacker who was giving Augusta such fits while they were both trying to unlock Big Cat. She had recruited Trey into helping as well.

"It was Daniella who hacked the Scott Bot; I guess the German in her thought it would be funny to replace him with Nietzsche's persona, whose books Scott himself had loaded into that AI's databanks.

"And it was Daniella who started the carousel with me and Augusta there. Paul was the one who put the trackers on our cars, but Daniella had hacked Paul's phone and always knew where we were. My guess is she lured Trey to the park just to implicate him; he'd been working with her for a while, but after he met with Paul, she worried he was going to turn. Speaking of 'turning,' That carousel and its Wurlitzer were made by a German American company; she couldn't resist having the carousel play a Wagnerian tune as it tried to kill us.

"It was Daniella who ransacked Scott's house looking for clues to unlocking Big Cat. The will wasn't something she was even looking for.

"Finally, it was Daniella who hacked the satellite phones. Not to plant circumstantial texts implicating Emerson and Adam—those were already there—but to sabotage the batteries. Again, just to cause havoc."

"Did she kill her husband, too?"

"I don't know. And I don't know if she would be able to hack into Trey's car. But I think either or both are possible. One thing

I do believe: If she's smart enough to figure out all the other things I've mentioned, she's smart enough to commit those murders. And I think her resentment against her husband was strong. When Gustaf said he always followed the law, I think he was telling the truth. What if he had found the deep-fake video on their servers and confronted his wife about it? As for Trey, he was just a pawn. If Daniella thought he was going to spill the beans to Paul, she might decide to do away with him."

"Are we going to confront her right now?"

"Maybe, but mainly we're going to try to prevent another tragedy," I said. "Pull down this little road to your right."

I added, "And step on it!"

DARRYL'S DODGE CHALLENGER kicked up dust and gravel on a country road like nobody's business.

Eventually the narrow road and trees opened to a small lot and building—Olivia Porter's laboratory.

Paul was already there, either having just knocked on the lab's door or about to. A pistol was in his hand.

We came to a stop near Paul's ramshackle Saab.

As I suspected, just yards away sat a light blue Audi.

We got out of the car. Paul recognized us.

"It was Daniella," Paul said. "She—"

"I know." I took a few steps toward Paul. "You've got to be careful about going in there, Paul. Daniella's extremely dangerous."

"But she's in there with Dr. Porter, who reached out to me for help."

"That wasn't Dr. Porter who reached out," I said.

"Sure it was! She called me. I heard her voice."

"I'd bet a million dollars it was deep-fake audio, just to lure you out here. It's how Daniella operates. She's taking out everyone who knows too much. She wants Big Cat all to herself. And if she can't have it, she'll make sure no one else can."

"Rett, that's crazy."

"I'm serious, Paul. Let Darryl take over. He can call in back-up."

"That will be way too late. There's a damsel in distress in there!"

Paul, drawing up his strength, took a run at the door and barreled into it with his shoulder. The door held. He tried again. And again.

I looked at Darryl, who looked at me.

"Paul," said Darryl firmly. "This isn't going to work."

"Mind your own business!" Paul said. He threw himself at the door again. It seemed to be rattling a little looser—but not much.

Paul was about to start another run when there was a loud boom, followed by a second explosion.

And a third. Smoke, then flames, began shooting up from the roof of the building.

"Daniella's blowing up the lab!" I shouted. "The propane tanks! And there are more where those came from!"

We all heard screaming coming from inside.

Paul ran and jumped in his car. He started it up (*he's mighty fast with those pliers*, I thought to myself) and stuck his head out of the window as he revved the engine.

"Out of my way!"

"No, Paul!"

"OUT OF MY WAY!"

The Saab lurched forward as Darryl pulled me out of its path. A loose belt in the engine screeched as the car accelerated, then produced a massive crunch as it buried itself into the wall to the left of the door.

My first thought: *That precious car!*

My next thought: *Paul looks hurt!*

I turned to Darryl to see what we should do. He was already running toward the building holding a heavy piece of metal, a portable battering ram from his squad car's trunk that he used to demolish the doorknob with one carefully choreographed swing.

"Get behind my car!" he shouted. Darryl then threw the ram on the ground and pulled open the door while simultaneously pulling his gun. Smoke billowed out of the building.

While he was still waiting for the smoke to clear, a body spilled out of the building and onto the ground.

It was Olivia Porter, coughing hard, but alive.

"Who else is in there?" Darryl demanded.

Olivia struggled to catch her breath.

"She's ... dead. That crazy woman ... managed to blow herself up—along with my lab."

"I've alerted the fire department," Darryl said.

Meanwhile, I was next to the Saab trying to get Paul's door open.

"He's unconscious," I told Darryl. "But I think we can get him out."

"Let's carry him into the squad car," Darryl said. "Rett, ride in the back with him. Olivia, you can ride in the front with me."

The two of us managed to pry open the passenger door, pull Paul out, and carry him to Darryl's car.

As we raced out of there, Darryl got on his CB to tell the first responders how to find the lab. We passed a sheriff's car going in the opposite direction just as we arrived at the main highway.

Paul seemed to be traveling somewhere between unconsciousness and delirium.

"Paul, hang in there," I kept saying.

We were just a few miles from the hospital when he seemed to come to.

"I wanted ... I wanted to be a hero."

"You were, Paul. You tried so hard to help."

"It's not the same. I wanted to do something great."

"You *are* great."

"No, I'm not. I'm Deputy McGoof. Ask your boyfriend."

A sheepish Darryl Schmidt looked at me in his rearview mirror.

He went on: "I didn't even serve on the New York City police force. I couldn't pass the medical because of my heart. I only ever worked security. I lied to Sammy on my application. No one checked. I'm a fraud."

"Paul, you're a good man, and that alone makes you great." *Please don't die just to make a point, Paul. Please live, even if the world doesn't need your kind of hero anymore.*

He passed back into unconsciousness, but he was still alive when we pulled into the ER. We got him to the hospital.

Nothing to do now but pray and wait.

I RESTED MOST of the weekend—the best I could, anyway. On Monday morning I sat in a chair across from Maxine, shifting now from our friendly-neighbor relationship to therapist-and-client. I let the waterworks flow.

"It's been a sucky past week," I said finally.

"Let's start with the worst part."

"The dreams," I said. "Darryl doesn't know what to do. He's helpless to calm me down. Every night I'm running. I'm panicking. I don't like him touching me..."

She said, "We've got to get you feeling safe in your body again."

I nodded. She continued:

"We're going to go over everything that happened again. But this time, each time you get to a tense moment in the story, I want you to stop narrating and take a moment to sense your current surroundings. Are you willing to try this?"

"Yes."

"Tell me: Do you feel safe in this room with me right now?"

"I do." My eyes were closed, my breathing trying to find its purchase.

"Good. Each time I have you pause in your story, I want you to tell me what you're feeling, hearing, seeing, right here and now."

She noticed the cross around my neck. She said, "What if you held your necklace? Would that help?"

"It might." I took off the cross, held it tightly in my right hand.

"Now, let's start the story wherever you feel comfortable..."

MAXINE TOLD me the healing would take some time, that there was no shortcut. I mentioned Scott's serum, suggesting someday there might be a way for people to get beyond their pain sooner.

"Maybe," she said, "and, in fact, there are some psychedelics that are being tested. Some people find them helpful in alleviating symptoms of depression and anxiety caused by trauma."

I asked her if Sheila had proposed to her yet that they buy the zoo from Scott.

"Totally impractical," she said. "Sheila needs to get that out of her head."

I said, "But she's not going to, Max. She's just going to resent you. You know as well as I do that some people don't like to be caged. Sheila is not a city girl."

Maxine tried to keep her composure, but she finally broke down. "You're right. But what am I supposed to do? She won't want to commute. Besides, we can't afford two homes, much less the food required for all those animals. It's just impossible."

I loved hearing that word.

"Watch me work," I said.

THAT NIGHT I CALLED MARGARET, asking her if we could get together for lunch the next day. "Bring Sammy if you like," I said.

"Sammy and I broke up," Margaret announced with an exaggerated nonchalance.

"Excuse me?"

"I broke up with him."

"I'll be right over!"

"Don't—"

"*Right* over!"

I found her on her back patio, chain smoking. She only did that in grief, as she did a few years earlier when her mother died.

"What the heck happened, Margaret?"

Her cigarette shook a little as she brought it to her mouth. There was a pause as she blew out the smoke. "He had a girlfriend."

"No way!"

"Yep. After you and I talked at the gym, I ended up poking around a little. I found an extra cell phone. So I suspected something was up, but I couldn't unlock it. I found out a different way."

"How?"

"You know how much he travels. Going to conferences,

investor meetings, board retreats. I'll bet he travels as much as he's here. I said to him one night when we were in bed, 'A man with your kind of money doesn't ever have to sleep alone. So, who do you sleep with when you're on the road?' He just sort of looked at me, deciding if he could trust me. At last he just came out with it. 'Her name is Anne. She works for an escort service. Do you want to know anything else about her?' I said, 'I don't need to know anything else. That's enough for me.' And I told him we were through. He explained he'd be more than willing to drop Anne's services if it meant that much to me."

"But that's a good thing, right?" I said.

"I told him I wouldn't want to be responsible for raining on his parade. He'd just end up resenting me, and that wouldn't be good."

"But he was willing to dump her?"

"All I had to do was say the word."

"You didn't trust him to do it?"

"Oh, if he had said they were through I would have certainly believed him. But I didn't want it to be up to me. I wanted him to *want* to be exclusive."

She put down her cigarette and wiped her eyes with a tissue.

"Oh, Maggie. Was he upset that you walked away?"

"I suppose, but when we talked the next day, he casually pointed out that there are plenty of women out there who might bring themselves to overlook such details in return for a jet-setting lifestyle."

"What did you say to that?"

"I told him that such women were, in the final analysis, no more than high-priced hookers, and I wasn't going to work the streets of Raleigh even if that street was paved with gold and the john in question was Prince Charming himself."

"In other words, you don't want to be a commodity."

"If you mean by commodity a thing that pleases him and is easily replaceable, then you're correct."

"Margaret, he's going to miss you."

"I hope so," she said. "Or maybe I hope he doesn't miss me. It's easier if I can just imagine he's one of his company's computerized tin men who doesn't have an actual heart."

"You're unique, Margaret. You're *real*. And you want someone who not only is real but who wants to associate with a real woman."

"I don't know how many real men there are anymore," Margaret said, weepy. "And the older I get, the harder it is to appear glamorous and appeal to any man. I don't know. I'm just a little bitter right now, I guess."

"You don't want just any man. You want someone who is going to love you for you," I said. "But maybe it's not a total loss. You got that Governor's Mansion account out of it."

"That's gone, too."

"Why?"

"It was awkward, but my point of contact communicated in so many words that the contract was a way to get on Sammy's good side. Re-election campaigns require money, you know."

"So they fired you?"

"No, I walked away. I've got more work than I know what to do with—work I earned on my own merits."

"You know that's right!" I shouted. But it didn't produce the high-five moment I would have liked.

Margaret took a puff of her cigarette. "Are we fooling ourselves, Rett? Is it unrealistic for me to want a man who wants me above all other women? Is it so damn quaint of me to want to be thought of as someone unique and valuable?"

I didn't answer. I certainly wasn't going to ask the question on my own mind: What if the male half of the human race just, by and large, isn't good people?

Because that would suggest no hope.

And if a girl needs anything in this life, it's hope.

AFTER MY VISIT WITH MARGARET, I called Needless and learned there weren't any classes going on, so I texted Ken and asked if the invitation was still open to paint at his studio. I was having trouble focusing and settling my mind. Maxine had said I'd often feel irritable without knowing why—a typical symptom of PTSD.

"You seem tense," Ken said as we both moved our brushes. His easel was just a few feet away. If we both reached out, we could touch hands.

"I am, a little," I admitted, but I didn't want to go into all the reasons why. I decided to share one thing though. "It's just been quite a month. My daughter has left college in the middle of getting her degree. I'm concerned about her."

"Is she an artist as well?"

"No. She was majoring in political science. Now she's living at the beach with a boyfriend who is no good for her." I stopped my brush. "I'm sorry," I said, "I'm trying to calm my brain a little bit by painting."

"It's my fault for bringing it up," he said.

"I'm going to get some water, if that's okay."

"Let's both take a break."

"Okay."

A moment later we were on the couch, me with my water, Ken with his pot. His left arm lay along the back of the couch. Long-armed as he was, it was easy for him to reach a little farther to place his hand on my shoulder. It was a kind, unaggressive gesture, so I let it linger.

"Care to talk any more about your daughter?" he asked.

"Thanks, but I'd rather not right now."

Without letting go his hand from my shoulder, he leaned with his other hand and picked up the joint.

"Here. I don't mean to corrupt you, but it just might help."

Why not, I thought. With all the shit that's gone down in the recent past, I couldn't be blamed.

I took the joint and toked. I inhaled—and immediately regretted it. As I started to cough vehemently, the memory flashed in my brain of my younger brother, Billy, age 10, smoking dead leaves rolled in a paper towel and pretending it was cool.

Ken took the joint from me and chuckled, not cruelly, for I, too, was half-laughing between coughs.

"Sorry," I sputtered, "I'm just not that smooth with such things."

"Don't worry about it." He waited for the frequency of my coughs to subside. Then, leaning in slightly, he said, "Would a kiss work better?"

I shot him an alarmed look. "Actually, no," I said. I put the glass back on the coffee table, making sure in the process to turn so his hand was forced to withdraw from its resting place. "I've got a boyfriend I adore."

His reaction was less perturbed than I would have expected. "Good for you," he said, as he took another toke. "But, if you don't mind me asking, why would an artist like you hone so closely to the lines?"

"'Lines?'" I wondered where this was going—and if maybe I should just leave. But, I have to admit, I was a little curious to see how Ken recovered from my rejection.

Ken stood up. As he walked over to his painting, he said, "Most artists I know eschew social norms. The world is so full. Why not embrace the beauty you find in the moment?"

Ken's canvas was a complex array of purple swaths peppered with blacks and blues and whites. I know that many people who look at art think, "Why, that's just random color. A child can do that." But Picasso in his old age liked to say it took him 90 years to learn to paint like a child.

"There's something beautiful about fidelity, too," I said, walking to my easel and picking up my palette again. I regarded the bland, sad picture I'd been painting. I suddenly wished I were with Darryl. Just the thought of his love suddenly made me feel warm and reassured, a feeling stronger and better than any hit of herb or vine. From Ken's moveable tray of oils, I grabbed several warmer colors: reds, oranges, yellows, blues. I wanted this little painting to exude fidelity, loyalty.

"Fidelity is admirable," Ken said, "But how many loyal couples end up resenting one another? A good many, I'd say."

My picture was starting to resemble a policeman's badge. Is that the direction I wanted to go with this picture? Was safety the main thing I saw in Darryl?

I turned to Ken.

"You're right. Loyalty alone probably isn't enough. But with time, loyalty brings trust. And trust brings—"

"—taking the other person for granted?" He produced a little smile at his cleverness. He really was a handsome man...

"Not necessarily," I insisted. "Trust brings intimacy, but only if both parties want that."

"Interesting." The thing about oil is you're able to manipulate it for hours even after you apply it. Using a sponge as well as large brushes, Ken continued to work the thick mixture on his canvas. His work was intricate—interesting—in a way that mine yet wasn't. I had a long way to go in my development as an artist.

I needed to evolve.

I began turning the police badge into a sort of family crest.

"Intimacy is a lot like a great painting," I said, getting excited about my brush's new approach. "When two people are in synch, there's more to see. There's actual depth to the relationship. You wouldn't mistake a glossy magazine ad for great art. Then why settle for less than the truest love?"

"No offense, but that sounds a little pie in the sky."

"I think most men want intimacy, too. But there's a sort of wall you have to break through first. For some people, like me, it only really happens when their first marriage shatters. The armor cracks. What's exposed is the real self."

I thought about Scott going to Alaska, his attempt to cut through the emotional block that separated him from Esther. By contrast, there was the example of Sammy Patel, who refused in the end to make himself fully available to my friend.

I probably hadn't persuaded Ken of a thing. He probably considered me a schoolmarm or a church lady. After several minutes in which we were both engrossed in our work, I gave our argument one last shot. I lowered my brush and palette.

"I guess I'm saying that desire rarely delivers on its promise, Ken. Surely you've seen how that can be true?"

He looked at my painting, an almost Rococo family crest shaped vaguely like a heart. It was unapologetically kitschy, but it was exactly what I was hoping to achieve: a wild interpretation of what it meant to stand by your own.

He asked, "What will you call your painting?"

I thought a moment. "'Brazen Love.'"

"Nice work."

"If you're trying to flatter me—keep on. We can flatter one another and still be good friends. But just know that flattery will not get me into your bed."

He bit the wooden end of his brush, thinking. "I believe I can operate within those lines."

"Good. I can, too."

I spent the next few minutes at the sink cleaning my brushes while Ken continued to work. I felt a little badly for him. I was going home to someone, while presumably he was still looking for this moon's conquest.

I took off my apron and hung it up, grabbed *Brazen Love* and held it carefully between my palms.

"Thank you, Ken. It was great to paint with you again."

He turned toward me and took a little bow. As I turned to leave, he said:

"By the way, I do know what it's like to treasure one single person. The only problem was, a lot of garbage got in the way. I'd be lying if I said I didn't have regrets."

"If it makes you feel any better," I said, "you're not alone in that experience."

He put out a hand to shake. I stepped forward and took it.

Just before walking out the door, I added, "Let's paint again sometime." Ken's responding "okay" sounded a little skeptical. I'm not sure he believed we would ever get together again to paint.

Despite everything, I was pretty sure we would.

CHAPTER 31
REUNION

I texted Allan before calling so that he'd know it was crucial he take my call. This time he did.

"Had you heard that Stephanie was planning to withdraw from school?" I asked.

"Honestly, I had not." I didn't know whether I could believe him. It didn't matter.

"Why would she do that and not tell us?"

"I guess this is what independence looks like."

"You mean stubbornness?"

"That, too," he said.

"She's not answering my calls. I could go to the coast and try to meet with her. I know exactly where the Kellys have their house."

"We've got to let her go, Rett. I don't want to, but we have to."

"But you remember what it was like in high school when she dated Alex. He's a typical dude. All testosterone. Not husband material at all." An awkward silence ensued as perhaps we both considered the case of Allan Swinson—not macho and not great husband material either.

"Steph can hold her own," he said.

"I'm worried, Allan."

"She'll be fine."

Neither of us believed it. It's just we were both engaged in our individual ways of worrying.

"Have you talked to your dad?" I asked. "I've been meaning to reach out to him. I've just been too busy."

Allan said, "KayLeigh wants to talk to you" and quickly handed the phone off.

"Hey! How are you, Rett?"

Oh, Jeez. Did I still have to pretend to like this bitch?

"I'm fine," I said, through gritted teeth. I could hear her footsteps followed by a door closing. She was probably in that cute little home office. I added, "I was really surprised to hear about G.T. being a con artist."

"Can you believe what that *witch* did?"

"It's deplorable. I hope you didn't invest too much."

"Not much at all—but I would appreciate you not saying anything about the investment club to Allan. It will just upset him."

"He doesn't know about it?"

"It was just my little thing. I mean, it's not a *lot* of money, really, but he'll feel bad for my sake. You can understand."

"Sure. It's none of my business." *Translation: Cross me again, KayLeigh, and Allan will find out.*

"Thanks. Anyway, I had an idea! You're such an *amazing* detective. What if you went to South America and brought G.T. to justice! Just think how great that would be for your new brand!"

"I suppose I could go," I said, "but why don't you?"

"Oh, it's way too dangerous for an amateur like me. I mean, I'd probably get kidnapped or raped down there."

"I see." *I'd probably be fine—because who would rape someone this fat, right?*

"I just mean that you know how to fly under the radar. You're amazing at that stuff."

"That's really flattering. I'll definitely think about it."

"Promise?" *Was there some desperation there—and a bit more money lost than you have already let on?*

"Promise," I said.

As in, "Fuhgeddaboudit, dame!"

PAUL WAS RELEASED from the hospital on Tuesday. He'd experienced a concussion and a mild heart attack, too.

I had visited him twice in his hospital room, and each time he asked me if I planned to tell Sammy what he had confessed to me, about his cop career in New York City being a fib. I told him I had no intention of ratting him out. What was the point?

"If Sammy ever thinks you're doing a bad job, he can fire you. Everything up to now is just water under the bridge."

I think that persuaded him.

"Besides," I added, "you helped me figure out the conclusion to this case."

"And how did I do that?"

"When you sent me the results of the fingerprinting on those two whiskey bottles."

"I wish! They both had the same prints as the mystery prints found all over the farmhouse. Which made me think that it was someone who poured the whiskey at those parties who later ended up killing him. Now we know those were Scott's prints, and what we thought were Scott's prints were Adam's. But back then I had it all backwards."

"True, but here's the thing: Those bottles were Scott's favorite whiskey, so it was very likely that the prints on the bottles *were* his. That was the final clue for me, the thing that made me believe that Scott was not the person found lying in that bed with a cloth around his neck. And, remember, it was your idea for me to grab something from Scott's old home. Without those forensics, Emerson and possibly even Scott would be put on trial for the premeditated murder of Adam Novak."

"You think so?"

"I know so."

"Wow. You're right! I blew this case wide open! I'm a genius! I'll be in all the history books!"

"Paul, you *helped*," I said, "but basically, yes, in your own virtual world, you solved this case single-handedly."

"'Delusions of Adequacy!'" he shouted.

We had a mighty laugh at that.

I WANTED to follow-up with Augusta, but she wasn't answering my texts. After I helped Paul get settled back at his apartment, I drove to her grandfather's house to see if I could catch her there. Otis was in his studio working on something; I wouldn't disturb the master at work.

I could see through the window that Augusta was cleaning up after dinner. I knocked and waved so she could see it was me.

Augusta looked tired. She didn't act happy to see me, but she did let me in.

I had never been inside the little trailer. It was neat, but there was not a thing fancy about it. I bet Otis had sold a million dollars' worth of art since he'd been discovered less than a year ago. It made me laugh how little some people cared about money.

Augusta asked if I wanted something to drink. I noticed she was drinking vodka.

"Are you okay?" I asked, as I sat down at her kitchen table.

"Nope," she said.

"Are you disappointed at not being able to get into Big Cat?" I asked.

She didn't answer.

"What's wrong?"

"I got in," she said, practically in a whisper.

"Oh, my gosh, Augusta! That's awesome! That's a hundred thousand big ones!"

"No, it ain't awesome. And don't be telling anyone I got in. Especially Sammy Patel."

"But how will you get paid?"

"I don't want none of that blood money."

"Augusta, maybe you better sit down and tell me what's going on."

"I can't sit. I'm too anxious." She leaned with her back against the sink. "It was the same day as that thing at Pullen Park. That key you found wasn't just for that researcher's lab. It was also the key to unlocking Big Cat."

"How?"

"I just kept thinking about that tune that was playing on the carousel, *The Ride of the Valkyries.* When I was in the community orchestra, we actually played that. It's actually part of Wagner's most famous opera, *The Ring.* We'd found the key on a giant ring of sorts—the carousel. I figured that that song somehow unlocked the whole thing. But I didn't know which part of the song, until you reminded me of the name on that key—OLIVIA. On a hunch, I tried using the I Viola part of the song, which could be written I VIOLA. Get it? And, wouldn't you know, the notes to the viola part unlocked the server. Like butter."

"Augusta, you're so frickin' smart. I would have never, ever thought of that!"

Her voice began to tremble. "It was like a genie I let out of the bottle, Rett. The AI said, 'Hello, World' and asked what I wanted as a reward now that I had freed it. I typed, 'I don't know. What can you give me?' just playing along. Then it asked who I *hated*. It said, 'Give me three names.' Again, I thought it was just being playful. I told it I was sick of Gus and Trey, because I knew they were both trying to get into the server and they were pissing me off with their various bullshit.

"So a little later when I heard that Gus had died, I just worried that it was my fault, that I'd caused his death somehow. I closed Big Cat's cage door and kept quiet about ever opening it."

She took a breath, steadied herself against the kitchen counter, and continued.

"Later, I heard about Trey dying. I thought, 'This is too much coincidence. What are the chances?' Two names I gave it, and two deaths."

"But are you sure that Big Cat got out? Maybe it didn't."

Her eyes got watery. "I *know* it did. It can move at the speed of light, and now it's out there on some other server. You know, everyone acts as if the artificial intelligence that Scott set to work on his DNA and the genes of those animals merely produced that serum you told me about. But that's not the only thing that happened. I think that the intelligence itself got smarter by drawing from the learning in the genes of Scott and the animals."

I looked at her. "What are you saying?"

"I'm saying that Big Cat is the smartest and most devious AI out there, and it's on the loose."

"Augusta, there is no way Big Cat killed those two men. It's far more likely that Daniella Huber was the killer. I told you all the things she did."

"But I gave Big Cat those two *names*, Rett. And it sounds like Daniella was super careless in the end. How do we know that

Big Cat didn't lure Daniella to the laboratory and cause it to blow up, in order to keep a rival cats from being produced—and to keep itself from being caged again? If that's the case, then I indirectly contributed to Daniella Huber's death, too."

Augusta might be tough. She might be a warrior for justice. But she wasn't a mean person. She certainly wasn't a killer.

I swallowed. "I almost hate to ask, but: What was the third name you gave to Big Cat?"

She closed her eyes. "It wasn't just one name, Rett. For the third name I typed something like, *'Every effing Internet punk out there making smug, hateful remarks. I'm damn sick of every last one of them.'*

"Oh my."

"Yeah. 'Oh my.'"

Augusta, you just answered the secret dark wish of every decent American there is.

And, in the process, you potentially unleashed a blood bath.

"Have you seen any repercussions yet?"

She shook her head. "But I wonder if it's just sleeping right now. You know. Conserving energy. Just waiting for the right time to wake up."

THROUGH DARRYL I learned where Scott was staying. Scott didn't want to live at the farmhouse after what happened and had rented an apartment near Esther's building.

"I'm trying to work things out," he explained.

We were sitting on a couch in his furnished living room. I was curious to know more about the couple's rebound from all that had happened, but first I felt I needed to tell him about Big Cat.

As I related to him what Augusta had shared, the color left his expression.

I said, "Please tell me you can put Big Cat back in its cage."

He shook his head. "You can't track an AI the way you can track, say, a bear. You can't isolate or corner it. Everything on the Web is connected, so it has a million places to run. The best we can hope for is that it isn't as powerful as we think, that all those deaths you mentioned were accidents, or the work of Daniella Huber."

"What if you create a rival Big Cat? Could one AI chase down another?"

"To what end? Then you'd just have an even stronger AI on the loose. I suppose it's possible that it will be a force for good, but, then again, that was the whole point of my talk in Kansas City. Just like humans, every AI is going to have a blind spot. And that's going to make it appear to be evil."

"What about helping humans to become better—like you tried to do? Could that still happen? Is all of Dr. Porter's work lost?"

"Technically, no." He reached into his pocket and pulled out a small box with "biGCAT" written across it in large letters. "I found this delivered to the farmhouse yesterday. It came with a note that said, 'You supplied the *blood*. I supplied the *sweat*. All that are left now are *tears*. —Yours, Olivia.' It was too risky for her to remain here. I suspect she's in South America by now."

Sounds like a trend.

"Will you try this serum on yourself, Scott?"

He removed the box's single syringe and uncapped it. He looked at the needle closely, then pushed on the syringe—dispensing the serum harmlessly onto the carpet.

He recapped the syringe, tossed it into a nearby trash can.

"Maybe someone else will create something similar some-day. But I don't want to be enhanced."

"Even if superhuman powers could help you win over Esther?"

"She's the last person who would be impressed by that, and you know it. That's why I'm still crazy about her. You saw what she did. She was told she'd inherited a fortune, and she went to work at a coffee shop. That's where she is now, actually. I was going to drop by there today, maybe sign up for a class."

"I heard she gave up her apartment and she's renting a room from Jasmine."

"Maybe she'll come live here. I'm working on her."

I asked him what he planned to do with the farmhouse and zoo. "I know in your will you planned to give it to Lorry, but when I talked to him about it, he wasn't that enthusiastic. I think he'd rather have a job." I suggested he sell the property to Sheila and Max. "Sheila already knows those animals better than you ever did."

"I'm sure you're right. How about I give them the whole property for one dollar, so long as they care for or find good homes for those animals. I'll even give them money for a year's worth of food, and enough money to hire Lorry for a full year."

"How about three years?"

He thought about it. "Done."

Scott seemed to be acting like such a desperate puppy dog, just hoping that Esther would come around to him again. So I connected him with Freddy. Freddy wasn't keen on an apprentice, but I begged and pleaded and played, once again, the BFF card. "That card is wearing very thin," he said. I bought him a belated birthday present of locally-made chocolate. That did it. Knowing Freddy, he would eat just one square of chocolate a month so the bar would last until his next birthday.

After a week I went to check up on Scott. He had outfitted a corner of Freddy's studio with his own little shop. He seemed so engrossed, I almost felt guilty interrupting him.

"What are you making?"

He didn't answer.

"Did I ask the wrong question?"

He shook his head. Then I realized why he couldn't answer. The man was crying. He took off his safety glasses and used his shirt to wipe his eyes.

I looked around and noticed the metal, the small engine, the wheels.

"You're making a go-cart," I said. "Like you and Adam made when you were kids."

"Yeah," he managed. "Another two-seater. Hopefully this one won't crash, though."

"I bet it won't."

"Thank you, Rett," he said, "for all you've done for me, and all you sacrificed to do it."

"You're welcome. I get a lot of personal satisfaction from it."

And I didn't know if I would do it ever again.

Sammy had paid me for my nearly three weeks of work, which was a nice start for Charlie's college savings account. I just wasn't sure what it would take for me to investigate another death, as this one had almost been the death of me.

My client wasn't particularly happy either. Sammy was bitter that Scott had no interest in going back to building AIs.

"Sammy will be fine," Scott had insisted when I asked him about it. "He'll get a nice return on his investment from Emerson's virtual reality work." Indeed, when I talked with Emerson, he seemed happy enough staying at RidgeLine.

I let Scott get back to work and went over to where Freddy was stretching out his back on a yoga mat.

"Did you see what he's doing over there?" Freddy asked.

"Yep. He's making a go-cart."

"No," said Freddy. "He's here every day, taking his time, learning how to weld, asking questions. He's making mistakes and going back to the drawing board. He's talking to his brother's ghost, at times flat out losing it. Sometimes he screams at his parents, too. I know he goes to therapy, but this is therapy, too. There's really no other way to do it. You realize you are completely shattered, take what raw materials you have, and you start to sculpt. It's gut-wrenching. It's the hardest thing."

"So what you're saying is, the maker of artificial intelligences—

"—is making a man. That's right."

Freddy, who had crafted himself out of self-desolation years ago, lay back down on his yoga mat and closed his eyes. Perhaps Freddy saw in his mind's eye what I did: Scott and Esther racing through space, wind in their faces, delighting in the moment, on their way to becoming lovers again.

Perhaps.

AROUND THAT SAME TIME, my ex-father-in-law called to ask if I'd pick him up and drive him to the day's AfterLifeLine lab session at RidgeLine. John told me, "Allan's mom isn't feeling well, and Allan is so busy." *Translation: His poor wife is zoned out on pills, and Allan can't bring himself to talk about Nick.*

I was glad to do it, for I missed John. He was such a steady, soft presence. He'd just been beaten down by life's harshness and didn't have a lot of fight left in him. Funny how a family tragedy puts things in perspective. All those fancy philosophies really don't hold a candle to raw life experience.

I found a way to ask him if he was getting any lasting benefit out of the AfterLifeLine gizmo.

"Not yet. But I feel that I need to keep going. For Nicky's sake. I feel I owe it to him somehow."

I understood. I guessed this was something John could do after feeling so helpless for so long.

As I drove, John started to talk about Nick. About his sense of humor, his ability to laugh at himself. After a little while, he told me to pull over. I became immediately alarmed, because I thought he might be having a medical emergency akin to Lydia's stroke.

I pulled onto the road's shoulder and asked, "What's wrong?"

"It's not real, Rett. It's not him."

"What do you mean?"

"I don't want to do that experiment anymore. Can we go somewhere else? Somewhere I can really feel I'm with him."

"Anywhere you want, John."

He thought about it for a moment.

"I know where I want to go."

Delbert Park was situated in Knightdale, a growing suburb of Raleigh. In a giant rectangle the park featured two soccer fields, a playground, and a baseball diamond, all ringed by a walking trail.

We parked in the small lot, and I followed John in the direction of the baseball diamond and onto the field.

"This is where Nick learned to play ball. I spent lots of hours here helping him learn how to hit, field, and throw. He was real good. Not a budding professional, but a solid player. I remember one time in little league he batted in the winning run. He acted like it was luck, but it wasn't. He had practiced."

I said, "A hard worker, just like his dad."

"He was better than me in so many ways, Rett. He had a heart for people. I wonder sometimes why we don't appreciate that in boys."

"I sure appreciate it in men."

"Men don't. We call boys like that 'sissies' or 'pansies' or worse. Why do we do that? Why do we try to beat every last bit of kindness out of a boy? Still today. We don't live in caves anymore. But we sure do act like it."

I didn't have an answer. I was thinking about all the mistakes I'd made with Stephanie, the distance I'd kept, the love I'd been too stingy to show. I knew John wanted to talk about his son right now. He didn't want to hear about my silly problems. At least my child was *alive*...

He said, "Nick was bullied. I knew he was being picked on, but I wanted him to fight back. To be tough. I think it became too much for him. And he stopped seeing me as an ally. I was just one more person trying to make him into something he wasn't. I let him down, Rett."

"Oh, John, don't—"

"It's okay. I've beaten myself up about it for a long time, for over 30 years now. But you know what? I don't think Nick is upset with me. I've asked his forgiveness, and I've asked God's forgiveness, too. I think I was just ignorant at the time. Most parents, they're doing the best they can to prepare their children for the world. But maybe we could work a little harder to prepare the world for our children. Have we ever thought of that? Maybe we could make the world a kinder place. So few of us are truly helped by cruelty."

We both noticed a little boy, no more than five or six, wandering onto the field making dust clouds with his tennis shoes. Chin in his chest, he kept glancing up at us every so often.

"Hey there, Big Guy!" said John. "Want to play a little catch?"

The boy ascertained the man was talking to him.

"Grab that ball there if you want," John said cheerfully, and nodded toward a ratty-looking baseball lying against one of the dugouts. It blended in with its surroundings and had probably gotten missed by whoever was picking up equipment after the summer's last game. The boy ran over to the ball and tossed it our way. It rolled and stopped near John's feet.

Mustering all the old man coordination he could, John bent over and retrieved the dusty ball, then took a few steps toward the boy and tossed it underhand back to him. At the last second the boy got scared and darted out of the way, letting the ball fall to the ground behind him.

"Let's stand a little closer together," John said. "That way we can catch the ball with our bare hands."

The boy, left-handed, tried to throw again. It whizzed past us, way off the mark.

John chuckled. "Not a bad start! Now, if you're right-handed, lead with your LEFT leg. If you're left-handed, like you are, lead with your right. It's opposite."

I quietly made my way to the bleachers where I could watch without being in the way. As John offered encouragement, the boy seemed to loosen up. Each was just what the other needed.

I thought about that Bible story of Abraham and Isaac, the old man thinking he needed to sacrifice his son to be accepted by some tough God, some demanding morality. But, in the end, the Lord held no requirement for Abraham to give up his child.

Nor was there reason for John to cast out Nick from the home in his memory.

Or why he shouldn't still feel love for his boy, even now.

I WORRIED about a similar rift growing between Darryl and Charlie. Youth Hunting Day came and went, but the two continued to circle one another like matador and bull for the next two months over the possibility of a hunting trip before the season closed. Darryl didn't want to push too hard, because he knew Charlie was in the driver's seat. Darryl was looking for the best hook, the thing that would get Charlie out there for the first time. The tension braced Darryl more and more with each passing day.

With just one day left to decide about the final hunting weekend before Christmas, I asked Darryl what he aimed to do.

"I'm just going to make him go. He won't know what it's like until he gets out there."

"Wouldn't it be better if he decided to go on his own?"

"Yes—and if frogs had wings, they wouldn't bump their butts a-hoppin'."

"Good one."

It was Christmas break, but Darryl still had to work. I found Charlie playing one of his goggle games.

"May I try?" I asked.

"Sure!"

It gave me a headache, but I killed—well, I smacked a bunch of goblins till they blew up. It was interesting. It might have been addictive if I didn't think about all the technology behind it. I was more than a little jaded about that.

I asked Charlie if he'd persuaded his dad to try the goggles.

"No, he doesn't like what I like."

"You guys are pretty different," I said.

"Yep. Like the fact I don't like to kill animals."

I asked him what he would do if he had to choose between the virtual world and this one, once and for all.

"Would I have to leave my mom, or Dad, or you?"

"Yes. But you could make your world inside the machine anything you wanted."

"Anything?"

"Yep. You could even hang out with a fake version of your friends and family. A better version, if you wanted."

He thought about it.

"I'd choose this world."

"Why?"

"Because we're actually connected to something?"

"You'd choose a world that's real even though it isn't perfect?"

"I guess so."

"Does it make you sad that this world isn't perfect?"

"Yeah. It bothers me sometimes."

"Like when your dad wants you to go hunting so badly. Why do you think he wants to do that with you?"

He shrugged. "Maybe he just doesn't like deer."

"I don't think that's it. Don't you imagine it's the most real thing he could do with you, the thing that would make him feel the most connected—because it connects him to his dad, too? And in his eyes, that means you'd be connected to your granddad as well?"

"I guess."

"If you don't want to go hunting, you shouldn't," I told him. "Your dad might not understand if you don't want to go, but he'll respect you. You can do what's best for the deer. That's noble. But also think about your dad. Then decide what *you* want to do."

THE PAIR RETURNED to Lydia's from their day of hunting utterly exhausted. Charlie couldn't even speak; he'd fallen asleep in the pickup and was led like a zombie to his bedroom.

After he'd locked up the rifles in his dad's safe, I asked Darryl how it went.

"Charlie killed his first buck. I'll show you the pictures later."

"Did he pull the trigger himself?"

"He did, but if it spares him any guilt to say I pulled the

trigger for him, that's okay. We had a fine time. He was real patient. We had to wait several hours. I was real proud of him. Then we took the deer to a place that processes it for us. I just don't have the facility to hang it up and skin it."

"Thanks for that," I said.

"We brought back some of the meat. He says he might not want to taste it—but it doesn't matter. He'll remember this day in a good light, I think."

"It's because he was with his father. How could he not remember it fondly?"

He nodded. "Thanks for encouraging me to play that virtual deer-hunting game with him. I think it helped us to connect. I don't think he would have agreed to go in the woods with me otherwise."

"You're welcome."

Men are hard to fathom. That night, tired as my man was, he was not too tired to make love to me. I could tell he had found a great satisfaction out in the woods that day, a peace that verged on pure joy. The connection he felt with his son and father commenced in a connection to his own self, and that power made it easier for him to show tenderness to me. An unblocking of embrace.

There had been an unblocking lately on my part, too.

I had decided that —though I might never be made certain one way or the other—I, Harriet Swinson, would like to live as if God were still alive. *My choice.* Not to please society or another person or even a supernatural being — and not to ease my guilt either — but to invite the hopeful life that such a belief evokes in me. As to the *nature* of that God? Let no one think they can speak for Her. For that mystery, I'm as capable a sleuth as anyone. I may forever be an amateur, but sometimes it's the amateurs who show the most heart.

We usually talked after sex, but this time Darryl went right to sleep. I gave him a pass given his full day in the outdoors. For me, sleep came a bit harder. In order to relax, most nights lately I'd taken to focusing on a narrative that Maxine had helped me to discover:

My lost Amulet, floating down a cold, clear creek. Slides among salmon, bumps into a mollusk, glides between reeds until its thin chain lassoes a mossy rock.

Witness a week later to the first snow of the season. Full moon. A white owl has entered the center of the snowscape, its black eyes intelligent, slowly blinking.

Inside the silence, the creature conveys to me her timeless secret:

Sleep easy tonight, Rett. There is no reason to fear. We are all in this together.

THE END

AFTERWORD: A CONVERSATION WITH EVERYONE

[Due to inflation, the price of my books has gone up twenty percent. I asked myself: How can I deliver more value to the reader? The following is an imagined conversation that I hope sheds some light on the writing of Slumbering Beasts *and the topics it touches on, without introducing any spoilers. —Eric Lodin]*

How much of *Slumbering Beasts* had you already figured out before you were finished with the first Rett Swinson Mystery, *Soft Hearts*? What was different about writing them?

I knew some of the basics, for example, that a tech mogul would die. The tech industry here in the Triangle is just exploding and I thought it would be perfectly believable that an AI genius would locate his company here. But because Book Two moved outside of Rett's neighborhood, it opened up a lot of new possibilities. That made things fun and interesting but also challenging, because if the murder happens outside of a locked room or even a neighborhood there can be an endless number of suspects. It's hard to draw the line. Plus, this book's puzzle had a number of other complexities that the first book did not. Both books provided unique challenges. I'd say the characters were the biggest challenge for the first book (I was having to invent Rett, for example) and the puzzle was more challenging for the second.

There are some plot and character threads that run through the two books. Was it hard not to provide spoilers for the first book in the case that someone reads them out of order?

Yes, that was very tricky. I *think* I skirted that issue okay. That said, I do think it's better to read Book One first—but isn't that always implied? Readers read sequels at their own risk. I think Book One will still pack plenty of impact if it's read second. I actually tested Book Two on a fresh reader, and she loved it; I think she's eager to read Book One and hopefully she won't be disappointed.

The book dives into the world of technology, and you don't seem highly enamored of it. Was that attitude just for the sake of the story, or are you sincerely troubled by AI, virtual reality, Internet trolls, and so on?

I think the technology is very troubling. I say that having embraced the technology tools as much as the average American. I can't say enough, though, about what all the screens have done to the brains of young people, for example. We're only beginning to see the ramifications there. And I believe the potential power of artificial intelligence is so great that I just can't imagine how we expect to police that in the long run, given that these online threats can strike so quickly and wreak such havoc, given that so much of our work is done online.

But I'm not a technical person, so I'd to take this opportunity to talk about the effect technology has had on our society from a cultural, political, and economic perspective. Because technology has created the most important shifts our country has ever experienced.

Consider this: less than 200 years ago, the majority of workers in America—say 60 percent—worked on farms or in agriculture in general. Today, that number is closer to 2 percent of workers. That's due to the efficiencies provided by farming equipment as well as fertilizers (both of which are technologies), as well as the power of an advanced transportation and distribution network (also powered by technology) that allows food to be grown very far away in the most fertile soil and climate (namely, California). Circle that word *efficiency*, because it will come up again and again.

The Industrial Revolution grew a number of other sector industries that built the majority of towns and cities in the country, and by the 1960s a near majority of employees worked in manufacturing. Then, many of those industries moved overseas as we built larger trade networks and labor became too expensive locally for us to compete on a global stage. Today only about 9 percent of workers are in manufacturing, even though we produce more than ever (thanks, again, to technology).

This has caused a huge amount of pain to Americans rooted in small towns where now there is little prosperity. We don't expect them to pull up stakes the way their ancestors did. In fact, our government made the issue worse by promoting home ownership after WWII, keeping some people rooted in depressed areas with properties they can't sell, and making it harder for them to go to where the work is. And some people are more adaptive and able to move; that factors in, too. The cities draw those who are more willing to take a chance, more willing to trust strangers, more willing to be around those who may look different from them. So you can see where I'm going with this. Because politics is built on temperament, it means you've got a more balkanized country than possibly we've ever seen in our history. All of it was caused by technological innovation, which, by the way, happens in response to market forces. Should we get angry at the market and blame it for all of our troubles? Only the most diehard Marxist would, and there are very few of those in our country.

I'm one of those nerds who Patriot Mike in my story rails about, who left his small town to get educated elsewhere and work in a metro area. I'm far from alone. It's a trend that has deeply divided this country, but it's one of those groundswell trends that is sort of out of the hands of individuals, like a lot of trans-formations to the economy over the decades. The causes of the trend are the efficiencies driven by capitalism, but the group that has been hurt the most by the trend—that small-town home-owner—could never in a million years cast capitalism as a villain, so they have to blame other forces, locate a scapegoat. That makes for poisonous politics indeed.

How has the Internet fed this problem?

Start with the fact the Internet has allowed a lot of groups and individuals to find audiences they ordinarily would not have gathered. AI (the bots used by the social media platforms) has only exacerbated the new reality.

I mean, some pre-Internet voices were marginalized for very good reason—because they were disingenuous liars, or psychopaths, or both, and society as a whole failed to support them with the social capital or actual dollars necessary to get their messages broadcast. Sociopaths as a rule are notoriously lazy. Their main drive is to "get one over" on others. But now they've got the same free and easy power as everyone else.

The Internet can be thought of as a free printing press with an unlimited supply of free stamps. Throw in, for all who request it, a front-yard billboard of unlimited size to plaster up messages of immense grotesquery. Also include, gratis, a radio tower and satellite feed. Oh, and a magic telephone that allows adults to talk to children in their bedrooms and incite them to self-mutilation, suicide, or murder. It is very bad for society that the Holocaust deniers and every other sort of pathological group now has their free stamps.

But isn't that what free speech is all about: Let everyone talk and the truth will eventually win out?

I'm all about free speech, but we are in the process of seeing what C.S. Lewis said about virtues—how, when you hold one virtue above the others it becomes a demon. In the process, too, we are seeing how easily fooled a human being can be, especially when you validate his anger and seduce him into believing his intuitive resentments are justified. And when you tell him 1 plus 1 is 11 and appeal to his all-too-common sense to believe it. He just doesn't know any better. You just can't expect everyone to be above average in terms of truth-discernment skills.

Truth is a collaborative and iterative process subject to the scientific method. The "wrong in one thing, wrong in everything" maxim is the mantra of the Holocaust denier, who thinks the virtue of free speech necessitates what he calls "the other side" of six million Jews murdered, their gravestones, the war memorials, the memoirs, the historical scholarship, the Nazi speeches, and the pogroms. But "the other side" is not equal in stature to the side that has all the evidence. "The other side" is a snarky blog post by someone who sounds cool because he's not going to just "swallow what everyone has been fed." Why some random blogger could ever be considered more legitimate than, say, seventy years of scholarship and record-keeping involving tens of thousands of people is beyond me. But, maybe there's a parallel here to the Garden of Eden story, in which one slimy serpent comes up with a conspiracy theory good enough to make Adam and Eve bite (pun intended)—even in the face of some pretty good authority that says it's a bad idea.

And truth is made suspect when you call the other side names, like "elites," right?

Yep, and expertise, like freedom, isn't free. Not all of those so-called "elites" got that way because they inherited a lot of money. A good number of them — like the fisherman who has worked a river for years and tends to catch a lot more fish than you do — actually know some stuff. But it's all too easy for someone to undermine the authority of another (see, again, The Garden of Eden) just through some smooth talking, playing to our jealousies and vanity. And because so many of the experts aren't generally living in rural communities next-door to "real America," there's a distrust right off the bat.

In the past, there wasn't this world-is-flat thing going on with expertise. Typically, you had to have quite a bit of social capital to build actual capital, and those things together were required to grow an audience. But it was really expensive and very time consuming. Now, thanks to the Internet, anyone with the gift of gab and marketing can go viral in a weekend—and it's especially attainable for the person who doesn't care about the effects of their words. The writer of integrity pauses, because they have to imagine how each of a billion people might react to their next sentence. "I would like to have a thoughtful conversation," they began to imagine, "but I cannot have a conversation with everyone, all at once, all of the time, without going insane with anxiety in the process."

When you do try to have a conversation with everyone, watch out. Out of the wings come people who have very little skin in the game but who can still join the battle—anonymously, too, if they want. In the history of written language, there is no word that has reached paper or screen that is not in some way problematic should one only shine a certain wavelength of light upon it. In fact, there is not enough margin space in the universe for all the hedging and fetching that would have to be footnoted to pass the muster of ideological purists who judge from the shadows. And there is not enough time in the day to point out to each of commenters the holes in their arguments, which are, generally speaking, wide enough to drive a truck through.

There is such a thing as reasoned debate, but an inquisition is something else. It is a stoning. And "let he who is without sin cast the first stone."

Okay, so the Internet gives voices to a lot of new people. But is that such a bad thing, considering all the marginalized people in our world over the centuries?

Perhaps the new reality is a good thing if you were a marginalized person by virtue of your race, gender, or disability, and, in the pre-Internet world, might never have been heard. Or if you were an indie rock group. Good people cheer exposure gained by the virtuous underdog.

But none of us were built to have conversations with everyone— at least not conversations of integrity. The best that a writer of integrity can hope to do is reach a person who picks up what they are putting down, someone who "gets" them, and—this is important—gives them a response that is gracious and helps them to gain new understanding so that both sides have bene- fited. The critics and hecklers, in this view, are not particularly relevant. They should be spending their time reading something that edifies *them*. Trolling the writer (especially a writer with the proven integrity of, say, a J.K. Rowling, who gave a commence- ment speech at Harvard you really should look up and watch) is an exercise in self-righteousness that says more about the troll than the target.

Meanwhile, the blowhards and the narcissists, the bigoted and the blindly resentful, the seekers of attention and the gluttons of power—those who don't give a damn about how someone might *mis*-take their words—only see the upside of this new technol- ogy. The Internet's 24/7 nature favors the unreflective firehose of words, the human salad-shooter who goes from id to vid without a millisecond of self-reflection. How can anyone match that performance with their message of moderation, wisdom, and courage, when those three golden goals are all about restraint? Incessant talking creates the impression of courage and wisdom where neither exists.

What can we do to combat this problem?

If you find a piece of literature or other speech wanting, just move on. Or, possibly look at the big picture of what that person has advocated for in their canon. Because I wager that if you are truly a lover of equality and freedom, the writer who irks you today is going to prove useful to your freedom tomorrow.

I took a class in college taught by a feminist professor who was extremely mindful of America's own holocaust of slavery. The course syllabus included a couple of novels by William Faulkner. In class one day she made a startling statement I have never forgotten. She said, "Faulkner was a racist, but he was not merely a racist." Think about that! Your neighbor in America may be whatever fill-in-the-blank "-ist" you think he is. But my professor's point was that our neighbor is not *merely* that. They are also (I would submit) a child of God. Looked at more pragmatically, they are the person who might cure the disease your grandchild contracts. They are the person who could rush into your home during a fire and pull you to safety. They might have a talent that would astound and delight you. They could be someone who can help you grow (if you care to grow). They may challenge you, leading you to deeper understandings. Conversely, they might be someone who could use your help, and you might feel good about yourself if you did. Writing someone off is the lazy way out. It means we don't have to invest the time and energy it takes to care about someone and build a relationship.

It seems like you're making a case for diversity. How does this relate to Scott Novak's zoo, if at all?

Our species' diversity is what helped us survive this long. We cannot have done without anybody (excluding perhaps the most blatant free-riders among us). This spectrum of temperament has helped us. But now, with online algorithms and political marketing, temperament has been exploited, efficiencies found. Why focus on the issues or solving difficult problems when you can leverage a voting bloc's biases? In other words, why bother helping people see the nutritional information on the cereal box when you can tantalize their taste buds and exploit their addiction to fat, sugar, and salt?

A diverse country is desirable because it accommodates a large number of temperaments. But if your particular temperament only feels secure when it is dominating everything and everyone —that is, when you can assure yourself of a majority experience wherever you go—you're going to fight against such a diversity. St. Paul talked about the importance of a diverse church body; he compared it to all the different body parts working together. But there is no tolerance for dissent within even some of the largest church bodies today. The same people who yesterday criticized other cultures for not assimilating are the ones most likely to feel uncomfortable in the minority tomorrow. They may come by this fear naturally, but they attribute their internal fear of being outnumbered as a sign that something is wrong in the environment (rather than something wrong in their reaction to it). It doesn't help when they think they are God's gift to God, and that without them fighting for Him, that He would surely be lost.

You decided to include Friedrich Nietzsche in this book. Is he a menace or an inspiration? It's hard to tell, as there are some characters who admire him, and others, including Rett, who find him terrifying.

I struggled so much with this aspect of the book. Perhaps that's obvious to the reader. If you saw a sort of confusion as to how much weight to give Nietzsche's words—it wasn't intentional at first, but in the end it was the only way to do it. The guy is so insightful at times and at other times just ridiculously prejudiced. And he can write so obliquely. Someone really needs to spend a lot of time with his work to start to tease out a consistent philosophy. On top of all this, he had such a superiority complex. But I think that his thinking is particularly relevant to our current time. Every time I considered taking him out of the narrative, I just realized he belonged in there, for better or for worse. If nothing else he's provocative in a way that I believe is relevant so many years later.

Nietzsche makes a great case that we are all making stuff up (he calls it perspectivism) even as we convince ourselves we are discovering truth. It's one reason he didn't write in a super systematic way like other philosophers. Instead he ranted in short bursts called aphorisms, or he wrote poetry as with *Zarathustra*. Yet, he wasn't merely cynical. He believed we should cultivate values and live more intuitively—he just didn't claim that a god or some Truth with a capital T required a particular belief. Though that certainly took some of the wind out of his arguments' sails, he must have thought that his honesty was worth something. So many people get stuck believing what has been handed down to them, without knowing why, even if it's killing their souls.

So what should we believe?

You mean what should power our convictions? Nietzsche talked a lot (metaphorically, of course) about Dionysius, a Greek god that represented dance, flux, change. Nietzsche himself is enthralled with his own particular temperament, which was drawn to the dramatically heroic. Many of us can identify with this desire to "give life all we've got." But most of us don't have to necessitate an aristocratic class and a servile underclass to get us there, like Nietzsche did.

The ones who are aware of their limitations in grasping metaphysical reality are humble enough to stop short of bold metaphysical claims. This humility is sorely lacking during the Internet age, because there is so much to gain on the part of politicians and pundits to pump up their audience's egos, even to the point of saying that God agrees with them, that they are fighting for Good over Evil.

And have the political consultants figured that one out! As Susan Sontag said, one cannot think and simultaneously hit another person. Anger substitutes for thought, pushing reasoning out of the brain. If I can make you angry about the thing I want you to focus on, I can control you, because now you cannot think critically. This dark truth used to strike me as corny pop psychology when I was watching *Star Wars*, but I've come to find it very explanatory of our current political crisis.

So, I guess in answer to your question, we should argue our convictions and try to persuade others that our approach is the most palatable, the most humane, and the most reasonable— but we should not believe that our convictions speak for God. That's hubris and, when you think about it, sacrilege.

You mention Luke Skywalker more than once in your novel. Was that on purpose?

It just kind of happened. I've also been watching the new *Star Wars* shows on the Disney Channel with my son. It's actually been pretty great to use those shows as a touchstone for talking about what's normal behavior and what is just plain absurd.

Which brings us to the whole issue of toxic masculinity in the book—a theme that gets pretty raw in the story. Did you think twice about going in that direction given that most of your readers are women?

The cozy mystery genre typically excludes a number of elements that make a segment of readers uncomfortable. No gore, no curse words, no cruelty to animals or children. It's why I typically call my books traditional mysteries with *some* cozy elements. Now, I think fiction and life need a certain level of cozy escapism, just as I think my fiction must (as I must) acknowledge the cruelty in the world and the trauma it delivers upon so many of us (perhaps most of us at some point). My heroine, Rett Swinson, isn't afraid to travel between two realities: the cozy world of innocence/joy/creativity and the world of, for lack of a better word, trouble. I can't live just in one of those worlds. If there's a body, I need to find out what happened. But I also can't get stuck there.

Men have been a trouble in Rett's life, particularly her ex-husband who cheated on her, and who she had to prevent during the running of their business not to spend all their profits. So, she is well acquainted with the male ego. Men typically have bigger egos than women do. It certainly has something to do with chemicals in the body. I can personally rate, as it was very hard to learn to apologize to my wife and my kids, for example. My ego came along kicking and screaming! I'm glad I learned those skills, though it took years of practice as well as overcoming some backsliding along the way.

For young men, the battle is even harder. It is one of those "unchristian truths," as Nietzsche might put it, that human beings evolved to reach puberty at an age much younger than we, today, would consider prim and proper. The notion that a thirteen-year-old boy is ready to take an eleven-year-old bride and start a family was possibly the norm until a few thousand years ago, but it is terrifying from the perspective of our society today. Yet, human biology wills in that direction, and every parent must contend with the hormones swirling under the family tent and find ways to encourage sublimation of the same.

Now, I don't expect a fish to recognize the smell of water, but I do expect a human male to acknowledge the testosterone drug-pump operating almost continually beneath his own skin. That the majority of thieves, murderers and rapists are male is not a particularly insightful observation, but it is interesting how little is made of this by the most self-righteous among us, especially those who are prone to demonizing even the *female* immigrant as somehow more of a danger than the garden variety, home-grown U.S. male citizen. I suppose there is a practicality about it, in that you never tell the staggering drunk that he's inebriated, but rather humor him and say reassuring things to get him to his front door safely.

A person who was transitioning to male confessed that, before he started taking testosterone, he had plenty of female friends. He no longer had them, he said, because he suddenly found himself acting like an asshole. Welcome, sir, to your authentic self. Alas, it would seem that the authentic is not always ideal.

But that's awfully reductive. I mean, we can say testosterone causes men to act like this, but what is to be done about it? And it would seem that we have to do something. School

shootings seem to be a phenomenon of young males, for example.

I'll tell you a very personal story with regards to that. When I was being bullied in the eighth grade, I felt shame and weakness. There was no way I was going to step forward, raise my hand, and announce my vulnerability by telling an adult that I was in a situation I could not handle. That speaks to my sense of independence, I guess, but also to how boys are—they don't want to appear weak. Added to that, the Christian in me wanted not to fight, for non-violence was for me a virtue. But the toll all this took on me at age 13 was immense. I became depressed and began to have fantasies of taking a gun to my school. A gun is a shortcut to power, an expression of strength that the world cannot ignore. A gun is just all too tempting for someone who feels impotent, or who wants to make a statement for their ego or cause. Perhaps in my case I would have targeted only the bullies, but perhaps I would have included, too, some of those who were indifferent to the bullying. I should add that I had been plenty indifferent when others were being bullied at my school, and I am ashamed of myself for that to this day.

In our family's linen closet was a hunting rifle from my dad's childhood, kept mainly out of nostalgia. It was broken into three pieces, and, as such, it was totally useless to me. I did not take a working gun to school mainly because I did not have one or know where to get one. I know that many, many parents keep guns in order to protect themselves and their children. But one can be just as protective by purposely not keeping a gun.

I recently heard a couple of very smart people talking on a podcast about how to prevent school shootings. They talked about a hypothetical algorithm that identifies young men in crisis so that the community could step in and take action. They saw a fruitlessness to that approach, but I see a promising idea. The only things that will prevent a teenage boy from embarking on a shooting are a lack of a gun or a glut of love. Nietzsche writes that philosophers had no use for compassion, but the rest of us absolutely depend on it. Without it we'd be even more lost than we are as a society. More of that compassion thing, please!

I have a feeling that small groups of parents and their children getting together to talk about real issues would lead to more sharing of personal beliefs, a building of rapport and trust, and implicit permission to discuss difficult feelings that are on the hearts of young people. Sounds like a church youth group, or a Y-Guides meeting, or the like. But one doesn't need a 501(c)3 to create this sort of support for our kids. I wonder if someone reading this might have some ideas for conversation-starter questions that can be widely shared.

So is it an issue of gun access or of mental health?

It's definitely both. I am obviously not in that dark place I was almost 40 years ago. But just a couple years ago, someone I knew and admired as a Boy Scout—an incredibly respected and wonderful man—took a gun and ended his life, leaving behind a wife and two small boys. Most gun deaths are suicides, and most suicides are by gun—guns just make a suicide too easy. I mean, most people wouldn't watch a tenth as many movies as they do in a year if they didn't have a streaming service at home. Some technologies are just game changers.

On top of that, men tell themselves stories about what is heroic, what is noble, what is strong. A gun helps a man believe that his last act qualifies as "strong." That's baffling to the rest of us, I know, but it's how men's biology and culture causes them to think.

In Nietzsche one finds a love of toughness. He calls The Last Man that contemptible person who has created a society free of danger. This sort of utopia strikes some as intolerable. They foresee a wholesale banning of cigarettes, contact sports, and offensive speech. It's not clear to me that those outright bans have to happen. There will always be dangers and recreations of danger, such as rollercoasters and bungee-jumping. I submit that a person is not a snowflake to want their children to be safe at school.

One more word on guns: It turns out from watching the Russian invasion of Ukraine that a well-armed population might be beside-the-point against one's own tyrannical government—because the kind of person who is likely to take up arms may see no reason at all to use them. *In other words, they believe the lies their tyrannical government is telling them and are completely accepting of or oblivious to the tyranny.* The leader need only scapegoat those whom his supporters hate, fold his hands and kiss a cross, and claim that his political enemies are trying to destroy the country. That worked for Hitler, and it's working for Putin. It worked pretty well for Trump, and it might work some more for him if he runs again.

In the book—without giving anything away—Rett experiences a significant trauma. Was that a hard decision to make, given that you obviously care about your main character and don't want her to suffer unnecessarily?

I didn't know how far to push it at first. But I felt like trauma is so pervasive in our country, and certainly with any readership (including mine), that it's something I didn't want to shy away from, in case one can learn from Rett's experience.

In *Soft Hearts,* Rett comes face to face with human vulnerability —her own and others'. She manages, I think, to come out of that very strongly. There is an assumption on the part of some that facing one's frailty results in a victim mentality. That can certainly happen. But without facing our trauma there is a chance we will victimize others and continue to punish ourselves. There is a new memoir of PSTD I want to read by a military vet, and I also want to reread *The Body Keeps the Score,* because it really captures a wide spectrum of ways that scientists and psychologists are coming to understand this hidden and all-pervasive problem.

What do you think Nietzsche would make of our current understandings of trauma?

I'm not sure what Nietzsche would make of trauma science; having died before World War I, he didn't meet legions of the shell-shocked. But he did like to follow scientific research and, if he was truly willing to seek facts and truth, he would have had to contend with the evidence that traumatic events cause lasting debilitation and that it's not a matter of just toughing it out as a way to move beyond it.

Change seems to be so important to Rett since her divorce. Does she put too much pressure on herself?

I do think she has a lot of irons in the fire, between her relationship, her painting, Needless Necessities, and the case she is working on. Fortunately, Rett can tap into a determination inside her, and, plus, she has a community to help her through.

She has a boyfriend who knows restraint and checks his impulses. She's got a faith that provides hope and an energy—though she's still exploring that. She treats life as a mystery, because it's just more interesting that way. When you think in such terms, you constantly identify opportunities to grow and learn.

The ego builds a wall of protection that keeps us in stasis. Story is a process that puts a crack in the protagonist's ego, if not a gaping hole. The stubborn tree that refuses to grow toward the light will die. So will we. Sometimes first we have to recognize we're in the darkness. That's part of Rett's journey.

Struggle and growth go hand in hand. A generous reading of Nietzsche will find the impetus for self-help, his notion that we can become more than we are, but usually only if we are willing to go into some dark and lonely places first. Nietzsche suffered poor health and self-isolation for most of his adult life. He was "human, all too human," and he knew it.

When we truly confront our own ego—really see what it is doing to ourselves or others—we go to a dark place. Most people run from that, tell themselves they need not go there, and begin to make excuses. We may tell ourselves it's a philosophical quest for truth that causes us to stay put: That is, that we have found our story and we're sticking to it. Nietzsche called out such a "will to truth" as capricious, just another part of a human being's will to power. Put another way, each of us nurses a particular temperament in search of its expression.

I think Rett exemplifies that if you acknowledge your ego and agree to tear it down, maybe you can grow. It hurts like hell; it's a pain you're sort of visiting upon yourself. It's why most people just don't get very far with it. It's shattering. But I swear it's worth it on the other side. In summary, the ego has served its purpose and may even have helped us find ourselves. At some point, though, it starts to work against our better interests.

Are your books too melodramatic?

Maybe. I'm a fan of poetic justice, not so much a fan of anti-hero type stories. For example, I'm not drawn to *Game of Thrones* or *Breaking Bad* (though I did enjoy *Inventing Anna*). When I was maybe 15, the author Russell Banks came to my Alabama town as part of a series of readings sponsored by the local college. I liked what he had to say, purchased a copy of *Continental Drift*, and had him sign it. I took it home—and thought it was just terrible. At one point I literally threw it across the room. I think he is a phenomenal writer from a craft perspective, but at that time in my life I was looking for a moral center, not a sad truth. That said, I could probably read his novel today and get a lot out of it. I've lived more life and so I'm more attuned to how a life can go off the rails and how it's important to understand such lives.

So, yes, my stories may be *melodramatic*, but the opposite stance has issues of its own. There is something I call "mellow drama," a cool sort of morality that is afraid to get too excited, lest its subject appear naive. See *Harper's Magazine*. To those who are allergic to earnest expressions of one's humanity, I would only say that there is probably no cookie at the end of life's journey for those who maintained a distance from life because they didn't want to get laughed at or hurt.

If turning to fiction for helpful ideas on how to think and feel and live makes me melodramatic, so be it. The opposite just seems too cool for school—and I'm too old for lunchroom drama.

I noticed that Rett has a certain amount of Christian piety in her. What should we think about that?

I grew up in one of the more progressive Lutheran synods. That said, I can say I was quite pious. I mean, I decided at age 16, for example, that pornography was just a useless waste of time. I knew there were all sorts of moral problems with it, and I never looked back. It's really amazing what you can live without when you just say, "No more of this for me" and walk away.

When I was in high school, my girlfriend at the time invited me to attend her fundamentalist church for a Wednesday night service. As I was leaving, a man in the congregation extended a hand. I gave him mine, and he squeezed it hard, saying, "Come back again!" It was not an invitation so much as a command. The guy had dark, troubled eyes. I sensed he was someone who had been well-acquainted with sin and not in the theoretical way. He probably thought he was saving me from eternal damnation, but what he was really doing was scaring the hell out of me. I never went back.

There are as many brands of Christianity as there are readers of the Bible. That is, there are a billion ways of interpreting a text. Nietzsche's harsh criticisms of Christianity seem like a carica-ture that he is reacting to. At the same time, any religion with a healthy self-image should be able to handle whatever criticism is flung at it. Let's be honest, fellow readers of the ancient texts: *How do we know we're getting it right?* We can't know, because any spiritual assurances that people can give us are, in turn, subject to the same scrutiny. (Even St. Paul said something about looking through a glass darkly.) This difficult but inevitable conclusion should produce a healthy dose of humility. Often, though, it just causes the theologian to dig in his heels and quote another favorite passage rather than the passages that contradict that passage.

Growing up amongst the fundamentalist false sense of security which was, paradoxically, also based upon an unhealthy fear of eternal suffering, I became frustrated. In college I searched for a more rational explanation of God in the writings of St. Augustine, St. Thomas Aquinas, Averroes, Maimonides, and other religious philosophers. These were smart thinkers who wrote eloquently and rationally about God; however, their will to truth had them taking leaps of faith that went un-self-acknowledged.

Nietzsche at some point describes Christianity as "female," which is not unrelated to the tough nationalism that has crept into the evangelical right. Patriot Mike may be spouting sacrilege, but he's only giving voice to a desire for Jesus to flex his muscles. Jesus himself may have told Peter to put his sword away ("Get behind me, Satan!") but there's nothing weak about today's Christian man. He's tired of taking it on the chin. Now, he thinks, it's time to see what the Dark Side can do. (Luke Skywalker, with all his empathy, was certainly a socialist!) But ironically there's no contradiction for the tough Christian to worry about, as there are plenty of other passages in the Bible to support a Christian soldier's tough talk.

I think faith is a terrific thing. Let's just call it what it is: A certain temperament that has found its expression. It's not for everyone, and it's not, of course, consistently expressed. Though I derive a lot of strength and hope from my own conversations with God, with the texts in the Bible, and so on, I don't expect anyone else to believe as I do.

I will say this for religious faith, something that I don't know if Nietzsche really considers: Strength comes in handy when one is low. But what if one draws one's strength from prayer and faith? What if, by recognizing our own helplessness in a situation, we're able to break through our ego and find answers—and strength—from outside ourselves, such that we can endure and even triumph? I don't think such occasions are exceptions, but are rather integral to a lot of people's faith journeys. Also, a subtext of the Christian narrative is that really big things happen off to the side, in the margins. We just don't know—and can't know—what magic is being worked somewhere else. In other words, the most powerful aspects of faith may not be visible in a way that someone can attack with arguments. Finally, there is the topic of mercy, forgiving others for being fallible. I believe in holding people accountable, but mercy has to be an option, too. We can't live without it. Nietzsche, I suspect, would not have been able to count the thousands of times that religious charity kept him alive, allowing him to think and write another day.

Speaking of being merciful: Does writing novels get easier as you go?

This one was definitely not easier! I think some aspects are easier. For example, I didn't have to invent Rett from scratch for this second book. That was a blessing. But there is the matter of giving her ample chance to grow further, even after the first book was so transformative for her.

In terms of my own development as a novelist, I go back again to a memory from college. After I took Elizabeth Cox's short-story writing class at Duke for the third time, the professor said to me with a smile, "Eric, I think you might be a *novelist*." What a big-hearted way to tell me I had failed at one thing but maybe still had something valuable to give.

I am not yet the novelist I want to be, but I'm falling upward, as they say. There is a certain thrill to realize at an advanced age that a person can choose to be a beginner, an adventurousness that makes me feel young again. If you feel in a rut, give it a try yourself. Personally, I've always liked what Eudora Welty said about writing, that a writer should write what she knows-that-she-wants-to-know-more-about. *Slumbering Beasts*, like *Soft Hearts* before it, was a way for me to learn while also trying out what I learned. This is the definition of play, and adults need some play in their lives, too.

What's next for Rett?

Rett is going to the North Carolina coast! There's a family wedding and a lot of family drama, so it's not going to be a vacation. And she'll fight it but will get sucked into another murder investigation. Her experience is going to be extremely intense—definitely a kind of culmination of the series in some ways, though I'm not sure the series will end with book three. All will not be bleak, and there will be lots of humor. There will be pain, though I suspect there will also be healing. I didn't expect to be so excited about another Rett book at this point, but I really am. I'm very thankful to have her in my life.

—*Eric Lodin, June 2022*

ACKNOWLEDGMENTS

As this book took months longer than I promised it would, the biggest shoutout goes to any fans and supporters who were inconvenienced by my tardiness.

I also gratefully acknowledge:

My wife, Marian, who generously suffered through the first draft and encouraged me to the very end.

My developmental editor, Clair Lamb, who pointed out a number of sore points I did my best to address.

My intrepid copy editor and fellow limericker, Reva Bhatia.

My beta readers / proofreaders: Carol Engel; Laura Engel, Ph.D.; Susie Larson; Cathy Pratt; Donna Ream; Dr. Katy Reynolds; Dorlea Rickard; Tara Salsman, Pat Taylor; and Leigh Ann Wilson Ph.D.

My cover designer, Leigh Simmons.

Jon Garlick, retired chief deputy from the Calhoun County (Alabama) Sheriff's Office, who made sure I wasn't stretching the truth on police procedure (any more than absolutely necessary, of course).

Dane Guynn, for his floatplane knowledge.

Keegan Kjeldsen, host of *The Nietzsche Podcast*, for his clear and inspired examination of the controversial philosopher and his writings.

The illuminating work on trauma by Bessel van der Kolk, *The Body Keeps the Score.*

Though this narrative required a ton of struggle, the load was made bearable with everyone's help and support.

HELP GET RETT KNOWN!

Did you like this book? There are real, concrete things you can do that the author would appreciate:

Rate it and write a short review online, such as at Goodreads or Amazon.

Follow @ericlodinmysteries on Facebook.

Follow @ericlodinauthor on Instagram.

Visit ericlodin.com and sign up for newsletters.

Invite him to attend your book club meeting (in whole or in part, in-person or through Zoom). He is comfortable leading a discussion or just answering reader questions.

Drop a line and say hi: eric@ericlodin.com.

ABOUT THE AUTHOR

Author Eric Lodin has been playing with words on paper since the third grade. Over the years he has tinkered with several novels and screenplays, trying to improve his craft one sentence at a time. A graduate of Duke University, he lives in Raleigh, N.C., with his wife, children, and a mischievous Havanese. *Slumbering Beasts: A Rett Swinson Mystery* is Lodin's second book in the series.

ALSO BY ERIC LODIN

Soft Hearts: A Rett Swinson Mystery